RUNNING

A novel

J. T. Cooper

RUNNING
©2019 J.T. Cooper

ISBN 978-0-578-47136-5 Print

2019

Published by J.T. Cooper
Distributed by IngramSpark

http://www.ingramspark.com/

1. FICTION / General / . 2. / Suspense. 3. / Artists.

**To Jim and Matthew
with love**

Chapter One

KEITH

He woke up too early and shuffled down the dead black hallway to the steps. By touch he scuffed downstairs into the front hall. From there, little lights guided him: amber, green, red. Nearly every electronic device and appliance had lit-up dots or numbers. So did the security system. He glanced at it for the first of probably a dozen times that day. It was armed. Good. Blue numbers on the stove's clock read four fifty-seven a.m. It was a long time until daylight.

He started a pot of coffee, a full one rather than his usual half. His daughter Kinley would want some when she woke up. Years of disappointment hadn't shaken his wife's hope that their girl, a grown woman now, would come home for a good, long visit. Ironic. Kinley had slept upstairs for weeks now, but Brenda hadn't been here to enjoy it because Kinley had come home to watch her mother die. Keith grabbed a mug and interrupted the coffee's flow.

He wandered into his studio, a sun porch originally, just off the kitchen, and inhaled the scents of oils and turpentine. His fingers clawed themselves into the right position for holding a brush. Not yet. He hadn't painted at all while cancer devoured Brenda. It was the least he could give her. And the most. Even now he couldn't allow himself to paint as freely as before her death. He must be vigilant. He was always careful, but now he must be more cautious than ever. Brenda's death might rip a hole in the secrets he'd worked hard to conceal.

Like it was any other day, he followed his routine and walked down the long driveway to the locked gate where he found the newspaper. He read it while drinking more coffee and eating the oatmeal Brenda said was good for him. He halfway expected to hear his wife stirring upstairs, getting ready for work. The silence was suffocating. A tremendous aching filled his body and mind. He couldn't give into it. Not yet. He rinsed his dishes and went to the basement to work out and do a mile and a half on the treadmill. He showered. He was already tired.

Finally Kinley came downstairs and headed straight for the coffeepot. "I'd forgotten how gray it is in Cincinnati," she said. "When was the last time there was sun?" She filled a mug.

Keith shrugged like he didn't know, but he did. It had been three days ago, the day Brenda died. The light had been exquisite.

"Seems like it would make it tough for you, Dad." Kinley sat across from him at the kitchen table. Her long hair, darker than her natural color, he thought, was caught up into a wide barrette. "You ought to paint in Colorado where it's sunny most of the time." She sipped the coffee and grimaced. Brenda had always said he brewed airplane fuel.

"According to you, everything's better in Colorado." He pushed the folded newspaper toward his daughter. Brenda's obituary was in it. Kinley had written and sent it before he'd been able to stop her. She'd included his name, only his first name, which might lead some people to believe his last was Williams, like his wife's, but their two children were listed as Kinley and Brendan Owen. Too close. It made him feel like a meteor was aimed at his house.

Kinley gave him a wan smile. "Everything *is* better in Colorado. Except for ice cream. No Graeter's."

Both Kinley and her brother had gobbled up Graeter's ice cream every chance they got. He liked it too. The chocolate chips were as big as miniature candy bars. "I might come out there some day," he said.

Her face said she didn't believe him. She changed the subject. "Do you need me to iron you a shirt or something?"

"No." He tried to make his voice gentle. "You know I'm not going to the funeral."

She didn't say anything.

"Don't think for a minute that I don't grieve for your mother."

She pursed her lips. The creases alongside her dark eyes were deeper now. Adding interest, actually, but she'd turned thirty in December, and Keith doubted that she shared his opinion. "Aunt Lily and Uncle Dave won't understand," she said. These were Brenda's siblings who'd traveled up from southern Kentucky for the service. "First they have to stay at a hotel when they know good and well how big our house is, and then you don't show up for the funeral." She set her chin. "Brendan and I may not like it, but we're used to you." Being eccentric, he finished silently for her. Kinley frowned. "They'll expect lunch. I don't guess we can bring them here."

There was no need to answer her. He went over to the counter and picked up his wallet. "Here." He pulled out two hundreds. "You and Brendan choose somewhere nice."

She didn't take the money. Instead, she stared at him. Keith figured his veil of secrecy had worn pretty thin with the kids. Head low, Kinley left the kitchen, and Keith tossed the money on the counter.

Later, when he heard the front door open, his heart raced, even though it was just Brendan who knew the security code and was coming to pick up his sister for the funeral. Perhaps Brendan thought he was driving his father too, but Keith doubted it. His son seemed to expect less than Kinley did. Keith's refusal to go would just be one more rejection, filed away with the soccer games and school plays he'd never attended. Brenda had told him more than once that it was strange that he could see colors and shapes so brilliantly but couldn't see into his children's hearts. He could. He just couldn't do anything about it.

Kinley was whispering to her brother, probably informing him of their father's latest deficiency. Shoulders sloped, hands in his pockets, Brendan looked at him over Kinley's head. He said, "People won't know what to think." He looked so much like Brenda. The same reddish brown hair. The same freckles.

"That's their problem," Keith said. He thought he heard a tiny snort from Megan. There was something hard about Brendan's wife, something rigid and relentless about the set of her mouth, although he'd never heard his son complain. Brenda hadn't liked her.

Brendan turned abruptly to Kinley. "You ready?"

She nodded. She wore a violet jacket over a black skirt. She'd ended up with nice legs, just like her mother. Keith wasn't sure he'd seen his daughter's legs since back when she wore the tiny Easter frocks Brenda used to buy her. It seemed like she'd always hidden them beneath ragged jeans.

"We'll be back after the service," Brendan said.

Kinley shook her head. "After lunch." She picked up the money on the counter.   Neither of his children ever turned down a buck, but he was glad to give them money. They couldn't complain about him being stingy. Megan watched the money disappear into Kinley's bag but never said a word, not about lunch, the service, or Brenda.

After making sure the front door was locked, Keith went to his studio, now full of gray, pearlescent light. He could do something with that, he thought, something subtle and mysterious, but started stretching canvases. The work was meant to be mindless, soothing, but he could almost see the nerves jumping under his skin. "It was too soon," he said aloud without meaning to. He shut his eyes, and, as always, saw pictures, this time of his wife. At first they were of her in the hospice bed, bald and wizened, dying by inches. He grimaced and blinked those away. He exchanged them with ones of the dozen or so times she'd posed for him, always uncomfortable, shy about it even when she was clothed. She wasn't an easy model, but she was what he had. And he'd made it work.

Then he envisioned her as he'd first seen her, in a droopy black and white waitress's uniform, handing him a menu at a little restaurant across the river in Kentucky. He'd immediately noticed the glow of her skin, the apricot freckles on her arms. It had been early summer, only a couple of weeks after he'd ended up in Ohio.

<u>1976</u>

Cincinnati was still a mystery. Keith didn't have a car but was reluctant to buy one, even though he had cash enough to do it. He rode buses to get a little bit of a feel for the city, graphing the neighborhoods in his head, scoping out the streets. Cincinnati seemed like a place where it would be easy to be anonymous. He lived in a two-room dump in Clifton, near the university, because buses were plentiful there and the population was liquid. He didn't plan to stay in that apartment.

He knew Kentucky was just across the Ohio River; he'd stared at it from the Cincinnati side and envisioned a picture or two. He'd never been in Kentucky. Never been in Ohio either until now. At Dixie Terminal he transferred onto a bus that lumbered across the bridge into Covington. Chili parlors, seedy taverns, brick and frame shotgun houses. It didn't look much different from Cincinnati. He got off on Madison Avenue and wandered up and down the commercial district. No one paid attention to him, which was good. While he was on the road, he'd chopped off his hair with scissors and then had a barber trim it up when he arrived in Cincinnati. Right away he bought several ordinary white and blue short-sleeved shirts and a couple of pairs of chinos. He figured he'd pass for a Young Republican or a student at a Baptist seminary.

He was hungry, so he slipped into a worn out restaurant around the corner from an old jewelry store with a huge clock outside. A hand-made sign said the diner was Pop's, breakfast and lunch. Keith figured the lunch crowd, if there'd been one, had left. It was nearly one-thirty; they were probably ready to close except for a pair of old men sitting in the corner booth. Little flags stuck in bud vases celebrated the Bicentennial.

"Hi," the waitress said, setting down a short glass of water and a typewritten menu. "Know what you want?" Her accent made him think of country music and rugged hills.

Keith supposed most of Pop's customers didn't need time to read the menu. "No," he said. "What's good?"

She shrugged a skinny shoulder. She was a tiny thing, bird-boned and short. A long braid of burnt sienna hair rode her back. "I like the chicken salad. The burger's okay. But the banana pudding is really cool."

Keith smiled at her, hoping to get one back. It'd been forever since he'd talked to a girl. This one wasn't especially pretty, but her coloring was like something from the Renaissance. All those golds and chestnuts and umbers. Pale blue eyes with nearly colorless lashes. Maybe sixteen. "Chicken salad, then. What's your name?"

"Brenda. You get chips with that." She scribbled on a pad. "What do you want to drink?"

"Coke." She intrigued him, or her coloring did, but he was afraid of scaring her off, and he didn't want anything to do with jailbait. "Say, how old are you, Brenda?"

She furrowed her brow. "Old enough. Are you a cop or something?"

This made him smile again. "No way."

At that, she grinned back with perfect teeth and a nice arc to her lips. "I'm eighteen, but everybody says I look like a kid."

When he'd finished the banana pudding, which was as good as she'd said, he asked her when she got off work and if they could do something. He had no idea what.

Glancing around at the now empty restaurant, she said, "I get off as soon as I wipe up your table, but I have to go home. I gotta watch my little brother." She acted sorry about it. There was no fear in her.

"Oh." He supposed he could ask for her phone number or come back the next day or maybe set up a date for the evening. Hard to do without a car. Or he could just forget it. Much as he'd like some female company, or even a female model, a woman might complicate things, and things were pretty damned complicated already.

Brenda was still grinning. "But you could walk me home. It's just six blocks. Unless you need to get back to work."

"Not working today," he said. Or ever again, if he could help it. "I'll wait outside."

Five minutes later, her black sandals were flapping against the hot pavement, and she was talking, waving her hands around for punctuation. Her drawl was more pronounced than ever. He mentioned it.

"Oh, we come from downstate Kentucky, almost Tennessee," she said. "Daddy moved up here to work across the river at the Ford plant, and Mommy got a job there too." She twisted her body to look up at him. "You're not from around here?"

"No, I've lived lots of places," Keith said.

"Like where?"

5

He didn't know how much truth to give her. "Far away. Illinois. Indiana."

She scrunched up her freckle-dusted nose. "Those aren't far away. I thought you were talking about some place exciting like California or maybe New York or something."

He laughed. For the first time in weeks. He'd told her the truth and was glad of it. "Nothing exciting about me," he said. But that was a lie.

She said she wanted to go to college, was saving money, but it wouldn't be happening for a while. She wanted to be an elementary school teacher. Her sister Lily was dying to be a beautician, but she was still in high school. Except, of course, it was summer and Lily was watching their brother David, who was twelve but no way capable of being left alone. Lily was going to the movies this afternoon, so that's why Brenda needed to get home. She hardly stopped for air.

"What do you do?" she asked.

"I'm a painter."

"Houses or pictures?" She looked up at him with her head cocked. She reminded him again of a pretty little bird, maybe a nut hatch or a house finch.

"Pictures."

"Ooh. That must be fun. All those colors." She smacked her lips like she could taste them. "Me, I can't even draw a stick man."

"Why would you want to?" This sent her off into a ripple of giggles.

They stopped outside a narrow two story house, heavy-headed hydrangeas leaning against the darkened bricks. He remembered his grandmother having the same plant by her fence, except that she'd called it a snowball bush. He liked the creamy, yellowy tint of them. White had so many variations.

Brenda asked him if he had a dollar bill, and, puzzled, he gave her one. She pulled a pen out of her pocket, scribbled her phone number on the buck, and handed it back to him. She told him to keep trying if the line was busy. Lily was always talking on the phone. And then she said, "Bye, Keith. It was fun talking to you," and scampered into the house. Despite the city traffic, it was suddenly very quiet.

He walked for hours, crossing the Licking River into Newport before finally catching a bus back to Cincinnati. He stopped at a little market near his apartment and bought a six-pack and a couple of frozen dinners. He was tired of eating by himself, but there was no remedy for it. He had no plans to make friends. But he did have plans. Lots of them. He climbed two flights of stained steps and unlocked his door. His silent apartment had trapped the afternoon heat. The beer was already sweating. Maybe he needed a wife. He smiled at this. Right. With the kind of life he was going to lead? He popped the top on his Bud and took a long drink. But being married might make some things easier.

He lifted one of the vinyl couch cushions and felt for the bag he'd stuffed behind the frame. It was still there. So was the one he'd hidden in the bedsprings. Ditto for the one in the oven and the other in a corn flakes box. He sighed and took another drink. A wife could buy a car in her name, a house too. She could set up a bank account with her social security number. It might just be a solution. He'd be free to paint. The thought of this gave him a rush that had nothing to do with beer. It'd been weeks since he'd held a brush. Finishing the beer, he left, locking up carefully, and went back toward the market where there was a pay phone. There was nothing special about little Brenda, but she was young. Maybe a naïve girl wouldn't be as nosy as one with experience. She might do just fine. He fished the dollar bill out of his wallet.

● ● ● ●

The studio was silent. Unnerving. Keith didn't figure listening to music would be disrespectful to Brenda's memory. She'd loved music, although not necessarily what he liked. His tunes were mostly Beatles and Stones, a little Dylan and Clapton. He'd always told the kids that nothing worth listening to had been written since the early seventies. He started up his iPod, and "Come Together" flooded the room. Back in Chicago, over thirty years ago, he'd tried to envision what the character in the song looked like. *Toejam football. Joo joo eyeball.* And he'd painted him in bold strokes and colors. Abstract. Almost scary. He hadn't painted in that style since. That part of him was gone forever.

Two paintings leaned against the painted brick wall that separated the sun porch from the kitchen. He'd finished them before Brenda got so sick. Well, maybe they were finished. He had a hard time letting go of his work, deciding when it was truly done. But Devonie was always begging for more. She said his paintings flew out of her gallery; plus she wanted one or two for an upcoming auction. He had two others he'd been holding back for even longer. Maybe those would suit her. Leon would help him frame and crate, but right then Leon and his wife and sons were at the funeral. Leon adored Brenda. Everybody did. Had.

A weak sun was fighting the clouds, laying a dull pewter on the studio. With all its windows, this room was the most vulnerable. More than thirty years ago, when he and Brenda had first moved into the house, he'd had a ten-foot privacy fence built around the backyard. He kept the door leading from the studio to the patio locked with a deadbolt. But someone could scale the wall, break the glass. He'd felt a little better when he'd had the security people include the wall in their system, but it still worried him. He had to have light, but light made him naked. He was folding rags when the doorbell rang, instantly pumping panic through his body. He froze. That damned Brendan hadn't reset the system when he left.

Pulling off the iPod, he opened the supply cabinet where he kept one of his guns. The pistol felt good and solid in his hand. Creeping into the kitchen, he peered outside through the slats of the shutters over the sink. He could see the circle driveway and nearly to the front gate from there. Parked near the front door was a silver car. Honda Accord. The doorbell rang again.

He tiptoed into the dim hall. Originally, long windows had flanked the door, but he'd had Leon turn those into wall the first few months they'd lived there. He'd left the semi-circular window above the door; it was harmless and Brenda liked it.

Hardly breathing, he fixed his eye to the peephole. It was a woman, and he wondered if it could be Dana. Crazy thought. He didn't think so, but it had been a long time since he'd seen her. This woman was shorter, he thought, although she was about the right age. Gray hair. Dana would've kept hers blonde. The woman was setting a potted plant on the front stoop. Keith took a deep breath. Probably one of Brenda's teacher friends, but why wasn't she at the service? And why would she think anyone was home? The woman walked off the porch, her beige coat wrinkled where she'd sat on it. Without looking back so Keith could get a good glance at her, she got into the Honda and started the engine. Probably okay, probably. But his heart was still thudding as he watched her drive to the gate and leave. From the house he closed the gates and set the alarm.

Over the years he'd Googled Dana, and Nick too, for that matter, but he'd never found a trace about her. She'd vanished. Keith smiled to himself as he went back to the kitchen. He wondered if Dana ever Googled him. The only reference Keith had been able to find for Nick was recent, just a few months back. He was listed as a survivor in an obituary for his father, but this brought Keith no relief. In his will, old Mr. Collins had probably listed every disservice or grievance he'd ever suffered, with specific, and violent, instructions about how to rectify them. Keith lowered the gun and walked back to the studio. Death attracted notice. Maybe it was time to hide again.

Chapter Two

KINLEY

She should've come home more often. The words kept sticking in her brain like a guilty mantra. Her mother had never said anything outright, but there was always a yearning in her voice when she called. Kinley had ignored it. Moving around her old bedroom, she hung up the clothes she'd worn to the funeral and slipped into yoga pants and a faded hoodie. She twisted up her hair and fastened it with the tooled silver clasp Michael had given her for Christmas. Her duties were done for the day, and it'd been one hell of a day. On the way home from the after-funeral lunch, a grim event with her grieving aunt and uncle, she'd made Brendan stop to pick up food for Dad. She'd brought it in, along with a potted plant that had been left on the front porch, and listened to Dad rant about them forgetting to close the gates and set the alarm when they'd left. Megan hadn't gotten out of the car. Dad had eaten what she'd bought and gone straight to the den to watch television. He'd been in there forever. Kinley supposed she should join him, but she didn't want to. Dad, not her mother, was the reason she'd rarely come home.

She remembered how happy, almost giddy, she'd felt when she left Cincinnati for college in Colorado. It'd seemed like running away, something she'd considered more than once during high school. At the time, she'd assumed her dad was nuts. After Psych 101, she'd decided he was agoraphobic. But Dad defied labels; he did leave the house occasionally. Last night, when it was good and dark, he'd walked for an hour on the well-heeled roads of their eastern Cincinnati suburb. She stared at the heavy drapes covering her window. Every window in the house had thick curtains or shutters or blinds. Dad thought there were enemies out there, so they'd had to live in a perpetual blackout.

She shook her head. Other than the family, Leon, and, by email, the gallery owner in New York, Keith Owen didn't interact with anybody. Maybe he was sane, but he certainly was strange. And brilliant. She glanced at the top shelf of her closet where all those sketchbooks she'd filled as a kid still sat. Mom wouldn't throw them away, and Kinley couldn't quite trash them either. Through the years, her mother told her again and again that she'd inherited her father's artistic talent, and, once upon a time, Kinley had believed it, thrilled on the very rare occasions when Dad would say that she had a nice sense of color or proportion. She'd signed up as an art major at the University of Colorado. Now, she wondered why she'd done so, and the only answer she could find was that she'd spent her entire childhood trying to break through Keith Owen's wall. Maybe if they shared something it would happen. Nope. He'd glanced at her freshman portfolio, said her work was disappointing, derivative, and then treated her to a cyanide silence she'd endured for about a week before she fled back to Colorado, switched her major to business, and quit college altogether before the end of her second year.

Kinley sat on the bed and looked around the room. Since the last time she'd come home, five years ago at least, Mom must've given up on the idea that her daughter was ever going to visit and decided to redecorate. God, had it really been five years? Nearly four years ago, she'd seen her mother at Brendan's wedding in Florida, what Megan had called a "destination wedding," complete with vows on the beach and tropical rum punch. Megan had looked absurd trailing her meringue wedding gown across the sand, but at least a beach wedding avoided some questions about Brendan's absent father. Until this trip, that was the last time she'd seen Mom or Brendan. She was a bad daughter, really bad. Kinley looked at the pale green walls and wondered where the Nine Inch Nails and The Cure posters had ended up. Probably in the trash where they belonged. The only familiar piece was her old desk, scarred with dings and ancient splashes of paint, a silent protest against the shiny new furniture.

Kinley turned on her phone, and, as she'd expected, there was a text from Michael, left hours ago. "Hey Sweetheart, hope it wasn't too bad. Thinking about you. Call me when you can." An almost tangible wave of yearning engulfed her. She wanted to go home, and this house wasn't where it lived.

"Where are you?" she asked as soon as Michael said hello. She wanted to place him, see him in her mind.

"Walking home from practicing. Are you doing okay?"

"I'm fine. It's over; that's the most important thing. Why aren't you riding your bike?"

"It snowed this morning. Did you make it through the eulogy?" Michael's voice felt like a warm blanket, but she'd never tell him that.

"I did. So did Brendan. But Aunt Lily couldn't quit crying." She swallowed at the memory. "So many people were there. Kids Mom taught years ago. All grown up now. Her teacher friends. Lots of people."

"She touched a lot of lives."

Kinley had been tough for weeks, constructing a barrier against the hospital, hospice, and her mother's deep decline, but Michael's words crashed through it. Her throat tightened. She wasn't sure whether she was crying for her mother or her screwed-up family or for Michael. She thought she was being quiet about it, but Michael knew. "I wish I were there with you," he said. She hadn't let him come. He had his senior piano recital in six weeks. Airfare was expensive, although Dad would've paid for Michael just as he had for Kinley. But Dad wouldn't have allowed Michael to stay at their house. Just too complicated. Too hard to explain. "I'll be home soon," she said, trying to keep the waver out of her voice.

"When?"

"I'm not sure yet."

"Your dad may want you to stay."

"I doubt it." She sniffed. "How's the music coming?"

"Bach is still kicking my ass."

She gave him a pitiful chuckle. "You'll get it. You know you will."

After they hung up, she glanced at her suitcase in the closet. She was ready to get on a plane tomorrow, tonight, but she'd had enough guilt to last a lifetime. Wiping her face, she stood and took a deep breath. She'd never know whether Dad cared one way or the other, but she'd go downstairs and sit with him. No more remorse, she told herself, even if it killed her.

In the den, the television supplied the only light, turning Dad's silver hair first blue, then green. Kinley could barely remember him having dark hair. According to her mother, Dad had been graying at twenty-four, when Kinley was born. He wore it combed back, and it was a little long. Mom had always cut it for him. Kinley wondered what he'd do now. When Dad saw her, he reached to turn on a lamp by the sofa. "Hi," he said. "You doing all right?"

What if she said she wasn't? Would he call an ambulance or see if a shrink would make a house call? "I'm okay. How about you?" She sat in her mother's usual place, next to Dad, at the end of the sofa. She wondered if he noticed.

He paused the TV. "I don't know." He waved his right hand, the hand that painted what critics called "modern masterpieces." One hell of a hand. "I miss her," he said. "But after all the chemo and pain and months of broken hopes. . ." His voice trailed off. He met Kinley's eyes. "Relief," he finished.

Kinley nodded. Maybe she should hug him. She'd done that as a child, wrapping her arms around his big, solid body and smelling sharp turpentine and earthy pigments. "Me too," she said. No, she couldn't hug him.

Maybe he sensed her decision. He gestured at the television, to a frozen screen of tropical plants and birds. "Look at those colors," he said. "South America. Colombia. Fantastic."

He'd always watched travel shows. Ironic. Kinley didn't say anything.

Pulling at the collar of his denim shirt, he kept his eyes on the screen. "You're welcome to stay as long as you want, Kinley." He paused. "I like having you here."

She believed him, as far as it went. She could stay as long as she didn't interrupt his painting or solitude or rigid routines. Dad had a million unpublished rules.

Before she could reply, he said, "But I would really appreciate it if you'd stay long enough to go through your mother's things, her clothes and all. I don't know what to do with them." He glanced at her and then back at the television. "Take anything you want—mementos, whatever. Brendan told me he'd like to have her diamond to keep for Cassie until she grows up. But anything else."

Kinley didn't want the ring. She couldn't think of anything she did want. "I guess I could do that. Spend a couple more days. Maybe pick out a few things to send to Aunt Lily and Uncle David."

He kept staring at the television, probably determining the exact mix of pigments for the leaves, the bird's plumage. "Sure. Good," he murmured.

She sat with him for an hour, but he never said another word about anything but the shows he was watching. Kinley was glad when her friend Sarah called. It gave her an excuse to leave him.

The next day she worked in her parents' room, and by afternoon she was nearly done emptying her mother's drawers of underwear, nightgowns, and socks. Echoing up from the basement came the sound of muted hammering. She knew what it meant. Her dad and Leon were packing up pictures to send to the gallery in New York. As she recalled, that nearly always happened just before he embarked on a painting frenzy. She hoped she was gone before it started. They'd hated those times. He'd hardly eat, shower, speak. Mom would take them out to the mall, the library, anywhere, just to keep them out of the house. And then, after dark and past their bedtimes, they'd come home. Kinley and Brendan would do their homework while Mom checked her third-graders' papers. They could make noise then, because when the light was gone, Dad didn't paint.

It wasn't fair that her mother had to die so young, only fifty, nor was it fair that her mother had to die first. She'd been entitled to some normalcy and peace.

Kinley started grabbing clothes from her mother's closet: slacks, tops, those cutesy embroidered sweaters and denim shirts that elementary teachers tended to wear. They were all size small, petite, something Kinley hadn't been since seventh grade when her father's height had asserted itself. She stuffed the garments into bags for Good Will. Tomorrow she was going home.

The closet was empty except for a few items stored on the high shelf. Kinley stretched to reach a hatbox containing ball caps left over from the sports she and Brendan had played all the way back to T-Ball. Brendan had been athletic, although she didn't think he was now. She didn't know, and she should. She blamed Dad for the distance between her and her baby brother too. Mom had come to every game, worn their team's hats, cheered. Kinley rubbed at her leaky eyes and put the lid back on. Brendan might want these. She glanced back up at the shelf. There were some quilts from Mom's family. She pulled these down. Aunt Lily should have them. Hidden under the quilts was another box. She had to stand on tiptoes to reach it; Mom would've needed a ladder. Opening the box, Kinley found a photo album. As far as she knew, there wasn't a family photo in the house. Dad had always forbidden them to take pictures. There were so many bizarre rules in their family that Kinley had never questioned it. She remembered how Mom had needed to beg him to allow their yearbook photos. Heart pumping, Kinley turned on a lamp and sat on the bed, spreading the album in front of her. The first pictures were really old, turning orange with age. There were Christmas shots of Grandma and Grandpa, with Mom no older than seven or eight and Aunt Lily two years younger. Uncle David was a toddler, supporting himself against a worn sofa while he gripped a toy airplane. Kinley studied every picture. She'd never seen any of them. As she turned the album pages, her mother grew up until there were five or six shots of her in her graduation gown with various people posed beside her, all smiling. Aunt Lily's dark hair was streaked with blonde. From under her mortarboard, Mom's hair poured halfway down her back. Mom had been cute, cheerful, happy. The way she'd always tried to be with Brendan and her.

And then there was nothing but blank pages. Kinley knew the dates. Mom had married Dad two months after her high school graduation. No wedding pictures. Nothing. But she felt something more in the album and flipped to the back where a large yellow envelope was taped to the cover, sticky now with age. Very carefully, Kinley pulled the envelope away from the album and fished out a stack of foreign pictures. She had to stare at them a while to realize that they were of her and Brendan as babies here in this house. One of her with her hair braided, looking over the top of infant Brendan's cradle. Dad had made that cradle. She supposed it was still down in the basement. Another of her and Brendan at maybe four and two, in swimsuits, aiming a hose into a wading pool. Nothing dramatic, but she couldn't believe she'd never seen the photos. Ever. Impatient now, she shuffled through the stack, seeing Brendan, herself, and occasionally Mom. The ones of her mother were off-center, blurry. Had she taken these? She had no memory of it. There wasn't a single picture of her father with her mother or his children. It was as if he didn't exist except as a sperm donor.

It was too weird, and that was saying something in their family. Before she could think any more about it, Kinley grabbed her phone and started to text Brendan. Then she remembered how he hated texts. He'd told her that texts were conversation condoms. She smiled and called him.

As soon as he said hello, Kinley started. "Do you think Dad is in the witness protection program? Or something like that? Maybe he was a spy or something? An escaped con?"

Brendan always spoke slowly. Sometimes it drove Kinley crazy. "Oh, sure. CIA. James Bond with a brush. He's never left the house enough to spy on anybody. What makes you think that?"

"I found some pictures of us I've never seen before. Pictures when we were babies, little kids, and there's not a picture anywhere with Dad in it. You know how he's never let us take his picture or any pictures for that matter, but I never considered why he wouldn't. Just another odd thing about our odd dad."

"Who took the pictures then?"

"Mom, I guess. Sneaked them when he wasn't here. Except he was usually here. Maybe those times when he ran away, I don't know." Kinley stared at one of her and Brendan in front of a Christmas tree. "I don't remember posing for any of these, but we were pretty little. Don't you think it's strange that he prohibited pictures? Do you think there might be some big secret? Or is he just nuts?"

"I choose nuts. He's always been a poster boy for the Eccentric Artist Guild. I expect him to cut off an ear any day." Brendan might've been waiting for her to snicker, but she didn't. Finally he said, "I don't think he has a secret identity or anything."

She could hear traffic behind Brendan's voice. "But think about it. Wouldn't him being in the witness protection program explain a lot?"

"If you want to give him an excuse, sure."

That shut her up for a minute. He'd always thought that Mom had gotten a raw deal in marrying Dad. She recalled how Brendan's jaw had worked, then tightened during the funeral. They both had loved their

14

mother, but Brendan and Mom had some special kind of radar. The two B's, she remembered them saying and laughing about it. Just like she and her dad had been the two K's. Right. No magic there. She swallowed. "I just thought it made sense," she muttered.

Brendan ignored this. "I'd love to see those pictures."

"Well, come on over. I've got chili simmering. Leon's still here helping Dad frame and crate."

"Uh, oh. You know what that means."

She scrunched up her nose before answering. "Yeah. But I'll be gone before he starts."

"When are you leaving?"

"Tomorrow."

Brendan didn't answer right away. "I want to see you again before you go. And the photos. Let me call Megan. Did you put meat in the chili?"

She growled at him. He'd always made fun of her intermittent attempts at going vegetarian. "Of course I did. Dad wouldn't eat it otherwise."

"I'll be there in fifteen," he said.

She took the pictures to her room, just in case Dad came upstairs. He might burn them or something. She glanced at the green garbage bags lining the walls. They seemed sadder than the funeral or even those last days in hospice. All those things, still smelling of her mother's laundry soap or perfume or even that faint spicy scent of her hair, cast off, unnecessary. Leon had said he'd get rid of them. She didn't think she could. Kinley slid the album under her bed and went downstairs. At least she wouldn't have to eat her last meal alone with Dad.

Grabbing a box of oyster crackers and a stack of bowls, Kinley set the table for three. She'd ask Leon to stay, but he wouldn't. She couldn't recall a time when Leon hadn't been all but part of the family, but she also couldn't recall him ever eating supper with them. The old story, according to Mom, was that Leon had worked for the landscaping company that finished the house when it was new; he'd set in the yews and maples that were either huge by now or long gone. He'd quit the landscapers and come to work for Dad right after they'd moved into the house. Back in middle school, when she'd been hooked on old-fashioned romances, Kinley had called him their "general factotum." Leon had laughed at this, saying it was a better title than "handyman." She never knew a time when Leon hadn't been part of her life. He loved to tell how two-year-old Kinley had tried to lick him once, thinking he was made of chocolate like the bunny in her Easter basket. He'd taught both her and Brendan how to throw and catch, how to change lightbulbs and tires. He still mowed the gigantic yard, did repairs and cleaning and ran errands for Dad. Kinley gave the burbling pot of chili a stir. Recluses couldn't get by without their general factotums. She had no idea how much Dad paid Leon, but it could never be enough.

"Supper's soon," she yelled down the steps. "Brendan's coming too."

"Smells good," Leon called back. Dad said nothing.

The two of them had just come upstairs when Brendan arrived, looking nearly as brittle as he had the day of the funeral. She doubted that Dad had any idea how much Brendan resented the fact that their mother was dead but Dad was still alive. Leon, though, seemed to size it all up and patted Brendan's arm. Tall and lean despite threads of white in his crinkly hair, Leon gave Kinley a little squeeze. She wondered if he had stayed for so many years out of allegiance to Mom or Dad. "I'll finish the crating tomorrow, Keith," Leon said, "and get those babies shipped." He put on his jacket.

Dad asked, "What time?"

Leon shrugged. "Whenever you want."

Dad turned his back and focused on washing his hands. "I was wondering if you could take Kinley to the airport. Her flight's at ten something."

Kinley felt a knot building in her chest. It wouldn't kill Dad to drop her off at the terminal. No one would see him. It seemed like the least he could do. But Leon said, "Sure thing. I'll be here by eight. Okay, girlie?" It was what he'd always called her.

It should've been a homey, family scene after all the upset and trauma. Steam rose from the chili, and spoons clinked against pottery bowls. Something out of Norman Rockwell, whom her father always belittled. But it wasn't one bit warm and cozy. For a while Kinley tried to make conversation, first with her father, then with Brendan. Her brother was a little more responsive, but each topic she tried went as flat as stale beer. Dad did say the chili was good. When she asked, he replied that they'd crated three paintings. And he said yes, when Kinley asked if Leon could mail a few of Mom's things to Aunt Lily. That was it. As soon as Dad finished, he escaped to his den. He and Brendan hadn't exchanged any words at all. Leaning back in her chair, Kinley stared at Brendan. He was still gorgeous. She remembered being disgusted with her high school girlfriends when they passed her little brother in the hall and gushed over him. He had Dad's square jaw and height with Mom's coloring. But his dark blue eyes were his own, the result of some lucky dive into an older gene pool. She wondered if the college girls crushed on their handsome librarian.

"What?" he asked, reaching for another handful of oyster crackers. He lined them up on his placemat, like he used to do his M & M's. "I'm not going to make nice any more. I only ever did it for Mom."

"I know that." She reached for her wineglass. The other two had drunk Coke, but she'd gone through several bottles of red the last few weeks. It helped. "She never complained about him."

"That's because she was a saint." Two crackers went into his mouth.

"She seemed to love him."

Brendan stared at the puffy little crackers. She noticed a pick or two on his navy blue sweater, and he'd picked up a little weight over the last four years. It wasn't like him to tolerate any sloppiness. She wondered about Megan. Mom had never said a word to her about Brendan's wife, but Kinley had seen how her mother's lips went thin when anyone mentioned her.

He said, "And that's because our mother was a good-hearted fool."

Kinley shook her head and drank off the rest of her wine. "Come upstairs and look at the pictures. You're going to be amazed."

He was more shaken than amazed. Holding each photo close to Kinley's bedside lamp, he marveled over them; she would've bet he was one inch from tears. "Look at us," he breathed. "I had no idea there were any pictures of us."

"Aunt Lily took some when we used to visit her and Grandma down in Kentucky."

"Yeah, and they all had to stay there, didn't they?" He held up another, one with Mom in it. "Who took these?" He frowned. "And where did the camera come from? Dad never let us have a camera in the house."

"Mom probably had one hidden." Kinley pointed to the blurry photo of her mother holding Brendan. "I think I took these. Look how bad they are."

Brendan raised his head and stared at her. "Why do you think he's always been so weird about pictures? Megan and I probably have a hundred of Cassie already."

Kinley dropped into the desk chair. "Maybe it would blow his cover." She held up a hand. "I know. You think I'm crazy, but do you see how I came up with the witness protection thing? It's weird. Almost spooky."

Brendan held each photo carefully with his fingertips even though they were faded and worn. Ignoring her, he said, "I have to have copies of these."

"Take them," Kinley said. "I don't want them."

He gave her a quick look.

"I don't. Really." He obviously thought her theory was stupid and she guessed it was, but she persisted. "Have you ever done computer research on Dad? I mean, more than just Google? When you're bored at the library or something?" He must have access to several databases at the university library. Hell, he was a reference librarian, the next best thing to God when it came to information.

Brendan was still concentrating on the photos. His eyes looked bruised. None of them had slept much the last few weeks, but Brendan had worked even when he hadn't slept the night before. "Yeah. I've done a pretty thorough job on him." He shook his head. "Nothing we didn't know. King of the Artists. Amazing talent. The gallery, the sales."

"I wonder if he's even met Devonie. I mean, she's been promoting his work for decades."

Brendan shook his head. "Nope. I asked Mom once what she was like, and she said she had no idea. Just an email address. He's never met her."

"Do you think Mom knew more about Dad than she told us?"

"Maybe. Not that it'll do us any good now." He slid the photos back into the envelope. "Whenever I asked her for more about Dad, she'd clam up. You too, right?"

Kinley nodded. "Which could mean that she knew but couldn't tell or that she was ashamed she didn't know more."

Brendan stood up. "You read too many mysteries in your misspent youth, Kin. He's just a jerk, a brilliant, reclusive jerk. That's all." He smiled to take the sting out and Kinley let it go. It wasn't like she disagreed. She stood too.

"I'll miss you," he said, hugging her.

"Come to Colorado." She spoke into his shoulder. "I worry about you."

He shook his head at her invitation. "I'm fine."

Chapter Three

She considered pumping Leon for information when he drove her to the airport the next morning. But halfway across the Ohio River, he'd started reassuring her that he'd take good care of her father and that she shouldn't worry and he sounded so sweet, so Leon, that she hadn't wanted to upset him with questions he either couldn't or wasn't supposed to answer. It was silly anyway. Her father was who he was for whatever reason, and if he'd let them all down fourteen billion times, so be it.

Still, she couldn't let go of her curiosity, Brendan's resentment, and the realization that their mother had provided a loving buffer between them and the worst aspects of their father's character. Kinley could hear her mother's voice, soft and southern. "Your daddy just doesn't like crowds, Kinley" and "Daddy's with you in spirit, Brendan." And worst of all: "You all should be proud to have such a talented father." The buffer was gone now.

Somewhere over what was probably Kansas, her fretting transformed itself into a dull ache, which had more to do with needing Michael than missing her mother. She'd thought about asking him to meet her at the airport but hadn't. That would've meant time away from his piano. Sarah was coming instead. It was okay; Kinley could wait until evening when he'd be hers, at least until morning when he had to leave early for his church job.

As soon as she saw the white-topped Rockies and the teepees of the Denver Airport meant to mimic them, she felt like she was home. She summoned Sarah from the cell-phone lot and waited, taking deep breaths of air that felt fresh despite fumes from all the traffic. The sky was Colorado blue, intense, fathomless. Pulling up to the curb, Sarah honked once and waved. Damn, she'd missed Sarah too. She'd been Kinley's first tenant five years ago. And she'd become her best friend and nearly an assistant manager for the ten apartments Kinley had carved from three old houses.

"What's going on?" Kinley asked as they set out on their drive to Boulder. "Anything new?" She definitely did not want to talk about her mother's death and funeral.

Sarah got it. She maneuvered Kinley's Scion around airport traffic. "Nothing much. The guys in the gray house had a big party last week. I had to go shut them down before the neighbors called the cops. A plugged up toilet at the brick house. Plunger duty. It worked." She raised her eyebrows over huge sunglasses that made her look like a bug. She was short, a little plump, and darted everywhere at top speed whether it was in a car, or her bike, or on foot. "Everything's cool. Went to see my advisor, and it looks like I'll have my big, bad Master's at the end of the summer."

"Yay." Kinley tried for enthusiasm. "Except you'll be leaving me then. Going back to Wyoming to meet a cowboy." Every time she made friends with her tenants, they left. They graduated or quit school or moved in with a boy or girlfriend. Michael too. He'd be graduating even sooner, in May. She'd lose him and Sarah at nearly the same time.

Sarah shook her head. "No damned cowboys, thanks. They need a speech therapist in Broomfield. I've got an interview at the end of the month."

"Super. But you'll want to move closer, won't you?"

Sarah shrugged. "Not necessarily. It's not far; besides, I gotta get the job first, don't I?"

Kinley stared at the concrete winding ahead. "How's my boy?" She shouldn't call him that; it was demeaning really, although Michael never seemed to mind. But he was a boy, to her at least. Twenty-two to her thirty. She was crazy for letting herself fall for him.

"Fine. Never home." Sarah would know. Kinley had divided the yellow house into three apartments: the entire first floor for her and two smaller flats upstairs for student rentals. Sarah lived in one, Michael in the other, although he spent most days and nights downstairs with Kinley. He fussed about it, saying he could move in with her and she could rent his place and get more money. He'd still pay rent or contribute one way or another. But she never agreed. It would be tempting fate.

"Always in a practice room, I guess," she said. Okay, she was searching.

"Probably." Sarah glanced sideways at Kinley. "I don't think he's ever given you reason to doubt him."

He hadn't. She was stupid, insecure, silly. Sarah started talking about a paper she was writing and then an exam she'd aced. Kinley tried to listen. As they neared her house, she watched for its yellow paint and broad porch like it was a talisman. She'd loved the place from the minute she'd seen it, biking down the street as a freshman. When it had come up for sale, she'd known she had to have it, somehow or the other. Dad bought it for her and paid for its renovations along with the gray house next door, despite the fact that she'd quit college. Sometimes it made her feel guilty about how she blasted him in her head. He'd always bought Brendan and her whatever they wanted. It made her feel a little better to reassure herself that she was doing her own financing on the brick house three blocks over. Sarah parked Kinley's car in back and climbed the wooden steps to her apartment, saying they should have dinner later or something. Kinley nodded, but they both knew she'd be with Michael. She hoped. Her kitchen smelled like herbs and coffee, familiar but at the same time foreign. She'd been gone a long time.

Everything was neat. Michael treated her place like he was a guest. She'd complained about it, saying he could put his dirty dishes in the sink rather than washing every spoon as soon as he used it; he could throw his towels across the shower bar. But he never did. She'd always considered her brother a neat freak, but he was slovenly compared to Michael. Midday light fell into the kitchen. Kinley touched the coffeepot. Cold. Michael had been gone a while.

The living room was dim, shaded by the front porch. She set down her bags and wandered to the front corner where she had a desk and filing cabinet. Ten apartments required a lot of paper. This month's rent checks were clipped together. Michael had done that, but there was no note. Nothing personal. Last night she'd told him when her flight was getting in. She'd hoped that maybe he'd be home to greet her, or at least leave her a slip of paper saying 'welcome home.'

She carried her bags to the bedroom. It was as surgically tidy as the rest of the apartment. The wide bed was made, not a bump or wrinkle. She picked up a pillow and sniffed. Essence of dryer sheet. Either he'd changed the bed or retreated to his Spartan studio upstairs while she'd been gone. Her gaze flittered over to the painting on the wall opposite the bed. Aspens in autumn against a Colorado sky. Her one original Keith Owen. The first few weeks of her freshman year, she'd begged her father for a painting, and he'd been agreeable enough, maybe even pleased that she wanted one. And then he'd fussed when she'd dictated the subject since he'd not seen it for himself. The picture would probably net a fortune if Devonie knew it existed.

She should unpack. She even went so far as to unzip her bag but walked away. Her steps clattered against the hardwood in the dining room: her studio. Boxes of cheap glassware stock lined one wall. Her paints littered the work table under the window. Dad painted masterpieces. Kinley painted grapes and cherries and holly on pitchers and wineglasses.

In the kitchen she opened a bottle of wine and poured some into an unpainted wineglass. The stuff she decorated was cute; it made some money, but she thought the fancy glassware was prissy, silly. The wine hit the back of her throat like a balm. Flying always made her thirsty. She should drink water, but what the hell. She glanced at the clock. Maybe Michael was planning a welcome home dinner. He was completely Italian and a great cook. She opened the refrigerator to see if he'd bought ingredients for shrimp fra diavolo or his yummy spinach and chicken dish. Three beers, a dried-up hunk of cheddar, and some grapes. Quit wishing for miracles, she told herself and threw back another slug of wine.

Five minutes later she was driving to campus. It was easy to find a parking spot on a Saturday, and although she didn't have a student sticker, the campus cops rarely gave parking tickets on weekends. She went into the music building and headed for the practice rooms. Many of them were being used, and a wild cacophony blasted down the narrow hallway. Violin, a reedy tenor voice, oboe or was it bassoon? She couldn't tell the difference. Michael always used the room at the end if he could get it. As she neared the last room, she heard him. The notes flowed and ebbed like waves. Must be the Mendelssohn, she thought.

She hesitated. Dad had usually shrieked when they interrupted his painting; she wasn't sure what Michael would do. She never interrupted him. She pictured Michael's fingers, running over the keys, strong and gentle at the same time, the tendons and muscles in his arms, hidden beneath his shirt, rippling like his music. Her breath came quickly. She went in, stopping his phrase, closed the door, and leaned against it. "I'm home," she murmured. The room was little larger than a closet and held only the essentials: a piano and bench, a music stand, a folding chair, and Michael's backpack and jacket on the floor.

He turned his head, eyes glazed from concentration, hands still hovering over the keys, but then he smiled and morphed into her Archangel Michael, one of those dark-haired, beautiful Italian boys in Renaissance paintings. "I'm glad," he said.

She didn't move from the door. "Take me," she said.

"What?" She didn't repeat herself. "Here?"

She nodded.

"Now?"

"Absolutely now."

Chapter Four

KEITH

He awoke with a start, the images still vivid. He hadn't dreamed of Dana in ages; he'd assumed she'd exited his subconscious just as she'd left his life over thirty years ago. He'd been Tom then, although Dana and Nick both called him Tommy. Twenty years old and bursting with unfulfilled passions. Perhaps he'd dreamt of Dana, and sex, since the two were all but synonymous, because he'd spent the last two days painting flesh, a woman's torso from the slightest whisper of her breasts' rise to the rounded belly just below her navel. But the headless body didn't belong to Dana.

Willing himself to calm down, he lay still for a few minutes. In reality, there'd be no more women in his life. He couldn't risk it again. That part of his life was finished. It was another discipline he'd have to accept for the sake of painting.

<u>1975</u>

They were driving a green Pinto to Memphis. It was his first run but not Dana's. He was driving. She was nonchalant, relaxed, her long, tan legs folded so her bony feet could rest on the edge of the seat. Hot air blew through the windows. Dana wore shorts. Tom tried to focus on the road rather than Dana's bare legs, golden, the calves echoing the curve of her arm, her cheek. He could paint that sweet curve. No face, no upper body, just her leg.

"Stop soon, Tommy. I'm dying of thirst," she said.

He nodded, switching lanes so he'd be ready for an exit. It was late afternoon, and they were about halfway between Chicago and Memphis, driving through flat farmland that reminded him of home. Their orders were to stay at a motel on this side of the city, and early in the morning he

23

was to take the package to TWA air freight. He was more worried about the motel than the mission. He wondered how the hell he was going to sleep in the same room as Dana without touching her. But he couldn't. Nick would kill him. Literally.

"Don't talk much, do you?" She shifted, stretching her legs out as far as she could. He forced his gaze back to the hot asphalt.

"I guess not."

"Always thinking about those amazing pictures you're gonna paint, aren't you?" He could sense that she was smiling, teasing him.

He spotted a sign for an exit. "Pretty much."

She lifted her heavy hair, blonde and as straight as a hippie chick's. "God, it's hot," she said. "Wish this stupid car had air conditioning."

He imagined sweat trickling between her breasts, pictured himself licking it. He had to quit this. He and Dana had a job. And performing it successfully would net him enough cash to pay a little rent on the studio he shared with Nick as well as living expenses. He might even be able to quit his part-time job at the hellacious pizza joint. And then he could just paint and paint and paint.

●●●●

Keith raised himself out of bed with a grunt. He'd bought himself a lifetime of painting; he needed to get his lazy ass moving and do it. It was still only five a.m. when he eased Brenda's car out of the garage and crept down the driveway. Out on the road there was no traffic, nobody to see him. He still had plenty of gas in the tank. No additional stops. He drove cautiously as he always did, apprehensive about being stopped by the police, although there was no reason to fear them. He remembered Brendan spitting out words like "paranoid" and "delusional," at him over Brenda's inert body, a few hours before she died. It had been early morning like this. His son didn't know what he was talking about, and Keith wasn't about to tell him, but he was sick of hiding. He just didn't know how to quit.

He pulled into the lot of a mega-grocery, open twenty-four hours a day. Leon had offered to do this for him, but Keith wanted to make his own choices. A cold wind cut through his jacket as he walked into the store. He picked up a small basket rather than choosing a cart. It would be enough.

The produce department blazed under bright lights, the fruits and vegetables glowing with such vivid color that they hardly looked real. He found the ruby grapefruit immediately and put two in his basket. Better to have spares. Then he found the avocados, black-skinned and rough. He'd have preferred the green ones with their glossy curves, but Leon had said that they were scarce around here. The coarse skin was ominous, ugly.

24

Probably a better choice anyway. Keith felt them for firmness; he didn't want overripe fruit. Again he chose two.

He saw another shopper, a man in work clothes, probably coming home from a night shift somewhere. The guy was buying bananas. Keith skirted him and glanced at the displays. What he was looking for wouldn't be in a large stack. Maybe the small shelves at the ends. He found mangoes, almonds, some kind of red gooey stuff to glaze strawberries. Not what he was looking for. He might have to go elsewhere, but he wasn't sure where. Leon said there was a produce market over on Montgomery Road, but Keith didn't want to venture that far afield, nor did he want to ask the clerk who'd just come out of the back room with a cart full of lettuce. There was one more place to look. Keeping his chin down, Keith passed the clerk and looked just past the plums and nectarines. There. Yes. He picked up two pomegranates.

This early in the morning there was only one cashier. Keith set the basket of fruit on the belt and turned his head, his fingers wavering toward the candy bars. He rarely ate candy anymore; Brenda said it was bad for him. Why did he crave sweets this morning? He grabbed a Snickers and a Hershey bar and slid them next to the grapefruits, ignoring the cashier's bored voice asking for a discount card and paying her with cash.

Once he got home, he arranged the still life. That's what people would call it, and they'd have no idea how correct they'd be. While he waited for what promised to be good morning light, he found Leon's contributions: a long board coarsely painted pinkish beige, and a shiny new scalpel. Leon always delivered the tough stuff.

He'd already cleared the table in his studio and placed the board on it. He angled it to catch the strongest sunlight. He wanted to imitate an operating room's illumination. Throughout the day he'd have to keep moving the board, maybe even using the mirrors he kept for heightened reflection. He tweaked and fiddled until all he had left to do was prepare the fruit. Keith took a deep breath. He could've used one of Brenda's knives, sitting slanted in a wooden block. Leon kept them sharp; she'd always bragged on him for that. But Keith had to use the scalpel.

He cut the avocado first, running the blade around the stone but leaving it intact. He discarded the empty half and placed the one with the bulging stone on the board. Then he halved the grapefruit, glad that beads of juice glistened on its pulp. He took one half and set in on the board, positioning it just so in relationship to the avocado. He'd consulted the Internet to learn how to cut a pomegranate. Who ate pomegranates? It was tricky, but the scalpel worked well, and he set it on the board, teasing a few of the dark seeds away from the fruit. He exhaled. Yes, that was what he'd envisioned. After washing the scalpel, he polished it until it gleamed with purpose and, perhaps, malice. He set it on the board by the fruits. Yes.

Turning to the canvas, he scrutinized what was already there. Over the years he'd painted and drawn nudes when he could get models. Dana twice, acts of relentless discipline. And he'd painted Brenda nude the one time he was able to coax the shyness out of her. While he'd worked on the torso he put Dana's golden-hued skin out of his mind and recalled Brenda's flesh, the whisper of pink under white. He'd got it right.

Leon arrived, but the sound hardly registered. He worked. He worked so hard and fast that he felt sweat ooze from his skin, and that was a good sign. Leon's board was the wrong color. Annoying, but he already had the flesh. Now it was just a matter of transferring the fruit onto the belly. He mixed his pigments with a sure hand. He had the flow.

He sensed when the sun moved straight up and wasn't surprised when Leon tapped on the studio door to offer him lunch. Raising his paintbrush, he moved it sideways along with his head. No, I'm not stopping. And he didn't stop until the only illumination came from overhead lights. Not enough, but he went on anyway. By now the picture was as fixed as a photograph in his mind. The fruits were drooping; they'd be mush tomorrow, and the spares would never look the same. He kept working even after his feet ached from standing. His back had stiffened, and his fingers cramped, but he went on until the shadows started wavering. He glanced at his watch. It was two-thirty in the morning. Standing a few feet back from the painting, he ate both candy bars, hardly tasting anything but cloying sweetness. He made himself turn off the lights and wander through the dark house, checking the security system and going upstairs.

1975

Nick had ordered him to get a room with two beds in Memphis. "Not that I don't trust you, man," he'd said to Tom with a grin that said he didn't trust him at all. "I wouldn't have her go at all, except well. . ." Except that Nick didn't trust him with the package either. Dana had made runs before. She'd show him the ropes, Nick had said.

It was dark, late when they reached the outskirts of town. Dana had insisted that they pick up burgers at McDonald's and take them to the motel. It was an ordinary cheap room: orange bedspreads and terrible paintings of ships over the beds. Dana opened the wrapper on her Big Mac. "It's gonna be a long night. Did you bring any weed?" she asked. She'd flipped off her shoes and sat on a bed, her feet tan and dirty as a little girl's.

He shook his head. He didn't have money for that, although he was happy enough to partake if someone else bought it.

She sighed as if this were a huge disappointment and then bit into the gooey burger. Her teeth were perfectly straight, a little wider than normal, like those of a small animal who needed to crunch hard things to survive. He grinned at the image and covered it by pulling on the straw of his Coke. "I guess we could get some beer," he offered.

She made a face and kept eating, not saying anything but looking at him the whole time she was chewing. He was uncomfortable as hell. He hated people watching him eat. He gobbled down his food, finishing long before Dana. Finally she balled up the wrappers and stuffed them into the grease-splotched bag. "TV is shit," she said, rising from the edge of the bed. He'd sat at the scarred table, keeping his distance. "I bet you're nervous about the drop-off, aren't you?"

He nodded.

"Who are you?" she asked.

He understood and pulled the fake driver's license from his pocket. "John Wethington," he said. "I'm shipping owner's manuals for office machines to a guy in Hialeah, Florida."

"Go ahead and put the fake in your wallet and stow the real one in your shoe or something. It's better that you don't have to think about anything in the morning. We're supposed to get there at six-thirty. Earlier than God."

He did what she said. "Why so early?"

She shrugged and the strap of her top slid off her shoulder. There was no bra strap showing. "Nick says the theory is that clerks are all half-asleep at that hour. But there's nothing to worry about. They never check the boxes. I've done it three times now. No problem." She grinned and walked over to him. "But it's best if you're relaxed." When her bare leg touched his jeans, she pulled the flimsy shirt over her head. He was right; no bra. God, he thought, beautiful tits. Then his brain started screaming at the risk. Nick.

Dana was reading his mind. "How will he ever know?"

●●●●

All day he'd painted a memorial to Brenda. Why was he thinking of Dana? Keith shook his head, trying to dislodge the pictures. He'd waked up with Dana and now she was trying to go to bed with him. Again. He didn't want her in his brain. He folded his paint-daubed jeans on the floor by the bed. He remembered telling Brenda, way back when they'd first married, that there was no sense in trying to get paint spots out of his clothes. He often wiped his brushes on his jeans. Smocks were for dilettantes. He shut his eyes and tried to harness his dreams, willing them to be about his wife.

All week he worked on the painting, finally getting out the spare fruit and slicing it, depicting the sliced flesh as obscene rather than appetizing. Occasionally Leon made him eat. And after that first night when he'd worked until long after dark, he quit when he lost his light. He'd found errors the next day. He was right to be a slave to light.

Finally he was able to surface into real life. Keith's mouth turned up into a grim smile at this. Most people would say he never experienced real life. But he returned Devonie's email from earlier in the week when she'd gushed about the new paintings, discussed when she planned to display them, told how she was calling someone to write about them. He shaved. He got into his basement safe, bolted to the concrete floor, and counted his cash. Not so very much. He liked to keep a sizeable amount in the house in case he needed to make a quick exit. It took too long to get money from Switzerland, but even securing local funds would be a problem now since the Cincinnati account was in Brenda's name, along with Brendan's. Everything needed to be put right. The death certificates had come. He emailed Brendan who wouldn't like taking care of his dad's business but could hardly refuse. Real life.

Chapter Five

BRENDAN

Grey rain fell from grey skies onto grey concrete buildings surrounding the library. His dad might've found something intriguing in the dim, soft light, but Brendan thought it was depressing. He sat at the reference desk with nothing to do. A few students trudged by him, heading for the long rows of computers, dumping their sodden bookbags on the floor. Most of them would be checking email or Facebook rather than working. It was the week after spring break; nobody had much motivation. He'd been amused by the students' tan faces, baked the week before in Florida or Mexico, now wrapped up in hoods and hats against the damp cold of March in Cincinnati.

Another hour or so and he could go home. There was some joy there; mostly in the form of Cassie who jumped up and down, tickled with her ability to do that now, and yammered, "Da-da-da-da." And a lot of gibberish he pretended to understand. Brendan smiled. At least his mother had known the pleasure of a grandchild for a while. She'd melted over Cassie, hugging her and crooning songs that he wished he remembered.

He moved his mouse, clicked a time or two, and checked his own email, watching to make sure the reference supervisor wasn't watching. Her name was Beverly Rappaport, so naturally he'd nicknamed her "The Raptor," bringing horrified giggles from some of the circulation and processing people. Beverly timed his lunch breaks to the half-minute and loved to remind him that he had neither sick nor vacation days left after the time he'd taken during his mother's illness. He wasn't singled out for her spite; she hated everyone, but she was his boss so her venom affected every hour he spent at work. His mail consisted of junk from the Health Center promoting cholesterol tests and a Student/Faculty 5K run in late April. More junk from the provost and the library director. He deleted several messages before he saw that one was from his mother. Well, not really. Like everything else, Dad hid behind her identity when he ventured into the world. Brendan clicked. It was spare, no greetings, no civilities. It was as if Dad thought excessive words might reveal his secrets. "Need to talk to you about business. Soon." Brendan shook his head and typed, "I work tomorrow evening, so I'll come in the morning around nine." No greetings, no civilities from him either.

It was still raining when he got home. Megan's car, her beloved Lexus, was snug inside the one-car garage. His Hyundai, eight years old and tired, deserved no better than sitting out in the elements, according to Megan. The minute Cassie heard him, she ran from the kitchen, a soggy saltine clutched in her hand. She jabbered. He kissed her cheek. Baby cheeks were irresistible. "Where's Mommy?" he asked.

Cassie pointed down the hall. Brendan took off his wet jacket and hung it on a doorknob. He found Megan in the bathroom, putting on makeup. It wasn't for him. "Where are you going?" he asked.

"I told you. We're trying out that new Thai restaurant."

She held a tiny brush to her eyelashes and stared ahead into the mirror. She looked good, maybe even better than when he'd met her up at Kent State while he'd been working on his library degree. She was slim, toned. After Cassie, she'd demanded a membership at a gym, one with babysitters, and she went three days a week. Putting down the mascara brush, she slid her eyes over to him. "Still raining?"

"Pouring."

Cassie came flying down the hall and crashed into the bathroom, grabbing one of Megan's legs. Cracker goo speckled the stylish black slacks. "Damn," Megan said, reaching for a towel. "Get her out of here, will you? I need to leave in fifteen minutes."

Brendan picked the baby up and nuzzled a soft spot under her spiderweb hair. "What are we supposed to eat?"

Megan shrugged.

It didn't matter. Most nights Brendan made dinner anyway. Megan did shop, sometimes; they always had yogurt in the fridge and blue boxes of mac and cheese in the pantry. He carried Cassie to the kitchen. Broken saltines littered the floor. Dirty dishes filled the sink. After Cassie, Megan had begged to quit her paralegal job. She wanted to be a full-time mommy, she'd said, but obviously not a housekeeper. She knew Brendan's salary was crap, but she'd persisted even after he said they'd have barely enough to live on and no luxuries at all if she didn't work. Ask your dad for cash, she'd said.

He got out the broom and started sweeping up crumbs. "What's my girl want for supper?"

Cassie pointed to the pantry. "Mac," she said.

"What did you have for lunch?"

She stuffed the cracker in her mouth. Lifting the trashcan lid, Brendan saw the blue box under an empty yogurt container and Diet Coke can. "I think we'll have something else," he said. "How about scrambled eggs?" She frowned. "And toast and jelly for your belly?" He gave her stomach a gentle tickle and made her smile.

Hours later, after feeding Cassie, cleaning up both her and the kitchen, reading a story and putting her to bed, Brendan sank onto the living room sofa. It was nine o'clock, but Megan wasn't home. Not unusual. He turned on the television but couldn't get interested in anything. He figured his dad wanted him to straighten out bank accounts, that sort of thing. He tried not to be jealous of the bucks Dad had socked away. He'd earned them, he supposed, but at an emotional cost to all of them. Brendan squeezed a plush rabbit Cassie had left on the sofa. He wanted to think that he'd do better as a dad.

At ten, Megan still wasn't home. She was rarely specific about her companions when she went out. Julie was nearly always part of the group, and she was the only one he'd met. An attorney at the firm where Megan once worked, Julie was gorgeous, rich, and divorced. Ambitious too. Megan warbled on about the cases Julie was assigned and how well she did with them. He'd thought Julie sharp to the point of dangerous. He didn't like her.

Brendan went into the silent kitchen and listened to the refrigerator hum. Megan wanted a bigger one and a gas stove, ironic since she rarely cooked. Megan wanted everything. A few months back, she'd pestered Brendan until he'd begged his father for her Lexus. God, he'd hated doing that, but Dad hadn't acted like it was any big deal. "She needs a good solid car for the baby," he'd said. Recently she'd been talking about a new house. Brand new with more bathrooms and bedrooms.

He rummaged around in the perfectly adequate refrigerator and found some salami and a half-full tub of low-fat cream cheese. Scrambled eggs, toast, and applesauce for supper didn't cut it. He made a thick sandwich and opened a Diet Coke. Megan wouldn't buy regular ones even though he preferred them. She said he was getting fat. He sat back down in front of the TV and watched basketball players fly down the court. He'd done that in high school, even played some intramural ball in college. He bit into the sandwich, flavors coagulating on his tongue, fat coating the roof of his mouth. His free hand went to the bulge above his waist. Megan was right, but he wasn't sure he cared.

At eleven she came home. He didn't bother to ask how it could've taken so long for dinner. They'd gone to a club or bar; Megan had been drinking for sure. But she wasn't close to being wasted, just friendlier than usual. She cuddled next to him on the sofa and slid her shoes off. "Have you had a nice quiet evening?" she asked. She had amazing eyes, almost aquamarine. They'd been the first thing he'd noticed about her.

"Peachy," he said. "Lots of *Goodnight Moon* and bathtub splashes."

Megan smiled and blinked at him. "Is little Brendan in a bad, bad mood?" He'd never been able to decide whether he loved or hated her baby talk come-ons.

"Not really. Just tired, I guess."

"Well, you can sleep in tomorrow morning. I'll keep Cassie out of your hair." She put her hand on his upper thigh. A signal he'd better acknowledge, not that he didn't want to. No matter how annoying Megan could be, he always wanted her.

"No, I can't. Dad asked me to come over."

Her eyes hardened. "Why?"

"Business. Bank accounts probably."

Megan tilted her head.

He said, "Mom's accounts had my name on them."

She'd been leaning against his shoulder but straightened. "I didn't know that."

Secrecy was a hard habit to break. Megan didn't need to know everything. "It didn't matter. It's not my money."

"But if your name was on the account. . . ."

Was she envisioning refrigerators or mansions? It was hard to tell with Megan; her imagination defied gravity.

"It's still not my money."

She gave this a second and then leaned over to kiss him. Strategic pause, he thought. Her blonde hair curtained his face. She smelled good, like wine and sweet fruit. He ran his hand down the silk of her blouse and was aiming for the top button when she pulled away and squinted at him. "What have you been eating?"

"Salami." He didn't mention the thick layer of cream cheese. "Bad, huh?"

This time she chose to consider it humorous. "My tubby hubby," she whispered. "Brush your teeth, baby. Please?"

The next morning when the alarm went off, Megan was already out of bed. Highly unusual. Brendan sat up and stared at his father's painting on the opposite wall. Dad had said that since he'd painted one for Kinley, he would do a picture for Brendan too. Whatever subject he wanted. Brendan smiled at the memory. He'd been in college then, full of himself, and intent on tormenting his dad at every opportunity. "Cows," he'd requested, thinking Dad would probably pitch a fit over it. He hadn't. He'd known what Brendan was doing. "Cows it is," Dad had said.

The canvas showed a rough pasture like the ones down where his mother's folks lived. Wintry hills clotted with black, bare trees filled the background, and the sky promised snow. Cattle crowded an old wire fence in the foreground, but in the middle was a lone, grazing cow with its back turned to the others, tail raised in insolence. If a cow could've thumbed its nose at the world, this one would've. Brendan had never told Megan how much the thing was probably worth. She'd want to sell it.

He had a vague memory of agreeing last night to talk to Dad about a new house, when he'd really been saying yes to the way she was moving on him. God, she was like quicksilver in bed. He had no intention of humbling himself to his father so soon after the Lexus, but Megan didn't need to know that. Brendan heaved himself out of bed.

In the kitchen, she was still working it. Cassie sat in her highchair, playing with Cheerios. Megan had on her gym clothes, the knit pants stretched tight against her firm ass. She smiled at him and kissed his cheek, a wisp of clean-scented lotion competing with the bacon she was frying. She never let him have bacon.

"I've got your breakfast ready," she said.

Most days he had to make his own coffee and usually grabbed a granola bar as he left, his girls still sleeping. If he didn't know better, he'd think Megan was having an affair or something. But she was mercenary not promiscuous. This was about his sex-induced promise.

She poured his coffee, gave him two eggs and buttered his toast. "What's the occasion?" he asked.

Megan pretended to pout. "Why should it be an occasion? I'd make breakfast for you every day if you didn't have to be at that stupid library so early."

It was always the dumb library, the stupid library. Back at college, she'd been impressed that he was working on his master's in library and information. Or maybe it'd been his Honda S2000 that had attracted her. Whatever. As soon as she discovered what librarians made, she'd disparaged his career, telling him to get into computers or corporate research or something that paid a living wage. He ate his eggs.

She gave Cassie a little bowl of strawberry yogurt and put a spoon in her hand. "Are you coming back home before you go to the library?"

Watching Cassie work a spoon was hilarious. "No. I'll probably need to go to the bank for Dad." He guided the spoon into the bowl for her. "There you go, sweetie. Now put it in your mouth." She grinned at him. It was a game.

"Well." Megan drew out the word and rested her hand at the top of his leg as a reminder. "Don't forget to talk to him about a house."

●●●●

Daffodil spikes poked up along Dad's driveway. The forsythia by the side of the house was ready to burst loose. It was still March, but Mother Nature

33

was doing a good job of teasing people into thinking it was spring. Brendan felt good, even if he did have to see his father.

Dad opened the front door before Brendan could get out of his car. "Isn't it a lovely morning?" Dad asked. He was smiling, cheerful. He must've finished the painting that was haunting him after Mom's funeral. Or taken happy pills. It wasn't the first time that Brendan had tried to blame his father's eccentricities on drugs rather than temperament. Except that he'd never leave the house to see a doctor. Or a dealer.

"It is."

"I thought we'd go out on the patio. Leon says I need sun." He poured both of them mugs of coffee. "I had him buy doughnuts." Dad gestured at the Krispy Kreme box. Despite his big breakfast, Brendan took one and folded a napkin around it. He'd start monitoring his carb load tomorrow.

They walked through the studio where a medium-sized canvas sat on the easel, totally draped. Brendan knew better than to ask to see it, although this smiley new Dad might show it to him. He got the feeling that Megan wasn't the only one playing him.

They sat at the wrought iron table. Cold metal ate through his trousers. Brendan wrapped his hands around his mug, but Dad didn't act like he was a bit chilly. He hadn't even bothered to put on a jacket. He said, "My mother used to say that air like this was a tonic."

Brendan figured he could count on one hand the number of times his father had said anything about his parents or youth. "It does cheer a person up," Brendan said, trying to figure out what his father wanted. Jesus, it must be big for his dad to be this cordial. Dad had brought along a thick manila folder and set it next to his coffee.

Brendan waited. He heard birds calling and wished he'd listened when his mother had identified songbirds by their tunes. She knew all that country, natural stuff. At least it would've been a topic for conversation. He'd never been able to make small talk with his dad. Any other father would be talking about the NCAA tournament or maybe the price of gas or even politics. Not Dad. Brendan took another bite of the doughnut and wished he hadn't.

Finally his father cleared his throat and opened the folder. An envelope from Columbus was on top. "These are death certificates. There are five. We can order more if we need them."

Brendan nodded.

Dad set those aside and picked up a bank statement. "Our accounts are in your mother's name, payable on death to you." A wry whisper of a smile played around Dad's thin lips. Brendan was glad he'd inherited his mother's wide smile. "It was in her name, but the account was ours."

34

That message was clear. "Of course," he said.

"I've never done the local banking." Dad raised his chin. "Nor do I intend to." Brendan had expected this. "I'd like you to go to the bank, show them a death certificate, and have the account put in your name with your sister as beneficiary." Dad waved his hand. "Pay on death. Whatever the wording is."

Brendan took the papers. "Okay, but. . .," he started.

Dad turned his head toward the thorny rose bushes at the edge of the patio. They looked dead. "I don't do the banking," he repeated. "But I occasionally need to make deposits and withdrawals."

The implication was that Brendan would do these for him. He nodded.

"I'd like you to withdraw fifteen thousand dollars for me."

Christ. That was nearly five months of paychecks for him. Just money to have around the house, Brendan figured. "Today?"

Dad nodded. "If you can."

"Sure."

Dad pointed to the envelope. "I've written her social security number here if you need it." A ruffle of breeze blew across the lawn and puffed his father's flannel shirt. He seemed hesitant. Everything so far had been easy enough, Brendan thought. Tougher tasks were coming.

Dad took another envelope from the folder, handed it to Brendan, and started speaking very fast. "Here's her will. She left everything to you and Kinley, although it really comes to me. But I must not be mentioned in any way."

Brendan didn't know whether his father wanted him to open the envelope or not.

"You'll need to see the lawyer who drafted this, get things moving. The house and car will need to be put in your name. And Kinley's." His dad thought for a minute. "Some investments, the cabin down at the lake."

Okay, Brendan was starting to figure it out. His job would be to handle all the business that his mother had done, just like Leon was now charged with all the shopping and errand-running that Mom used to do. Brendan bet his father wished Kinley lived closer; she'd be nicer about all this. He grunted, assuming his father would sense a reluctant yes. This was going to eat up every free minute he owned.

Dad tilted his head and nodded, which meant he understood that the task was onerous to Brendan. "I'll be paying you a thousand a month to take care of it all." Brendan was so surprised that he hardly noticed his father's changed expression. The smile had gone like someone flipped a switch. "Spend it, save it; I don't care. But set up a separate account. You should have funds that Megan cannot access. Take a thousand out of the cash you're withdrawing and do it today."

Brendan felt his body tense in defense of his wife. He started to protest, but Dad's face was stony. And it really wasn't a bad idea. He wasn't surprised that Dad saw through Megan; Mom had. But she'd never said anything so specific about her. He looked at his half-eaten doughnut and felt sick. His wife was greedy. Everyone knew it. He exhaled and said, "Okay."

Dad sipped his coffee and reached into the folder again to bring out a slip of paper. "I have an account in Switzerland," he said, his voice low now like he was afraid the squirrels would hear him. "Numbered. In a private bank."

This slammed Brendan's attention. Holy shit. Maybe Kinley was right. Maybe Dad was some kind of criminal who needed laundry services for his money. He managed to nod.

"This will not be your concern," Dad said. He smoothed the paper against the envelope from the state. "But if something happens to me, I want you and Kinley to have access to it." He paused again like he was bringing the words up from his toes. "The Swiss banker has my instructions. It's all organized."

Brendan didn't know what to say. He glanced at the paper. A series of numbers. A word. A name with a number after it. "Mr. Huber? That's the banker?"

Dad nodded. "Put this someplace secure. Really secure." He pointed to another set of numbers at the bottom of the page. "This is the combination to my safe. You'll need to get in there too." He pressed his lips together. "If I were to die."

"All right." Brendan folded the paper and put it in his wallet. Dad frowned. "Just for now," Brendan said. "Does Kinley know about this?"

Dad shook his head. "I suppose you could tell her. But you must impress upon her the need for secrecy." He covered Brendan's hand with his own and squeezed. Hard, like he was etching it into Brendan's skin. He couldn't remember the last time his father had touched him, but this felt more like a blow than a caress.

"I promise. Is that everything?"

Dad let go of his hand and nodded. "For now."

"Then I'd better go," Brendan said. "I have to be at work by noon." It was only ten, but he had to get out of there that minute.

Dad stood when he did. "Where will you put these?"

Brendan knew he meant the sheet with secret numbers on it. "I'm not sure."

"Don't let Megan see it."

He was right, but it still ticked Brendan off. He scowled and muttered, "I won't."

Chapter Six

BRENDAN

He drove toward the bank but hardly saw his surroundings. A Swiss bank account. Who on earth had those? Secret numbers and code words. It was like he'd been dropped into a Matt Damon movie. He had to call Kinley. She was right. This was crazy. Dad was crazy. Or not. He shook his head. No one but Kinley would believe this shit. *He* didn't believe this shit.

He parked at a convenience store and pulled the phone out of his pocket. But before he clicked on Kinley's number, he opened the bank statement his father had given him. He'd wondered how his mother had felt about keeping her maiden name. These days it was common, but it'd been an anomaly back in the seventies. If Mom had been some kind of righteous women's libber, it might have suited her, but she wasn't anything like that, and Brendan guessed it probably hurt her feelings.

He scanned down the column of ATM and automatic withdrawals, for cash, utilities, ordinary expenses. Dad must pay Leon in cash, which would figure—no complications like social security and taxes. Those could be traced. He hoped old Leon had saved some back for retirement.

The balance wasn't too bizarre. A payment to the funeral home had bitten a huge chunk out of the account, leaving about sixty thousand. More money than Brendan's account would ever see, but not absurd. Then he looked at the last page of the statement. In savings, certificates of deposit, and a brokerage account were another mill and a half. Brendan's throat went dry. God knows how much was sitting in a fairy tale bank in Switzerland.

"What are you doing?" he asked as soon as Kinley answered.

"Painting a pitcher." His sis was quite the wit. "Why?" Her voice was deep. It was early morning in Boulder.

"You aren't going to believe this." He told her everything, including the crazy stuff about Swiss bank accounts.

"You are shitting me," she said.

"No, I'm not. Can you believe there's even more money in Switzerland?"

"Incredible." She paused. "But he gets fortunes for his paintings even after Devonie takes her cut, doesn't he? And Mom made decent money teaching. They've never spent much."

"Yeah, yeah. But still. I'm beginning to wonder about what you said."

"About what? Witness protection? They don't set them up with a fortune, Brendan. Could it be something criminal?" The pitch of her voice went from early morning croak to a high squeak. "Damn."

"That's what I said. Anyway. I have to get to the bank, but think about it. Do you remember anything? Like from when you were little? Anything that might give us a clue about what's going on?" Kinley had two years more memory than he did. Maybe Dad hadn't kept things so close back then.

"I don't think so, but I'll try." She stopped for a second. "We knew he had money. . ." Her words trailed off. She was still shocked.

"Yeah, but this much money?"

"Exactly. Umm. Call me later, okay?"

Brendan figured her musician boyfriend must've come into the room. He'd never met the guy, and Kinley had never said much about him. Made him nervous. "Sure. Later."

●●●●

It all had gone smoothly enough at the bank. He'd mailed paperwork to Kinley on his way to the university and planted the key to his new safe deposit box in the bottom drawer of the desk in his office. The bank had given him a temporary debit card and a print-out of his account number. He stuck those in his messenger bag and then reconsidered. He wouldn't put it past Megan to go through the boring crap that cluttered up his bag. He'd think of something else.

Just before he had to go on duty at the reference desk he called his father, telling him he'd run out of time and asking if he could see him that evening or tomorrow morning. Carrying $14,000 around gave him the heebie jeebies, but there was no help for it. Dad said to stop by the next morning, which was okay by Brendan. He wasn't sure he could face the old man without demanding answers, and then there'd be an argument. It had happened before.

It was a dead afternoon on the desk. The weather had warmed up a little, and students had better things to do than sit in a dusty library. Two asked for help in finding a topic for research papers, and he directed them to *CQ Researcher*. Brendan yawned. He loved research, loved hunting and chasing after information, but what most students requested didn't stretch his skills at all. Researching his father was another matter. He doubted that there was an article written on Keith Owen that he hadn't read, but he kept trying. The Raptor had left at five; she couldn't bitch about it.

After hours of fruitless research, Brendan strolled out to the vending machines and got a package of cookies and a Diet Coke. Great nutrition, he thought. He really should start going to the gym or something. There was a fitness center on campus, but he'd never been tempted to use it. He ate in the library lobby where, during the day, students congregated around a cart selling overpriced lattes and over-caloried pastries. He'd succumbed to both a few times. He took a deep breath and his waistband cut into his flesh. Megan was right; he needed to do something about his weight. He would've kept that thought longer except that when he stood to throw away his trash, a solitary student, a beautiful girl, looked up from her laptop and smiled at him. She had long, dark hair with thick straight bangs nearly covering her eyebrows. Hair like an Asian girl, although she wasn't. He smiled back, lifted his hand a little, and watched her watching him. That hadn't happened in a while.

The student worker he'd left to man the desk closed her physics book as soon as she saw him walking across the library. Hell, he didn't care that she was studying and told her so when he sat back down. Staring at the computer screen, he tried to think of anything or anyone who could lead him to information about his father. He Googled his mother's name. Lord, there were about a million Brenda Williams. He tried narrowing his search but still got nowhere.

Maybe. He started typing so fast the student worker looked up. He'd try Devonie Goddard. He found several listings, mostly announcements for shows at her gallery. He went back and typed in her name along with his dad's. Several hits looked good. He started reading.

The fourth article was actually an interview with Devonie Goddard from January, written by D. K. Oliver, whoever he was. There was a picture of Devonie; sort of interesting since he'd never seen the woman even though her efforts had produced the huge bank balances he'd been fooling with. Devonie was no young chick. Probably Dad's age, fifty or so; maybe more if she'd had work done. And she'd made enough money off Dad's paintings to afford all kinds of work. Blah, blah, blah, he read. Keith Owen's skill. Keith Owen's versatility. Keith Owen's mastery of light and brushwork. Yeah, yeah, thought Brendan. His father was a genius. A whacked-out genius. He already knew that much.

The interviewer asked Goddard how she'd discovered Keith Owen, and Brendan finally found some meat in the article. She said that shortly after she started working at her father's gallery in New York, she'd been visiting a friend in Cincinnati. They'd gone gallery-hopping, but she'd seen nothing that impressed her. Of course not, thought Brendan. Cincinnati's a backwater to New Yorkers. Everything is. Then a friendly stranger told Devonie that she should check out a coffeehouse in Clifton (she explained that this was near the University of Cincinnati) to see work by some promising young artists. She went that evening and had been shocked and delighted at two paintings by someone who signed his or her work, *KOWEN*. No period. It'd taken her a while to find someone in the place who knew that it was actually K. Owen. Brendan nodded at the screen. Dad still signed his paintings like that.

The interviewer asked, and the rest is history?

Oh, no, Goddard replied. Brendan pictured her getting wide-eyed at this point. She said that she was stunned that the paintings in the coffeehouse were a mere hundred dollars each, and she was appalled that they were sitting unprotected in a damp, smoky atmosphere. She had to visit the place twice to get any information whatsoever, even though she wanted to buy the paintings. She wasn't about to give the shifty-looking café manager the money. She demanded at least a phone number for K. Owen. No go. It took forever for her to receive a mailing address.

And what paintings were these?

He'd bet old Devonie had been waiting for a drum roll before she answered: "'Day River'" and 'Vierge.' I sold them for scads more, and Mr. Owen agreed to let me handle all his work."

Brendan knew the paintings by reputation. He'd seen photos of them. Mom had been the model for "Vierge." He took a deep breath and noticed his student worker staring at him. Maybe he'd been muttering. He read on.

When was this?

Devonie replied that it had been in 1978.

There was one more question. Oliver asked Devonie how often she met with Owen. He said his readers would love to learn more about the mysterious artist. Brendan couldn't decide whether Goddard had scowled or preened at this question. He read her response eagerly.

"I've never met him," Devonie said. "In the beginning we communicated by mail, and now it's by email. I don't even have a phone number for Keith."

As intact as his virgin, Brendan thought. Even with Devonie. He read on.

"I can tell you that Keith is married and has two children. I can also tell you that he has not been painting recently because his wife is seriously ill. Anyone who studies Keith Owen's work realizes that he's become more symbolic, more fanciful in recent years. As far as I know he's continuing this trend, and I find it fascinating. Journalists constantly contact me to learn more about him. I don't know more about him, and I respect his privacy." Devonie finished with one more sentence. "It has been an honor and a pleasure to represent Keith Owen's work."

K. Oliver wrote some pap about it being an honor and pleasure to speak with Devonie Goddard. Blah, blah, blah. Brendan was amazed that the woman had dared to say this much. If he'd known, Dad would've laid into her about it, but hell, how many people read *Serendipitous Salon* anyway? There was nothing in the article to help him.

●●●●

When he got home Cassie was pink from her bath and pretty in a sweet little nightgown. She gave him a damp hug, and then Megan whisked her off to bed. He heard Megan humming as she tucked the baby in. She might drive him crazy, but Megan loved their child.

He was peering into the refrigerator when Megan came back. He didn't have a clue what his girls had eaten, but there wasn't much to choose from in the fridge. "There's yogurt and bagged salad," she said.

With his back to his wife, Brendan glared at the little yogurt cups and grabbed the milk. He'd have cereal. There was always cereal. Megan hovered while he got a bowl and spoon and stood wordless as he decided whether he wanted Cinnamon Toast Crunch or Cheerios. He'd prefer the first one but knew what Megan would say.

She sat next to him and let him get three bites down before she started. "How did it go with your father?" Her eyes, gorgeous bluey-greeny eyes, were wide and innocent. Like hell.

"Fine." He crunched, hoping she'd switch topics. Double like hell.

"Did you bring up a new house? Someplace big enough for kids to have some room? Surely your dad would approve of that."

He swallowed in a hurry. "Kids?" She knew he wanted more children, but she'd stated several times that one was enough when you were poor.

She looked down at the table and started drawing figure eights with her finger. "Someday maybe."

Brendan filled his spoon again. "No. There wasn't time. He had a bunch of banking for me to do, and I couldn't even get back to him before I had to leave for work. I have to go over there again in the morning before work."

He figured she'd be wheedling him again to bring up the house, maybe even touching him a little here and there, making promises in return for her expectations. So he was surprised when he looked up and saw disgusted creases settle around Megan's mouth. Her eyes smoldered with contempt. "You're such a coward. Scared to bring up anything to your precious, rich daddy." The words dripped with something akin to battery acid.

"Not precious, that's for sure," he protested. His spoon clattered against the bowl. He didn't want the cereal. "I didn't get around to it."

"You wouldn't have done it if you'd had all the time in the world." She breathed out a deep sigh of discontent. "Don't start in on your *pride* again." She made the word into an obscenity. "I don't know how you expect us to live on your stupid salary. " She paused for a second. Probably to reload. "Well, are you going to talk to him tomorrow?"

Rather than answering, Brendan scooted his chair back. He wanted to tell her that she could get off her ass and find a job if she felt so deprived, but it was better to walk away. He dumped the rest of his cereal down the garbage disposal.

She stood and waited until the disposal quit growling. "I'm warning you, Brendan. I'm not happy."

He finally looked back at her, wondering how he'd ever found her beautiful, desirable. "Are you ever?" he shot back, but he kept his voice low. He didn't want Cassie to hear them fighting.

Megan flounced off. He heard the bathtub running and later he heard her close the bedroom door, but Brendan stared at the television for another two hours. Hoping Megan was asleep by then, he went to bed, but he couldn't sleep.

He'd been in grad school when they'd met; she was working on an associate's degree to be a paralegal and had come into the library while he was doing his reference practicum. At first she'd been impressed by his imminent master's degree. He'd been impressed by her long blonde hair and mysterious eyes. She'd told him that she'd just quit dating a law student who'd bored her with all his hours of studying. She'd been a challenge even then, demanding more time than he had, wanting constant reassurances that he loved her. This translated into expensive meals, gifts, and countless text messages while he was in class or trying to study. He stared at the dim ceiling of their bedroom. Her texts had read like soft porn: promising, promising. And sometimes she'd delivered.

He glanced at his wife's back, only a size six, but a barrier as big as a boulder nonetheless. He didn't know whether she slept or not, but touching her would be like fondling poison ivy. Maybe he was a coward, with Megan, not his father. It was about pride, but he could never make her understand. Dad would agree to buy them another house; he'd bought this one and two for Kinley, although hers were a business. Brendan thought of his Kentucky kinfolk and how they abhorred the concept of being "beholden" to someone. He guessed it was in his blood. He didn't want to owe his father a thing.

At some point he dozed off but woke nearly an hour before he needed to get up. He'd told Beverly that he'd be a little late, that he needed to do some estate business for his father, and she'd uttered a sigh of the long suffering and said that he would need to stay late to make up his time. So much for sympathy. Still, Megan was asleep. The baby monitor was silent. He knew what he could do with the extra time.

Creeping out from under the comforter, he found sweats and shoes in the dark and went to the bathroom to put them on. A jacket. Gloves. A knit hat. He checked his watch as he unlocked the back door. He was going to run. Hadn't done it since high school when every sport he played required it, but he'd get some weight off. It would be one less thing for Megan to bitch about.

The sky was inky and strewn with pale stars. He remembered looking at the stars down at the lake when he was a kid. It was an entirely different sky in the country. He took off on the sidewalk and then switched to the street. Fewer cracks and bumps in the pavement. His feet hit the cold concrete in a pleasant rhythm. It felt good for a while, and then his lungs started cranking about the unusual activity and chilly air. He kept going. Newspapers lay in driveways. Streetlights gave him brief pools of light. God, he was in bad shape. He was gasping like a two-pack-a-day geezer.

Run through it, he told himself. Enjoy the solitude. His thighs were starting a slow burn, but he forced himself to keep going. Megan wasn't carping out here. His father wasn't frustrating him. He coughed and slowed to a lope, then a walk. Walking was okay, he told himself, as long as he went back to running in a few minutes.

Lights came on at one house as he passed it. He felt like a voyeur staring at what few yellow windows he saw. A dog barked at him. Someone started a car. He kicked back into a run, and it felt a little easier than before. Heat built beneath his jacket. He didn't feel cold any more. At the next streetlight he glanced at his watch. Lame. He'd been out for only fifteen minutes, but he turned to retrace his steps back home. Pacing, he muttered to himself.

As he neared his house, the discomfort faded. Well, most of it. His shoes were crap. They didn't look bad, but there was little cushioning left. Maybe he'd buy some new ones out of the thou Dad had given him. Paid him, he corrected himself. He slowed up at his driveway and gave the small house a critical glance. It wasn't such a bad place. Neat, maintained. He wasn't going to say a word to his father about a house.

●●●●

The gate was shut tight, so Brendan had to get out of the car to punch in the numbers. At least Dad hadn't changed the code as he tended to do every few weeks. When he settled back into the car, Brendan felt a faint tingle in his legs from the running. Good. He'd jump-started his circulation. He'd run every few days, he promised himself.

He spotted Leon's pickup parked in the circle. Usually Leon would hear him coming and let him in, but Brendan had to unlock the front door and hurry to disarm the system. He wouldn't put it past his father to install a retina scan soon. He called, "Hello?" But they ignored him. Dad was in the kitchen, standing by the window over the sink where he'd watched Brendan arrive, and, still wearing his jacket, Leon sat at the table with his hands woven together. He looked up at Brendan and asked, "Did you reset the system?"

Brendan nodded. There was enough tension in the room to fuel a generator. Both men looked worn out, old.

Leon raised his mournful, hound dog eyes. "C'mon, Keith. Calm down. It's okay," he said.

Dad's body was stiff, his fists clenched. Brendan glanced away from his father and saw a pistol laying on the countertop like a menacing kitchen tool. "What the hell's going on?" he asked.

Dad kept glaring out the window like he expected a commando attack any minute. Leon ignored Brendan and repeated, "Man, you gotta calm down. I'm sorry as I can be that I talked to the woman, but she said you two were old friends. I didn't know anything different." Leon bit at his lip, shoulders sagging against his chair.

Brendan's head moved back and forth between the two like he was watching a tennis match. "Would somebody tell me what's going on?" He opened his bag and counted out the cash his dad had requested. Then he reached in his pocket and set bank papers next to the stack of bills. "If you're still interested, everything's squared away."

Dad wrenched his eyes away from the window to give Brendan a quick glance and about half a nod. "I have to leave," he said, his voice flat. "Now."

Leon stood. "You've got the security system. I'll stay here. You don't have to leave."

His father's head jerked from side to side. "Keep watch, Brendan." He pointed at the window, snatched the gun, and left the room.

Out of habit, Brendan obeyed and stood in front of the window. Sun gleamed down on the two vehicles outside and a stiff breeze tossed the naked tree limbs. Peaceful. Quiet. "Are you going to tell me?" he asked Leon without taking his eyes off the driveway.

He heard the big man breathe out a sigh. "When I came to work this morning there was a car sitting right in front of the gate. I stopped, knowing your dad would have a fit if somebody sneaked in behind me. This lady got out. Probably about the same age as me and Keith. Blonde. She said she'd known Keith back in Chicago when they were young and wondered if this was his house. She said she needed to talk to him real bad."

Brendan shook his head. Leon had fucked up big time.

"So I asked her name and said I'd give him the message, but I told her that she had to leave."

"Thus confirming that this is Keith Owen's house." Brendan looked over his shoulder at the man. He had misery coming out of his pores.

Leon said, "Yeah." It sounded more like a moan. "I know better. But I guess I always thought. . . ." His voice trailed off.

"That all the secrecy was pretty stupid," Brendan finished for him.

Leon nodded, and Brendan turned his eyes back to the driveway. "What did she say her name was?"

"Dana."

The name meant nothing to Brendan.

"She made me write down her phone number." Leon pushed a slip of paper to the center of the table. It wasn't a local area code.

"Where's Dad going?"

Leon said, "I don't know, but I figure I better help him pack up." He stood and moved a step closer to Brendan. "Do you think he'll fire me?"

After thirty years of doing a crazy man's dirty work, Brendan thought not, but that was just it: his dad was crazy. "I hope not."

Leon went upstairs, and in only a few minutes both he and Dad returned carrying a suitcase and an empty duffel bag. Without saying a word, Dad marched straight into his studio, and Leon headed to the garage.

Brendan turned on the cold tap and ran water. Then he turned it off. He couldn't figure out if the situation was serious or an exercise in rampant paranoia. Dad emerged with a bulging bag of painting supplies and a couple of blank canvases. He must be planning on staying gone a while. Brendan could hear the garage door opening. "What can I do, Dad?"

His father set down the bag and stuffed the cash into it. Brendan could see the gun in the pocket of his jacket. "Drive out beyond the gate and make sure no one's there. Honk your horn if it's clear."

This wasn't what Brendan had in mind, but he nodded. "Anything else?"

"No." He motioned for Brendan to leave.

There was no one at the gate.

Chapter Seven

KINLEY

On Saturday morning she carried several boxes of painted glassware out onto the back porch. She'd promised the arts consortium over on Pearl Street that she'd deliver spring items by the first of April. They said her stuff sold like crazy. Kinley smiled to herself. Like her dad's paintings, right? She'd just opened up the trunk of her car when she heard a "Need help?" from the second floor.

"Wouldn't turn it down," she said to Sarah who came down the outside steps barefoot with a fluffy pink robe wrapped around her chunky body. She looked like a cloud of cotton candy.

Grabbing one of the boxes, Sarah asked, "Why isn't Young Mozart helping you?"

"Already slaving away in a practice room." Kinley set a box of margarita glasses painted with lemons on the backseat. Sarah handed her a taller box that contained two matching pitchers.

"So, what good is he?" Sarah grinned and hobbled over the rough blacktop for another box.

"He can cook," Kinley said.

Sarah cocked an eyebrow. "On all burners."

They carefully positioned two more boxes: salad plates and matching bowls decorated with tulips and daffodils, along with three dozen wineglasses wearing grapes and leaves. Mundane, thought Kinley, similar to crap painted in China that sold for a lot less, but they brought in some cash.

"Michael's bummed," Kinley said.

"About what?"

"He got an email yesterday about one of his grad school auditions." Kinley squinted against the sunlight. She should be more unhappy about his news. "He didn't get into the program at the University of Michigan."

"Damn." Sarah retied her robe. "Was that his first choice? With him being from Michigan and all?"

Kinley shook her head. "No, but it was his family's. Still, it's no fun being rejected."

"He has other ones out there, doesn't he?"

Kinley nodded. "Plenty. He'll get accepted somewhere." She turned to get into her car. "Thanks, girl."

Sarah waved a hand like it was nothing. "He'll want you to go with him wherever it is."

Kinley shook her head and ran her finger down the sharp edge of her key. "Well, see you. Thanks." Sarah nodded, and Kinley started the car. She appreciated Sarah for more than moving boxes. There'd been plenty of little friends in elementary school, and Mom had made sure that she and Brendan played sports, joined Scouts, and went to kids' activities at church. But by middle school, female social life gravitated toward sleepovers and hanging out after school. Dad had made that impossible. It was different for Brendan. His friends were teammates, and his life centered around the gym or playing field. She met girls for ball games or mall cruising, but she'd just never had the knack for easy friendship until the day Sarah filled out an application to be Kinley's first tenant. Before Michael interrupted things, Kinley and Sarah had seen each other every day. Yet Sarah never seemed to resent Michael like some friends would've.

Kinley turned into the alley behind the Pearl Street shop. She'd had the same problems with boys in high school. Yeah, she'd gone to prom, but only by persuading her mother to let her dress and be picked up at another girl's house. When she actually went out with a guy, she drove her car and met him somewhere. She couldn't imagine any high school boy willing to run the gauntlet of Dad's security systems, not that Dad would ever have allowed it. And in college, well, she'd gone a little wild her first year. She smiled as she pulled in and parked. Wild enough that there had been a long, remorseful dry spell.

She'd just opened the car door when her phone played its text chime. Michael. He wrote: "Nearly done. Want to meet at noon to do something?"

It was ridiculous how good this made her feel. "OK," she typed. "Where?"

"House? Cheer me up?"

She grinned. "OK. Smiles."

They'd been together for nearly a year now, which should indicate some kind of significance, but she was always convinced he'd find someone cuter, younger, better than she was. Sarah invariably rolled her eyes when Kinley expressed her doubts. You're not giving the guy credit, she fussed.

You're spoiling a good thing. Maybe. But Kinley had a healthy distrust of artistic men.

The clerks at the consortium oohed and ahhed about her glassware, which was nice, but Kinley knew the stuff was craft not art. She wandered through the store and then out onto the pedestrian-only street to look at the show that was Pearl Street. It was too early in the day and season for most of the street performers to be doing their thing. A few anti-war protesters stood in their usual spot with their signs. A brisk breeze off the mountains whipped their hair. A guy playing Spanish guitar sat in the sun. His open guitar case was still empty. She strolled down one side of the street and stopped to get coffee before she walked back. At the height of summer there would be painters, balloon artists, musicians, jugglers, and even more bizarre entertainers like the guy who impersonated a robot and the woman who moved a piano out into the middle of the street and played all afternoon. Badly. Michael shuddered every time he heard her. Kinley loved Boulder. Sarah said it was where nouveau hippies came to play and old hippies came to die. Kinley figured she belonged there.

● ● ● ●

"What do you want to do?" asked Michael. "It's a beautiful day." He'd headed straight for his laptop the minute he'd come home. No more audition news.

"I don't know. Do you want to hike, ride?" They often rode their bikes around town or up the murderous hill by Boulder Creek. She felt her age when they did that.

Michael shook his head. The sun streaming through the kitchen window caught in his black curls, shiny as blackbirds' wings. "I feel lazy today." He stared out the window at the sunshine for a minute and then said, "I know. This is the first Saturday in April, right? The farmer's market will be open."

"They won't have much this early in the season." Mom always had a garden patch, usually just some tomatoes and peppers, maybe a few zucchini plants. Every spring she'd announced that a country girl just had to dig in the dirt. She'd set out her vegetables in a far corner of the yard where they wouldn't get in Leon's way when he mowed. Kinley hadn't thought of her mother's garden in years.

"That's okay." Michael kissed her forehead. "We'll get lunch there, look around."

They walked together easily, both of them the same height. Michael talked about his morning practice, how he'd decided to do the phrasing differently on a portion of the Mendelssohn. She didn't really understand, but it didn't matter. He asked what she was planning to paint next. She didn't figure he really cared about that, but it was polite of him to ask. They got burritos at the market and laughed at each other's attempts to eat the drippy rolls. She'd been right; there were more shoppers than produce, but Michael got excited about some fresh lettuce and insisted they should buy a gigantic loaf of artisan bread because Kinley loved good bread. He'd cook tonight, he said. Whatever she wanted.

Kinley couldn't decide whether there was sympathy or guilt in his efforts to please her. Michael had hugged her hard and wept a little when Dad called to say that her mother was dying. She supposed he was imagining how dreadful it would be to lose someone from his noisy, affectionate Italian family. Out of habit or loyalty or something, she'd told him very little about her parents. He probably thought her family was like his. Or he might be feeling guilty because he'd spent little time with her since she'd been home. He shouldn't worry about that. She didn't expect anything else. Maybe he was just trying to cheer himself up after the rejection. Kinley didn't think Michael Belli had been denied much of anything he'd ever wanted.

"What about that dish you make with chicken and spinach and fettucine?" she asked.

He grinned. "You got it, baby. Except we have to go to the store to get ingredients." He turned to one of the flower booths and pointed at some red tulips. "Would you like flowers?"

Kinley laughed and shifted the loaf of bread under her arm. "Do you have any idea how many tulips I've painted this week?"

He made a funny face and pointed at a bunch of daffodils. "Those then? Or maybe the purple ones? I don't know anything about flowers."

"Irises. Those must've come from someone's greenhouse." The vendor nodded. "Sure, they're lovely, but you don't have to buy me flowers."

"Yes, I do."

He set down the bag of lettuce and pulled out his wallet. Kinley knew he was always broke. His student loans rivaled the national debt even though he had a church job, like most keyboard people, and made a pittance from accompanying voice and instrumental majors. Since last fall when he'd all but moved in with her, she'd been after him to quit paying rent, but he refused. She'd never been able to figure out if he was being fair or arranging an escape route.

They walked home from the grocery with the mountains at their back. Michael carried the heavier bags like he was being kind to the elderly. Kinley could just about hear Sarah saying, would you stop? But Michael looked so young, his skin fresh from the breeze and sun. She'd never been able to see why he'd want a woman eight years his senior as a girlfriend. Even the term was ridiculous at her age. Once when they'd been on their second bottle of wine, she'd asked Sarah the same question. She'd shrugged. "You'd probably say, free rent."

"Yeah, but he insists on paying it."

Sarah had raised her glass and given Kinley an evil grin. "Maybe you're just phenomenal in the sack."

Kinley had sputtered a full mouthful of merlot but hadn't been able to get anything more substantive from Sarah who'd finally said, "Give it up. Maybe he just loves you."

He said he did. On a regular basis. But Kinley had choked out the words only twice and regretted it both times. It was a hazardous phrase.

Early evening sunshine flooded the yellow kitchen, the same hue as the outside of the house. Maybe her paint choices were her way of rebelling against the dim, shaded rooms where she'd grown up. She volunteered to make the salad, something she probably couldn't mess up. Michael put on a cd of Debussy, dreamy music that came in waves like the ocean. She described it that way to Michael who said he'd never thought of it in those terms, but she was right. It felt cozy, domestic that they were cooking together. It didn't happen often, and she always let Michael suggest it. He was drizzling olive oil into a pan, and she was washing lettuce when her phone rang. She glanced at the screen to see if she could ignore it. Brendan. Nope, she had to answer him. "Hey little brother." She took a sip of wine.

"Hey yourself. Is it springtime in the Rockies yet?"

"It's trying to be. What's up?"

"I just wanted to tell you that Dad's gone walkabout again." Cassie was babbling in the background.

"Great. Where's he gone?"

"I don't know. He took art supplies and canvases with him." Brendan's voice sounded tired, or disgusted.

Michael looked up from the skillet, sensing something serious.

"Sounds like he'll be gone a while. Could be anywhere, I guess." She smiled at Michael and mouthed, no problem.

"Yeah. He got spooked." Brendan went on to tell her about some woman named Dana who had turned up at the gate and left a message for Dad with Leon. "Leon's feeling like a thousand kinds of shit right now."

"Poor Leon. He puts up with a thousand kinds of shit. I wonder who Dana is." Her fingers tapped against the wineglass. They didn't know anybody from Dad's past. As far as they knew Dad didn't have a past before he met their mother.

"Don't know," said Brendan. "It sorta adds to the mystery, doesn't it?"

"Yeah. Keep searching, Brendan. There's got to be something out there." He didn't respond. "Don't worry about Dad. Where'd he go last time? Florida?"

"Yeah, but I figure he went to the cabin." Brendan paused again. "Kin, he took a gun. I didn't know he had a gun."

"That doesn't mean anything." Michael was staring at her now, a wooden spoon held in mid-air. She thought back over what she'd said. Nothing that Michael could get much from. God, she was tired of all the secrets. "Really. How are you otherwise?"

She heard her brother exhale like he'd been holding his breath. "I'm okay. I've started running. I was just going to run every couple of days or so, but I've done it three days in a row."

"Aren't you noble."

"No. I just like it."

Brendan probably liked being out of the house as much as anything. She knew she couldn't live five minutes with Megan. Kinley asked about her, though, and Cassie. Then they hung up. Of course Kinley had to explain a few things to Michael. She left out the famous artist part and anything about the gun. Michael winced when he said it but asked if her father had been having an affair with this Dana. Kinley shook her head. Dad wouldn't leave the house enough to manage an affair. No, she said. Dana was evidently an old friend, from back before her parents married. Michael still looked confused about why this would make her father leave home, so she told him that Dad was something of a hermit. She'd already hinted at this when she'd dissuaded Michael from coming to her mother's funeral. He frowned and said she ought to convince him to get help. Things were bound to be worse since her mother died. God, Michael was sweet. And young. And uncomplicated. She kissed him and asked whether they should stay in and watch a movie or go out to a party with some of his music major friends. She felt like an outsider at those gatherings, but he had lots of friends and she didn't.

He said, "Whatever you want to do." He was adding chicken pieces to the skillet. It smelled wonderful. "I need to write a resignation letter to give to the choir director tomorrow. But that won't take long."

"So soon?" Annoyance crawled through her guts like a spiky worm. Dad. And now another reminder that Michael would be leaving soon. In the fall he'd sent audition cd's to eight grad schools, none of them west of the Mississippi. Early in March, he'd auditioned at four of them, getting callbacks and breezing through the interviews. Indiana University had already accepted him, but he was lukewarm about them. She was surprised that Michigan had rejected him.

"I want to give them plenty of notice," he said. "And it's not that soon. Mama wants her baby home for a little while before I do my usual stint at music camp. I'll probably leave right after my recital."

He'd asked her to go to Michigan with him. He wanted her to meet his brother and sister and parents. The thought of this nearly made her break out in hives. Of course he needed to see his family, especially since he would be heading to grad school at the end of the summer. She wanted every success for him; she just didn't want him to leave. She turned back to the red onion she was slicing. "You could've applied to CU's grad program. You like it here."

He shook his head. "Career suicide. I have to work with different piano instructors. It's essential."

And I'm not, she thought, straightening to go back to the salad. He must know how hard it would be for her to leave Colorado, her houses, her life. He just didn't care about her going with him, she'd decided. She took a hefty sip of wine. The other two schools were Juilliard and CCM, the Cincinnati Conservatory of Music. It would be her screwed-up luck if Michael ended up in Cincinnati, the city she'd run from for twelve years. Not that it would matter.

Chapter Eight

KEITH

He drove slowly through his neighborhood, keeping his eyes on the mirrors more than the road. He didn't think anyone was following him, but he scrutinized every white car he saw. Leon had said that Dana was driving a white Ford, but he hadn't bothered to get the plate number or even the state. Keith's heart was still pumping like he'd been sprinting. How in the hell had she found him? And what did she want?

He drove west, then east, finally settling on south and crossing the Ohio into Newport. Pulling into parking lots along the way, he watched the traffic behind him. No Dana. He couldn't imagine her being skilled at surveillance, but she might not be alone. Keith continued driving deeper into Kentucky. Traffic was steady through the little towns that bled one into another all the way to Alexandria where residential and commercial areas thinned out. No white Fords behind him. He let out a gusty breath. That had been close. Damn Leon. He loved the guy like a brother, but he'd been stupid. Of course none of them understood. They just thought he was paranoid. He couldn't tell them the dangers. The gun was weighing down his pocket. Careless to have a firearm so obvious. Keith stuffed it under the passenger seat. Accessible, but not immediately visible.

Dana's note, crumpled now from resting beneath the gun in his pocket, fluttered out behind the gun. He straightened it against his thigh. Just her name and a phone number. He didn't recognize the area code. Not Chicago.

He thought about going all the way to the Gulf, Alabama or maybe Florida like the last time, but decided against it. The kids would probably figure he was going to the cabin, but he wasn't about to tell them they were right. Sometimes he wondered if they, and he included Leon here, might be better about keeping their mouths shut if they knew more. But he couldn't risk it. Brenda had known a little more, a very little, but it hadn't mattered with her. She'd never told anything, not in all the years they'd been married. When he allowed himself to think of her, he felt as if someone had blasted a hole in his guts.

He turned the heater up and started looking at the scenery rather than cars. There weren't many at this hour of the morning anyway. It was cloudy and chilly. Sometimes spring was nearly as gray as autumn, but it was a different tint of gray. All the various greens contrasted with a cloudy sky differently than fall's reds, golds, and browns. His brain wanted to ingest the spring colors and keep them forever. Shades of green mixed into a pleasant blur, the grass, the shrubs, and the faint hint of tender leaves just budding. Brenda used to call this the "green haze." Yes.

He passed into Pendleton County, relaxing even more and looking at the farms on either side of the two-lane road. Kentucky land dipped and rolled, nothing like the flat Indiana fields where he'd grown up. Farms always looked peaceful from the road, but he knew farming, knew how it sucked the essence from a soul. Or at least that's the way he'd felt. His dad had loved his farm, a hundred and fifty acres of boring dirt located ten miles outside Muncie, Indiana. Keith knew corn, knew soybeans, knew chickens and eggs. His first eighteen years on earth had been spent toiling on that flat land. There'd been no time to draw, let alone paint. When he'd been in grade school, his mom had stuck his pictures on the refrigerator with Farm Bureau magnets, but later, after his parents questioned if he was getting a little old for "doodling," he'd hidden his work behind the old chifferobe in his room.

<u>1972</u>

During their senior year, he and all his classmates had trooped, homeroom by homeroom, to the guidance counselor's office where a weary woman tried to pigeonhole them into professions. Most of the girls yearned to be wives and mothers although they claimed they wanted nursing or teaching careers. Some would marry their high school boyfriends, but others needed at least a little college to find husbands.

It was different for boys. They'd grown up with Vietnam on the nightly news, so the military was a threat clouding graduation, especially for those with rotten lottery numbers. Except for his friend Larry and another handful of guys who actually wanted to serve in the armed forces, most of the males in his class said they planned to go to college for the deferment, even if they'd rather be fixing cars or working in a factory. He was the only one, male or female, who wanted to go to art school.

His ambition was different enough to fluster the guidance counselor. She looked over his records. "I don't see that you've taken any art classes," she said.

"No." His parents had always insisted that shop or even typing was more important to his future.

"Is this a new interest then?" She looked skeptical.

"No." He drew in math class. He drew in history. He'd done it for years and gotten into trouble enough over his pictures that his dad had said he had to give up drawing like it was beer or cigarettes or some other vice.

"Well." She stretched the word. "The state universities have art programs of course, and I think there are some art schools around." She didn't have a clue.

He did. He'd found a directory in the library that listed several schools, and the one that appealed most to him was in Chicago. He told her. Of course his family couldn't possibly afford it.

She glanced back at his records. He knew what they said. His grades were adequate. Just. And his test scores were worse. Nobody was going to give him money for college. But it looked to him like art schools were more concerned with ability than numbers. He told her as much.

This ticked her off, maybe because he knew more than she did. "Then I suppose you should write this school about scholarships." She picked up his records and tapped them against her desk. "Follow their instructions for admission." She was done.

It was winter, quiet on the farm, so he'd had time to work on a portfolio. It consisted entirely of drawings because he had no art supplies other than a sketchbook. He hid to do it, sometimes in the barn, sometimes sitting in his dad's truck in an empty parking lot, running the heater for ten minutes at a time. He sent off his work and waited, hatching the mailbox like a broody hen. The blustery March day when he got his acceptance letter was more exciting than when he'd received his driver's license, more heady than the time he and Larry had sipped stolen whiskey under the bleachers at Homecoming. Waving the letter from the Art Institute, he flew into the house and shouted for his parents. Nobody in his family shouted. Ever. His mother looked up from the meatloaf she was mixing. His father set aside his farm equipment catalog and asked, "Is the mail here?"

He laid the opened envelope on the table and sputtered, "I got in. They admitted me."

His mother washed her hands, taking hours to dry them. His father sifted through the typewritten papers and forms, saying nothing. Neither of his parents had known about his plans, so it took them a minute to catch on. But it didn't take a genius to figure out they were less than enthusiastic.

He felt like a balloon that had landed on barbed wire. His father frowned as he read the letter. Then he handed it to Mom.

She scanned it, biting at her lip like she did when she had to dig chicken shit off their shoes. "Why do you want to go to Chicago?" she asked. "Aren't there good schools around here?"

He was still standing, leaning against Grandma's pie safe that contained the good dishes and other shabby, important items. He stuck his hands in his pockets.

"Son, we can't afford this." Dad set down the shiny brochure like it was distasteful, maybe even obscene.

"I'll work," he offered. "I'll work all summer and then when I'm in Chicago."

His parents looked at each other, not him, and his mother went back to her meatloaf. "You'll work right here," said his father, no heat in his voice, but no room for dispute either. "And your pay will be what it's always been: the security of your family."

He looked at his dad's unrelenting face and swallowed twice, trying to hold back the bitter words that rushed to his mouth. It was his brother's fault. If Darryl were still here, if Darryl hadn't joined the Navy, if Darryl could do his share of the farm work, Dad wouldn't need help. Darryl had left with kisses and tears and blessings; he was serving his country, after all. But the military shouldn't be the only ticket out. He waited. Maybe there were some magic words that might change their minds, but he couldn't come up with them. There'd never been any magic in their house. They were plain folks, his dad said. As if he were proud of it.

Mom cracked an egg into her bowl and dripped ketchup over it. Then she worked her fingers into the slime. "Why art? What in the world would you do with art?"

"Paint," he mumbled.

"What, pictures?" She rolled the mess into a ball and plopped it into a loaf pan.

He nodded.

Again she locked eyes with his father, transmitting some kind of code.

"No future in that, boy." His dad had retrieved his catalog and turned a page. "But I don't have a problem with you driving in to Ball State and taking some normal classes. You might find yourself something sensible to do that would support a family. We could pay a little on that if you stayed here and pitched in."

"I want to paint." His voice trembled and he hated that. He also hated that his fingers shook when he scrabbled at the papers, brochure, and envelope.

His father chuckled. "Well, the barn sure could use a couple of coats."

●●●●

Feeling more and more certain that no one was following him, Keith stopped in Lexington and bought a bottle of whiskey and five packs of cigarettes. He felt safe enough down at the cabin to sip a little, but only when he was by himself. There'd been a few times when Brenda and the kids had come to the cabin too. It was near what Brenda called her homeplace, located in Pulaski County where she'd been born, had lived until she was twelve, and where her parents had returned when they retired. Any time they went to the cabin, she always wanted to see her sister and brother and their families. They'd come back 'home' to live years ago too. It made Keith nervous, but he couldn't deny her the comfort of family. He'd never understood the invisible tether that drew folks back to their roots. The last place he ever wanted to see was that farm in Indiana.

He exited the highway and drove country road after country road. Spring was further along down here, sending color to the hills. A tender shimmery green, so new it was almost yellow, patched the hills, with redbud pinks mixed in for contrast. He could paint that.

As he neared the lake he stopped at a small store, one of many that popped up every few miles despite the supermarkets in town. It was a holdover from the old country stores with pot-bellied stoves and pickle barrels, he guessed, but this one catered to lake tourists and carried more Doritos and HoHo's than meat and potatoes. Plenty of pop, lots of live bait. Keith bought milk, bread, cheese, eggs. And a box of those cheap white doughnuts that sifted onto your shirt with every bite. Once he felt secure enough at the cabin he'd come back and buy more. It wasn't far.

He wound his way to the cabin. Brenda's father had owned several acres of lakefront property; now it was split between David and Lily and Brenda. Or him, he corrected himself. Land had been cheap back in the sixties when Mr. Williams had bought it, and it wasn't worth a lot more now since there was no access to the lake, just a view. The others hadn't built on the land, so the cabin was isolated. Perfect. His tires crunched against gravel, and he rounded one more curve before pulling in front of the building, twice the size it'd been when he'd first seen it and covered now in dark green siding rather than raw concrete blocks. Holding onto the bags of groceries and liquor, Keith got out of the car and glanced first at the grassy area on the far side of the door. Brenda's hydrangea, the one she'd planted when they were first married, was nothing but dried-up reeds now, but he could see little green shoots fighting their way past the stalks. He needed to trim it.

Inside, the cabin was cold, musty, and dark. Keith paid Brenda's brother a little bit every month to watch over the place. Usually Keith gave him a heads-up when he was coming down so David could switch on the electricity and water. There hadn't been time this morning. Keith spent several minutes getting the place running and bringing in his belongings before he went out the rear to the screened-in porch. It had been nothing but a crude deck when Brenda had first brought him here. Keith had replaced the deck with a spacious porch at the same time he'd built on an extra room, installed utilities, and had the siding put on. He looked out over the lake, hazy in the weak sunlight, and focused on the island across the water. Some of the trees were little more than toothpicks, but several were leafing out among the blurry redbuds. Their flowers were nearly magenta, he thought. Not red. He looked to the right at the marina, quiet now and waiting for warm weather to bring what Brenda called 'the Ohio Navy.' He smiled and let out a deep breath. There was more of her here than in the house they'd lived in for over thirty years. He'd run to the right place.

Chapter Nine

BRENDAN

He'd always figured that his dad was just a crazy recluse, some kind of J. D. Salinger of art, but that woman, Dana, had been real enough. Leon had seen her, and he wasn't a lunatic. Brendan stared at his computer screen and worried through all the research strategies he knew, but he had nothing to go on, no leads. He checked his email, but there were no new messages. The one that came up was the old announcement about the university's mini-marathon; he'd read it three times. God, he was bored. The library was dead except for a few students peering at Facebook or YouTube. The scholars were somewhere else, just like his student worker who was taking a makeup exam or something. Not that he needed help.

He leaned his spine against the backrest of his chair and squirmed. The old hamstrings and glutes weren't completely happy with his new running regime, but his brain was. He clicked back to the message for the 5K run, proceeds going to breast cancer research. That's where Mom's illness had started. Heck, he'd give it a shot. He was nowhere near that distance yet, but the race was a few weeks off. Even if he had to walk half of it, having a goal would be good, and he'd talk some people into donating. Megan thought he was crazy, getting up so early and running in the rain and cold and dark. But she didn't really care. He'd about decided she didn't really care what he did as long as it didn't affect her. He remembered that she was going out with girlfriends again tonight. He'd better pick up something for him and Cassie to eat.

He was in the middle of registering for the race when he sensed a student at the reference desk. Actually he could smell her—rain and shampoo—and it was a nice scent. He looked up.

"Hi."

It was the girl who'd smiled at him the other evening. "Hi," he said. Her dark hair was swooped up into a ponytail and unraveling around the edges. She held a dripping umbrella. "Can I help you?"

"Oh, I think you could if you would." Her eyes crinkled up. They were mostly green with intriguing rusty spots. "Here." She slipped a piece of paper across the desk until it touched his hand, the one with the titanium wedding band. Written on the paper were her phone number and name. Hannah.

He could feel his eyes blinking like strobes. Heat came up in his cheeks. "Umm," he stammered. That paper he'd signed saying he would refrain from social contact with students flashed into his mind. He'd never considered it an issue.

Still smiling, she said, "I'd like to interview you for the student newspaper." She lifted one slim shoulder. Embarrassment piled onto his discomfort. He felt like a fool for misinterpreting her come-on. But then her smile turned what he could only call saucy, and she whispered, "Or maybe we could do something more interesting. We'll see." He hadn't misinterpreted a damned thing. She left, making her way out of the reference area with slow, measured steps. Trouble, pure unadulterated trouble, he thought, but he didn't throw the paper away. Forcing himself back to the race application, he took deep breaths and got out his credit card for the fee. When he finished, he slipped Hannah's note behind his driver's license. Six months from now he'd find it in his wallet and laugh.

Dana, he told himself. Focus on this Dana woman. He didn't think there'd been an affair. Brendan's wallet felt like a stone in his back pocket. He figured Dana was from way back in dad's history, the sort of story he'd love to know. Maybe there'd been a romance back then, back before Dad turned so weird. Maybe high school or college. Probably when Dad was at Ball State. This fired up a sudden hunch.

Fishing his phone out of his pocket, Brendan scanned the reference area to see if his supervisor was in sight. He'd caught her reading mysteries in her office when the library was this dead, but she'd ream him about a personal call. Sometimes he wished she'd fire him. This job was not only dead but a total dead end. The Raptor was only forty and relentlessly healthy. He'd be senile before he got a promotion.

He called Kinley. She'd have the info at hand. He was practically OCD about organizing stuff, but Megan lived like a tornado, rearranging things into the next county and blowing the roof off any system he devised. Kinley picked up. "Hey," he said. "What's going on with you?"

"Nothing. I just put wineglasses in the oven to cook."

Right. Her painted glassware. He wished she'd do some real painting like she'd done in high school. Dad's genes were hopping through her veins, but she wouldn't give them a chance. "I'm at work so I won't be a minute," Brendan said. "Listen, can you get to your birth certificate easily?"

"Yeah, I think so. Why?"

"I need something off it."

"You're weird, baby bro. You trying to prove you're adopted?"

They'd talked about that once when they were in middle school and trying to figure out why everything at their house was so strange. He heard Kinley's shoes against hardwood. Although he'd seen pictures, it was hard to imagine his sister's house. "Sometimes I wish we were. No, I'm just wondering if Dad's social security number is on it. Seems like I remember that they did that back in the day."

Kinley breathed a chuckle. "Way back when I was born? Guess that's why it's not on yours."

"I don't know if it's on mine. It's at home, and I'm at work." He heard her open a drawer.

"So are you going to hack into government records or something?"

"Doubt it. But Dad told us he went to Ball State University, didn't he?"

"Yeah. Dropped out after a year. Like me."

Dripping rain, a disheveled male student came to the desk, and Brendan looked up. "Where's today's *Wall Street Journal*?" the boy muttered. "I gotta look up an article." Brendan was able to point.

"Not like you at all," he said to Kinley. "You stayed two years."

"Big deal," she said. "Here it is. God, I weighed over nine pounds. Poor Mom." She paused. "It's here. Both of their social security numbers. Got a pen?"

Of course he did, Brendan thought, but Kinley could no more imagine his job than he could fathom her Rocky Mountains. "Yep. Go."

She read the numbers. "How's that going to help you?"

"As I recall, back in Dad's time, students' social security numbers were their student ID's. Back before identity theft and all that."

"Really?" She chuckled. "What a wealth of useless information you have in that tiny brain of yours. So you're going to try to get into Ball State's records?" She sounded intrigued. Good. She was the one who'd come up with all the conspiracy theories in the first place.

"Yep. Don't quite know how I'll do it, but I'll let you know what I find out." He paused. "How's it going with the young musician?" She'd told him maybe five sentences about the guy, but Brendan had known from the look on her face that he was important.

"Okay, I guess."

Brendan waited.

"It's all about decisions around here," Kinley said, her voice hardening with every word. "Michael's been accepted for grad school at both Juilliard and Cincinnati Conservatory of Music. CCM. Isn't that funny?"

This time her chuckle was brittle. "Anyway, I haven't figured out whether I'm part of the decision-making process or not."

"Rough. Another self-absorbed *artiste* like Dad?"

"Maybe. Not sure." Which meant she didn't want to talk about it.

Kinley deserved better. Hell, he deserved better, but his self-absorbed partner was interested in money, not the arts. "Gotta go," he said. "Hang in there, sissy."

Kinley's voice turned funny. "That's what Mom always said to me."

"I know."

He put the phone back in his pocket and brought up the Ball State University site. It took a few clicks, but finally Brendan found a listing of the library's staff. Then it was a matter of choosing the right librarian. His instincts sent him to the reference people, information specialists in librarianese. But while wading through these listings, he found several that were little more than clerks. He didn't want the head of reference; his request might be a little shady on privacy issues. But he wanted someone who knew enough to delve into old records. He scrolled down the names of personnel until he stopped with what would've been a long screech in a Roadrunner cartoon. Zachary Wingo. Good Lord, Zack friggin' Wingo, who'd been the chief techie nerd in Brendan's information systems classes at Kent State. He'd wondered where Zack ended up. Profoundly odd and socially inept, Zack had also been scary smart. Brendan was one of the few who'd bothered to discover it. Most of Brendan's classmates, not particularly ordinary themselves by most standards, called him 'Zack Weirdo.' At Ball State, Zack's job title was 'Archivist.' That figured. Zack had a strong preference for machines rather than people. Using the reference desk phone, Brendan punched in Zack's number. This was a reference question, he reasoned, not personal business.

"Archives. Wingo." Yep, it was Zack. He still mumbled. Probably didn't make eye contact either. Brendan wondered if Zack wore his fuzzed-up black toboggan to work at Ball State.

"This is a voice from your past," Brendan said, lowering his pitch to announcer tones. "Your Kent State past." He didn't want to freak Zack out. He'd had a real penchant for believing in UFO's.

There was a hesitation, and then Zack shouted, "Brendan! It's gotta be Brendan." He sounded happy, which made Brendan sad. He should've found where Zack had ended up sooner and called him every now and then.

"Yup. What's happening, Zack?"

"Not much." Brendan could hear him swallow. "Well, I got a job."

Obviously. "Ball State. Good for you."

Zack sounded disappointed. "Oh, yeah. I guess that's how you found me."

Brendan kept his voice hearty. "Sure is. Do you like archives?"

Enthusiasm again. "Yeah, I do. I'm digitizing all their old records. Scanning like a madman."

"Cool. Been there long?"

"Almost a year." Zack paused. Brendan wondered if he was chewing on his pen like he used to do in class. "It took me three years to get a job. I'd about given up."

Brendan wasn't surprised. Zack Wingo would never excel at interviews. "So what did you do in the meantime? Backpack Europe? Hack computers for the CIA?"

Zack giggled. "No, man. I lived with my mom and worked at a computer repair shop. It was okay. Hey, did you marry that pretty girl?"

"I did. We have a daughter now."

"Cool. What's her name?"

"Cassie." Zack would go on like this for an hour if Brendan didn't stop him. "Hey, I need your help, buddy. Can you search Ball State's records and see if a person attended there back in the seventies?"

"Sure. We got those digitized a few months ago. What's the name?"

Brendan heard him clicking. "Keith Owen."

"Some long, lost cousin or a rich uncle?"

"Not exactly."

Zack was humming. He'd done that in grad school too, even during exams. "Let me double check something," he said. Brendan waited. "Nope. Nothing here," Zack said. "I assume Keith is a relative."

"Yeah. My dad. But I know he went to Ball State in like 1972 or 1973. Could the records be faulty?"

"Any records can be faulty, you know that. But I don't show him. I even reversed the name: you know, Owen Keith. And nothing."

Brendan was surprised that Zack didn't recognize the name, but then art to Zack would probably be anime.

Zack was still talking. "People lie, Brendan. Maybe he made it up. Not to disrespect your dad or anything."

Oh, Brendan could easily believe that his father had lied. But he decided to try another tack. "Did Ball State use social security numbers as student ID's back then? Could you look up a student by a number?"

"Weird. They might've. Let me see." Brendan heard the light click of teeth against plastic. "Nine digits. I'll be damned. Looks like they did. Man, that was stupid, wasn't it?"

"I don't know. Back then nobody worried about identity theft. Pre-internet and all that."

"Dark ages, huh?" Chew. Chew.

"You got that right," said Brendan. "So, if I gave you a number, could you see if that person attended Ball State?"

"Sure. Shoot."

Brendan read him the number. Zack hummed. He said, "Sure is lucky that we started doing this project. Otherwise you would've had to go through administration, and I'm not sure they would've searched for you. Privacy, you know."

"For sure. I really appreciate this."

"No problem. You still doing reference?"

"Yes."

"Your library digitizing its records?"

"I think so."

"They should." Zack started preaching about how the process reduced physical storage, made arcane information accessible, streamlined searches. Brendan took a couple of deep breaths. He was glad Zack loved his work.

"Here we go. Uh, oh."

Brendan tensed. "What?"

"That social security number doesn't belong to your dad. The student's name is Thomas Vickers. Enrolled the fall of '72. Ever heard of him?"

Brendan frowned at the pad of paper where he'd written the name. "No."

"Address is a rural route in Emory, Indiana." Zack paused. "Hey, that's just down the road from here. Local boy. Sound like your dad?"

It did, but who was Thomas Vickers? "I don't know," he said. "Do you think there might be something else in your records about Thomas Vickers? Class schedules? Clubs? What sorts of things are you archiving?"

"Digitizing," Zack corrected. "Lots of stuff. Meetings, reports, fraternities, all kinds of information."

"Could you search for Thomas Vickers or that social security number through your databases?"

"You bet. Except I still have dozens of boxes to scan."

Brendan's spirits fell. He wanted info now. "Would it be too much trouble to look through what you've already processed?"

"No problem. Might take me a few days though. Is that okay?"

"Of course. Hey, Zack, you're a pal for doing this."

"Happy to do it, buddy. Good to hear from you. Give me your number. Maybe we could get together sometime."

●●●●

When Brendan got home, Megan was dressed to go out and looking hot. She wore heels with skinny black jeans and a bright blue cardigan. The shirt under the sweater was cut low, low enough to show a sweet shadow when she bent over to get Cassie's stuffed rabbit. Did women dress up sexy for other women? It seemed odd to him. "You're late," she said. It was more of an observation than a criticism only because Megan was pumped about going out. He could tell. Cassie wasn't as enthusiastic. She held her bunny to her neck and stared at her mother.

"I picked up supper for Cassie and me." He set the grocery bag on the counter.

"Okay," Megan said. "I need to leave in five minutes."

"Fine." Brendan shrugged out of his jacket. "You and Julie are doing dinner, I assume?"

Megan nodded. "Then we may go to a movie." She picked up her purse, a new one. Coach. She loved brand names, expensive designers. He'd bought her a black Coach bag for Christmas, but this one was pale gray. She saw him staring at it. "Julie gave it to me," she said. "Said she never used it."

Brendan thought it was a mighty expensive hand-me-down, but Julie always had money, and a lot of women, or at least Megan, had a tendency to tire of their things long before they were worn out. "Do you have money for dinner?" he asked.

Megan grinned, kissed Cassie's cheek, and said, "Yes, Dad. I've got my lunch money." She gave him a quick peck, almost a kiss, and left in a wave of perfume.

Cassie looked up at him and said, "Cookie?"

"No, dinner. But let Daddy get changed, okay?"

Two sweaters sprawled on the bed like they'd been pitched across the room. Megan must've had a hard time deciding what to wear. Brendan pulled out some jeans and an old hoodie. He didn't understand Megan's need to go out with friends at least twice a week. But then he didn't stay at home all day with a toddler either. It was cheaper than dinner out for the two of them when you added in the babysitter. Far cheaper. But he would've liked to go out with his wife occasionally. She always said they couldn't afford it.

"Mac?" Cassie asked hopefully when he went back into the kitchen.

"Nope. We're having salad with chicken and big bread." It was what Cassie called French bread.

She looked apprehensive. "Salad?" There was a w in the middle.

He opened a bag. "Look, baby carrots. What baby bunnies like to eat. And celery. I bet I can make mine crunch louder than yours."

Later he put a warm, clean, sleepy baby girl in her bed. She was out as soon as she'd sighed once and clutched her bunny to her chest. He turned on the television and flopped onto the sofa to fold laundry Megan hadn't finished. Only then did his mind travel back to what Zack had told him. The information wasn't conclusive yet, and Brendan wasn't sure it mattered anyway. But he was enough of a reference librarian to enjoy the hunt. He muted the TV and called Leon.

"Hey, Leon. It's Brendan. It's not too late, is it?"

"No. Course not. How're you doing? Is everything okay?"

"Fine, fine. Have you heard from Dad?"

"Yeah. He called yesterday. Asked if I got those canvases sent out. Old Worrywart. Course I did." Leon paused. "He said he was down at the lake."

"That's where I figured he'd go."

"That's as good a place as any to grieve for your mama. She loved that cabin."

Brendan raised an eyebrow, glad Leon couldn't see his skepticism. "He still mad at you?"

"No. Didn't seem to be."

"Good. Have you seen or heard any more from that Dana woman?"

"No." Brendan figured that despite Dad's change of mood, nice, old Leon was still burning from his brief lapse in security. He wouldn't want to talk about it.

"That's good. Don't worry about it, Leon. It was probably nothing." Brendan was folding one-handed: tiny jeans, yoga pants, Megan's panties. These days he saw Megan's underwear in the wash more than on her body. Sad commentary, he thought.

Leon always spoke slowly, but he took even more time before he replied. "It can't be nothing, Brendan. Just the fact that she found him means there's a leak somewhere." Another pause. "I just can't figure out where."

Brendan rolled socks. "No sense in trying to." He got to the point. "Listen, have you ever heard of a Thomas Vickers? Maybe Tom Vickers?"

"No. Somebody else from Keith's past?" Leon's voice went up half an octave. "Has somebody gotten in touch with you?"

"Nothing like that. I was doing some research about Dad's college days, and that name came up." Brendan didn't want to go further with it. "I just wondered."

"Can't say as I have," Leon said. "Oh, a couple of bills came today. You want me to send them to you?"

"No. I'll stop by later in the week."

And that answered that question. Brendan had never figured that Leon knew anything. He set his phone aside and picked up the laundry basket. Under it was one of those real estate booklets they had at the grocery. He glanced at the pages that were dog-eared. Megan had good taste. She'd chosen mansions, literally mansions, all well over half a million. One was near Dad's house. Brendan shook his head. The only way they were making it on his pitiful salary was that they had neither a mortgage nor car payments.

He threw the booklet on the sofa. Even Dad wouldn't go for those kinds of prices. And Brendan wasn't going to ask. Emergencies, health problems, sure. He'd get over his pride for those, especially if they involved Cassie, but Megan might as well forget her house campaign. He was getting awfully tired of her repeated argument that Dad had bought Kinley two houses. His sister hadn't cost Dad four years of college and grad school. Kinley. He grabbed his phone and called her. She answered on the second ring, and he told her what he knew. "Thomas Vickers?" he asked. "From Emory, Indiana?"

"No, I'm sure I've never heard that name, but Emory, Indiana sounds familiar," she said. "Wait. Isn't that where Dad's from?"

"I think so."

"Thomas Vickers," she murmured. "No. What does all this mean?"

"I don't know, but I'm thinking maybe Dad changed his name at some point." Brendan started picking up Cassie's toys, dumping them into a bin. "But that doesn't tell me why."

Kinley snorted a laugh. "I'm still betting on the witness protection program."

"I can't imagine what he would've witnessed. Maybe he's CIA." Brendan waited for Kinley to laugh. "Did you realize that all the bank accounts are in mom's name? I'm wondering about other things, maybe the house, car."

"It was her car. And she wrote all the checks. It sort of makes sense. Are you doing that now?"

"Yeah."

"Bummer."

"Not really, and, umm, he's paying me." Brendan felt guilty about this, like he was getting more than his sister, but she couldn't have done the work from Colorado.

"Well, he should. That takes time." She paused. It sounded like she was loading a dishwasher. "You still running?"

He said yes, and told her about the race. She asked about Cassie. He asked if Michael had decided on a grad school yet. She said yes but nothing more. After insisting that he tell her anything he learned about their father, she hung up, and Brendan felt empty. He wished Kinley lived closer. He wished he could make Megan happy. He wished for a lot of things. He took the laundry back to the bedroom, checking on Cassie as he went. He got out clean sweats for his morning run, set out his shoes, and put away the rest. Picking up one of the sweaters lying on the bed, he folded it. It was new. A price tag dangled from the label. $258.00. The other one was even more. He'd bet the one she'd worn was new too, and sure enough, he found the tag in the bathroom trash basket. It was only $225. He sank down on the bed. He liked expensive clothes too; hell, that's all he'd worn before they married. And he liked Megan to have what she wanted. Still, they couldn't afford purchases like these. Maybe she planned to take back the two with the tags still on. But even the one she was wearing was beyond their means.

Brendan rubbed his face. He'd talked and talked to her about running up their charge cards. Sometimes she'd laughed about it, saying he could ask his rich daddy for help every now and then. Sometimes she'd yelled at him, saying was cheap, stingy. She never would accept that they simply didn't have the money for what she thought she needed. He went to the kitchen table and booted up their laptop, a gift from Mom before she got so sick. Logging onto their bank site, he checked back for over a month and saw nothing resembling the sweater extravaganza. Probably on the charge card. If she didn't have to pay for something immediately, Megan tended to think she didn't have to pay for it at all. Sometimes it felt as though she had a vise around his chest and was slowly squeezing the air out of him.

He didn't want to look at their Visa account, not tonight anyway. Maybe Megan's talent for denial was rubbing off on him. He shut the laptop and made a decision, probably a stupid one, but being stupid was better than feeling miserable. Going back to the bedroom, he picked up his wallet from the dresser and dug out the slip of paper. He glanced at the two sweaters and punched in Hannah's number. He almost cancelled the call before it connected. Almost.

He walked back into the living room. There was a beer commercial on the television. Beautiful people danced, flirted, had fun. He'd forgotten fun. Somehow it had vanished behind his mother's death and Megan's constant harping. Hannah answered. "Hey Brendan." Damned Caller ID. Her voice was stronger than he'd remembered, but this afternoon she'd been whispering. People did that in a library.

"Hi." He felt like a fool, a guilty, sinful fool.

"Whatcha doing?"

"Nothing," he said, feeling like he was fourteen. "You?"

"I'm at work," she said. He could hear clattering and music.

"Where do you work?"

"Starbuck's."

"Oh." Why was he doing this?

"Do you like Starbucks?"

"Yeah." He couldn't afford them. A quarter bought him a cup of acidic brew in the faculty lounge. "Listen," he started, not sure what he was going to say. Then it came out in a rush. "I'd like to do the interview. Maybe over coffee or something."

She laughed. "Coffee? Okay. But not here." She named a place near campus and asked if he knew where it was. He did. "When?" she asked.

That was tough, but if Megan could run around doing whatever she pleased, so could he. "How about tomorrow after I get off? Maybe five-thirty? Would that work for you?"

"Sounds good," she said. "Strange time of day for coffee, but I'll take what I can get." She laughed again, making him feel warm and cold at the same time.

"Okay. See you then."

God, he was sweating. It wasn't like they were meeting at a hotel or even a bar. It wasn't like it meant anything, but he still felt like he'd jumped off a bridge. And was, despite the terror, enjoying the fall.

Chapter Ten

KINLEY

She gave the countertops a swipe or two with the sponge. With each minute she was more overwhelmed by a longing for her mother. Talking to Brendan made her miss him too. Actually, seeing her brother for the horrible weeks while she'd been home made her realize that she'd missed him for years. But who she wanted right then was her mother, despite the fact that they'd never been in the habit of holding those cozy chats some of her high school pals had shared with their moms. From what he was saying these days, Michael had evidently assumed that Kinley would go with him when he left for grad school. She didn't know whether his assumption made her feel wanted or taken for granted. She also didn't know what kind of advice her mother would've given her about Michael. It could've gone either way.

Her apartment was quiet. It was amazing how much noise Michael generated just by being there, his shoes against the floor, his easy conversations, the music he played. Kinley liked the noise. She wasn't sure what she'd do without it. Making a quick decision, she grabbed an unopened pint of Ben and Jerry's Cherry Garcia from the freezer and climbed the steps up to Sarah's apartment. Kinley knew she was home.

When Sarah opened her door, she grinned and asked, "Is this a party?" Kinley shrugged and opened the ice cream.

"Where's Michael?" Sarah gave her a spoon.

"Playing for the Presbyterians."

"Oh, that's right. It's Wednesday." First Kinley, then Sarah stuck a spoon into the carton. "I guess the choir will be missing him soon."

Kinley nodded. She pressed a chocolate flake against the roof of her mouth and let it melt. Heaven.

"Well?" Sarah's eyebrows climbed up her forehead. "Has he made his decision? Is this a celebration or a pity party?"

Kinley slid another spoonful into her mouth before she answered. "Both. He chose Cincinnati because he thinks I'll go there with him. I could go home, he said, be with my family. He just assumed I'd want to. Never even asked." She stared at Sarah's orange curtains.

"At least he wants you to come with him. He's not dumping you, Kin."

Kinley made circles in the air with her spoon. "The boy isn't thinking about what I'd have to give up." She looked back at Sarah. "Selfish? Him or me?"

"He's a man, not a boy, and maybe you're both a little self-absorbed." Sarah frowned. "Why can't you go?"

Kinley shook her head. "My work's here." Sarah's frown deepened. "Oh, I could paint glass anywhere, sure, but the houses, my tenants. I have to be here." She looked again at the curtained window next to Sarah's door. She couldn't see them, but the mountains were out there. The grand Rockies that represented everything she loved about Colorado.

"That's not necessarily true. You could hire an apartment manager, someone who'd live on-site. A grad student would love to do that for free rent."

Kinley concentrated on a cherry.

Sarah pointed her spoon at Kinley. "You don't want to go back to Cincinnati."

"No, I don't." The ice cream had left a film in her mouth. She licked her spoon and set it down on the table. "But it's more than that."

"Okay." Sarah got up, put the half-empty carton in the freezer, and poured two glasses of water. "I'm guessing it's your father. You've never had anything good to say about him." She sat again. For such a short woman, she was a formidable presence.

"Yeah, my father."

"It's not like you two would have to live with him or anything."

Kinley shivered. "I'd never live with him. Never, ever, ever."

"Okay. Like I said. It can't be your brother; you seem to think he's pretty wonderful." Sarah twined her fingers together and set her hands on the woven placemat. She was willing to wait. She was determined to wait.

Kinley started, "You know how Michael's all compulsive about his music. Always practicing. Never here."

"His senior recital is next week. There've been all the auditions. Come on, Kinley, be fair."

"I'm not talking about the last three months. Think back. The music comes first." It was time. She was ready to open something she'd been schooled all her life to keep shut. "Art always came first with my dad. Not us, not Mom. I think he's probably done some pretty terrible things for the sake of his art, worse even than ignoring his family."

"Art?" Sarah scrunched up her nose, and Kinley could almost see her thoughts tumbling over each other. She gave her time enough to piece it together. The aspen painting, Sarah's art appreciation class. Sarah's face went red. "Your dad is Keith Owen? Jesus Christ, Kinley."

Feeling her jaw tighten, Kinley managed a curt nod. "Yep, and God help me, I have to beg you not to tell a soul, especially not Michael." Sarah nodded. "Dad's amazing, but he's nuts. He's an obsessive recluse who poisons everything around him for the sake of his creative genius. Everything has to be secret. Nobody can know who he is or where he lives. All for his art. I don't know how my mother lived with him, always, always coming second." Before she knew it, she was spilling even more secrets: the security measures, her prom, her brother's games, the fact that, other than trips to the cabin, Dad never had gone anywhere with his family. No vacations, no photographs. She'd raised her hands and was counting his crimes on her fingers.

"Jesus," Sarah breathed again. "Keith Owen?"

Taut as one of Michael's piano wires, Kinley said, "I won't live that way."

"You really think Michael will be like that?" Sarah shook her head. "I don't see it. Yeah, he's dedicated, ambitious, but you wouldn't have him any other way, would you? I can't see you hooking up with a slacker."

"Why not? I am."

Sarah hooted. "Oh, cut the crap. You're no slacker. You run these apartments like a machine. You meet your glassware deadlines. You work hard."

But I don't paint, Kinley thought, and that's what I should be doing. Her hands were shaking; agitation had her heart banging. "I need to go. Keep the ice cream."

Sarah went to the sink, rinsed the spoons, wiped her hands. "Look, I don't pretend to know Michael as well as you do, but I think he loves you. These buildings are nothing compared to that. I know you love the mountains, but they aren't going anywhere. They're nothing compared to love either. Some people manage a relationship along with their art. I'm certain Michael can." Sarah turned to look at her. "He's not your father, Kinley."

She stood and pushed in her chair very carefully. "I can't risk it."

BRENDAN

When the alarm went off, he moved like a robot, putting on his socks, sweats, and shoes. Megan groaned and rolled over. She hadn't come home until 2:30. Long movie. Yeah. He sneaked out into the hall and closed the bathroom door before turning on the light. If Cassie woke up, he wouldn't be able to run.

He managed to get out of the house without disturbing anybody and stood in the driveway to stretch. He'd run for forty-five minutes three days in a row now. He'd try for fifty or even fifty-five today. It was clear and cold. Stars freckled the sky. He started at a moderate pace, setting his pedometer as he went. By the end of the block his muscles were warming up, smoothing out. He liked to imagine himself as a machine, to picture his joints as cogs, his muscles as belts. In the dark, with no distractions except trashcans on Tuesdays, he had to occupy his mind some way, but he'd forbidden himself to worry while he ran. The trouble was he couldn't stop fretting about Megan's demands and purchases. Not to mention her late night. Then there was his date with Hannah. What an asinine thing to do, he thought, even if the interview was legit rather than pretense. He'd call her this morning and cancel. And he'd ask Megan what was going on. It was all probably innocent. A voice in his head said, "Really?" about both decisions. But he ignored it. His new shoes were good, really good. No worrying, not while he was running.

He liked to watch lights come on in the houses he passed. He had them timed now and knew which ones would be lit up or dark as he passed. The white house with the huge pine tree was erratic; sometimes lights were blazing and other mornings all was dark. He'd figured a newborn baby must live in that house.

He was warm now, sweating under his knitted hat. Good. He'd weigh this morning. In three weeks he'd already lost eight pounds. Pretty good. Megan wouldn't be able to rag on him about his weight much longer. Megan. The sweaters. The evenings out. She never asked for money for drinks or movies or dinner. Who paid? Julie worked full-time. Could she go out that often? Until 2:30? His breath was coming harder. That was okay. He'd push until the end of this block. He wouldn't think about Megan. Or Hannah. Or Dad and his mysteries.

Just then his calf seized up into a cramp so strong he nearly fell. Hopping on the other leg, he felt the pinch extend both up and down his leg. It took a full minute to make himself use the cramped leg, stepping cautiously and grinding his teeth against the agony. Even though he'd been out only thirty minutes, there was no way he was going to run any more today. Limping, he backtracked toward home.

Up ahead he saw his house and a strange car in his driveway. Weird. It was a four-door, probably black or navy. It was still too dark to make out much more. As he lurched forward, the driver backed onto the street and turned on his headlights. Strange, but probably just someone turning around.

●●●●

His shower finally released the taut muscle. Hamstring, he figured as he dressed. Cassie and Megan were still asleep. He opened one of the ever-present yogurt cups and sat at the laptop to eat. Bringing up their Visa account, he searched for charges during the past month. Nothing resembled a bill for the sweaters. Maybe she'd opened a department store charge. He knew she had one from Penney's, but those sweaters were a little out of Penney's league. Megan's purse, the gorgeous Coach bag, sat right there on the table, tempting him to do research a lot sneakier and ignoble than running background on his father. He'd always trusted her. He'd never checked up on her. Dipping into the bag for her wallet, he felt his face heating up, but he did it anyway, shuffling through her cards and finding nothing but what he'd expect. He frowned. Could Julie be charging things for her?

Before putting her wallet away, he checked her cash compartment and counted out $200. Shit, where was the money coming from? He slipped the wallet back into her purse, stared at his yogurt, closed the laptop. He didn't understand, but he was getting a very bad feeling about all this. Throwing on his jacket, he crept back to the bedroom and told Megan he was leaving, that Cassie wasn't up yet. She nodded, mumbled okay, but didn't open her eyes. He didn't kiss her. Maybe he'd meet Hannah after all.

Chapter Eleven

KEITH

He felt safe now. The first night he'd prowled the cabin, keeping the gun in his pocket, afraid to build a fire or turn on lights. Despite the baseboard heat, it had been cold and miserable. The sounds of wind and nocturnal creatures kept him jumpy. By the next night, he'd loosened up, had a whiskey before his grilled cheese and soup supper. Smoked a cig after it. The day after that, he'd started painting.

It was another Brenda picture. He'd set up his easel on the deck, which caught decent light most of the day as long as he took out the screens. He remembered fussing with Brenda about screening in the porch when they'd renovated the place. She hated mosquitoes and suffered more than most from their bites. But the light, he'd said. Even at their vacation cabin, he'd need light. God, he'd been stubborn. They'd finally compromised on screens he could remove.

He planned to set the picture on the island across the lake, to capture the newborn green of the leaves, the deep hue of the redbuds, and the contrast of dogwood blossoms. All day he'd been working on the lake water, trying to catch it in the morning sun, blending his pigments just right to get the grays and browns and greens. Water was rarely blue. Why did people persist in thinking it was? Amateurs painted blue water. He was pleased when he stood back and gazed at his work.

Keith thought he'd pair this one with the cancer painting he'd left shrouded at home. He'd forbidden Leon to touch it. There were always a few adjustments, some tweaking before a painting was finished. He needed time to remove himself from it before he varnished it.

He wasn't sure he'd ever send that one to Devonie. The cancer painting was risky; it revealed too much. The style ventured far from his usual work these days. Maybe that's why he liked it. It was reminiscent of his painting back in Chicago before he'd forced his art down another path.

He was at a stopping place; might as well quit before he lost all the light. After cleaning his brushes, he poured a little bourbon over ice, lit a cigarette, and sat at the oval chrome and formica table that had occupied the cabin since Brenda's father cobbled the building together in the sixties. The chairs were covered in rust-colored vinyl, a slit or two in nearly every one. He'd told Brenda several times that they could get new furniture for the place, but she liked it the way it was.

They'd come here for their honeymoon. Back then it had seemed primitive, dark, even squalid. Two small windows opened onto the deck and allowed very little light into the place. The walls were unpainted concrete blocks plastered with cobwebs. There'd been only one room then, with a rudimentary bathroom that needed priming from a pump beneath the floor. Back then there'd been no heat except the fireplace, but they'd married in early August. They hadn't needed heat.

1976

They said their vows on a Friday afternoon in front of a justice of the peace in Covington. Her parents and siblings were there, along with Brenda's two best friends from high school and the Williams' next-door neighbors. Keith had nobody to see him wed. He'd told Brenda that his parents were dead, his brother in the Navy. It was partially true.

Keith had bought a suit. The tie felt like a noose, although Brenda hadn't put a rope around his neck. She was a perky little thing and easy to get along with. Holding a bouquet of yellow daisies, she winked at him before the ceremony. She had a sense of humor. He wasn't sure he did. She'd said that she'd had to cry and raise a big ruckus to reassure her daddy that the quick wedding wasn't because she was in the family way. Keith hadn't heard that phrase since his grandmother died.

Brenda's parents had been cautious but friendly. They wanted them to wait. They were bewildered when Keith marched their daughter into a bank and set up an account in her name, which led to a trip over the river where little Brenda paid $75,000 for what she called a 'palace' on the east side of Cincinnati. During the six weeks he and Brenda dated, Keith had asked everyone he met where the finest houses in Cincinnati were located. Three out of four people had named the same suburb where huge houses were being built, so he took Brenda there one Saturday afternoon and asked her to choose the one she liked best. She'd danced around the nearly completed houses, laughing and clapping her hands like a child. She was a child, but that was okay. At least the money was safe now. Keith could relax, and so could Brenda's parents, although they seemed more pleased that Keith had paid her college tuition than they were about the house. Go figure.

The wedding party had an afternoon reception at Pop's, and his new wife held his hand throughout the meal, brushing his knuckles against her thigh, just at the hemline of her short white dress. He'd been looking forward to that part of having a wife too. He'd been careful during their short courtship. A kiss or two, a little bit of necking. He didn't want to scare her off, and he could wait. He was good at waiting.

Mr. Williams had offered the cabin to them for a honeymoon. Although Keith could've afforded most any trip Brenda might've dreamed up, she wanted to share her favorite place with him. She'd said that they could visit all her kinfolk down there; she could show him off. But Keith had said no. He wanted her to himself. It wasn't the first time she'd given him a baffled smile. It wouldn't be the last either, Keith reckoned.

They'd driven down to the lake in the new silver Mustang II Brenda had chosen and bought outright with Keith's money. Like the house, it was in her name. This confused her for a while, but she was so pixilated, that was her word, by all the extravagance that she'd let it go, saying only that the car had to be a Ford so her Mommy and Daddy could keep their jobs at the plant.

When they arrived at the cabin, she parked the car, and Keith unloaded their suitcases. He'd bought those too. Brenda, still in her short white dress, bounded over to the cabin's rustic door and unlocked it. "Now don't be disappointed," she cautioned. "It's not like our new house. It's plain." It was plain all right. Not much more than a fishing shack.

He kept his mouth shut, though, and brought in their bags along with a few groceries and a bottle of cheap champagne the Williams' neighbors had given them. Mrs. Williams had frowned at the gift and hissed, "Catholics," near Keith's ear. "We're Baptist. Tee-total," she whispered.

Brenda opened the door to the deck and glanced around the place. "We gotta turn on the generator for the fridge and stove to work. Daddy said there was enough gasoline for a few days." She went back outside. He heard noises from underneath the floor. Soon the refrigerator was humming and water gurgled in the pipes. She came back into the cabin wiping webs from her arms. "I got the pump working too. Come on," she said, pulling at his hand. "Look at the lake. Have you ever seen anything so pretty?"

There were probably two hours of light left. The sun had mellowed out over the water, throwing glitters up toward the trees. One caught in Brenda's ring. It was a nice stone, a good investment in Keith's mind. She saw the sparkle too and held up her hand. "You spoil me to death, Keith

Owen." She wound her freckled arm around his waist. "I swear, I feel like a princess in a fairy tale."

"Good," he said and kissed her. She tasted like the cream soda she'd guzzled on the way down.

She grinned at him, but he figured there was fear behind it. "I reckon I'd better get sheets on the bed." And she backed away, leaving him to watch the light play on the water. Silver, gold, dun. It was pretty. He'd paint soon. Very soon.

Shallow alcoves flanked the stone fireplace with bunk beds crammed into the front one and a double bed in the other. She fussed with the big bed and then took a broom to the pine plank floors. Keith opened the refrigerator, wishing there was beer, but when they'd stopped at a little store to buy their groceries, Brenda had told him the county was dry. "We could drive down to the line tomorrow and get beer if you want it," she'd said so shyly that he figured she was more afraid of the mysteries of drink than sex. He put the champagne in the freezer to cool.

"Are you hungry?" she asked, scooping dirt and leaves into a dustpan. Her bare arm looked like an extension of the broomstick.

"No."

She spent nearly an hour wiping things down, taking dishes from the single cabinet and washing them, and somehow managing to keep her dress clean. In the bathroom she set out towels and soap she'd brought from home, chattering the whole time. Maybe they'd go fishing. Maybe they'd go into town to eat one night. She knew a great place for catfish. Her high-heeled sandals clattered against the floor as she rushed from spot to spot. She was stalling, but Keith didn't mind.

The light had nearly faded by the time she perched on one of the old chrome chairs and raised her hair off her neck. "I've worked up a sweat," she said and then colored. Brides shouldn't sweat.

He smiled at her. "You need something cool to drink." He opened the freezer to get the champagne, chilled enough he supposed. He didn't know any more about champagne than Brenda. He wasn't sure how to open it but managed without breaking the cork. Pouring some into two Flintstones glasses she'd just washed, he urged her to raise her glass, like they did in the movies. "To us," he said. "To Brenda and Keith."

She giggled, nodded, and took a sip. "It don't taste like the road to perdition," she said. "I mean, it doesn't. Kinda like ginger ale, isn't it?"

He nodded and confessed, "I've never drunk it before either."

She laughed. "Aren't we a pair? I figured you grew up on this stuff."

Keith thought about the orderly farm, his dull, serious parents. "No, not at all."

Brenda drank hers down quickly and asked for another sip. She was nervous, but she was also brave. Laying her hand on his, she said, "I just want to tell you that I love the new house and the new car. I love being able to go to college, and I love you." Her eyes looked serious and gray in the low light.

He wouldn't lie to her, not any more than he had to. He said, "I want to make you happy, Brenda." And he did. He was immensely grateful for her name and social security number. He could paint safely now. He could hide rather than run, thanks to Brenda. Gratitude was nearly love, wasn't it?

The sky over the lake turned to slate. Brenda jumped up and went to a shelf by the stove where she pulled out four Mason jars with squat candles inside, setting two on the table and two by the fireplace. Fingers shaking, she struck one kitchen match and then another to light the four. "We got lamps," she said. "But I thought this would be nicer."

Light flickered against the concrete walls and rough floor, softening the dismal cabin. Brenda stood by the table and upended her glass. Then she reached behind her back to unzip her dress. "I reckon I'm ready if you are," she said, her voice a little hoarse.

The bed smelled of clean sheets and musty mattress. And girl. Fresh, young girl. There was candlelight in her eyes. Keith kissed her. "Have you ... do you know?" He couldn't quite ask her. It seemed impolite.

Her mouth curved up in its usual way, a beautiful arc. "I've never been with a boy," she said. "But I know what happens."

"Your mother?"

"Lordamighty no. My sister. Lily's been fooling around with her boyfriend for months. She told me all about it." She snuggled closer to him, her bright hair tickling his cheek. She flattened her hand against his chest like she was testing his skin. "It'll be okay, Keith." And then she'd moved her hand down.

●●●●

He'd never forgotten the unconscious grace she'd shown that night and for the three days afterward when she had him laughing and easy for the first time in years. He glanced at his empty glass. He hadn't been aware of finishing the whiskey. Standing, he turned on lamps and went out on the deck to bring his canvas in for the night. There was just enough light for him to see the outlines of it. Eventually he would paint Brenda in the trees, among the redbuds and dogwoods and poplars and pines. She'd be a ghost, a pre-Raphaelite vision in a long white dress, her hair the color and length it'd been when he met her. She would be nearly as thin as the saplings he'd paint, and hazy, misty. Part of the woods and island. There and not there.

He threw a cloth over the canvas and looked out at the darkness. He could barely tell water from island. Stretching out his fingers, he fisted them and opened again. They were stiff from holding a brush all day. It was all so much harder now.

●●●●

A few days later he awoke to rain and was almost glad not to paint. Last night he'd drunk too much, for something to do as much as anything. With no television, not even any music, the evenings were far too long. He'd go into Somerset today; he needed groceries anyway. Maybe he'd pick up a book, although he wasn't much of a reader. He dressed, ate the last two white doughnuts, and shook the powdered sugar off his hands. Maybe he'd buy some ibuprofen or something for his hands. He straightened the kitchen, made his bed, wandered around the cabin. It was only six-thirty. Stores probably weren't open. Back home he would've been pleased with the early hour. Back home he worried about being followed or recognized, but after this long he didn't think it was an issue in Pulaski County.

Maybe, he thought, he should move. He could sell the house for a bundle, maybe just rent an apartment somewhere. North Carolina appealed to him, either mountains or beach. And he'd thought about Arizona. He'd heard that arthritis improved there. Moving might be smart. He could pick right up and disappear again. If Dana had found him, Nick Collins could too. Keith felt in his jacket pocket for the paper with Dana's number on it. He couldn't decide whether she was benign or malignant. His face creased into a sour, ironic smile at the words. Part of him wanted to call her, just to see what she wanted. But he couldn't risk it. Things were dangerous now. He'd stayed in the same place too long, but Brenda had always argued that it wouldn't be good to uproot the kids. And she liked her job. He would've hated to leave Leon.

He went outside, locking the cabin door behind him. The pines dripped. The road was black with wet. He started the car, glad to have the radio for company. The little store not too far from the marina was dark, but he'd decided to go to a supermarket anyway. He was tired of living on sandwiches and canned soup. At the cabin, there were a few pots and pans he could use for simple cooking. The first morning of their honeymoon, Brenda had made coffee and then held up a large cast iron frying pan. Her skinny wrists looked hardly strong enough to lift the skillet. "I've always wanted to make pancakes for a man," she'd said. Brenda had been a good cook. "It's just another way of making love," she'd said when he complimented her. Despite the white doughnuts, he wanted pancakes.

After eating a stack of them at a little restaurant attached to a downtrodden motel, Keith went to Wal-Mart and bought a cd player and all the cd's he could find that wouldn't turn his stomach. Most of the selection had been country. He hated country music. He put these in his cart with a couple of books that looked like spy thrillers. Maybe he'd pick up some tips, he thought. This brought a ghost of a smile to his mouth, and a middle-aged woman with a grandbaby riding in her cart smiled back at him. Keith immediately adjusted his mouth. Then he bought food: frozen meatballs, jarred sauce and pasta, lettuce and carrots. He added what he needed for hamburgers along with a frozen pizza and some fruit. Along the way he bought more white doughnuts, a few chocolate bars, and ibuprofen. He peered at the mishmash of items in his cart. He'd never been domestic, and he was too old to learn. But he wouldn't starve.

By the time he left the store, the morning had lightened up as much as it was going to. Rain was still coming down. He drove around, reluctant to go back to the cabin. He spotted a laundromat. He'd need that eventually, depending upon how long he stayed. He even thought about buying a television, but he'd need cable to get any channels down here and he wasn't willing to fool with that. He drove south on Highway 27, crossing a bridge over another end of the lake, and wandered through little burg after little burg until he entered McCreary County. Then he kept driving until he was in Tennessee. Right over the line was a cluster of sordid beer joints. After last night's whiskey, he wasn't interested, but the establishments were open. At nine in the morning.

He was shaking his head and looking for a place to turn around when he noticed a pay phone sitting outside yet another little store that definitely did not have beer signs in its window. The local Baptists, he thought. His eyes went back to the pay phone, a dinosaur if there ever was one in this day and time. His left hand fumbled with the slip of paper. Dana wouldn't have any way to find him if he called from a pay phone. He parked the car and turned off the ignition, but he didn't get out. The little store was open. Around the side of it he saw two parked cars, probably employees. They'd notice if he sat too long, but he couldn't make up his mind. He never knew how Dana felt about what he'd done. Thirty years ago, he was certain that Dana liked him a little, or at the very least, respected his work. He stared at the empty shelves shoved against the store's front wall. They'd hold flowers and tomato plants once it was warm enough for planting.

It was nearly midnight, but Nick's studio had enough overhead lights to fake daylight. Besides, he didn't need natural light for the abstract he was painting. Hearing two sets of feet shuffling up the metal steps, he figured Nick was bringing in yet another woman. Having a studio was Nick's status symbol with girls, outranking the fast car, swank apartment, and ready cash Mr. Collins supplied to his little boy. Nick rarely painted.

Tom had already stilled his brush, waiting for the interruption, but he hadn't been prepared for the girl to be beautiful. Most of them weren't. She had long blonde hair and wore a gray coat that nearly touched the ankles of her high-heeled boots. With the boots she was probably five inches taller than Nick who was a skinny, fast-talking Irish shrimp sired by an older fast-talking Irish shrimp who had barrels of money.

"Hey Farm Boy, this is Dana. Isn't she outstanding? What're you painting?"
Nick shed his coat and pulled the girl over to Tom's canvas.

He gave Dana a brief smile. It didn't pay to get too friendly with Nick's women, and keeping Nick sweet was his bread and butter. He stood back from his painting.

Nick gave it a glance. "Cool. Oh man, you are so good." Nick turned to Dana. "Farm Boy had no place to crash, so he's been living here a while now." He pointed to the shabby Japanese screen at the end of the huge room. Behind it sat a cot, a refrigerator, and an apartment-sized stove. "I'm trying to get him a job with my dad," Nick said. He grinned. "Might beat washing dishes at a restaurant, right?"

He had no idea what sort of employment Mr. Collins might give him, so he didn't reply. At that moment he didn't care. The girl smelled like cold night along with a tang of something sweet and spicy. He wished she'd take her coat off. She was still gazing at his painting. "Not finished," he mumbled.

"Amazing," Dana said. "Fantastic." She switched her gaze to his face and looked at it nearly as intensely. "Original," she murmured.

"Dana's in art history at the Institute. Wants to do gallery work along with busting artists' balls with critiques, don't you babe?" Nick was high on something. Not unusual.

He nodded, forcing himself to look away from the girl. It was like she was swallowing the painting, and him, with her eyes. Nick didn't seem to be noticing, but it didn't pay to take chances. He turned toward Nick and asked, "You want me to leave?"

Nick did a little dance that involved squeezing Dana, sniffing the air like a hound, and darting his eyes around the studio. "Yeah, man. I hate to ask, but my brother's staying at my apartment just now and well, you know..."

He knew. Nick liked his sex loud and athletic; besides, he thought girls got off on doing it in a studio. Nick always promised he'd paint them, but when they took their clothes off, he never got around to picking up a brush. Whether it was his Irish charm or Daddy's money or the fact that Nick was damned handsome with a romantic, poetic sort of vibe, his line was successful with lots of women. Dana was giving Nick a nice, hot look.

"Yeah, I'll clear out." He cleaned his brush, stepped behind the screen to get his jacket, and smoothed the blankets on the cot. He'd have to change the sheets tomorrow.

As he neared the door, Dana asked, "Where will you go?" She'd taken her coat off. All the right curves, broad shoulders, long legs. She looked Scandinavian, which meant luscious and loose, according to all those art movies he'd heard about.

He shrugged. "Somewhere. Don't worry about me." His only choice was a crappy hotel six blocks away where he begrudged the cheap room rate but figured he was still ahead even if he had to resort to the slimy desk clerk and lumpy mattress five or six times a month.

With the advent of Dana, he slept at the hotel so many times the desk clerk knew his name. But by January, Nick's brother got his own place, and Dana moved in with Nick. Sometimes when Nick actually went to classes at the Art Institute, Dana sneaked off and stopped by the studio. She never said much to him, but she would stare at his work and say smart things about it. She liked his broken eggs picture.

"Symbolic, right? The cracks, the shells, all the runny mess," she'd said. "Death before there's a chance for life?"

He nodded even though he wasn't entirely sure what he'd meant by the painting. The whole trick, he thought, was to let people come to their own conclusions.

"Did you really grow up on a farm?" she asked.

"I did."

She smiled at him and he nearly risked his free living quarters by kissing her. "Did the farm have chickens?"

"Yeah. Dirty old things."

It had been one of those false spring days, unusually warm for February, so he'd opened all the windows in the studio. Dana shivered. "You cold?" he asked. Without waiting for an answer, he rushed around the room closing the heavy oversized windows. "You want some tea?"

"Sounds good." She sat in the one upholstered chair that their models used, on the rare occasions that they hired models. He couldn't afford them, and Nick didn't paint enough to need them.

He filled a pan with water and put it on to boil. Dana was looking at the canvases leaning against the walls. She pointed at the three that were obviously Nick's. "Nick Collins can't paint for shit," she pronounced but smiled like she didn't care.

He shrugged. "You have to work to get good."

"And Nick never works," she said.

"Doesn't have to."

Dana leaned back in the chair and focused on him. Her eyes were green, the green of old glass. "Not like the rest of us." She gave him a lazy smile, almost a come-on, although he might be wrong. He didn't know beans about women. He ducked behind the screen to watch the water boil.

Keith smoothed the slip of paper against his jeans. He still didn't know beans about women, especially this one particular woman, but he decided to chance it. He found a quarter in his pocket and dialed.

It rang. The area code might belong to a state that was two or even three time zones different from Tennessee. It crossed his mind that he might be waking her, and that almost made him hang up. But he kept listening. Four rings now. Then the tinny, computerized voice of an answering machine told him that Ms. Dana Oliver couldn't come to the phone just then. He should leave a message at the beep. Keith set the phone back in its cradle.

Chapter Twelve

BRENDAN

It was nearly quitting time. He'd heard nothing from Zack, but he hadn't expected to. Digitizing was probably slow and painstaking. Despite Zack's enthusiasm for it, Brendan figured the process was deadly. He'd chosen academic libraries as his specialty, envisioning vibrant discussions with grad students and challenging research requests from professors. It hadn't worked out like that. What contact he had with professors and grad students amounted to their emailed requests for books and articles. He glanced at a stack of those on his desk. He might as well work at McDonald's. He'd been wondering for weeks if corporate research might be more satisfying. Those jobs paid better than academic libraries, and Megan would like that, he guessed.

Just now he was more concerned with his wife's mysteries than his dad's. And then there was Hannah. He looked at his phone and then the clock. Now or never if he was going to cancel. Who was he kidding? He'd worn his best shirt and made sure his socks didn't have holes. He not only intended to meet her, he figured they'd end up in bed. Hannah's signals predicted it. That morning he'd left Megan a note that said he was eating with some of his co-workers, an informal dinner meeting he called it. He wouldn't be home until at least nine, he wrote. He'd never been unfaithful to Megan, never even considered it. Somewhere along the line he'd turned into a total and complete shit.

His workday finally stuttered to a stop, and Brendan decided to walk to the coffee shop. A warm breeze whipped at naked tree limbs and tossed the daffodils by the library. Few students were stirring at that hour, giving the campus a cozy, park-like feel. He'd loved college when he'd been a student: the old buildings, the hidden spots perfect for lunch or studying; just the setting made him happy. Maybe he'd thought he could preserve those feelings forever by working at one. He'd been wrong. He wasn't happy about anything these days.

But as he neared the coffee shop, and Hannah, a familiar motor resurrected a pleasant humming in his body. The search, the quest. He hadn't felt this sort of excitement for years, and he liked it. He told himself it was just coffee. So far, he'd done nothing wrong. Megan was hiding things from him; this was no worse. But the pulse in his blood knew the truth. Before he opened the door, he smoothed his hair and straightened his shoulders.

He was early, and she hadn't arrived yet. The place was nearly empty. He ordered coffee with a splash of skim milk and a muffin from a bored barista. He'd be missing dinner, unless that's where he and Hannah ended up. There was nothing wrong with that. Just dinner. Choosing the most remote table in the room, he sat facing the door, figuring he could tell a good bit about Hannah's intentions by the way she walked in. Spying on his father and wife, secretly meeting a gorgeous girl--he ought to look for a job with the frigging CIA. He took a sip of coffee as bitter as his humor.

As soon as she came in, Hannah caught his eye, nodded, and went to the counter. She was wearing tight jeans, a low-cut top, and a cardigan— nearly the same outfit Megan had worn the night before, which deepened his doubts about what Megan was up to. He heard Hannah order a green tea latte and a brownie. He was getting courage from caffeine; she was doing it with sugar. Strolling back to the table, she said, "Hi. I thought you might stand me up." She dropped her book bag and sat. Utterly calm.

He shook his head like it'd never crossed his mind. She arranged a notebook and pen next to her drink and looked up at him from under her heavy bangs like she expected him to start everything. Her pale skin was creamy, almost thick. His dad would enjoy the contrast between her hair and complexion.

"So, is this really an interview?" he asked, throwing her the smile that had worked so well in college.

She shrugged, and the movement forced a bit of cleavage to blossom above her blouse. He pinched off a bite of his muffin. It was stale. She opened the notebook and fiddled with the pen, laying it at a precise angle to the paper. "If that's what you want," she said. "You fascinate me. I wanted to get to know you before it's too late."

It was a good line. "Too late how?" Resting his elbows on the table, he leaned toward her.

Hannah's dark hair lay in parentheses just at the tops of her breasts. "I've been noticing you for ages." She lifted a hand and wiggled her fingers. "Ever since I was a sophomore. I graduate in a month, and then I'm out of here. Carpe diem and all that crap." Her cheeks were flushed. Appealing as hell.

"So interview me. What do you want to know?" He kept smiling. He was in the groove now. "My middle name is Claude. That's pretty fascinating."

She laughed. "Your dad's name?"

A *frisson* of wariness crept up his spine. "No. My maternal grandfather's."

"Are you from around here?"

He gave her his résumé while she nibbled on her brownie. The notebook paper was still blank. "A hometown boy. I would've thought you were from someplace else. Somewhere exciting." She sipped her tea but kept her eyes on him.

"No. Are there rules for this? Do you get to do all the asking?"

She set down her tea. "Ask away. I'm boring."

"Never. Where are you from?"

"A suburb outside Columbus."

"Why didn't you go to big, bad Ohio State?"

She shrugged again, and the same thing happened with her breasts. He wondered if she'd practiced. She said, "I wanted to get away from home. You didn't, though. At least for undergrad." None of this was important, not even interesting.

"I lived in the dorms. I might as well have been a hundred miles away from home." He leaned back in his chair. Okay, she was attractive, but the high he'd felt was evaporating by the minute. It felt wrong, silly even.

"So you wanted to get away from home too."

His shrug revealed nothing.

She tilted her head. "Do you still want to get away from home?"

Here we go, he thought, and spoke before he could change his mind. "Look, I'm married, and I have . . ."

She interrupted him. "I know."

He wondered for a crazy moment if she was fulfilling a dare to seduce a faculty member before she graduated. Something resembling panic sparked his nerves faster than the overbrewed coffee.

"You have sad eyes, Brendan."

She was still trying. Had to give her credit for determination. And she was damned attractive. "Really," he said. "Well, my mother died six weeks ago. That's enough to make anybody sad." It was cheap, but he was done. She wanted him to spout some cliché about being misunderstood by his wife. Even if it was true, he wasn't going there.

It threw Hannah, but only for a second. Her eyes widened, "Oh, I'm really, really sorry. I didn't know that."

"How could you?"

She shook her head and sipped her tea. "That would kill me. Mom and I fight all the time, but I can't imagine losing her." This was genuine.

"My sister and mother fought a lot too. Mothers and daughters do."

"So you have a sister?" She'd picked up her pen but only to make loopy doodles.

"Yeah. One. You?"

She shook her head. "Two brothers."

"Poor you."

That made her chuckle.

He was tired. He wanted to go home. This was flattering but exhausting. He took a deep breath. "Do you really write for the newspaper?"

"I really do. I'm a journalism major. And no, I don't have a job lined up." She ate another bite of brownie. "Everybody asks that." She swallowed. "Speaking of jobs, why did you become a librarian? I always think of them as snotty old ladies shushing everybody."

"Yeah, everybody does," he said, paralleling her words. "I love the game of it, the search." This much was true, even though his work rarely measured up. He smiled. "There are lots of male librarians."

She knew her fish was getting away, but she seemed okay with it. "Don't you need something more exciting in your life than a library?" It was said with curiosity, not the contrived tone she'd tried at first. He thought. He wasn't sure.

"Maybe I do." He toyed with the sad muffin. "I've started running. I played a lot of sports in high school and missed the exercise."

"Running." She gave him a knowing smile.

He ignored the innuendo. "In high school I played most of the sports they offered, except football. Liked basketball best."

"Which high school?"

He told her, but he was just trying to be polite now. Hannah sensed it. After several minutes of sports talk, she stuffed the notebook and pen in her bag and said, "Okay, I think I've blown this. I guess I stink at the art of seduction. That's obvious, isn't it?" She gave him a wry smile. "But I haven't given up yet. I will see you again somehow." She covered his hand with hers.

"You can always find me in the library," he said. He thought that might bring a frown or even a scowl, but she was still smiling when she pushed in her chair.

"You can run, but you can't hide, Brendan," she said as she left. He expected her to look back when she reached the door, but she didn't.

His coffee was cold. Daylight had faded. As he walked to his car, he told himself he hadn't done anything wrong. Maybe Megan hadn't either.

Maybe she'd just been out late flirting like he had, a sorry statement about their marriage but essentially harmless, he told himself. He checked his watch. It was still early. He'd be home before seven, he thought as he started his car. Traffic had slowed down. It might even be earlier. He'd tell Megan that they'd ended up canceling the meeting. A little lie but a lot better than what he might've done.

When he turned onto their street, he noticed the plum trees blooming at the house four doors down, white petals stark in the twilight. Spring. April. New beginnings. He didn't want his marriage to fall apart. He and Megan had to talk. He'd keep his temper, be fair. He'd been tempted too. As he neared his house, he spotted a silver car parked in the driveway. Different from the one he'd seen this morning. He slowed. A Mercedes. He couldn't think of anybody he knew who drove one. He tried to swallow, but his spit had dried up. Megan didn't expect him for another couple of hours.

He drove past his house, following his running route until he'd gone around the block. Parking down and across the street from their house, he called Megan. It rang several times before she picked up.

"The meeting got cut short," he said. "Just now left to come home. You need me to pick anything up?"

She said, oh, and then, hmm, and finally said they needed milk. "Did you eat?" she asked.

"Sort of."

"I didn't cook. You might want to pick up something for yourself."

"Okay. I'll do that. See you in a little bit."

He waited. Three minutes. Five. Ten. The front door opened and a man came out, pulling a suit jacket on as he walked. Average height. Dark hair. He couldn't tell much in the near dark, but he was sure he didn't know him. The Merc's lights came on. Brendan jotted the license number on the back of a gasoline receipt. Megan thought it was stupid to save gas receipts. The man backed his car out of the driveway and sped down the street. Brendan watched him until he disappeared.

At first he drove without knowing where he was going. His pulse banged against his throat. Try as he might, he couldn't think of any logical reason why a man might be at his house, especially a man rushing out of his house when the husband called. Some other part of his brain guided him to the grocery. He parked but sat staring straight ahead. What had they done with Cassie? Her presence would hardly be conducive to romance. He glanced down at the scribbled plate number. Leon had a nephew who was a policeman. Reference librarians didn't have access to that kind of information. He punched in Leon's number and went through the usual greetings. No, Brendan hadn't heard from his father. Everything was fine. Well, maybe it wasn't.

"Does your nephew still work for the Cincinnati Police?" he asked. Leon said he did.

"Could he look up a license plate and tell me who a car belongs to? There's been an unusual vehicle parked in front of our house at odd times." God, Leon would think he was getting as paranoid as his father.

"I don't like that," Leon said slowly. "Not with the baby in the house."

Brendan agreed. Oh, how he agreed. "I just thought it might help to find out who it belongs to. I've asked the neighbors. . . ." His voice trailed off.

"Sure thing," said Leon. "You know, I haven't heard or seen anything more of that Dana woman. You don't think this might be connected, do you?"

"I doubt it," said Brendan. He read off the plate number and took a deep breath. "Well, thanks a bunch."

"Yeah. I'll call him. And then I'll get back to you. Take care."

The lights in the grocery hurt his eyes. Brendan picked up a half gallon of milk and thought about getting a nuke meal or some dried-out fried chicken for his supper, but he couldn't fathom eating anything. He paid for the milk and got back into his car, once again going on auto-pilot toward his house. By the time he got home, he still hadn't decided how he was going to approach Megan or what he was going to say.

She was sitting at the kitchen table leafing through a catalog. Brendan thought about kissing her to see how she smelled: fresh from a quick shower or dripping perfume. But they hadn't been kissing much lately. He hung up his jacket. "Where's Cassie?" he asked.

Megan kept her eyes on the pictures of pretty women in pretty clothes. "Julie took her to the mall to ride the merry-go-round."

Weird, Brendan thought. Julie didn't usually schedule play dates with his daughter. But it was convenient. He went back to the bedroom to change clothes. The bed was made. Nothing was out of place, but then he'd given her better than a half-hour. The shower was dry. He returned to the kitchen and opened a beer. To hell with the calories. "When's Julie bringing her home?" He sat at the table with Megan.

She still didn't look up. "After while."

Probably after Megan called and told her to. Once again, convenient. He didn't want to start any kind of traumatic conversation with Cassie around. But he was about to boil over. "Out late last night, weren't you?"

Color came up in her face. Megan blushed easily. He used to think that was charming. "Oh, I drank too much." She made it sound like an apology. "So I stayed at Julie's and watched a movie until I sobered up.

Didn't want to drive." There was little he could say to that. He watched her linger over the damned catalog. She must've been memorizing every stock number. "We need to talk," he said.

She looked up. "About what?" She was wary now. Her eyes were cold as stones.

He heard a car pull into the driveway. "You know what." A car door slammed. "But not until Cassie is asleep."

Tired and cranky, Cassie ruled the next hour. Megan didn't ask for Brendan's help like she usually did and stayed conveniently out of his way until the child was asleep. Then she went to the kitchen and lingered there, turning on the dishwasher, running water. Brendan stared at a chaotic sitcom without seeing it. Beer, coffee, and anxiety flared in his stomach. After waiting as long as he could, he went into the kitchen and leaned against the counter. "Who's the man?" he asked. He didn't really care what the guy's name was.

"What man?" She rubbed a towel over the countertop. Laminate rather than granite, much to Megan's displeasure.

Brendan looked down at the floor. There was a smear of something purple on the vinyl. "I'm tired, Megan. I don't want to play guessing games. I came home early. I saw a silver Mercedes in our driveway. I called you, and a man rushed out the door. Who is he and how long have you been seeing him?"

She didn't turn around. He waited while she folded the towel, hung it on the oven handle, and straightened it. "Megan?" He didn't want to yell and wake Cassie, but sharp metal crept into his voice.

Finally she faced him, staring at him like he was a stranger, even worse, a detestable excuse for humanity. "I have nothing to say to you," she said.

"You saw him last night too, didn't you?" Acid rose partway up his esophagus. "Answer me."

She turned back to the sink.

"Don't lie to me." That was pretty absurd since she wasn't even bothering to speak. He *would* get a response, damnit.

Reaching for a paper towel, she rubbed at the purple stain on the floor and then threw the towel away. Then she glared at him again. Her mouth was set in a straight, ugly line. "You lied to me. Or the same as." She lifted her chin. "All those expensive dates, the honeymoon in Italy, your fancy job at the university, your rich parents. You made me think there'd be plenty of money, that our life would be fun and exciting." She was shooting words at him like bullets. "Our life is crap. Poor, boring, stupid. You have no ambition, no drive. We'll scrape along like this forever. Nothing's ever going to change. I won't put up with it." She walked past the table, toward the hall, and spat over her shoulder, "You played me false, Brendan. You're the liar."

He slept in the guest room, what little sleep he got. There were no sheets or pillows on the bed so he brought a throw pillow from the sofa and used a wadded up duvet cover for a blanket. Nobody had stayed in the spare bedroom since Cassie's birth when Megan's mother had come, and the room had become a repository for junk. Scrapbooking supplies littered the floor. The vacuum cleaner sat in the middle of the room. He'd cleaned it a few times, but his efforts dissipated in days. Even as a kid he'd always felt compelled to tidy up his room before he could go to sleep, so the mess kept him awake. Then he fretted that he might not hear the baby monitor. Megan could doze through a tsunami and rarely heard Cassie crying even with the monitor. He worried that he'd oversleep. But he could not bring himself to lie down with Megan in a bed that he felt sure had been occupied by someone else a few hours ago.

The next morning he ran on reluctant legs. In the rain. He played his mind game of telling himself not to worry while he ran, but it didn't work. Yesterday's conflict about Hannah seemed ironic, even frivolous, and his father's mysteries were the last thing on his mind. All he could think of was Megan and that man. Their marriage was a sham. There was nothing left, but he couldn't help but hope that she would cry, say she was sorry, that she'd never do it again, and the chaos would go away. He hated chaos.

Tired after only a mile, he pushed on, wiping the rain off his face with a towel and thinking of things he might do to make Megan happier, but he wasn't sure she'd be pleased with any of it. It was his fault. Back when he'd met her, he'd liked his women gorgeous, hot, and a little bit stupid. Megan qualified. He'd made a bad choice. His breathing became ragged, and he slowed his pace. She was right. He'd misled her. Well, he had a little more money now with the payment from his father. He could spend more on her, maybe even ask his dad about a house, although it would choke him to do it.

Managing to shower and dress without waking either his wife or child, Brendan drove to work and closed his office door. He organized the papers he'd left on his desk before meeting Hannah and wiped down the shelves with a dust cloth. He thought about telling Beverly that he was ill, that he needed to leave, but he didn't know where he'd go. He was staring at the rain splashing his window when his phone rang. Leon.

"Hey, buddy." Leon sounded cheerful.

"Hey yourself. How's it going?"

"Pretty good for a rainy day, but I'm worried about this guy hanging around your house. You don't think he might know that Keith's your dad, do you? Trying to kidnap little Cassie for ransom or something?"

Brendan didn't think that at all, but Leon would be more upset if he told him the truth. "I doubt it. Did you get the guy's name?"

"Yeah. Scott Klein. Lives in Hyde Park. Want his address?"

"Sure." Brendan jotted it down.

"My nephew says you ought to file a complaint or at least talk to the police if he keeps hanging out." Leon's voice deepened with concern. "I think so too. I don't want anything happening to that baby girl of yours."

"Me either. We'll see. Maybe this Klein has some connection with one of our neighbors I didn't talk to. I'll check it out. You at the house?" Brendan drew a line under the name and address he'd written. Klein sounded familiar.

"Yeah. I'm keeping busy. Doing a little cleaning around the place this morning. I'd drown if I tried to work outside."

"That's for sure. I ran in it this morning."

"Fool." It was said with a chuckle.

"Yep. Thanks a bunch, Leon. I'll be over this weekend to pay you."

Brendan doodled around the name and then hopped on Google to research him. It didn't take two minutes for him to realize why he'd recognized the name. Scott Klein was a partner in the law firm where Megan had worked before she quit to have Cassie, where Julie still worked. Easy. Obvious. Brendan wondered if the affair had been going on for years. Leon was right. He was a fool.

Chapter Thirteen

KEITH

After he tried to call Dana, Keith's nerves were bad the rest of the day. Late in the afternoon Brenda's brother David stopped by, and Keith nearly grabbed his pistol when he heard the truck. Actually, he'd expected to see his brother-in-law since he paid him a pittance every year to come up and check on the place occasionally. It seemed like he paid everybody for something.

Keith's presence at the cabin didn't surprise David either, nothing much did. He asked about Kinley and Brendan, wondered if Keith needed anything, and suggested they go fishing on the weekend. Keith said he might, although he knew he wouldn't. He could sense that David felt kinship with him in their loss: his wife, David's sister. But the last thing Keith wanted was a long pity session with Brenda's brother.

After a bit more chatter and some stifled tears, David took off his ball cap and rubbed at his balding head, telling Keith that he was smart to come to the lake before the summer crowds scared off the fish with their big boats and bikinis. He grinned at his own joke and left. They'd always managed to be friendly. David had said once that his sister might've married young, but she married smart. Keith took it as an innocent compliment. Might've been different if they truly knew him.

After David left, Keith went back to his canvas. He had maybe one more hour of decent light. Brenda's ghost was done, but he was still working on the water and adding touches to the sky. He'd decided to call this one "The Lady of the Lake." It didn't have anything to do with King Arthur or any of that nonsense, but there were always critics who liked to play with symbols and interpretations. Titles, names—they weren't important to him.

Brenda wore a faded sundress that fell loose from her shoulders to accommodate an immensely pregnant belly. Absurd on such a tiny girl. It was late summer, hot, and despite the industrial-sized air conditioner that cooled their big house, Brenda's ankles were as swollen as her stomach. He poured her a glass of sweet tea and sat with her at their new kitchen table. She smoothed the oak with her finger. "Now we have a table and four chairs and a television, a sofa and a lamp table and a lamp." She lifted her finger to count off their possessions. "And a bed and a chest of drawers," she finished. "My granny would say we're living high off the hog." She smiled at him.

He'd painted furiously for months, turning out canvas after canvas, but he'd sold nothing yet. The money was holding out, but it wouldn't last forever. Brenda was satisfied using cast-off pots and pans from her mother and a few linens from K-Mart, but Keith wanted more for her. "We need to get a baby bed soon" he said, "and some clothes and stuff. Don't we?"

She nodded. "Soon is fine by me." She stretched and the bulk of her belly raised like the hump of a strange animal. It fascinated him when she put his hand against her rigid stomach to feel the baby's oddly violent movements. "Three more weeks," she said on a sigh. "And we haven't figured out a name yet."

He didn't care what they called it. He wasn't much interested in a baby, but not long after they married, Brenda had started talking about having a kid, even though its arrival would interrupt her classes. But only for a semester, she'd sworn, and she'd take summer school next year to make it up. To be honest, he didn't suppose a baby would disrupt his work much. Brenda was careful never to disturb him while he was in the studio. She'd make sure the baby didn't either. "You keep changing your mind about names," he said. During the last month he'd hung four of his paintings at different venues, all free, in various locations around the city. He might have more luck if he went in person to some of the small galleries in Cincinnati or even tried peddling them in New York. But he couldn't do that.

Brenda pressed her hand against her dress and rubbed circles around the lump. "Here recently my mind keeps going back to this girl who was in my biology class last spring. Her name was McKinley. I liked her name."

Keith made a face, but Brenda was staring at the window. "I was thinking that if we got rid of the 'Mac' it might be a pretty name. Kinley? Do you like that?"

He liked it as well as Amy, Alisa, or Jennifer, ones Brenda had suggested over the last few weeks. "Sure," he said.

Brenda rolled her eyes at him. "You don't care, do you?"

"Not much. I mean, I care about the baby, just not the name. What if it's a boy?"

She shifted in the chair. He didn't see how she could ever be comfortable. "We could name him after you. Keith's a strong name."

He shook his head. "What about your dad?"

She laughed. "I'm not hanging Claude on any poor defenseless baby. Except maybe as a middle name." She squinted up her eyes like she did when she was thinking hard.

The lowering sun touched her amber tea and gleamed against the varnished oak. He'd quit working early because she'd said she was hungry, but she'd made no move to start supper. He guessed it didn't matter. Here recently she'd been interrupting him a little more often, wanting his company he supposed. Maybe she was scared about having the baby, but he didn't know how to comfort her. He asked, "What if we name a boy after you?"

She tilted her head at him.

"Not Brenda, of course, but Brendan. It's a nice name. Sort of modern."

Her cheeks turned pink. They were plumper than he'd ever seen them, making her look even younger than twenty. "That's a fine name," she said. "I like it."

"That's settled then. Do you want to shop for a baby bed tonight?" He'd go out this once, even though it made him anxious.

"No. I'm too tired." She'd twisted her frazzled braid into a clip at the back of her head. Wisps of hair caught the slatted light from the shutters. Sipping her tea, she looked at him and then down again at her non-existent lap. She had more on her mind than names or a baby bed, but she was having a hard time spitting it out.

He stood. "I'll fry some bacon," he said. "Make us some BLT's. Does that sound good to you?"

She nodded. "Wait, Keith. I got something to say."

He sat again.

"I hope this baby is going to be Kinley Owen or Brendan Owen." She paused. "It bothers me some that I'm still Brenda Williams at college and on the deed to this house and at the bank. I'd rather claim being your wife."

He interrupted her. "Lots of women choose to keep their maiden names these days, call themselves 'Ms.' even if they're married."

Her pale eyes flashed. "Well, I ain't one of those women, and I didn't choose to do it. You told me to." Her grammar always slipped when she was upset. Keith kept his mouth shut. She went on. "I don't reckon I mind, but I want my baby to have his or her daddy's name. I'm not some unwed mother who doesn't have any name but her own to give her child." Her last words were defiant.

He hadn't thought about it. He hadn't weighed the danger in it. If Brenda got her way, the child would register for school with the last name of Owen. He, or she, would graduate and go on into life with the name. Did it matter? It did to Brenda. Maybe he could use his old social security number on the birth certificate. That might throw somebody off. Or not. Hell, he didn't know.

She didn't wait for him to comment. "I'm not stupid, Keith. You've done something, something that got you all this money. I don't know what, and I don't want to. I worry sometimes that you might end up in jail, and I might be right there with you for helping you hide." She ran a finger down the condensation on her tea glass. "I'm willing to do it," she said. "But I'm not willing for my child to wonder why he don't carry his daddy's name." Brenda rested her arms against the top of her belly.

He wished he could tell her he wasn't in trouble with the law. But he couldn't explain without letting her know more than he thought was prudent. No, she wasn't stupid, and he should've realized that she'd figure a few things out. "Okay," he said. "You're right. The baby should have my last name."

He expected her to smile, but she didn't.

"And we're going to buy that bed tomorrow morning before I get so tired. I'm not able to wait and do everything in the evenings when I'm so swelled up. Just this once I'm interrupting your painting, and you're going out with me." She pinned her eyes to his face, not giving him a chance to object.

●●●●

A week later he completed the Brenda painting and spent the morning sketching a remarkable spider web attached to the railing of the deck. In the mornings the lake's breeze made it shiver, the clinging dewdrops glistening with light. The geometry of the web intrigued him. He would paint it soon. After lunch he swept the cabin's floor and gathered up his dirty clothes. He couldn't delay going to the laundromat any longer.

He'd forgotten how boring it was to watch clothes wash and dry. He went outside and walked a block or two in either direction to pass the time. He smoked a cigarette. He thought about the paintings presenting themselves in his head. He saw paintings everywhere, but he dismissed most of them as trite or unchallenging. He'd be bored before he finished sketching. And he wondered about Dana, whether he should fear her and how on earth she'd found him and what she wanted.

After folding his clean clothes, he drove again to the Tennessee border. This time he went into the little store and bought cheese, lunchmeat, and cigarettes. He smoked only six or seven a day, not so much. They helped him to relax; besides, he didn't figure cutting his lifespan short at this point was any big deal. Throwing his purchases in the car, he went once more to the pay phone. He didn't need the slip of paper any more. He'd memorized the number. Taking a deep breath, he punched it in and waited.

"Hello," she said. Her voice was deeper than he remembered.

"You asked me to call." His heart was pounding.

"Thank God. I've been waiting for weeks."

He didn't say anything.

"Are you in Cincinnati?"

"You know I'm not going to tell you that," he said.

"Okay. You don't need to." She said this quickly, like she was afraid he'd hang up. "Listen, you need to be careful. Very careful."

"What do you mean?"

"Nick's looking for you. He didn't, you know, after you disappeared. His father searched all over the place, but Nick didn't start until a few months ago."

"Why now?"

"I'd rather tell you in person. I could come to Cincinnati. I don't imagine you travel."

"No."

She was silent for a second. He guessed that she didn't know what he was saying 'no' to. "Things haven't turned out well for Nick. He blames you."

"After all these years?"

"Yes," she confirmed. "More than ever."

"Are you still with him?"

"No."

"How did you find me?"

"I have my ways." She still had the same little laugh, but her voice turned serious in an instant. "Please. Be careful. Tell your children to be careful."

"My kids?" A chill started at his scalp and crept down his body. "He knows I have children and who they are?"

"I don't know what he knows, but he has people working on it."

"I gotta go." He hadn't felt this scared when she showed up at his house, when he'd run. He'd never felt this scared. A car pulled into the store's parking lot, adding panic to fear. The driver was a teen-aged girl, but it could've been Nick, he thought.

"But I need to see you," she protested. "There's more."

He hung up.

●●●●

Alert for any sign of a car following him, a suspicious stranger, anything, Keith drove back to the cabin with his fingers clamped around the wheel. His logical side told him he was safer down by the lake than anywhere. Only Leon, and probably his kids, knew he was at the cabin. Then his stomach clenched at the thought. The kids and Leon were in danger because they knew where he was. Dana said they were in danger no matter what they knew. He needed to get home.

Once inside, he packed up his painting supplies, stuffed his clothes into bags. He could call Kinley and Brendan, but neither would pay attention. They thought he was crazy. He started loading the car, his mind red-lining with decisions and plans. He needed a different car, a new phone. He wished he could persuade Brendan and Kinley to live at the house with him. He could protect them there. At that thought he stopped in the middle of easing the "Lady" painting into the back of the Subaru. He really was crazy. He needed to warn his children and then distance himself as far away from them as possible. Maybe he could leave one tiny clue, a false one, to lead Nick's people away from his kids. He shook his head. He had a three-hour drive to work it out. He actually remembered to turn off the generator and gather up his food to stow at the nearest dumpster. He wasn't panicked, he told himself. He had everything under control. He sped into the night.

Chapter Fourteen

KINLEY

She'd spent the morning working in the yards of her three buildings. When there were plumbing or electrical problems, she had to call people, but she did all the painting, cleaning, and yard work herself. The chores brought back pleasant memories of trailing patient old Leon as he mowed, dug, and trimmed. After lugging bags of yard waste to the curb, she wiped her dirty hands on her jeans. She'd have to get cleaned up soon. Michael's senior recital was at three. He'd already picked up his clothes and gone to the music building for some last-minute rehearsing. She would've liked to arrive with him, give him an encouraging kiss, all that lady behind the stage stuff. Instead, she'd be going with Sarah.

Her phone was on the kitchen table where she'd left it before she went outside. Stupid. Michael might've needed something. She had one message, from Brendan, and it was two hours old. She played it. "Kin, call me as soon as you get this. It's important, really important." His voice was tight.

She washed her hands and poured a little wine. She'd need it if something traumatic had happened. Hell, she'd need it to get through Michael's performance. She was more nervous than he was. The recital was like a giant exclamation point at the end of his college career. He'd completed all his classes and exams. He'd finished his church job. Although he hadn't said anything about his plans, Michael could be leaving for Michigan as soon as tomorrow.

She glanced at the clock. A little after one, three in Cincinnati. Brendan would still be at work. Surely he'd answer his phone if things were as important as his message indicated. He did. "Where were you?" he demanded.

"Outside. Trimming and raking. I was afraid my phone would slip out of my pocket. What's up? You sound like doomsday."

"I don't know what to think. Dad's back. He called me late last night, made me come over. He was pacing, wound up. He said a lot of things about it being his fault and how guilty he feels, but it all boils down to the fact that he thinks we're in danger. All three of us."

"Oh for crying out loud," Kinley said. It was one of her mother's expressions. "What's he having, a panic attack? I swear we need to get him to a shrink. We've needed to for years." She shouldered her phone and picked at grime under her thumbnail. "You had me scared."

Brendan's voice was dead serious. "He has me scared. He called that Dana, and she told him to be careful. Someone's looking for him. Someone from the past."

"And you believed it? God, Brendan. Why would anyone look for him?
Did he steal brushes at the art store when he was a teenager? Come on."

"I think I do believe him."

She didn't know what to say.

"He didn't tell me much, but for Dad it was quite a bit. He did something years ago, he said, before he married mom. Wouldn't say what. And he thinks someone's out for revenge."

Kinley rubbed her face. "Okay, let's just say it's true. Why would anyone wait thirty-two years to get back at him?"

"I don't know. You're the one who thought he had a past."

"I know. But it was silly. It doesn't make sense." She paused to take a sip of wine. "Vintage Dad."

"You should've seen him. He kept telling me I had to make you believe it, that he couldn't stand it if anything happened to us."

"Well, that's real sweet, baby brother, but it's all part of his sickness. Did you ever hear anything from that guy at Ball State?"

"Not yet. He said it would take a while." He paused. "Well, it wouldn't hurt you to be careful, Kin. Lock doors. Notice if you're being followed. That kind of thing."

"Okay, okay. Lord, I wish I'd never brought up the witness protection program or spy versus spy stuff. Now you believe it more than I do. But they're going to be hauling you off to the looney bin along with Dad if you go along with everything he says. Honest, Brendan. Relax."

"Sure." He didn't sound convinced. "Yeah." Actually, his voice sounded all but dead.

Kinley frowned at the phone. Maybe she could distract him, cheer him up. "How's my favorite niece?"

"Good."

Usually when she brought up Cassie it was Brendan's cue to tell hilarious, little kid stories. Something else was bothering him. "What's going on besides Dad?"

He didn't respond.

"Tell me." She drew out the words like Mom had. She heard a deep sigh.

"I think Megan's seeing someone. Actually, I know she is."

"You're shitting me."

"No."

"God, that's rotten. Like a full-fledged affair? What makes you think that?

"Lots of things."

"Aw, Bren. Shit." Of the two of them, Brendan was the one who'd always craved a Disney family. "Take off work," she said. "Come out here. I'd love it. Bring Cassie. Get away."

"I don't know if I can do that," he said. "Besides, that would just make it easier for her to see this guy."

"If she's set on seeing him, she'll do it no matter what. Really, Brendan, come to Colorado."

"Well. Maybe." He paused. "Look, I have to go. But seriously, do be careful. Maybe you're right about him being bonkers, but the old man had me nearly convinced." He clicked off.

Dismissing her father's ridiculous paranoia was easy. Her brother's situation was another matter. She thought back to Brendan's wedding. Via a terse email, Megan had sent Kinley the obligatory invitation to be a bridesmaid. Kinley had refused. She'd flown home and then flown to Florida with Mom who hadn't warmed up to Megan much either, although she'd never come right out and admitted it. During the flurry of festivities, Megan had seemed to care more about her makeup and dress than her new family, or even her own family, Kinley thought. And she'd positively gloated over the stacks of gifts. A material girl indeed.

Kinley showered and dressed, fixed her hair and spritzed perfume. Michael had said that a bunch of the music majors were going out for cocktails after the recital. She'd smiled at his word: cocktails. She would've just said drinks. Once she was ready she went to the kitchen and opened the refrigerator, grabbing a slice of cheese and eating it at the sink. Her heart ached for her brother. He wouldn't have said anything if he hadn't been sure about Megan. She wondered what he would do.

●●●●

She and Sarah sat in a small auditorium, four rows back from the stage.

Kinley wanted Michael to see her if he looked up. The professors who'd be judging him sat two rows ahead of them, right in front of where Michael would play. Kinley figured they'd probably want to see his hands. Or maybe not. She had no idea. The faculty had their pens ready and sheets of paper resting on notebooks in their laps.

Kinley's fingers were cold and damp. She hoped Michael's weren't. She never remembered his hands being cold, even during a Boulder blizzard. That's when they'd first made love, during a freakish October snowstorm two months after he'd moved upstairs. His hands had been flames that night.

"Do you think Michael's nervous?" asked Sarah. "I figure with all the auditions this is getting pretty routine for him."

"I don't know," said Kinley. "But he's been up here for hours." Several more people had entered the auditorium. He'd said that music majors were required to attend a certain number of recitals, but she didn't think all these people were fulfilling a credit demand. She looked back at Sarah. "The recital is just a formality at this point. But Michael wouldn't want to look bad."

"Michael *couldn't* look bad," said Sarah.

He'd just come onto the stage and there was a scatter of applause. Kinley's eyes ate him up. She'd bought his black suit before all the auditions, calling it a graduation present. His white shirt sparkled, and the lavender tie held a hint of insolence. His audition uniform, he called it, shrugging when she'd complimented him.

"Hot," Sarah breathed. "You can't tell me looking good didn't have something to do with all those colleges saying yes."

Michael grinned, his hands limp at his side. Did they shake in anticipation of their work? She couldn't imagine learning all those pieces. It has to be the whole package, he'd said to her. The performance, the look, and the skills. She smiled back at him and touched her lips. For one unfortunate moment she remembered her mother watching Brendan and her at their sports and activities and saw the similarity. She erased the thought and smiled.

He'd told her he would start with the Mendelssohn. He could play it in his sleep. Did he play in his sleep, Kinley wondered. And he'd bury the damned Bach in the middle, he'd said. The music started. She didn't know enough to judge his technique, and she figured that wrong notes hadn't been an issue for Michael since he was in middle school. He always told her to let the music take her, like a lover, he'd said. And she did, imagining pictures and stories to ride the sounds. He owned the piano, driving it like a long-distance trucker might manage a semi. But with grace and nuance.

Michael was several selections into his program and had managed the Bach before Kinley noticed the professors scribbling on their papers. She wished she could read what they were saying. It had to be good. Sarah had at least taken piano lessons, although she said she'd spent more time cursing her metronome than playing. During the Copland piece she'd squeezed Kinley's arm and nodded. Their boy was doing well.

And then it was over. Michael stood, smiling at the clapping audience, winking at Sarah and Kinley. The judges tapped their papers together and stood, but Michael didn't move from the gleaming grand piano. "With your permission," he said, nodding at his judges, "I'd like to play one more song that's not on my list." The professors hovered and sat back down. "This is for my lady," he said.

Sarah's was grinning wide at Kinley's hot face. "I don't think this is quite the done thing," she whispered. "But it's cool."

Kinley had no idea of what to expect. The audience didn't either. Michael waited a few seconds for everyone to settle down and then started with a familiar bass pattern. It was "My Girl" with flourishes and classical touches that the Temptations never dreamed of, but the driving rhythm they'd created. Cheesy, corny, wonderful. A collective laugh and enthusiastic applause rose from the audience, and Michael smiled as he played. The professors smiled too, and Kinley was glad they were good sports. Sarah pressed a tissue into her hand. "Here. You're crying."

Michael finished, stood, and blew a kiss to Kinley. There was thunderous applause and a couple of "bravos" shouted from the back of the hall. Then a ragged clutch of admirers rushed the stage, hugging Michael and giving him flowers. She should've brought him flowers. She hadn't known. Sarah said, "Do you want to brave the masses?"

Kinley shook her head. "We'll wait."

In a matter of minutes most of them had left, some shouting that they'd see him at the bar. Sarah said, "I'll catch a ride." And Kinley was alone with Michael. The auditorium seemed more than silent.

"Mr. Belli," she said, "that was fine music."

He spread his arms and she went to them like a bird to a nest. "Cute," she whispered against his dark curls. "Sweet." A thrum still ran through his body like an unreleased sustain pedal. He'd taught her what that was.

Holding her out from him enough to see her face, he asked, "Did you like it?" His eyes were wide, hopeful.

"Of course I liked it," Kinley said and kissed him.

"I do love you," he said against her mouth.

"I love you too." Every time she said it, the words came more easily. God knows they were true.

He worked at the knot of his tie and unfastened the top button of his shirt. "Shall we go? I'm ready for a drink."

●●●●

Kinley sat alone at a table close to the bar, nursing her second glass of wine. A few tables away, Michael was verbally replaying the recital to a bunch of his buddies, pausing now and then to swig at his beer. He looked deliciously disreputable in shirtsleeves and loosened tie. Sarah was flirting with the baritone Michael sometimes accompanied. It looked as though she was having some success with the guy, and Kinley was glad. Sarah hadn't had a boyfriend in months.

I'm an observer, Kinley thought, but she didn't mind the exclusion. There was still enough daylight to pick out the rich colors of the liquor bottles behind the bar, the bright coral of Sarah's blouse, the contrast between Michael's snowy shirt and his tanned neck. Her father could do something with all this, she thought, although she'd never known him to paint crowds of people. He never saw crowds of people.

Holding a drink, Sarah flopped down in a chair by Kinley. "Are you sulking?"

Kinley smiled. "Not at all. Are you flirting?"

"You better believe it. We're going out tomorrow night." Her round cheeks glowed.

"Did he leave?"

"No. Just went to the bathroom. I thought you looked lonely."

"I'm not."

Sarah frowned. "He's definitely not your father, you know. Michael is all about his music, but there's room for you. He proved it."

Kinley saw Michael glance her way. He'd done it several times, always with an apologetic grin. "I think you're right."

"Look, I can manage the apartments, at least for a while especially if I get the job in Broomfield. I'm figuring you'd give me free rent." She lifted an eyebrow at this. "And that would be worth the gas money. Go with him, Kinley. Give it a chance." Sarah touched her arm.

She might. She just might.

"Colorado will still be here if it doesn't work out. Go when he does."

Kinley shook her head. "I'm not going to Michigan with him. Three tenants are leaving. I have apartments to clean and paint."

Sarah waved this off, and the light made prisms from her earrings. "I don't mean Michigan. Ugh," she said, "I wouldn't want to meet the Belli Mafia as possible wife material either."

"Is that what I am? I don't think so."

Sarah eyed her as if she'd said something stupid.

Kinley saw the baritone approaching. "I'm thinking about it. Go get your singer."

People started leaving, going home or to dinner. Finally Michael collapsed into the chair by Kinley and threw his arm around her shoulders. He was more than a little drunk, but she'd expected that. "How's my sweetheart?" he asked.

Such an old-fashioned term. "I'm fine. And proud of you."

His grin was a little lopsided. "Good. I always want you to be proud of me."

"And I always will be." She grabbed his hand and kissed his fingers. Amazing fingers. "Do you want dinner? Are you hungry?"

He looked puzzled at first and then grinned again. "You know, I think I am." But he made no move to get up. "Say, I have a better idea."

"What?" She dug her car keys out of her purse.

His mouth settled into a curve, a closed-mouth smile like a cartoon character's. "Let's get married," he said. "Tonight. Right now."

Chapter Fifteen

BRENDAN

He felt bad about yesterday's call to Kinley. He should've asked courteous questions about Michael's recital, which she'd been talking about for weeks, and done more chitchat with his sister. But his brain was as fried as an ancient motherboard. Right after the conversation with Kinley, Dad had called and asked him to bring the paperwork and meet Leon at a nearby car dealership to trade in Mom's car and buy a different one, any late model that would hold a little cargo. Something innocuous, although Dad hadn't used that word. Brendan assumed that Dad thought the bad guys knew he drove a Subaru. No wonder Kinley was skeptical. Oh, and for safety's sake, Dad wanted Brendan to get a different car too, trade in the old Hyundai, and do it that afternoon. Brendan had begged off work, claiming illness. Beverly had scowled.

The least of his worries, he thought as he tied his running shoes. This morning was his race. With all the issues concerning Dad and Megan, he'd thought about blowing it off but decided to go ahead and run. After he finished, he'd come home and sit Megan down for a Come to Jesus while Cassie was napping. She'd been out late another two nights, no excuses, no apologies. This had to stop. Last night he figured she'd be pleased that he was driving a pretty nice late model Civic, purchased by his father, but she'd given him one of her stingy shrugs and walked away.

She and Cassie were still asleep. He filled a water bottle and made sure to lock the door when he left. Maybe Kinley was right to scoff at Dad's warnings, but he wasn't going to be careless, not with his wife and daughter. As he backed out of the driveway, he glanced at the closed blinds at their bedroom window. He'd been sleeping in the guest room for a while now, sort of married, sort of not. It would've been nice if Megan had gotten out of bed to wish him luck or even promised to greet him at the finish line. She'd known about the race for weeks. But these days he and Megan were about as chatty as cloistered monks. About as sexy too. He drove to campus thinking about seventeen things at once, none of which had an easy solution. And he still felt guilty about not mentioning Michael's recital.

Thank God everything about the race was straightforward. He parked, found the starting point, received his number and instructions, and stretched. The day was dry and a little chilly, which suited him. He recognized some of the other runners, faculty, staff, a few students. Brendan figured sweating with his fellow university employees might be considered 'collegial,' a plus on his yearly evaluation, although Beverly would blast him anyway. Megan would probably like it if he got fired and was forced to find a more lucrative job.

As the runners gathered to start, a few weak cheers rose from family and friends lining the route. One woman held a little boy about Cassie's age and forced the kid's arm up and down to wave at his daddy. Brendan's jaw tightened, and he had to do some good head-talking to get it loose again. Surely Megan's straying had been plotted to get a reaction out of him. Surely they could find a way to settle things, for Cassie's sake if nothing else. He took a deep breath and anticipated the start. The bystanders cheered again as the runners took off. Setting a medium pace, he concentrated on moving smoothly. Unlike most things he'd done in life, he wasn't in this to win. Not that he had a prayer of doing so. Ahead of him, he watched a woman's ponytail swish back and forth against her spine. They were doing nearly the same pace, well behind at least a dozen other runners.

He fought for air and slowed up. Ponytail pulled farther ahead of him, but then he got his wind back and stayed a few feet behind her for probably half a mile. His goal was to finish, he kept reminding himself. Even if he had to crawl in. But although he slowed as he went, he was still running or at least jogging at the three-quarter mark. He tried to keep his mind on the rhythm of his feet and the steadiness of his breathing, but he had the craziest vision of someone darting out from the sidelines and burying a knife in his chest. He shook it off. God, what had Dad done all those years ago? He wished Zack would call. At least that would be a little information.

His thighs were burning, and even though he could see the end up ahead, he had to slow even more. Disappointing, but he'd finish. Many were already done, wiping their faces and drinking. He'd forgotten a towel. Sweat rolled down his neck and cheeks. It didn't matter. He wasn't sure what mattered at this point. He crossed the line and rested his hands against his knees. Not bad for a beginner he thought. Someone pressed a cup of water into his hand, and someone else threw a towel over his shoulder. "Looks like you could use this," she said.

It was Hannah, her thick bangs nearly meeting her eyelashes. No makeup today. No cleavage either. Brendan wiped off. "Thanks. I forgot a towel," he said through broken breaths.

She smiled. "I stole one from a stack over there." She pointed. "I don't keep towels in my book bag."

He grinned, still trying to catch his breath.

"You did okay," she said.

"Not bad. For my first try." He supposed she'd come to cover the race for the paper. "You doing an article on this?"

She shook her head. "The newspaper received a list of participants, and I saw your name. I thought I'd come cheer you on. Did you hear me?"

"No." She walked with him toward where he'd parked, about a thousand miles from the finish line.

"That sucks. I hoped it would encourage you."

"I was too busy wondering if I was going to make it."

She smiled. "I knew you would. Nice legs, by the way."

They weren't. They were as white and skinny as pieces of chalk, and he felt clammy wearing the sweaty towel over his soaked shirt. He probably smelled bad. "Right."

She giggled and stopped walking. "I need to go. Got one last paper to write."

"Need to do research?"

She grinned. "I've already done it."

"Too bad. I'd be happy to help." He meant it. "Well, thanks for coming." It really had been sweet.

Her reply was a quick wave, and she crossed the street. He watched her for a minute and then kept walking until he reached his new car. Okay, he was happy to have it, and he didn't feel the pull of guilt so much since Dad had insisted. Pulling exercise pants on over his shorts, he thought that maybe this wasn't just a conquest for Hannah. He wasn't sure how he felt about her, but it certainly wasn't bad.

He started to call Megan to see if she needed him to pick anything up, but she hadn't been answering his calls recently. Besides, he didn't feel like traipsing through a grocery in his sweaty running clothes. While it was going on, the race had invigorated him, but now his limbs felt like noodles. He thought again about Hannah and how nice it'd been to see a friendly face at the end of the race. He liked the kinder, gentler Hannah a lot more than the sexy one. God, he might just be turning into an old man at twenty-eight.

He pulled into his driveway. Megan's Lexus wasn't there, but that wasn't surprising. She was probably out shopping or at the gym. Meeting up with the fabulous Scott Klein would be difficult with Cassie in tow.

Brendan glanced in the rear view mirror and saw the grimace on his face. Today. He and Megan were sorting everything out today.

The house was more of a wreck than usual. Dirty dishes filled the sink, and the laundry basket perched on the kitchen table. All he saw inside were his wrinkled undershirts and unmatched socks. He'd deal with it later. Craving a shower, he undressed as he went down the hall, noticing that Cassie's stroller, usually parked by the door of her room, was gone. Maybe they were at the mall.

Since he'd moved to the guestroom, he'd shifted most of his things to a drying rack in the basement, but he wanted a pair of sweat shorts from the chest of drawers in the master bedroom. He noticed that Megan hadn't made the bed, nothing unusual about that, but when he looked at the open closet, he came to a dead stop. It was empty. A couple of hangers lay on the floor; otherwise the closet was bare. Even the shelf was wiped clean. He stared at the space and then rushed to Cassie's room to open drawers and check her closet. Empty. Her baby bed, usually crowded with stuffed animals and a couple of special blankets, was cleared out. In the bathroom he could see no evidence of Megan. Her makeup, hair dryer, perfumes: all gone. He sat on the edge of the unmade bed and tried to think. He could go to the basement to see if the suitcases were missing, but he knew they would be. It amazed him that she could get everything packed up so quickly, but then he remembered the evening before when she'd holed up downstairs doing laundry and talking on her phone. He'd played with Cassie, given her a bath. Megan was probably packing even then.

For a horrific minute he wondered if they'd been kidnapped. Dad's paranoia flooded over him in sickly waves. He shook his head, looking at the shoes he'd kicked off. Kidnappers wouldn't have allowed her to pack her entire wardrobe. Hell, they wouldn't have let her take anything. She'd deserted him. Pure and simple. He wondered if she'd left a note. Would she? His eyes jittered around the room. Nothing there. He could try calling her, but she probably wouldn't pick up. Did she have money? This thought withered before it became a worry. Of course she did. She wouldn't have left if she hadn't. A better question was whether she was with Scott Klein, but Brendan felt sure he knew the answer to that one too.

KEITH

"I know you don't like me asking questions," Leon said. "But I can't help it. Who are we fighting here? Are we in the right? I don't care, but it might help me to know who the enemy is."

Keith thought that Leon must be plenty worried to voice his concerns. Thirty years ago he'd asked Leon Perry to work for him, making it a condition of employment that the big man never asked questions. He hadn't. Keith wondered if it was time to give him a little something, other than money, for the years of devotion. "What caused this happened years ago," he said. "Before I knew you. Before I married Brenda. I thought it was over, but I was in the habit of being careful so I kept it up. Now it's a problem again."

Leon was leaning against the kitchen counter. His face was blank.

Keith ran his tongue over his teeth, searching for the right words. "The bad guys are bad. Truly bad. And I challenged them, made them unhappy. There were serious repercussions, but the law's not after me." It sounded like a B grade gangster movie from the fifties, but Keith didn't feel he should say any more.

Leon nodded. "Okay. That's something."

Keith stood. "We're going to get out all the firearms in the house and place them strategically. They should be loaded."

Leon nodded again.

"Then we're going to frame and crate up the painting I did at the cabin, along with the ones I've been saving back, and we're going to ship them all to Devonie."

Another nod.

"And then you're going home, Leon. You're going to stay with your family and be safe."

Leon shook his head. "I can't do that. Someone's got to be here with you."

"No. I'll be leaving anyway before long."

Leon rolled his eyes. "We'll see," he said and left the room.

They put the shotgun in the bedroom. One pistol stayed in the studio; another was hidden in a kitchen drawer, under the dishtowels. Since they'd be in the basement working on the paintings, Leon suggested that the rifle might live down there until they finished. They double-checked the security system and closed what shades and blinds Leon had opened while Keith had been at the cabin. "It looks like we're preparing for a siege," Leon commented.

"We are," said Keith.

Leon said that he was ready for lunch even if Keith wasn't and made turkey and bacon sandwiches with lettuce and tomato. Keith hadn't intended to eat, but he did and felt better for it. "You had to have been a kid when you did whatever it was," said Leon.

"I was. Young and stupid." Keith looked at the crumbs on his plate. "Except..." He stopped.

Leon's dark eyes were shrewd. "Except you never could've had the freedom to paint if you hadn't done it. It isn't tough to figure out, man. My guess is that you took something that didn't belong to you."

Keith neither confirmed nor denied it.

"But if that's true, somebody sure has a long memory."

1974

He'd already made arrangements to sell his car to a guy from his damned English class. That and the $148 he'd managed to save were all he'd have to see him through in Chicago. Minus the bus ticket. His parents always went to bed not long after supper, living by Franklin's motto of early to bed, early to rise, and all that crap his father was fond of quoting. So, it was easy to pack up what few things he'd take with him without them suspecting anything. He stuffed clothes and his sketchpad into his gym bag, wrapping the few brushes he'd been able to buy in toilet paper and cushioning them with his underwear. He threw in a cheese sandwich he'd made on the sly. He figured Mom and Dad would receive the letter from Ball State tomorrow, and he didn't see any need to be here for that aggravation, especially since he was planning on leaving anyway.

Fully dressed, he lay down on his narrow bed and listened to the trucks going down the highway by their farm. He'd thought about hitching a ride; it would be cheaper, but the idea scared him a little. And he could imagine it taking long enough to get a ride that one of his dad's agricultural buddies might pull up and say, "Son, your daddy wouldn't like you being out here like this."

As long as he could remember, the walls in his bedroom had been papered in blue and beige stripes, fading over the years until there was hardly a pattern. He'd shared this room with Darryl until his brother had escaped. He hadn't ended up in Nam; he'd seen California and Alaska, enough variety that he probably wouldn't ever come back to the farm. As the younger brother, Tom would always get the shorter straw, but he had no intention of being his father's fallback plan. He'd write them eventually from Chicago so his mother wouldn't worry, but they'd probably guess where he was going so he wanted a healthy head start on any kind of search they might make. After they received the letter, he doubted that they'd bother.

When the glowing green hands of his clock showed that it was three-thirty, he crept downstairs and got into his car without closing the door or turning on the headlights until he'd pulled out on the road. Then he'd floored the old jalopy and sailed into Muncie. The guy who was buying the car lived near the university in an apartment with about a half dozen alternating roommates. Somebody would be up to let him in.

Once the Greyhound pulled away and headed toward Chicago, Tom began to relax. Daylight made the sky rosy, and it looked like it would be a pretty spring day. Excitement accelerated his pulse. He'd never been to a city or anywhere on his own like this. In Chicago he would be an artist. It would all begin there. He would paint all the time, whenever he liked. No one would stop him.

As the bus lumbered along the highway, he studied a map of the city until he knew where to go when he arrived. He headed first for the Art Institute and received a reduced admission fee to the museum with his student identification. That made him smile. The pictures made him breathless. Somehow he would manage to get into the academy. He'd attend classes there, he'd work in their studios. Still dreaming, he spent the day gazing at the colors and brushstrokes. At closing time he had to leave, and it was then that his spirits faded. After the warm museum, the chill breezes off the lake made him shiver, and the tall buildings reduced him to a small, backward stranger. He had no idea where he'd sleep that night.

He walked until he found a dingy restaurant and ordered the cheapest thing on the stained menu. He started to ask the waitress if she knew of a place he could stay, but he was too shy. He trudged along for miles, cold concrete seeping into his shoes. Unaware that he'd walked in circles, he found himself near the museum again, coming at it from a different direction. There was a hotel nearby. He'd never stayed in one and suspected that most were nicer, but he could afford this one, for one night anyway. The radiator hissed and the sheets had holes. Maybe tomorrow he'd find a job or a rooming house. His aunt in Muncie took in student boarders. He'd look for something like that.

By the third day he'd become bolder, but it hadn't done anything but make him more frustrated. The mangy hotel was eating up his money, and the place gave him the creeps. Old men lived there, coughing and mumbling, and he sometimes saw women that he suspected were prostitutes. He'd never seen one to know. That evening he gobbled the cheap hamburger that was the first food he'd eaten since the night before, and in desperation entered a bar not far from the museum. It was warm and smelled of beer. He liked the posters on the walls, old psychedelic ones advertising hippie bands and newer ones with geometric patterns. He also liked all the young faces he saw. He began to suspect that art students hung out there. Maybe he could buy one beer, even if he wasn't old enough, and he could talk to them.

Sitting at a table near the loudest and most exuberant group, he ordered a Budweiser and was served. He remembered his father purchasing one whole six-pack when Darryl was home on leave. His father had told him that he wasn't to drink any of it, that "they obeyed the law in this house." Darryl had smuggled one up to their room and given it to him.

A tall blond fellow with hair stringing to his shoulders said, "So what media can encompass more than one sense? Other than movies of course."

A bored brunette wearing a knit hat and a load of eyeliner gave him a dry look. "Provided we agree that movie-making is an art."

There was a roar of disagreement. He sipped his beer and felt good for the first time in days.

"Can music create pictures?" This came from a pudgy guy, older than the rest and the only one drinking something other than beer.

"In the imagination." Two or three chimed in on this.

"But they can all merge in the imagination," the tall guy said. "That's not my question. Can an author write visual art? Can a musician make a picture?"

A slightly built fellow with a bright smile and an abundance of dark hair turned to include him. "Don't remember seeing you," he said. "I'm Nick Collins."

He nodded. "Tom Vickers," he said, but he didn't know whether to extend a hand or not. It seemed so lame, so after-church. "I'm new. Just got to town."

"At the Institute?" Nick asked.

"I hope to be."

Nick turned back to the discussion. "Man," he said. "I can paint music. I know I can." He was nodding, eager, the kid trying to be teacher's pet.

The brunette acted as though Nick wasn't worthy of the air it took to correct him. "You can't paint a can of crap, Collins." She murmured it, but everybody heard.

He saw Nick's face redden, but the guy kept smiling. "Fuck you, Claudine," he said with no rancor whatsoever. "Time will tell."

Tom was a long way from Indiana. The group kept fussing, declaiming, and insulting each other. They tolerated Nick, made a pet of him, he realized, despite the insults, so he was surprised when the guy said, "Let's clear this joint. You want to see my studio? I just got it last week."

Tom nodded, stood, and fished for his wallet. Nick shook his head. "I got it."

Although he would've liked staying in the warm bar listening to the art students, he thought he might've found a friend. It had been easy enough. Nick talked non-stop, describing all the characters from the bar, what media they used, and who was sleeping with whom. It went on for several long blocks until Nick stopped at a black-painted door, unlocked it, and led him up three flights of poorly lit wooden stairs. "It's all mine," he said. "Most of them have to work at the Institute or maybe share with a bunch of other people. But this is mine." He unlocked another door and turned on what looked like a hundred blazing lights.

It was a dream. The studio consisted of the entire top floor of the building with tall windows lining three walls. Two easels stood on a paint-scarred wooden floor. There were shelves and pegs and tables as well as an upholstered chair, not new but decent, at the other end. Tom peeked behind a screen and saw a small refrigerator, sink, and two-burner hot plate. "What do you think?" asked Nick.

He was able to choke out, "Fantastic." A person could create masterpieces here. But he saw no works in progress, just a row of clean stretched canvases against one wall. "What do you work in?" he asked, pretty sure this was the way it was asked.

Nick was prowling the gigantic room. He didn't stand still much. "I like oils, but I suck at those. I'm trying to get into watercolors."

Tom had sneaked into a studio at Ball State as often as he could and played with watercolors a few times. He thought they were insipid, but he nodded. "Man, would I love to have something like this."

Nick was bouncing on his toes. "I know. I'll be able to do good stuff here. I'm certain." He blinked a couple of times. "Want a beer? A joint? Got both."

He'd never smoked grass, although he'd been around it once or twice in Muncie. "A beer, I guess."

Nick rushed to the refrigerator and pulled out a couple. "So where are you staying? You got someplace to work? What medium do you like?"

Tom said that he hadn't found a place yet and that he wanted to paint with oils. Nick's eyes were jumping around the room so much that Tom wasn't sure the guy had heard him. "Oils are what the big boys use," Nick said, downing about half his beer. "When I try to paint with them I end up with a fucking mess." He laughed. "You know, kinda like somebody blew up an omelet."

Tom laughed. Nick grinned back at him and sort of twitched all over. "You know, if you want to crash here for a while, you can." He jerked a shoulder toward the far end of the studio. "There's a fold-up cot back in the closet. Even got sheets and a pillow." Nick winked. "In case I ever get a chick up here, you know what I mean?"

He nodded.

Scratching at his cheek, Nick looked at the massive windows. "Hell, you can work here too, if you want to. Might have to charge you some rent eventually. I work for my dad sometimes so I get a little dough from time to time, but. . ." His voice dropped off. "I'm not here much. I gotta be gone when I'm handling Dad's business and then there are classes."

Tom didn't know what to say. It was too good to be true.

"I got an apartment I share with my older brother," Nick went on. "So I don't sleep here. Usually. Except when he's being a tightass and objects to me bringing home women." He upended his beer. "But then he's gone a lot of the time too. Brothers. You got one?"

Tom nodded. "He's in the Navy."

"Cool." Nick crushed his can. "So what do you say? You seem like a good dude. Tell you what, you keep the studio nice and clean in exchange for rent, throw me a few bucks now and then, and it'll be a good deal for both of us." He frowned for a second. "You won't be dealing drugs from out of here or nothing, will you?"

He shook his head hard. "I'm not interested in drugs at all."

Nick raised his eyebrows. "Oh, everybody's interested in drugs, but we don't want that going on here. Just pure art, right?"

A week later, it was as though there'd never been a problem. No, he wasn't enrolled at the Academy, but he had a safe place to stay and a job bussing tables and doing dishes at an Italian restaurant three blocks away. And he could paint almost all he wanted to. He rarely saw Nick. Tom wondered if he painted at all. When he did see him it was at the Two Keys, the bar where they'd met. He went there on his nights off and managed to learn the names of most of the art students who drank there. They said little to him but accepted him as Nick's friend. The group didn't respect Nick much, but he was so easy with his smiles and money that they found it hard to dislike him.

A couple of weeks into June, Tom was painting when he heard Nick unlock the studio door. He skittered into the room, looking more serious than Tom had ever seen him. "Man, you got to help me," he said.

Tom put down his brush.

"My dad's coming up here this afternoon. Says he wants to see what he's paying for." Nick chewed at his lip. "He doesn't think art is worth doing. Not for his son anyway." He looked around the vast studio. "I don't have a thing to show him."

"Have you got anything over at school you could bring here?"

Nick shook his head. "If you want to know the truth, I haven't been going to classes much here recently." He brightened. "But I'm going to do better next fall if they let me come back."

Tom felt a thud in his stomach. His perfect nest was going to be ruined. "What can I do?"

"For one thing you can lie and say you're paying me rent to work here, if he asks. Dad's not real big on freebies, you know?"

Tom nodded.

"And I was thinking maybe you could start a painting and say it's mine." Nick looked miserable. "I know. It's cheating. You don't have to finish it or anything. Just make it look like I've been doing something." He glanced around at Tom's canvases leaning against the walls. "Some of those could be mine, you know."

"Not with my name on them." He resented the suggestion.

"Okay, but could you start one? You know, without a signature. Something kinda dopey and conservative." Tom's paintings were mostly abstract.

"Okay," he said slowly.

Nick brightened. "Cool. You're a pal. He's gonna be here in a couple of hours. But you can slap some paint on a canvas by then, can't you?" He rushed over to get one and set it on the other easel. "We can fake him out, right?"

Tom's answer was to pick up a clean brush. Nick was staring out the bank of windows at a dramatic sky—heavy, purple thunderheads rolling in from the lake with sunshine still bathing the city. Odd shadows. Vibrant colors. "Look," said Nick. "It would be fine to capture that, wouldn't it?"

He had an eye, no doubt about it. "Why don't you try for it?" Tom asked.

Nick scrunched his nose, shrugged. "Gotta run some errands for my dad before he gets here." He shuffled toward the door. "Just the start of one, right? Thanks, man."

Two hours later, Tom had more than a beginning of a still life. It wasn't bad, just ordinary. He'd cleaned the brushes he'd used for it and gone back to his own work. He'd cheated before, got caught at it actually, but he'd never cheated art. "A man should have a code of ethics," his father had said with annoying regularity. Tom guessed his own code had to do with art, and he'd broken it. But if this was a means to a greater end, he didn't regret it.

Mr. Collins was no taller than his son who trotted along behind him like a terrier. The man looked like a businessman in a dark blue blazer and an unfashionably narrow tie. He didn't smile all the time like Nick. Lowering his brush, Tom nodded at him and said, "Tom Vickers, sir." Collins hardly acknowledged him.

"Tom does abstracts, as you can see, Dad. I know you don't like that style much, but he's really good. I'm trying to get him to show a couple at Art in the Park next month." Nick chattered on and on, showing his father the studio's amenities.

Tom said nothing. Mr. Collins wore shiny cordovan shoes, a little flashy with his conservative clothes. They clicked against the floor and stopped at Tom's easel. "What's this supposed to be?" he asked, frowning.

"A window inside a window inside a window," Tom said. The lines were precise with flat light deep inside. He was playing with dimensions.

Mr. Collins twitched his nose like he was allergic to pigments. "And this is yours, Nicky?" He turned to the other canvas. Tom had thrown together a pottery bowl, a couple of bananas, and an apple that was more withered than he'd painted it. The colors were dark, what there was of them. He'd done little but sketch out the fruit. "This would look good in our dining room," Collins said. "If you finish it." He gave Tom a brief nod and turned like a soldier on parade. He was ready to leave.

"Oh, I will." Nick looked like he was promising his soul to God. "And I'll have more soon. Just been sort of blocked here recently."

Tom knew he'd have to finish the still life. Free rent, he thought, time to paint.

It didn't end there, though. A few months later, Nick hatched the idea of opening up their studio for a gallery party. They'd exhibit, he said, and maybe ask one or two other art students to bring their work. Tom wondered what Nick would contribute. He had the completed still life Tom had painted for him, signed by Nick, and a couple of charcoal drawings. He was good at those; they'd probably gotten him into the Institute. Sure enough, Tom was in charge of cleaning the studio, hanging the work, and painting a couple of "little things" for Nick. He did them.

Tom hoped Nick would invite faculty from the Institute. Personal interest was probably his only hope now of getting in. He didn't. Dozens of artistic friends, cases of wine, and pounds of fancy cheese and crackers were what Nick provided for what ended up as a party. Nick's brother Joe came but not the old man. Tom didn't know whether he'd been invited or not. Joe was a heavier, older, and less flighty version of Nick.

"I like this," Joe said, pointing to Tom's window painting. "But there's no price on it."

Tom shrugged. "This isn't really a gallery."

"Might as well be." Joe scrutinized the canvas. Nick had mentioned that his brother liked art but was a "bean counter," who managed the financial end of their father's vast real estate holdings. "How much? I'd like to buy it."

Tom had no idea. He was pleased enough that someone liked his work. "Maybe fifty?" he said.

Joe looked down his thin Collins nose. "You need to learn the marketing end of this business, and it is a business. You should know that."

Tom gave him an affirmative twitch. He supposed so, but that end of art seemed mundane, almost obscene.

"I'll buy it for two hundred," Joe said. "And consider it an investment. You have the magic, you know."

Tom could only nod.

"And even if nobody else is, I'm aware that you painted those two over there with my brother's name on them." He smiled to take the sting out. "I love him, but he could never paint that well."

Joe pulled out a slim wallet and fished two hundreds out of it. "I'll pick this one up next week. Wouldn't want to leave a blank space here."

Joe left, and Tom stashed the money in his back pocket. That was enough cash to last him months.

●●●●

From the basement, Keith heard Leon running the saw and then hammering. How long had he been sitting there staring at the crumbs on his plate? He rarely thought of himself as Tom any more. Tom had died in 1976, when he'd become Keith. He wasn't sure they were the same man. He rose with a grunt and took his plate to the sink. He doubted that Nick was the same as he'd been back then either.

Clenching and unclenching his hands, Keith looked at his phone and thought about calling Dana. God, he still couldn't believe she'd married Nick, but because she had, she'd sure as hell have the answers he wanted.

Chapter Sixteen

KINLEY

She grinned at him. "Let's get you something to eat." She found his suit jacket and handed it to him. She'd already paid their bar bill.

"I mean it," Michael said. His face was flushed, his curls tangled. Incredibly appealing. "I want to marry you. You're beautiful, wonderful, exciting. . . ."

"And you're drunk."

He was walking pretty well, although listing a little toward the right. She maneuvered him outside, and he breathed in a great gulp of Colorado air. "Life is very good," he said. The words weren't quite precise.

"Yes."

"It went well, don't you think?" He'd already asked her this three times.

"Phenomenal. Wonderful. Aren't you happy with your performance?"

He nodded and looked remarkably like a little boy who'd tied his shoes for the first time. "Wish my parents had been able to come."

"Me too. They'd be so proud."

"Did you like your song?"

She squeezed his arm. "Of course I did. I loved it."

They walked a block and a half to the French bistro both of them liked. Kinley gave the waiter a firm negative when he offered wine or drinks and kept pushing the breadbasket toward Michael. "There's grass in the butter," he complained.

"Parsley, I think. That's new." She broke a roll. "Of course we haven't been here in a while."

Michael had kept a perpetual grin on his face for the last couple of hours, but it disappeared. "My last time," he said, suddenly bereft. "I'll never come here again."

"You can if you want to," she said and buttered her bread. "You can stay here this summer or fly back any time you want." She wanted to say that he never had to leave, but she'd accepted that this wasn't true. He did have to leave. He had to ride his talent as far as it would take him.

"I can't do that." He would've said more, but the waiter returned to take their order. Michael was sobering up by the minute. He sipped his water. "I need my summer job, and even with that and what the conservatory is offering me, I'll still be broke."

He'd climb up on his pride if she said that she'd pay for his ticket, Kinley thought. She admired it, she supposed. "A starving artist," she murmured and covered his hand with hers. It was warm. How was she ever going to let him go?

"I meant it, you know."

"Meant what?" She took her hand away.

"I want to marry you. Now, if you want. Later if it suits you better."

Kinley looked away at the plants by the front door. "Mama Belli wouldn't want to miss her boy's wedding. That would break her heart."

"I'm serious, Kinley." His eyes certainly were. And they looked very, very focused. "The only reason I haven't asked you before was that I was afraid you'd say no." He shook his head a half inch. "It's no kind of life to expect you to live, me busy all the time at the conservatory, no money." He chewed at his lip. "You've never said that you'd come with me. But maybe you were waiting on me to propose."

She'd invested so much of herself in her houses, her tenants, Boulder. "It's complicated," she said. And then there was her fear, dissipating now but still hanging like a poisonous fog in her mind. She feared she'd disappear behind his art.

The waiter arrived with their salads, and she hoped Michael would switch the subject.

He ignored the salad. "It wouldn't have to be. Hire a manager. Or sell the houses. You could move with them still up for sale if you had a manager here."

Before thinking she said, "Sarah has offered to do it."

His face broke into a huge smile. "See? Easy. Just pack your clothes, and we'll live on love."

She lifted her fork but didn't touch the salad. "I won't spend the summer with you in Michigan. That would be a disaster whether we were married or not." She nearly choked on the words. Had her father promised Mom a lifetime of romance and love when they married? What he'd given her were the chores of keeping his gate and guarding his cave.

He dug into the lettuce and radicchio. "Okay, I can see that. Living with my parents would be annoying, and I'd be up at camp most of the time.

Besides, you'd probably want to put everything in order at the apartments."

She allowed herself to envision it: the painting and repairs, the finances, the realtors, the packing. "Huge job," she said. Her salad suddenly looked as appealing as fungi.

Michael was stabbing the greens and chewing away. Happy. "We'll get married in Cincinnati," he said. "Or Michigan, I don't care. Just before classes start. Your dad and brother are already in Cincinnati." He snapped his fingers and repeated the word: "Easy."

Her response was slow enough that he looked up, met her eyes, and said, "I love you, Kinley. Now that it's about to happen, I can't stand the thought of leaving you."

But you are, she thought. Her mouth was dry. She drank some water before she said, "I love you too, Michael." She did. She could give him that much.

Their food came, and there was the fuss and bother of shifting their salad plates, answering the waiter. Michael was still staring at her when the waiter left. She started to say that the food looked good, something innocuous, but he deserved better than that. "I don't know," she said and glanced at her plate. "I'm too old for you."

His mood changed, quick as lightning. "Piss on it." He scowled and cut into his steak like it still needed butchering. "Forget it. Just forget it. You could fuck up paradise, Kinley." And she heard him mutter something about her ruining the best day of his life.

Her insides scrunched until her belly cramped. "I didn't say no."

He ignored her.

"Had you planned to ask me today?" She hadn't touched her food, but if she didn't, the waiter would be hovering again. She dipped her fork into the potatoes but didn't manage to get it to her mouth.

"I was going to do it tomorrow. Make a big dinner. Have wine. Do it up all formal." He finally looked up. His anger seared her. "Is that what you wanted? Is this not good enough? I don't have a ring either. Were you wanting a big diamond or something?" Sour words.

"Of course not."

"I figured maybe I was wrong about assuming you'd come with me. Maybe you wanted to be asked, I thought. I could understand that. You're always giving me all these lame excuses. I couldn't figure it out. And then I thought maybe you weren't sure because I hadn't said anything about marriage. Maybe you wanted more of a commitment." He speared a bit of meat. "I didn't want to propose without an income or prospects or anything, but I thought, what the hell. That's old-fashioned and stupid." He was muttering again. "I'm the one who's stupid."

"No, Michael. You're not stupid." She wanted to touch him. "Let me think. I wasn't expecting this."

He was still truculent. "Yeah. You think real hard." But she glimpsed a tiny lightening in his expression. "And you'd better think quick," he said. "I'm leaving on Wednesday."

●●●●

She'd barely put the key in the door when he started unbuttoning her blouse. In minutes they were making love, although it was more like grappling than coupling. Michael's anger had ignited a fire in him that she would've enjoyed if she hadn't known the reason for it. When they finished, he slept. His ability to fall instantly asleep, after sex or not, amazed Kinley. She envied it. She stared at the window's vague patch of light and knew relaxing was impossible.

She wandered to the kitchen and made a cup of herbal tea, carrying it to the dining room. Maybe she'd work a while. It was mindless and might soothe her, although she didn't think anything could lull her brain into ignoring a marriage proposal. She turned on the bright lamps. Her sketchbook was open to the drawings she'd done the last week: leaves and pumpkins for the fall pieces, holly and snowmen for Christmas. Cute. Deadly cute. About as profound as emojis. For years, she'd sketched nothing but little figures for her glass pieces, even when Brendan, and Michael, had scolded and cajoled her about doing more than pitchers and plates.

She flipped to a clean page and picked up her pencil. Without thinking, she started sketching the bar where they'd had drinks. She drew Sarah leaning over to pick up a glass from a table, her hair falling forward into deep curve. Michael's head tilted to one side, giving him a crooked smile. She liked outlining his jaw. Her pencil flew over the page as she recalled the scene. It wasn't perfect but evoked the shapes better than she could've hoped. When Dad used to try to teach her how to draw and paint, he'd said that an artist had a camera in his brain. Working from life was always better, he'd said, but it wasn't entirely necessary.

If you're truly an artist, Kinley thought. Dad never said that, but it was certainly implied. Her tea was cold. She pushed it away. She'd never been very good at drawing people. Not like Dad. But these figures didn't try to be realistic. In her head they were mobile shapes with elongated appendages and unfinished faces. Sketching in the baritone's curved back as he'd leaned toward Sarah, she caught a forgotten wave of euphoria rolling through her brain.

She should be sleeping. Really, she should be thinking about Michael and their future. With her pencil, she revisited his figure, sketching in details she'd left out, giving him more life. Perspective, she thought. Light. And she started shading the other characters, the empty chairs, the geometric panels of lowering sunlight on the floor.

She took a deep breath, and lifting her pencil, waited for the old frustration to set in. She wasn't any good. She had no talent. But it didn't come. Her only complaint was that the scene needed color. She wanted to catch the sepia tones of the room and the lavender of Michael's loosened tie. Slamming her pencil down, she stared at the doorway into the kitchen. She hadn't felt the slightest inclination to paint in nearly ten years. Why now?

She knew why. Among other things, she wanted to capture Michael, to keep him. Maybe this was why Dad had painted Mom so many times. Kinley's mouth twisted at this. But there was more to it than that, she thought. Lifting the sketchbook, she gazed at what she'd drawn. It was good. Even Dad would think it was good, although it was nothing like his style. It was hers.

Taking her tea into the kitchen, she reheated it in the microwave. The clock said two-thirty. Again, she tried to convince herself to go to bed. Instead, she sat at the kitchen table and cradled the mug, warming her hands against it. Maybe Michael's proposal had amounted to some bizarre kind of shock treatment, something that had jolted her brain into sync. It felt superstitious to think like that.

Tomorrow she'd buy pigments and brushes and canvases. Ten years ago she'd thrown away all her art supplies. Now she wanted them, at least to paint this sketch. It might be the only painting she'd ever do, she thought. She shook her head. It sounded like she was warding off a jinx. No, she had her art now. It wasn't going away.

When she heard Michael get up the next morning, she gave him a few minutes and then shuffled into the kitchen, draggle-tailed, her mother would've said. Michael glanced at her and then back at the bacon he was frying. "Did you stay up all night?" he asked.

"Most of it," she said, pouring coffee and sitting in the same spot where a few hours ago she'd listened to the refrigerator hum and thought about moving to Cincinnati. When she'd finally felt sleepy, she'd huddled on the sofa, spreading an old blanket over her legs. Even then she was too wound up to doze. "Hungover?"

He shook his head.

"That's good." The scent of bacon was making her hungry, giving her a kind of energy she didn't deserve on so little sleep. "What are we doing today?"

He shrugged, nothing more than a twitch of his tee shirt. She couldn't see his face, but she imagined it as stony, probably still angry. He'd rarely been upset, at least with her, during the time they'd been together. Kinley wondered how long he could hold onto a hurt. "I want to go to the art store," she said. "Buy some canvases and supplies."

He turned at this, as surprised as she was.

"Hang on." She jumped up and brought the drawing to him.

Setting down the fork, Michael stared at the drawing but let her hold it. "Kin," he said slowly, "this is amazing. It's just like the scene last night, but. . . ." He couldn't find the words.

"But in a different tempo or key or something, right?" She grinned at him.

"Exactly." He turned off the burner, his eyes still on the sketch. "What came over you anyway?"

"You," she said. "You did it."

He set the pan back down. A smile teased at his lips, but it didn't seem like he was sure how to interpret her words. She said, "I thought about us. Most of the night actually." She grabbed one of his hands and squeezed. "And I've made up my mind. Let's get married at the end of the summer."

Chapter Seventeen

BRENDAN

He wandered through the house in a daze. In the living room he picked up Cassie's toy bunny, the current favorite of all her stuffed pals. Surely Megan knew this and wouldn't have forgotten the bunny. She couldn't have just left it. Or him. His fingers dug into the plush fur. He should shower, change clothes. He should eat.

Opening the fridge, he poured a glass of orange juice. He'd been buying it recently to ward off cramps. The juice had become another part of his routine. Megan had said once that his entire life was a series of organizational rituals. "God," she'd complained, "it's a wonder you don't arrange the pantry by the Dewey fricking Decimal System."

Maybe he was as compulsive as his father. Not a pleasant thought. He closed the refrigerator and noticed a slip of paper stuck under the koala bear magnet they'd bought Cassie at the zoo. The words were in Megan's writing, but before he could read them, he puzzled over her putting such an important note where they usually placed their grocery list. He wasn't sure what this meant, if anything. He shut his eyes for a second and then began to read.

Do NOT call me. I will NOT pick up. I'm leaving on a cruise and won't be back for 10 days. Cassie is at my mother's. I want a divorce.

Brief, to the point, typically Megan. No signature, but there was no need for one was there? His legs felt weaker than they had after the race. The house was suffocating him. He threw the note on the counter, drank the juice without tasting it, and ran a hot shower, scrubbing his body raw. A cruise. He wondered where—the Caribbean, the Mediterranean. Megan had taken all her clothes, too many for a cruise. Were the rest at her mother's? None of his questions had answers, nor were they important.

After he dressed, he didn't know what to do. For fifteen frantic minutes he made the bed, picked up toys, filled the dishwasher, and wiped off the kitchen counter, holding Megan's note with his fingertips so it wouldn't get wet. He was raising the lid on the washer when he realized the only dirty clothes were the ones he'd worn that morning. He grabbed his phone. Damn it, he would call her, whether she liked it or not.

The call went to voice mail, but he didn't know what to say. He thought about calling Megan's mother, to ask about Cassie mostly, but he didn't know when Megan had left. They might not have arrived yet. Standing at the living room window, he watched rain that had started without him realizing it. He wanted to run again, but he'd probably injure something doing it twice in a day. Besides, it was raining.

His phone rang, making him jump. Kinley. "Hey," he said, trying for normal.

"Hey yourself. How did your race go?" She sounded lively, happy.

"Pretty well. I finished it at least. How was Michael's recital?"

"Beyond fantastic. I have news. Wonderful news."

He forced out a chuckle. "That's great. Tell me."

"Two things. And somehow or the other they're related. Psychic forces or something."

"Don't tease, Kinley."

She laughed, one of her big, strong-throated ones he hadn't heard in a long time. "First of all," she said, "I'm marrying Michael late this summer and we'll be living in Cincinnati."

His initial reaction was to beg her to reconsider. Marriage was for fools. And then the larger surprise sank in. "You're coming back here?" He couldn't believe it. "Isn't Colorado absolutely the only place in the world to live?"

"Yeah, I know. We may not stay in Cincy after Michael finishes grad school. Really, I doubt that we will, but for a while I'll be able to see you, brother of mine. And my adorable niece too."

If she's here, Brendan thought. His jaw tightened. "Congratulations," he boomed, hoping the joy didn't sound fake. "I'm so happy for you." It would be good to have Kinley close.

"Thanks." It was a bright little word. "I haven't told Dad yet. Don't want to just yet, so don't let on, okay?"

Brendan said, "Hey, you've got me confused with somebody who speaks to his father on a regular basis. He's holed up right now planning his escape."

"That's why I don't want to talk to him yet," she said. "Maybe he'll settle down into what passes for normal with Dad."

"You still don't believe there's any danger?"

"No. Do you?"

Just then he figured hell was waiting right outside his front door, ready to gobble him up any minute. It might consist of Dad's bad guys or it might come in the form of Scott Klein bearing divorce papers, but it was threatening to drag him into the worst nightmare he'd ever had. "I'm not sure," he said. This was certainly not the time to tell his sister that Megan had left him. "You said there were two things. What's the other earth-shattering news?"

She giggled. "You won't believe this." He halfway expected a drum roll. "I'm painting. Again. For real. And I don't mean pissy little wineglasses and salad plates. I'm painting pictures."

"You're kidding." He'd never understood why she'd quit. Dad had been tough on her, he supposed. But no worse than a half-dozen coaches he'd had. "That's almost more wonderful than a wedding." He paused. "But still not as great as you moving back here."

"Hmm. Selfish priorities?"

If she only knew. "Maybe. But it's all super. I'm thrilled. Really." He went on making happy noises until he felt his throat dry out.

She must've heard something suspect in his enthusiasm. "What? Is something wrong?"

"No. I'm just tired from the race. I'm very happy for you. Very."

This seemed to satisfy her. She yammered on for a few minutes about Michael's recital and shopping for art supplies and deciding what she'd do about the apartments. She wasn't sure about a wedding, probably nothing big, but then there was Michael's Italian family. He listened, but when she ran out of steam he was thankful. "Give Cassie a hug for me," Kinley said.

He wished. After stowing the phone in his pocket, he wandered from room to room. Had he really been that much of a disappointment to Megan? Was he that much of a loser? Questions bombarded his brain until he wanted to punch something. He found himself sitting on the bed in their room, staring once again at the empty closet. Its contents had been important to Megan, more than Cassie's toys. Bitterness came up in his throat, and he regretted the orange juice. He deliberately shifted his eyes away from the empty space and drew in a quick breath. Since he'd come home from the race, he'd gone into the bedroom a dozen times, noting the obvious signs of his wife's departure, but he hadn't noticed another item missing. The cow picture, his father's painting, was gone.

●●●●

"I'm coming over," he said when Dad answered. The dismal day had turned to evening.

"What's wrong?"

130

Dad's question didn't surprise Brendan. He had never just stopped by to shoot the breeze with his father. His mother maybe, but never Dad. He wasn't sure who to blame for that. "Plenty. I'll tell you when I get there."

Dad was standing at the stove, pouring a jar of spaghetti sauce over frozen meatballs. His pistol rested in the middle of the kitchen table. Right by the salt and pepper shakers. "I thought you might need something to eat," he said. "Sit. Has someone tried to hurt you?"

Yeah, he thought as he sat, attempting to ignore the weapon. "I'm not sure," he said. On the trip over he'd pondered whether Megan had taken the painting. She knew his father was an artist, but Brendan had never mentioned that his father's paintings were valuable, and Megan wasn't exactly the type to read the magazines that swooned over Dad's gallery prices. Maybe Scott Klein did. Then again, Brendan hadn't slept or even entered the bedroom for weeks. The painting could've been gone a while. "Megan's left me for a lawyer who's taken her on a cruise. Says she wants a divorce." The words spewed out like vomit.

Dad winced. "Where's Cassie?"

"At her mother's house." Brendan wondered if Dad was going to give him a fat bunch of 'I told you so's.'

He didn't. "Did you know she was fooling around?"

What an innocuous euphemism. "Yeah, but just recently. This guy is one of the partners in the firm where she used to work. It could've been going on for years."

Dad stirred the sauce.

"She left while I was at the race. A note on the refrigerator. That's it."

"Get something to drink," Dad said. He ran water into another pan and set it on the stove.

Brendan wished his father drank; he could've used something stronger than the Coke he grabbed from the refrigerator. He started talking about the toy bunny, the empty closet, the note. Dad kept working at the stove and then put plates on the table. "Just a few days ago I confronted her, but we never really talked about it," Brendan said. "All she would say was that she wasn't happy."

"That kind of woman is never happy," Dad mumbled.

Brendan tapped his fingers against the icy can. He wondered where his father had come by this knowledge. Mom wasn't Megan's kind of woman at all. But he'd come to tell his father that the picture was gone, not to get his views on women. "Here's the kicker, Dad. I didn't realize it until just before I called you. She took the cow painting, the one you did for me. Or somebody did. It's gone."

His father turned slowly from the stove. "What?"

Brendan repeated what he'd said.

"Does she know its value?"

"I don't see how. I always gave her vague hints that you took an early retirement to paint." Brendan thought this might amuse his father in some dark way, but it didn't.

Dad stared at the meatballs. "Did this man ever come to your house?"

It was an embarrassing question. Humiliating, actually. "Yes."

Picking up the pasta, Dad broke some into the water. It wasn't boiling yet; it wasn't time, but Brendan didn't stop him.

"Maybe he knew," his father said. "And told her."

"Or wanted it to sell himself?"

Dad nodded.

"Or maybe this Scott Klein was hired by your enemies?" The word stuck in his throat. Kinley was right—Dad's conspiracy theory had to be nonsense. Brendan couldn't believe he was buying into his father's delusions. He stared at the gun. He also couldn't believe he'd come to his crazy father for comfort.

Dad stirred the sauce, took his time answering. "I believe there is real danger for all of us, even if you're dismissing it." He gave Brendan a long look. "But using Megan seems a little far-fetched for the people I'm concerned about. I can't believe they'd go to such trouble. And expense, for that matter. A cruise?" He shook his head. "What made you start suspecting her of adultery?"

That word. "I don't know. A feeling, some expensive gifts. And then I came home early one night and saw Klein leaving." It sounded so sleazy. Mom would've said 'common.'

Dad repeated his objections. "Too much time. Too much money."

"Not if they sell the painting."

Dad shrugged. "Maybe. But they'd have trouble selling it. Anything new of mine has always gone through Devonie. It would be suspect."

Brendan hadn't thought of that. God, he couldn't think at all.

The water started bubbling, and Dad stirred the pasta. "You could probably prosecute her for theft." His back was to Brendan. "If you wanted to."

Brendan didn't know what to say. He couldn't contemplate it.

Dad didn't speak either. He stayed silent all through the cooking and draining and serving. "Eat," he said as he set a plate in front of Brendan. "It helps."

Brendan wasn't sure anything would help, but out of habit he dipped his fork into the spaghetti and lifted it to his mouth. Hot. Rich. He cut into a meatball, chewed, and swallowed. After several bites, he still felt bruised but not paralyzed. And he absolutely didn't want to talk about Megan any more. He gestured at the gun. "You know how to shoot?"

Dad nodded.

"Did you learn on the farm as a kid?"

A faint smile loosened his father's mouth. "No. My father didn't hold with guns, except for the military."

Brendan figured that was a direct quote from the grandfather he'd never known. "Then who taught you?"

"Your mother." Dad's smile was wider at this. "I called her 'Dead-Eye.'"

Brendan stopped his fork halfway to his mouth. "You're kidding."

Dad shook his head. "She used to go hunting with your grandfather. I bought her rifle from him years ago."

Brendan set down his fork. "She hunted with a rifle?"

Dad nodded.

"I'm surprised a rifle didn't knock her down."

"You're thinking of a shotgun. Besides, she was tougher than she looked."

Brendan silently agreed. Living with Dad had been absurdly difficult, and then she'd faced an even worse battle with cancer. Old grief layered on top of new, or was it the other way around? He wiped his mouth, sipped the last of his Coke. He couldn't eat any more.

Dad kept pushing reddened noodles into his mouth. His rifle, Brendan thought. God, did he have an arsenal in the house? "Do you still have the rifle?"

"Yes. And a shotgun and two handguns." He said it like it was of no importance.

"You think you need all that firepower?"

"I might." Dad frowned at Brendan's plate. "Is that all you're going to eat?"

Brendan shrugged.

Dad glanced at the pistol. "I remember your mother fussing at me, saying if I could see sixteen colors in a snowbank I should at least be able to size up a target." He chuckled. "Come to find out, I'm left-eyed. Unusual. She figured it out, and then the instruction went much better. Want ice cream?"

Brendan shook his head.

Dad cleaned his plate and sat back in his chair. "You should call Megan's mother. Make sure Cassie's there."

Brendan glanced at the kitchen window. The shutters were tight, but he could tell that it was dark outside. Megan would've arrived hours ago. And probably left again. He nodded. Rhonda had always seemed to like him, and she adored Cassie. Still, he wondered what she thought about having a kid dumped on her for nearly two weeks. She and Megan's stepfather Dean worked full-time and probably would until they dropped. No money in that house. As Rhonda's phone rang, he thought about how he'd love to relieve her of her babysitting duties.

Dad left the kitchen before Rhonda picked up, and Brendan appreciated the privacy. Her hello was tentative; she'd seen who was calling. "Just checking on my baby girl," he said, trying to sound cheerful.

"She's fine. Ate a good supper," Rhonda said and then took off on a long discourse about Cassie's nap and her playtime with Grandpa . In detail. Over the years, Brendan had come to like Rhonda more than he'd expected, but she was a talker who required a certain amount of patience. From all her chatter, though, he was able to glean that Klein had accompanied Megan and Cassie, and that the two of them had left for Chicago shortly after dropping Cassie off. They were taking a late flight to Florida.

"I could come up tomorrow and get her," Brendan said. "You two have to work. Taking care of Cassie on top of that will be tough."

For once Rhonda's words failed her. It took several seconds for her to reply. "Megan wouldn't like that." Her voice was hushed, pained. "I don't want to get in the middle of this, Brendan. I care for all of you and am as sorry as I can be about everything." She choked off words he knew she was dying to say.

He didn't want to upset her more than she already was. "I understand, but remember that I can be there in three hours if you need help with her."

After a few more reassurances that did nothing to make him feel better, Brendan laid his phone on the table and stared at the gun. He didn't have energy enough to move. Dad came back to the kitchen and asked about Cassie. Brendan told him that Rhonda had refused his offer to come get the child.

Dad gave him a stern look. "You're going to fight to get custody of her, aren't you?"

Brendan raised an eyebrow. "Of course, but Megan does have a lawyer. She sleeps with him."

"We'll get you a better one. Do your research. Find out who's the best divorce attorney in town. I'll pay."

Brendan appreciated it. Hell, he couldn't afford a lawyer. He nodded and started thinking about going home. Dad had shown a generosity that didn't have serial numbers on it, but Brendan didn't want to test it too hard.

Dad leaned against the counter, hands in his pockets. "Stay the night," he said. "I just now put clean sheets on your bed."

Brendan stood and shook his head.

"You don't need to be alone tonight."

So, he stayed. For three hours they watched World War II shows on the History Channel like they'd been handed down by Moses. They didn't talk. Dad offered ice cream again, and Brendan refused again. His father fixed a heaping bowl of butter pecan covered in chocolate sauce and sucked down every bit of it. If Brendan had been capable of humor at that point, it would've amused him. When he couldn't take another grizzled veteran reliving the horrors of war, he told his father he was going to bed. He doubted that he could sleep, but as much as anything, he wanted the day to end.

The walls in his old room were bare. He'd stripped the Michael Jordan posters from the walls and emptied trophies from the shelves when he'd left for grad school. Mom had stored them in the basement, but Megan never let him bring them into the house. Junk, she said. Megan had a lot to answer for. He lay in his old bed, watching the hands of his ancient alarm clock creep around the dial and thinking that he'd been at fault too. He'd let her get away with it.

Early the next day, he went home and ran in the Sunday sunshine, carrying his phone, hoping to hear that Rhonda had changed her mind about the baby. He knew better than to expect a call from Megan. On Monday morning he ran again, thinking the early morning gloom was more appropriate than sunshine. He turned on the television while he showered and drank his juice. Noise was good.

At work he went through all the correct motions. There'd been little joy in his tasks before; now they were downright onerous. He thought about Hannah. He'd almost called her Sunday evening, not to start something but to tell her that Megan had left him. When he thought about it, though, calling her would be too much like whining for sympathy, so he didn't. Besides, it would be starting something.

He was in his office when Zack called, not bothering to hide his enthusiasm even through his mumbles. "Hey Brendan, how are you doing?"

"Not so bad, Zack. How about you?" There was no point in honesty.

"Good, good. Listen, I got info about Thomas Vickers. Big info."

Brendan held his pen over a notepad. "Okay. Tell me."

"Wait, I gotta ask." Zack's mumbling grew worse. "Okay, is your dad the Keith Owen who paints?"

Brendan shut his eyes. It had to come out. "Yeah. Looked him up, did you?"

"Yeah. Well. No shit?"

"No shit."

"I don't know much about artists. Maybe Van Gogh, da Vinci. But he's your dad?" Brendan heard him gnawing on a pen. "I mean, he's famous. A rock star."

"I guess you could say that. Listen, could you keep it on the down low, Zack? Privacy and all that?" Brendan had to say it. He'd been well trained.

Zack mumbled 'down low' like he didn't understand and then hummed a little. "Oh, for sure. No, I won't say a word. Who would I tell anyway?" Who, indeed?

"So, about Thomas Vickers?"

"Right. He enrolled at Ball State fall semester 1972. From Emory, Indiana. I told you that, didn't I?"

"Yes." Beverly the Raptor came to the door and pointed at her watch. It was time for him to man the reference desk. He smiled apologetically and mouthed 'five minutes.'

"Art major," Zack continued. "First semester he had a .31 GPA. Flunked everything but an art class. On probation."

Brendan took a breath that shuddered a little at the end. This had to be his father. "Okay," he said.

"If that wasn't gruesome enough, second semester he was brought up before the dean for disciplinary action. It even made the college newspaper. Probably wanted to make an example of him. Plagiarism. Evidently he plagiarized during his first time in Freshman Comp and flunked the class for it. He did it again when he re-took the class, and they kicked him out. April, 1973."

Wonderful. It was Dad. And what a fine role model he was. Brendan threw his pen across the desk. "Thanks, Zack. Good research."

"Well." The word had several syllables. "Was that your father, Brendan?"

This time he had to cover up. "Maybe."

"Why'd he change his name? Ashamed of being kicked out of school?"

Brendan rubbed his hand along his jaw. "Look, I'm not sure. This is sort of dramatic, you know. Kind of shocking."

Zack's mumbles ran together at top speed. "I'm not saying nothing. To nobody, Brendan. Really. You can trust me. And it's not that big of a deal now that everything's said and done, is it?"

But everything wasn't said and done, Brendan thought. Not by a long shot. "Right. Promise? I really do need you to keep this confidential.

Celebrity shows, hell, paparazzi." This was far-fetched, but he had to make Zack understand.

"I got it. Sealed. Zipped." He changed track in an instant. Pure Zack. "Hey, think we could meet up one of these weekends? I could drive down or something. Be fun to get together."

Brendan assured him they'd do that very thing soon and almost meant it. He wouldn't have much of anything else to do on weekends. "Gotta go now, though. Talk soon." Fearing that his supervisor was dealing with dozens of reference questions, he rushed to the information desk, but there was no one there, no one needing him at all.

Chapter Eighteen

Needles of frustration pricked at his brain. He'd wanted Brendan to stay longer. He'd been able to persuade him to spend the night and kept him a while longer the next morning with coffee and doughnuts. He hated that they were stale. But then Brendan left for his lonely house, unprotected and vulnerable. Brenda had always done the comforting. She would've known what to say to Brendan. All he could do was offer him a bed and bad food. Keith felt his shoulders slump. He needed to protect his kids, not an easy task when one of them had doubts about his warnings, and the other didn't believe there was a threat at all. He had a hazy plan: to put the house up for sale in a visible manner, to announce who it belonged to and then leave. But even if he wasn't very good at being supportive and even if leaving was the smart thing to do, Keith hated to abandon his son.

He put off thinking about it and worked on the spider web painting. Getting the dewdrops right would be tricky, but he knew how to do it. He was using a smaller canvas than usual and making everything sharp and precise. He liked the challenge. This was the only painting in the house. Everything else had been shipped to Devonie.

His bags were packed. His papers and money were in order. He told himself he'd leave as soon as the spider web painting was done, but that was a lie. Setting aside his brush, Keith stared at the canvas. Maybe he should call Dana, find out what she knew. It was risky. It might be a trap. Years ago he'd felt a connection with her, but he doubted that it had been any stronger than the web he was painting. He felt better about Dana than he did Megan. He couldn't do a damned thing about Brendan's sorry wife. Keith smiled. Those would've been Brenda's words. He wondered if Megan would try to sell the cow picture. Maybe he should email Devonie about that. Somehow he had to find a way to guard his children against the dangers he'd passed to them along with his DNA. Even though the light was perfect, he left the studio and stared at the pistol on the table.

Brenda had been typing a paper for Freshman Composition. He had sour memories of that class. Every minute or two she'd stop, cuss under her breath, and hunch over to apply the *Wite Out* brush. They'd been married a little over a month. It was late afternoon, and he'd just gone out to get the mail, which included a copy of the Chicago newspaper he subscribed to. As usual, he pored over it, looking for any mention of the Collins family, Nick, his father, his brother Joe. In the two weeks since he'd been receiving it, all he'd seen were rental ads for Mr. Collins' many properties.

"Shit," Brenda muttered. Her braid had unraveled and her cheeks were pink. "I can't type a lick." The scent of *Wite Out* drifted over to him.

Keith smoothed out the creased front section. He ignored sports, didn't pay much attention to the society page either. The Collins family had money enough for it, but they didn't travel in those circles.

"I hope you hadn't planned on a fancy supper," Brenda said. "I got two more pages to go." She glared at the handwritten draft she'd scrawled the night before. It was a wonder she could decipher it.

"No." He scanned the front page. Nothing. That was good. He wasn't sure what he dreaded finding. Nothing he'd done would make the paper.

Brenda's erratic pecking continued. He turned the page and lost his breath. The headline read: "Businessman's Son Shot Dead." The businessman was Nick's father; the son was his brother Joe. He read the article twice. It was short, didn't say much. Joe had been in the parking garage next to the building that housed Mr. Collins' office. He'd been getting in his car to go home. He'd been shot twice and was dead when the ambulance arrived.

Keith didn't notice that Brenda had stopped typing. "Keith," she said, making him raise his eyes before he could read the article for the third time. "What is it?"

"Somebody died," he said. "Someone I knew."

She left the typewriter and stood behind him, putting her hand on his shoulder. His sweet, convenient little bride. Now he'd put her in danger too. She figured out which article and read it for herself. "You knew Joseph Collins?" she asked. "In Chicago?"

He nodded.

"A friend?"

He shook his head.

"Sounds like an assassination." He made no response. Her fingers dug into his muscle. "What do you know? What have you done?" Her voice was a whisper.

He shook his head again.

"What are you messed up in?" This was a little louder.

"I need a gun," he said.

She moved back to her chair so she could see his face. "Have you killed someone?" Her face was so pale the freckles looked like dots.

Joe. He'd killed Joe. Or his actions had. "I need a gun," he said again. He had to protect her. And himself.

Brenda stood again. "I'll call my daddy," she said. "He's still got my rifle."

●●●●

He couldn't shoot cancer, but otherwise he'd done pretty well at protecting Brenda from all he'd done and been. His early precautions had been sensible, but from the day of Joe's death until now they'd been imperative. Leon had found him the pistols and shotgun. They were loaded, ready, but he could only protect his kids if he quit stalling.

Keith went back to the studio and was able to get some decent work done on the painting before he lost the light. He wandered around the house, feeling more lonesome than he had since Brenda died. Maybe it was having Brendan there the previous night. He opened the refrigerator, ready to heat up the leftover spaghetti from last night, when the phone rang. It was Kinley.

"How're you doing?" Her voice sounded years younger.

"Not so bad." He paused, thought a second. "You?" he added.

She laughed. "Too good to be true. Are you ready for a couple of big surprises?"

She was getting married. She was moving back to Cincinnati, at least temporarily. Brenda would've been ecstatic. He fought to find the words she would've used. "I'm over the moon, Kinley," he said.

Kinley giggled. "You sound like Mom. Even a little bit Southern."

He smiled at the phone.

"But it gets better." She told him that she was painting, that she'd sketched a couple of pictures and was working on them. She'd bought supplies but didn't like the brushes she'd found. Maybe she needed to order some from the company he used. Could he give her the email address?

He sank into a chair. His words wavered, but it didn't matter. "I'll send you brushes. You want ones like mine? Small, large, what?" He cleared his throat.

She didn't want the very large ones, not now anyway. It was all muscle memory, wasn't it, she said. It was like she'd never stopped holding a brush. Then she giggled again. "Of course I didn't, did I? All those pitchers and wineglasses."

"They count," he said. "There's still technique to it."

"Just barely." Her voice was breezy. "I was going to wait to tell you, but I just couldn't. I called Brendan yesterday and made him promise not to say anything."

It didn't even hurt that she'd told her brother first. It seemed right, actually. "That's fine," he said. She must not know about Megan. He debated telling her, but Brendan hadn't wanted to spoil her joy. He wouldn't either. "I'm proud of you," he said.

It was her turn to pause. When she spoke again, her voice was thready. "Thanks."

Chapter Nineteen

KINLEY

She woke very early on Wednesday and was happy about it. Michael had postponed leaving by a day but said he must leave on Thursday. Kinley wanted this day to last far more than twenty-four hours. Leaving him asleep for at least a little while, she made coffee and carried a mug to her desk. All but one of her tenants had told her their plans, whether they were staying over the summer or moving out. She needed to get dates on her calendar for inspections, cleaning, painting, all kinds of little details. Normally she liked this sort of organizational work; she called them her "Brendan jobs," but now she just wanted to paint.

Dad had overnighted a huge selection of brushes so beautiful she wanted to pet them. She'd already made a good start on the café painting, wanting it to have a French feel, a sort of *Boating Party* done abstract. But she'd set it aside to work on a sketch of Michael while he was still there. She'd begged him to pose for her. "Naked?" he'd asked with a huge grin. "Nude is the correct term," she'd said. "And yes, mostly."

He'd liked the idea; actually that's why he'd postponed his departure. She'd made him lay on a white sheet, another one pulled nearly to his waist, his arm resting down his side with his hand splayed on his covered thigh. His other arm was stretched in front of him, palm up, fingers curled. What she wanted most were the curve of his back and his hands. Always his hands. "Damn," he'd said. "You don't want to paint the good parts?" An evil laugh. She'd said, no.

On her way back to the kitchen to get more coffee, she stopped in the dining room and studied her sketches—two of him and two each of his hands. She was pleased. More and more she understood what her father meant when he'd said that she must see the complete composition, everything, before she picked up a brush. Her eyes slid over the curve of Michael's back, imagining the sheen of his skin and how she would achieve that. The white sheets, the ivory skin, the tan of his hands. She knew what she wanted to say.

While Michael sat in classes or practice rooms, she'd have her painting. That was what she'd come to realize that night after he proposed. And it had solidified with the passing days. Michael believed in her ambition, her talent. He wouldn't swallow her up with his.

Kinley made herself go back to the desk. Ten apartments, not including hers. Michael's was pristine; it had hardly been used this year. For a moment she considered moving her work up there, just for the summer. It had better light, and they'd sold or dumped what little furniture he'd had. Maybe. She stared at her notes. Five apartments would be vacant in the next week or two. She'd have to clean, shampoo carpets, maybe even paint those. Four were staying, and one of those gave her another reason to smile.

Sarah had pounded on their door last night, bobbing, bouncing, and shaking a piece of paper like a pompom. "I got the job in Broomfield," she'd exclaimed. "And, even better, my days won't start until 8:30, so I can easily commute from here and manage the apartments if you still want me to."

Kinley certainly wanted her to. She'd decided to put the brick building on the market right away. Its apartments had perpetual plumbing problems, and she, or Sarah, couldn't keep an eye on it like the yellow and gray houses sitting next door to each other. If it sold, she'd have the bit of equity she'd established the last couple of years. She wasn't sure what she and Michael would live on. The rents, of course, but she'd pay Sarah along with giving her free rent, and there'd still be the upkeep costs. Her glass painting had never paid much, but it had been a nice trickle of cash throughout the year. She supposed she could still do it, but she didn't want to. Michael had said they could manage without it. He'd get a church job; he always did. She needed to quit worrying.

Michael made pancakes for breakfast, and she helped him pack the rest of his clothes and music. Every task seemed significant. Every kiss seemed important. Her shirt smelled of his cologne. She wondered how long it would linger. All day they hardly left each other's sides, talking, touching. They made plans for the evening. He would cook, he said, and then they'd go to bed early. He wanted to hit the road by seven. She worried about his old car and whether he would make it safely to Michigan. Maybe he should take hers. Way too complicated, he said. The car would be fine.

A soft breeze was easing through the open door when they sat down to Michael's veal marsala. She poured wine for them. He spooned out salad. "Maybe we should've invited Sarah," she said.

"I thought about that, but I'm selfish." He touched her hand. "And we drank to her new job last night."

With her mouth full, Kinley could only nod. She swallowed. "I'm thrilled that she's going to take care of the apartments."

"Yes. Good news all around. How's it going with her and Will?"

"Will? Oh, the baritone?" Michael nodded. "Fine, I guess, except that he's leaving next week to go home for the summer. I guess we'll be music widows together."

Michael smiled. She'd have to be careful when she painted him. It would be too easy to make him a Renaissance dreamboat. She was considering his resemblance to Michelangelo's *David* when he said, "I'm glad you two will have each other for the summer."

"I'll be busy enough," she said between bites. "I have some glass orders to finish and work to do on several apartments. And there's the painting." The words made her cheeks warm. She was an artist

"Yes." He smiled at her again. "The painting."

She hated that he was leaving, but she was happy. Very happy. "And we'll call all the time, right?" she asked.

"Of course. And you'll come up to Michigan as soon as you can. We'll need to plan the wedding." She nodded, a little unsure about this part.

He said, "My mother will want to be part of that."

"Small, though, like we decided?" She'd told Sarah that she didn't see a thing wrong with eloping or arriving at a judge's office in jeans with maybe a white shirt for tradition's sake.

Michael set down his fork. "Sort of small. Do you have any idea how many cousins I have? Mama will want to plan the reception and the food and the cookie table." He swung his arm out in a large gesture. "All that stuff."

She felt a wave of panic. She wanted Michael, not all the people who went with him. But then look who she was bringing to the table.

"Will your father come?"

"No. And that has nothing to do with you, Michael. Really. Brendan will, though. And he'll bring his wife." She recalled how Megan always looked like she'd bitten into a very sour pickle. "And little Cassie."

He smiled again. Such very white teeth. "It'll be great fun. I'll see to the music, of course. And you'll want a chocolate cake, right?"

She grinned. He'd brought eclairs home from the grocery today. "Absolutely," she said.

They lingered over dinner, took breaks for kisses while they did the dishes, sat on the front porch in the dark, huddled in jackets. When they came back inside, he offered to pose for her again, joking, saying that surely she needed to see him *nude* again. She said that she'd like that, but she had no intention of doing any sketching just then. Their lovemaking was sad and sweet and occasionally fierce, as if they wanted to leave marks that would last through the separation.

●●●●

She heard a sharp noise that made her hand creep toward the alarm clock, but the sound wasn't right. There was an odd smell too, not immediately identifiable, and a low rustling noise underneath the alarm. In less than a second she was beating on Michael, shrieking, "Fire!"

He jumped up more quickly than she did, but soon they were both fumbling into clothes they'd left on the floor. Kinley turned the switch on the lamp but nothing happened. The power was out. "Call 911," Michael yelled.

She knew her phone was on the table by the bed, but she couldn't see it. Her fingers fumbled over useless items, tissues, jewelry. She knocked over a glass of water before she found it. The light from her open phone was reassuring for a second until she realized there was more light now, coming from the bathroom at the back of the house.

"Call as you walk. Come on," Michael shouted.

She punched in the three numbers as she fled the bedroom. There was still a smoky path to the front door, but flames were licking at the doorway of the kitchen, snaking across to the dining room. The dispatcher answered and Kinley had to cough before she could speak. Michael was ahead of her, opening the front door. He kept up a hoarse chant of "Come on. Come on. Come on."

Kinley stopped at the door and screamed, "Sarah!" Michael disappeared.

She had a minute, maybe one true minute. Flying across the living room, she grabbed her sketch book and unfinished canvas, hooking the strap of her purse over her arm at the same time. The heat was horrendous. Tears streamed from her eyes. She turned to look toward the kitchen and saw the fire dance across the hardwood and gnaw on the woodwork. Once outside, she gasped at the clear air. She sprang across the cool porch floor and slipped in the wet grass, dropping the sketchbook. She clutched it back up and kept running toward the back of the house. Through the dining room window she could see fire devouring the room in shimmers and waves. There was a loud pop, a flash, and glass from the window blew out onto the driveway and Kinley. Turpentine, she guessed. There'd been a nearly full container of it in the dining room.

She kept moving down the driveway, yelling Michael's name. The other side of the house blazed in a continuous roll of flames. She looked up. It hadn't engulfed the second story yet, but fire was licking at it, creeping up the walls. Despite the smoke, the unnatural light allowed her to see the upper deck. Sarah's apartment door was open, but Kinley couldn't see either Michael or Sarah. "Michael! Hurry!" she yelled, but the crackling flames were louder than her voice.

She watched as the bottom step was engulfed. They'd be trapped if they didn't hurry. He should've taken Sarah to the front. They could've come through a window and slid down the porch roof, maybe dropped down okay. Maybe they had. Oblivious to the broken glass glistening in the eerie light, she ran down the driveway to the front of the house. Smoke billowed out the front door. She looked up at the window over the porch but saw no one. "Come this way," she yelled, but no one seemed to hear her. Above the constant roaring of the fire she could detect a thin siren. Not close yet, she thought, not close enough. She ran to the back again and moved toward the steps. Maybe she could help. But the wall of heat forced her back.

Where were they? The blaze was climbing the steps, inching up in spurts of flame. She screamed for Michael again. The siren was loud now, and brakes squealed in front of her house. Firemen thudded down the driveway. Kinley shouted at them and pointed to the upstairs. A fireman grabbed her arm. "How many people in there?"

"Two," she said on a sob. "Upstairs." She pointed again. A huddled figure staggered out onto the deck. Flames licked at the two poles supporting the deck and outlined the shapes in harsh relief.

Michael was carrying Sarah like a baby. He had a blanket draped over his head and held around her.

Other firemen ran down the driveway carrying a ladder. "Get her out of here," one shouted. Kinley guessed they meant her, but she wasn't moving. She didn't see how Michael could climb down a ladder holding Sarah. Kinley's face burned with the heat.

The firefighter standing below the deck yelled, "Drop her. I'll get her. Drop her. Now."

Michael hesitated. The fireman climbed a couple of rungs, but he'd noticed the fire eating at the supports too. The whole deck would collapse any minute. The blaze had advanced nearly to the top of the steps. Surely Michael didn't mean to walk through the flames. He could use the ladder if he dropped Sarah. Kinley's voice was a harsh shriek when she echoed the fireman's words. "Let go of her, Michael. Please!"

When he unwrapped Sarah, the blanket slipped from his head. His face was an unearthly white against the rolling smoke. Holding Sarah at the railing, he bent over her and then rolled her over the edge of the rail. Another fireman ran up to the first one's side, and Kinley watched them brace as Sarah fell, the edge of her nightgown catching fire as she went down. One fireman batted at her smoldering gown with his glove and heaved her over his shoulder. He sprinted down the driveway. The other one shouted, "Now you. Get down that ladder, man. Now, damn it."

One of the deck's support poles looked no more substantial than a toothpick. Flames were at Michael's feet and eating away the boards of the deck. He shrugged off the blanket and grabbed the railing, but before he could swing over onto the ladder, the deck crashed into a shower of sparks and hissing flames. Kinley screamed and started to run to Michael but somehow, from somewhere, another fireman appeared at her side and took an iron grip on her arm. "Go, now," he ordered and propelled her down the driveway. She didn't want to leave, but neither could she bear watching them dig Michael from the burning debris.

She flew toward the flashing lights of the trucks and ambulance and didn't stop until she'd dodged all the hoses and shouts. She crossed the street and stood on the sidewalk where she could see the back of the ambulance. Sarah must already be inside. EMT's pulled out a stretcher and rushed it to the back of the house. He was dead. He had to be dead.

The firefighters hollered to each other as they positioned themselves to fight the blaze. She shivered, waiting. Then the paramedics appeared with the stretcher, hurrying down the drive. She moved toward the ambulance with every intention of climbing into it with Michael and Sarah, but an EMT blocked her. "We'll send one for you. Stay right where you are," he ordered as he jumped in the back and slammed the door. She wanted to tell him that she didn't need an ambulance; she needed to be with Michael. The vehicle sped off, siren blaring.

So far the gray house had not caught fire even though there wasn't much distance between them. The firefighters aimed a mighty hose between the two houses, making a wall of water. She saw her tenants from the other house gathered on the far side of the yard, peering at the flames. The girls were crying. Some carried bags or belongings. It was a nightmare. Shimmers of heat rose from the inferno, but Kinley couldn't quit shivering. A policeman spread a blanket across her shoulders. She clutched at it and then panicked all over again. Where were her things? She turned and saw the woman who lived across the street standing behind her. She held the canvas and book. "I'll keep them safe," the woman murmured. Kinley's purse was still glued under her arm. She coughed until she gagged.

Somebody yelled and there was a gigantic whoosh as the house collapsed upon itself. Victorian frame with gingerbread trim. A pretty yellow house. Tinder. The woman's husband handed Kinley a bottle of water. She couldn't quit coughing. The policeman asked if she owned the house, and she couldn't speak for the retching spasms that shook her body.

She drank half the water and managed to croak out her name when he asked.

"And the other two people?" he asked.

"Sarah," she managed. "Sarah Akers. And Michael Belli."

"Students?"

No, they were her best friend and her future husband. She rubbed at her face with the coarse blanket and nodded.

The hoses were winning now that there was little left to burn. The firemen spread out. One came back to the rig and spoke to the guy who seemed to be in charge. "I'm betting this is arson," he said in a low voice. "Scorch marks on the walls. Accelerant cans."

Kinley's feet burned. Her throat was a raw wound. She pulled at the water container until it collapsed. Arson? It made no sense to her.

The policeman gave her a long look, all the way up and down. "Is another ambulance on its way for her?"

He pointed at the sidewalk. Dark footprints marked the concrete. Her feet were bleeding.

"Should be here any minute," he said.

It was. The ambulance's siren sputtered to a stop in front of Kinley. The paramedic jumped out and opened the back door. She didn't need to get in there. She wasn't hurt. "Can you walk?" he asked her.

She nodded. He put a gentle hand on her back and led her toward the ambulance. At least they would take her to the hospital where she could check on Sarah and Michael. God. Michael.

The EMT made her lay down, attached an oxygen tube to her upper lip, and told her to relax. She had shards of glass in her feet, hair, and clothes, he said. Dozens of little and big cuts, he added. She didn't feel them. She asked him about Michael and Sarah, but he didn't know anything. Or wouldn't say. She kept coughing.

They rolled her into the emergency room and put her in an examining room. She asked everyone she saw about Sarah and Michael, but no one told her anything. They made her take her clothes off, and tiny bits of glass showered onto the floor. When they worked on her hair, countless more fell into a basin. They bathed her, and then they began the tedious process of digging shards from her body, mostly her feet. It hurt, and she guessed she got pretty agitated, because they gave her a shot that made everything blur at the edges. For a second she wondered if she could paint that way.

Later, her feet bandaged, her head still wonky, they said she could go, but she couldn't do that until she found out about Michael and Sarah. Besides, where would she go? Her tee shirt and pants were bloody and dotted with broken glass. A social worker came in with sweats and shoes for her and said she'd booked her a hotel room. She also said that she'd call her a cab, but Kinley couldn't leave until she heard something. The social worker took her to an empty waiting room and promised to give her news when she could.

A huge clock on the wall said it was five o'clock. The room was dim, silent. Clutching her phone, Kinley huddled into a chair. When she shut her eyes, she saw flames and Michael holding Sarah against the upstairs railing. And then him crashing down into the sparks. She made herself get up and hobbled to a coffee pot across the room, figuring it was empty or cold, but it wasn't too bad. The sign above the deserted desk said this was the Surgical Waiting Area. Did that mean that Michael, or Sarah, was in surgery? She shut her eyes.

Afraid of missing the social worker, Kinley sat, staring at the clock. Dread kept welling up in her. She needed to walk. After pacing a few steps, she had to stop. Her feet burned like she was walking on needles. Sitting again, she focused on the toes of her borrowed shoes. Arson. She'd hardly noticed when the fireman said the word. She shook her head. Why would anyone want to burn her house down? With her in it? She was the only one who'd benefit from the insurance. She looked down at her hands, peppered with scabs and cuts. Unless the fire's purpose was to hurt her.

Her eyes flew open. This was her father's fault. His enemies. It didn't matter that he'd warned her. It didn't matter that she'd ignored him. She called him. When he answered, she said, "You've killed Michael and maybe my friend too. You've burned down my house. You're a wicked, horrible man." She clicked off before he had a chance to say a word.

Chapter Twenty

KEITH

He'd smiled when Kinley's name came up on his phone. It was very early in the morning, but maybe she was calling to tell him about an artistic breakthrough or to ask a question about technique. He'd love that. He'd even welcome a chat about wedding plans. After he heard what she said he was no longer smiling.

He immediately called her back and got no answer. He couldn't bring himself to leave a message. He rinsed his breakfast dishes and folded up the newspaper. Kinley's house had burned; he got that much. She, however, was okay, and for that he was so grateful that he had to sit down and take several deep breaths. She was assuming it was arson. She was also assuming that the arson had been committed by his enemies. He picked up his phone and tried her again. Nothing.

So, he called Brendan who didn't need more troubles, that was for sure, but maybe Kinley would answer a call from her brother.

Brendan was on his way to work. "Kinley called," Keith said and quoted her exact words.

"What the hell?" Brendan didn't say anything for several seconds. "But she's okay?"

Keith said that he thought she was.

"Did your bad guys do it?"

Keith shut his eyes. Thirty years ago it had seemed like such a good idea, and it had paid off, not only for his art and earnings but for his family too. They'd never wanted for anything. He'd made sure of it. "It's possible," he said. "I'm glad Cassie is with her grandparents." He heard Brendan mutter something profane.

"Would you call Kinley?" Keith asked. "She needs somebody, and she doesn't want me."

"Yeah. Sure." Brendan's voice was gray, blank.

"Call me back and tell me what she says. And Brendan? Please be careful. Very, very careful."

Keith stared at the pistol sitting on the kitchen table. He had to put a stop to it. This was not his children's debt to pay. He picked up the phone again and entered Dana's number. Her area code was for Boston, he'd discovered. Not that it mattered.

She answered on the third ring. He was already wondering how to phrase a message to her, and this time he would've left one. "I need to talk to you."

"Tommy?" She sounded as if he'd awakened her.

"You know where I live," he said. "How soon can you get here?"

"What's wrong?" She was alert now.

"A lot."

She hesitated. He remembered how she squinted when she thought hard about something. He wondered if she still did. Finally she said, "I'll get the first flight I can manage. Tonight?"

"As soon as you can," he said.

"I'll call you."

She hung up.

BRENDAN

He couldn't take much more. His father, his sister, and yesterday he'd received Megan's petition for divorce in the mail. It was a shit storm, he thought. Traffic was so horrendous on I75, he didn't call Kinley until he'd parked his car. He listened to her phone ring as he walked across campus. The call went to voicemail, and he barked, "What's going on, Kinley? Call me."

He powerwalked to the library and arrived only three minutes late, but Beverly was hovering at the reference desk, making a show of looking at the clock. "Good morning," he said and ducked into his office to ditch his bag before heading to the desk. Of course Kinley chose that moment to call.

"Brendan." Her voice was hoarse, low. He didn't know whether that was from tears or the fire. Probably both.

"What's happening, Kin? Are you sure Michael's dead? I'm worried to death." Their mother's phrase.

She told him about the fire, about Sarah and Michael and going to the hospital.

"And you?" he asked in a hushed voice. "Are you okay? What happened?"

Her feet were cut up, she said, but she was okay. She didn't sound it.   "Where are you?" .

151

"Still at the hospital. They promised to tell me about Michael, but I've been waiting and waiting."

"Maybe he's okay. Really."

"I don't know." Her voice broke. "If you had seen him. . ." Her voice wavered.

"Don't borrow trouble," he said.

"I know."

Beverly came to his office door and frowned. He held up one finger and tried to look apologetic. She flounced off. "Listen, I'll call you on my lunch break. You'll know more then."

"What did Dad do?" she asked. "We shouldn't have to suffer, Brendan. It's so screwed up." He could tell she wanted to talk on and on about it, but he couldn't even tell her what Zack had discovered. Not now.

"I know. I'll call you. Take care." He hung up, took a deep breath, and headed for the reference desk where Beverly stood.

"I'm sorry," he said. "My sister's house burned last night, and her fiancé may be seriously injured." He couldn't say the word *dead*.

Beverly didn't sympathize, but she didn't fuss either. Good thing. Brendan wasn't sure how he would've reacted if she had. Taking a deep breath and collapsing into his chair, he thought that at that moment what he wanted more than anything was to pull a Forrest Gump and run all the way to the Pacific Ocean, turn around, and run back. Just run forever.

KINLEY

The waiting room clock finally made it to six. She'd tried calling Sarah's phone twice before she realized that it had probably burned up in the fire. And she'd panicked when she realized that she'd turned hers off after calling her father, missing Brendan's call, but more seriously, perhaps missing one about Michael. But she hadn't. After talking to Brendan, she rose, her feet protesting the decision, and started limping to the elevator. She'd go to the main desk, maybe back to the Emergency Room, somewhere, but she couldn't sit another minute.

Her phone and the elevator dinged at nearly the same moment. Kinley didn't recognize the number. Her heart kicked up its pace. "Hello?" She let the elevator go.

"It's Sarah." Her voice sounded rough as a gravel road. "Are you okay?"

Kinley told her and asked the same questions.

"Yeah. They've been giving me breathing treatments. I'm up in Respiratory Therapy."

Kinley could hardly form the words. "And Michael?"

"Nobody would tell me anything about him. You either, for that matter. But I did overhear someone saying he was being taken for an MRI."

Kinley sank into a nearby chair. Alive.

Sarah kept talking. Her parents were on their way from Wyoming to take her home. She remembered nothing about the fire and made a small noise when Kinley told her what had happened. "Dear God," Sarah whispered.

Kinley nodded and promised to call as soon as she had news about Michael. Then she punched the elevator's button again, went to the information desk, learned that he'd been admitted, and was told his room number. She took a deep breath before she opened his door.

It wasn't Intensive Care. It wasn't the morgue. All this she rejoiced over, but he looked like hell. His eyes were shut. Patches of hair had disappeared from his head. Two cherry-red splotches marked his left cheek and jaw. She glanced at his hands. The room was dim. She stepped closer. There was a bandage on the palm of his left hand, some scratches on the back of his right. Kinley let out the breath she'd been holding.

She said Michael's name, but he didn't move. As her eyes adjusted to the dimness she could see some kind of strap at his shoulder, mostly hidden by the hospital gown. His arms were okay. Down near his feet, she lifted the sheet and saw more bandages but no casts. He'd walked out into the fire wearing only shorts. Of course his legs had been vulnerable. She'd been standing there a while, looking at Michael, at every inch of him, when she heard a noise behind her. Sarah was creeping into the room. She was pale but solid. Her hug was strong. "You're sure you're all right?" Kinley buried her face in Sarah's hair. It smelled of fire.

"I am," Sarah croaked. "How's our boy?" A cough rattled up from Sarah's chest.

Kinley looked back at Michael. "I don't know. He's alive."

Sarah moved closer to the bed. "His hands?"

"I think they're okay."

Sarah nodded. "Looks like it." She ducked her head. "I had to check on him. He saved me." She scrubbed a fist across her cheek. "My parents are waiting. I need to go." She turned and then stopped. "I guess we'll have to wait to see how things turn out, won't we? Our plans?" asked Sarah. Her eyes were rimmed in red.

"Yes. Call me. I'll call you. Every day."

Sarah frowned. "Sure. Yes." She paused. "I have to get a phone." Kinley could feel Sarah totaling their losses. But she said, "We're all okay, Kinley."

Kinley looked at Michael. "Yes. We are."

After Sarah left, Kinley slipped off the borrowed shoes and curled up in the big chair next to Michael's bed. It was a relief to free her stinging feet. She leaned her head against the chair and closed her eyes. Not five minutes later, a young man brought in Michael's breakfast. "Should I wake him?" Kinley asked.

The guy shrugged, so she let the food sit, smelling coffee and eggs. She lifted a lid and saw two pieces of toast. Michael wouldn't mind if she ate one. A nurse caught her at the second crunch, and Kinley quickly set it down. The nurse smiled. "Are you his girl? He was asking about you."

Kinley nodded. "How is he? Is he supposed to be sleeping like this?"

"Yes. He's concussed. Although we do wake patients with brain injuries every hour or two to make sure they're all right." She took Michael's blood pressure, counted his pulse. "Otherwise he has a broken collar bone, bruises and lacerations, and scattered burns, especially on his legs and face."

"Lasting damage?" The two bites of toast stuck in Kinley's throat.

"Shouldn't be if the concussion doesn't get any worse." The nurse clicked numbers into the laptop she'd brought with her. "There may be some scarring on his leg. One of those burns is severe." A thermometer went into Michael's ear. "The doctor wants us to watch him for a day or so. They may do another MRI to see how his brain is healing."

Kinley took a deep breath. "It's okay that I'm here?"

"Of course. I understand that his parents are on their way, but I don't know when they'll arrive." She smiled. "Eat his breakfast. He won't want it."

Kinley finished the toast and then she dozed, waking every time the door opened. Michael slept through it all. A hero, she thought as she gazed over at him. A damned hero. She opened the blinds a little to let in the morning sunshine. The cuts and pallor looked worse in the light, but his chest rose and fell in a steady, reassuring rhythm. More than anything she wanted to crawl into bed with him and hold his damaged head against her heart. How had she ever considered living without him? She gripped the side rail of his bed and let her eyes drink him up. He must've sensed it, for his eyelids fluttered and opened, finding hers immediately. A smile curled his lips. "Hi," he said.

"Hello yourself." Damnit. Tears were running down her cheeks. "How many Kinleys do you see?" she asked.

His smile widened. "Six. And they're all beautiful."

Chapter Twenty One

KEITH

He made a grocery list for Leon. He didn't know how long Dana would stay. He didn't know what she'd eat, if she'd eat, but there was nothing much in the refrigerator. Finishing the list, he paced the house until he heard Leon's car. Keith thrust the paper into Leon's hand the minute the man walked in the door. Leon whistled. "Wine? Chocolates? You having a party? Is Brendan coming over?"

Keith muttered, "Dana. She's coming in tonight."

Leon stuffed the list in his pocket. "Okay." The word had about seven syllables. "Still want me to mow after I go to the store?"

Keith nodded.

Leon's frosted eyebrows raised nearly to his hairline. "Okay," he said again and pointed at the gun on the table. "You want me to get you some flowers for a prettier centerpiece?"

It was all a joke to Leon. Maybe he'd been a joke to Leon for years. Keith said, "I wish Brendan was coming over. Megan left him and went off with another man. Dropped Cassie off at her mother's."

There was no laughter in Leon's face now. "Brenda never liked that girl."

Keith went on. "And someone set Kinley's house on fire last night. She's okay, but people have been injured, maybe killed." Leon's eyes were wide. "I have to talk to Dana. I have to know what's going on."

Leon had turned gray. "God, Keith. Kinley? And the fire's because of you?"

Keith gave him a curt nod. "I'm pretty sure."

"But Kinley's okay?" Leon needed a repeat.

Keith shrugged. "She's well enough but blames me for all of it." He stared into Leon's puzzled eyes. "And she's right."

"Are the two connected? Megan and the fire?"

"I don't think so." Keith's voice lowered to a whisper. "I don't know."

Leon left, and Keith went from room to room, trying to straighten, dust, anything to keep moving. He tried calling Kinley three more times. She didn't answer. He didn't leave a message. He was scrubbing the hall bathroom upstairs when he heard Leon return. He assumed it was Leon. Once upon a time he would've rushed downstairs, pistol in hand, to make sure. Not now.

Keith threw towels in the washing machine and checked his watch. Brendan had promised to call Kinley again on his lunch break and report in. He'd sounded harried, and Keith was sorry for that. He was sorry for everything, but he was anxious to hear whether Kinley's Michael was dead or alive. Keith closed his eyes. God help him. He'd never intended for it to come to this.

He waited until the washer started agitating before he made himself busy again. He wasn't sure what Dana could do for him other than give him Nick's phone number, something Brendan probably could've located for him. But Keith wanted to know how she'd found him, how Nick had found him after all this time. Had someone ratted him out? Devonie? Megan? Hell, Leon? Keith wasn't convinced that both Dana and Nick had been able to locate him separately. For all he knew, they were working together. He shook his head. It didn't matter how they'd seen through his elaborate subterfuge. All that mattered was giving Nick what he wanted.

He watched the clock and touched his phone every few minutes. He was counting on Brendan. The phone rang at twelve-thirty. He didn't bother with hello. "How is she? Michael?"

Brendan's voice was low. "Michael's alive. Bad concussion. Broken collarbone. Not good but alive. Kinley's got cuts from flying glass, but she's okay, I guess. The house is a total loss. They're saying it's arson. She has to go to the police station this afternoon."

"So they do think it's arson."

"Yeah. Kinley heard the word from the firemen at the scene."

Keith winced.

"I'm sure they'll ask if she knows any reason why someone would set her house on fire." Brendan paused. "She doesn't know what to say."

"She should say that she doesn't know anything."

Brendan didn't speak.

"I'm not protecting myself now," Keith said. "She really doesn't know anything. Neither do you."

"All right." The words were frozen.

"I'm setting it all straight. Today. I'm taking care of it."

"If you say so."

Keith gripped the phone. "I'm sorry," he said.

"Yeah."

"For everything."

"Right."

For long seconds, neither spoke. Then Brendan said, "I got divorce papers in the mail yesterday."

"I'm sorry for that too."

"I don't think you're to blame for that mess, but hey, maybe you are." He paused. "Let me know when we're all safe, Dad. If ever." And he hung up.

Keith squeezed the silent phone. Kinley wouldn't take a call from him, but he could text her. He was clumsy with it, had only ever tried to do it a few times while Brenda was sick. And his fingers were as trembly as an old man's. "Glad everyone is okay," he typed. "Sorry for everything." He'd started to ask if she needed money, but that's all he'd ever done.

He heard Leon's mower. Everything sounded peaceful. He could almost pretend that seeing Dana was a reunion. Stupid, he thought, but despite everything, over the years he'd never been able to quit wondering about her. She'd always had that effect on him. But now there was a lot more going on than curiosity.

<u>1975</u>

Thanksgiving Day. Chicago was gray, chilly. He was painting, working up a sweat despite the cold. The restaurant where he washed dishes was closed for the holiday. Nick was feasting with his family. The day was his. He felt no nostalgia for the turkey his mother was roasting, nor for the long prayer before the midday meal when he would undoubtedly be mentioned. So far, he'd made two solo runs for the Collins family, one to Detroit and one to Minneapolis. He'd sent postcards to his parents from both places, assuring them that he was okay. He figured that was enough.

In the afternoon he heard feet on the steps outside the studio, and his spirits sank. He didn't need Nick, not today. But there was a tiny knock, not the sound of a key, and he let Dana in. She was wearing her Dr. Zhivago coat. It was winter again. God, he'd been here almost a year now and was no closer to achieving his dreams. He'd given up on getting into the Institute, didn't see the point. But other than the sale to Nick's brother Joe, he'd sold no paintings, attracted no attention. So far, so good, bumming off Nick, but eventually he had to sell to afford to paint.

"Such a long face, Farm Boy," Dana said, unwinding a sky blue scarf from her neck. "I thought you'd welcome some company on a holiday."

She was gorgeous. He wanted to count the different colors of blonde in her hair. She was also Nick's. There'd been no repeat of the trip to Memphis when she'd invited him to bed. Every time she came to the studio alone he thought it might happen again, but all she ever wanted was to look at his work. Flattering as hell, but. Sure enough, as soon as she'd taken off her coat, she walked over to his easel and scrutinized the canvas. "Nice," she murmured. "Stunning brushwork." It was another cityscape; he'd been hooked on those for weeks now. He stood behind her, remembering what she looked like beneath her sweater and jeans. She took her time scrutinizing other canvases he'd set against the walls. Never said much, but her eyes shone when she looked at them. Then she turned her back on his paintings and smiled at him. "But I'm more interested in you today," she said, turning and unbuttoning his paint-smeared shirt.

It wasn't safe. Nick could turn up any minute, although he hadn't seen him in over a week. He said so.

"He's at his parents'. Big Thanksgiving with all the cousins and gangsters. I try to avoid those gatherings, so I said I had a fever." Her mouth puckered. "And Joe's going to announce his engagement today. We're safe." She grabbed his hand and pulled him to the cot behind the screen Nick had painted with psychedelic flowers. What a waste of paint.

She kissed him and he plowed her hair with his fingers. There was paint on them. She broke the kiss to take off her boots.

"I figured you and Nick would be doing that soon," he said, toeing his way out of his shoes. His breaths were coming quick.

She looked up. "What, getting engaged? We talked about it. Maybe Christmas. We didn't want to steal Joe's thunder. He's the only decent person in the family."

She tucked her fingers into his waistband to unfasten his pants, but it didn't light him up like it should've. "Why are you marrying him? You know I'm crazy about you."

Her fingers were busy. "I'm crazy about you too."

"Do you love him?" He let her pull down his jeans.

She stood. They were nearly the same height. Her eyes were full of light. "No, I don't love him. He's a kind-hearted fool with no talent and a bad habit of doing everything his daddy wants, and that, not particularly well." She pulled her sweater over her head, the moon and sun of her hair catching on the wool. "He's sweet to me, okay?"

She reached behind her back to unfasten her bra, beige lace, two shades darker than her breasts. He could see the veins under her skin. "I can manage him unless his father has other ideas, and most of the time Nick amuses me." He could tell she was bored with talking. She crossed her arms under her breasts. The room was cold. "Is that enough truth for one day?"

He slid out of his shirt. "Why did you come to me then?"

"Nicky amuses me. You amaze me." She released her arms, raised them to touch his shoulders. "I'll marry Nicky because he's rich. And then I'll buy your paintings."

He didn't ask any more questions.

●●●●

Keith rubbed at a smear on the kitchen table. That had been the last time he'd seen Dana. She and Nick had skipped the engagement routine and married at New Year's. Mr. Collins had bought them a big house, and Nick visited the studio only to give Keith instructions for his runs and to pay him. One time Nick had mentioned that he was going to be a father, grinning about it, all proud. He'd winked and said his father was tickled, had given him and Dana a big chunk of change to furnish their house. He'd said that he didn't have any use for the studio any more, but the rent was paid up until July. Tom could stay until summer if he wanted.

Keith shook his head to clear the memories and went to the studio. Pulling off the drape, he exposed the spider web picture. He'd finished it a couple of days ago, but he stared at it, looking for any changes he might want to make. Kinley hadn't responded to his text. He didn't know how to explain what he'd done and been. Obsessions couldn't be justified. He nodded at the painting. It was done. Dana would want to see it.

BRENDAN

He couldn't remember suffering through a longer day. He wanted to call his mother-in-law to check on Cassie. He wanted to fly to Colorado to help his sister. He wanted to punch his father in the face. And all he could do was help students who'd waited until the day before a research paper was due to come to the library. He directed one to the right database and another to the correct area of the stacks for a book, but mostly he watched the clock.

He hadn't seen Beverly for hours, although she might be lurking in some dark, cobwebby corner waiting to catch him goofing off. He didn't care. He researched Cincinnati's divorce lawyers and made an appointment with one for next week. He'd hesitated for about a minute before he'd made the call but figured there was no sense in trying to reconcile with a woman who'd run off on a cruise with her lover.

Finally his workday ended, and he drove home. He pulled into his garage and went into the house, wary now that Dad's warnings had been proved valid. Nothing. That was the trouble. His house held nothing. Calling Rhonda made him feel a little better because she talked about Cassie. Come hell or high water he was holding onto his daughter. Cassie was fine. She'd spent the day with Grandpa Dean. Everything was fine, Rhonda said. But it wasn't.

"What happens when they get back?" he asked. "Did Megan say?"

"I'm not sure." Brendan could imagine the woman squirming.

"What about Cassie?" His head was pounding. "Is Megan picking her up or are you going to keep her after they get back?"

"Oh, I couldn't do that." This came out before Rhonda could think about it. "I mean, I love her, but I'm having to take vacation days and so's Dean and. . . ." Her voice faded.

"Okay. I just wanted to get an idea. You sure you don't want me to come up and get her?" He didn't know how he'd manage. Things were already sticky enough at the library, but there were day cares. He'd manage.

"No, we're set for now. Don't worry."

Of course not. Why should he worry about the crap that was tearing up his life? As he was changing out of his work clothes, he decided to put on his running gear and do a quick one. He'd run that morning, but he'd go again. Anything to rid himself of this dread enveloping him like poisonous gas. The conversation with his father had been odd, almost like he was saying good-bye forever. An oral suicide note. A good son would drive over and talk to his dad, get the truth out of him, find a way to resolve things less dramatically. Brendan shook his head. He couldn't believe the inveterate survivor would give up that easily. He probably was getting ready to hide again. Not for the first time, Brendan felt a sudden spark of anger that his mother had died and left them. He took a deep breath. Unfair. Ignoble. He tied his shoes.

Chapter Twenty Two

KINLEY

By early afternoon, Michael had been awake for a while and seemed lucid. She leaned against his bed. He was so banged up she was afraid to touch him. "Did you talk to your parents yet?" she asked.

"No. The people down in Emergency called them for me. Guess I lost my phone. Burned up." He coughed.

She reached for the water pitcher but he shook his head. "You've got more of your belongings than Sarah and I. You'd packed up nearly everything for the trip to Michigan, remember?"

"Yeah. That's right." He frowned. "You lost everything?"

"I got out with my phone, purse, sketchbook, and canvas." There might be something in the rubble, but she doubted it.

"Damn. I'm sorry. You loved that house." It was a whisper. Talking wasn't good for him. He was getting paler by the minute, but she couldn't resist keeping him awake a little longer.

She asked, "Your throat hurt?" His eyes had started darting around like he was agitated. Kinley straightened up. "What, Michael?"

"Sick," he murmured and started vomiting. She fumbled for the pan hospitals always kept nearby and tried to hold his head up at the same time. He didn't need to choke. Very little of it went in the pan; a lot ended up on Kinley.

"I'll get a nurse," she told him. "Don't worry."

Handing Kinley a wad of paper towels, the nurse said she'd see to Michael. He was due for a pain shot anyway; maybe Kinley should leave and let him rest a while. She was probably right. Kinley limped down the long hall. She'd have to get clothes for sure now, and it was better for Michael if she left him alone anyway. In more ways than one, she realized. Being around her was dangerous.

She got a taxi to her house that was no longer a house. She shaded her eyes against bold sunshine and looked at the wreckage. One of the upstairs bathtubs stood on its end. A few bits and pieces were recognizable. Otherwise, charred garbage. Borrowing a broom from one of the gray house tenants, she swept ash off her car, wondering if it would start. It smelled of fire. She smelled of fire and puke. She drove farther than she had to, all the way into Broomfield to a mega-mall where she could fade into its vastness. She bought jeans, shirts, underwear and socks. It was hell trying on shoes, but she made herself do it. Somehow she had to summon up the energy to talk to the police in a couple of hours, and she'd have to add more lies to the mountain of untruths she'd built over the years because of her father.

Brendan had called on his lunch break and told her that neither Dad nor he knew for sure why she'd been targeted. "We don't know enough to make sense," he'd said. "It's too awkward to explain to the cops, and Dad swears he's going to take care of it. You don't know anything, Sis. Really."

"How's Dad going to make it stop?"

"I'm not sure, but I think he's going to quit hiding. Be Thomas Vickers."

"Who?"

Then he'd explained about what his friend had discovered in the Ball State archives. It hadn't surprised her. There'd been nothing noble about any of it, nothing of redeeming value like spying for his country or providing evidence for law enforcement officials. Whatever his name, Keith or Tom, her father was at best a liar, but more probably a criminal. And definitely a son of a bitch. She'd said as much to Brendan.

"Yeah." Silence. "You're right."

"What?" she'd asked. "You sound like you feel sorry for him."

"No. Maybe. You know what's probably going to happen if he lets these people find him, don't you?"

She didn't care.

"They'll probably kill him."

She'd closed her eyes. Angry as she was, she couldn't wish him dead. She hadn't known what to say except to tell Brendan to be careful, to keep Cassie and Megan safe. Then he'd told her that Megan had left him, had filed for divorce, and she wished she could have one of the shots they were giving Michael, something to make it all go away.

KEITH

Leon finished the yard and left reluctantly. Keith thought about Nick, about finally meeting him again. He wondered if Nick would actually come or if he'd send one of his henchmen. Opening the dish towel drawer, Keith slid the pistol under some pot holders. He showered, changed clothes, and stared at the food in the refrigerator. He couldn't eat. He'd wait until Dana arrived, whenever that would be. He'd had bags packed and ready in the car for days. He could leave before she got there, just up and disappear. But he wouldn't do that now.

He opened a bottle of wine. Leon had bought white and red. Keith had no idea which Dana preferred. He found wineglasses in the dining room cabinet. Brenda had bought them for company he never allowed. They were dusty. He washed them and filled one halfway with red. He took it into the den and tried to distract himself with a travel show on Thailand. He muted the sound.

Every time the refrigerator switched on, he jumped. He nearly had a heart attack when his phone rang. "I'm here," Dana said. "Outside your gate."

For some reason he looked at the clock. Nine-seventeen. "Okay." He went to the front hall to disarm the security system and listen for her. The hallway was dark, but he didn't want a light. He unlocked the front door but didn't open it.

She tapped on the door rather than ringing the bell. That seemed right; she was expected even though he didn't know what to expect. Would she be alone? He hadn't bothered to peer out the kitchen window to find out. Would she carry a gun? He gripped the knob and turned it. Damp air blew in around her, and he smelled faint perfume. "Tommy," she said. Her smile was like a memory, familiar but not quite real. She strode into the dark hallway and he followed her, this woman who was, and yet wasn't, Dana.

She turned into the kitchen as if she knew the house and his habits. She sat and gazed at Brenda's prized granite counters, cabinets, copper pot rack. He'd had to spend two weeks at a crummy condo in Florida when they were installed. "Nice," she murmured. Her eyes landed on the open wine bottle. "Could I have some?"

"I have white too," he said. "I didn't know which kind you like."

"Red's fine."

Her hair looked the same, still long and blonde, worn up in a twist at the back of her head. She wasn't quite as slender but neither was he. He willed his hand to quit shaking while he poured and set the glass in front of her. Then he had to go to the den to retrieve his. Awkward, and stupid as well. She could pull a pistol from the huge bag she'd set on the floor and have it ready to fire when he returned.

But she was sitting at the table, quietly sipping her wine when he came back. Her lips were thinner, her chin sharper. Time had sculpted her features to the edge of hardness. He sat across from her. Wrinkles made parentheses at her mouth and etched the skin near her eyes. She'd lost the soft flesh that conceals the cords and tendons of the neck, but her eyes lit up when she looked at him. "So talk," she said.

163

He wasn't sure what to say first. "You said I should be careful, my kids too." His voice wavered a bit, and he hated that. "You were right to warn me. Someone set my daughter's house in Colorado on fire. She, her boyfriend, and a tenant got out, but she lost everything and people were hurt."

Dana clenched her eyes shut. "He said he'd target your children. That's why I tried to see you."

"How did you know? What do you know?"

She took a huge gulp of wine, making him think she wasn't quite as collected as she was acting. "What kind of fool makes enemies of the Collins clan? You'd seen them, knew what they could do. You should've known better."

He waited.

She went on. "It wasn't about the money. You knew that, didn't you? Back then they had more money than God, but the people down in Florida, the ones in Bolivia, they didn't call up and say, 'Our package is late. Has there been some kind of delay?' No, they started their threats immediately. At first old Donald was sure they were cheating him and accused them of it. So he delayed another cash run. Roughed some people up. Because his boy Nick trusted you, he trusted you. But you disappeared. He tried sending money, but by then it was too late. They wanted more than money." She shook her head, and the crystals in her necklace flashed drops of light onto the table. "They shot Joe."

He took a deep breath. "I know. I hated it." So far she hadn't told him anything he hadn't figured out on his own.

"Such a shame. Joe wasn't stupid. He knew his father's business was more than real estate, but he kept his nose clean as much as anybody could in that family." She held up her glass, and he stood to get more for her. "Did you ever meet him?"

He handed her the filled glass. "He bought one of my paintings."

"I'd forgotten. Yes, he hung it in his living room. Nick cut it up with a razor after Joe died." Her jaw tightened. "I tried to save it. Told Nick it was like burning money, but he didn't listen to me. He rarely did after the first few weeks we were married."

"It didn't matter." He finally took a tiny sip. "You and Nick divorced?"

"Oh yeah. Long time ago."

She closed up then, drank more wine, stared at the shuttered kitchen window. She hadn't answered his questions yet.

"Did you ever get tired of running? Hiding?" she asked.

"Yes."

"What did your wife think about it?"

He didn't know. Brenda had sometimes lost patience with his reclusive ways, especially when they affected the children, but she hadn't questioned him much. "I guess she got used to it," he said.

Dana made a little noise back in her throat. "I haven't eaten in hours," she said.

He jumped up and started pulling cheeses and meats from the refrigerator, bread and crackers from the pantry. He felt her eyes on him for a minute, and then she stood too, using some sort of sure-handed radar for locating plates and silverware. He arranged food on a platter and broke open a bag of chips.

She sat and unfolded the paper napkin he gave her. There were cloth ones somewhere; Brenda preferred cloth. "Did you ever go back to the farm?" Dana asked. He supposed she had questions of her own but was surprised that she cared enough to ask them.

"No. Never."

"Your parents?"

"I didn't know anything for years, but then the Internet came along."

"Made it harder to keep secrets, didn't it?"

He nodded. "I found out they both were dead. Within ten months of each other. My brother Darryl sold the farm."

She folded up a slice of ham. "Did that make you sad?"

He shrugged. "I'd left them a long time ago."

"You're good at that, aren't you?"

He kept quiet, plucking a pickle from the platter. Sour juice flooded his mouth.

"Did you Google me?"

"Yes. Couldn't find a thing."

She lifted her wine again. "I bet you looked for Dana Collins."

He nodded.

"I've used my maiden name for everything from the start, even when Nick bankrolled my first gallery. For my articles I used my initials: D. K. Oliver."

"Oh." It didn't matter. "So you got what you wanted."

"Like you, Tommy, I did. I have a small, select gallery in Boston. I've established myself as an expert on contemporary works. And to do it I used Collins money. We have a lot in common."

It was said with bitter irony more than any kind of pride. He forced himself to eat a few bites. Reaching for the chocolates, he opened the box and put it where she could reach it.

"Lovely," she said.

The kitchen was silent. She continued to eat steadily, her fingers picking pieces from the platter, then the candy box. Finally she crumpled her napkin and reached into her bag. He felt sure now that it wasn't for a gun. She held up cigarettes and a lighter. "I'll go outside," she said.

He shook his head. "You don't have to. I smoke sometimes."

"I'd rather get some air," she said.

She glanced around the studio as they walked through it to the dark patio, lights from the house illuminating only a spot here and there. He smelled the fresh-mown grass. She offered her pack to him and he took one, watching the curve of her cheek in the lighter's flare. "Much better," she said on an exhalation.

They stood on the rough stones, and he felt the night air creeping up his pants. It was late. Would she stay the night? She'd brought in only that huge coppery bag.

"Devonie and I are friends," she said. "We help each other find pieces for our clients." Dana looked down the yard to the shadowy trees, just filled out. "I interviewed her about you. You have her well-trained. She said very little."

He flicked ash toward the boxwoods. "She knows very little."

"We're your original fan club. We wouldn't do anything to impede your art."

He shook his head but wasn't sure she could see it in the dark.

She touched his hand, the first time their skin had made contact. "You have to know you're magnificent. All the potential I saw back in that squalid studio has bloomed beyond anyone's expectations." Her voice was different now, younger, higher. "You had to free yourself to paint. I just wish you'd done it a different way."

He tossed his cigarette to the ground. "I didn't think it through. I didn't consider the consequences." He took a deep breath. "And I did it before I knew my work would be any good at all."

"Yes, you did," she murmured. "You always knew."

"You act like you think it was worth it. My children wouldn't agree. Joe either." He heard his voice go hard. She'd moved close enough that he could see dots of light reflected in her eyes.

She leaned toward him and brushed his lips with hers. He didn't move, and she stepped back and shivered. "I was so angry when you left. Not for Nick and his father, not even for Joe. For me. I wanted to see the paintings as you did them. Do you have any paintings here? Is there anything I can see?"

"Just one. I've sent everything else to Devonie."

166

She took her time with the spider web painting, making him turn on all the studio lights, pacing back and forth in front of the easel, praising, analyzing. Then she announced that she was tired; they'd talk more in the morning. Following him up the steps, she ignored the other bedrooms and joined him, hesitating only for a minute and asking, "Is this okay?" It was more than okay. Their silent coupling seemed like a dream he'd tried to remember.

After she slept, his mind churned with the questions she hadn't answered. He was counting on her for a solution, but maybe this was all there was. They'd enjoy a little time together, and then he'd call Nick Collins and offer himself as ransom for his children. If only he could be sure it would be enough.

In the morning he was able to sneak out of bed without waking her. He made coffee and cleaned up the mess they hadn't bothered with last night. He ate two chocolates with his coffee instead of oatmeal. He checked the security system. Not that it mattered any more. An hour later Dana breezed into the kitchen, poured coffee, and waved away his offer of breakfast. She carried towels outside to dry the wrought iron chairs and took her coffee to the patio. "Winters are long in Boston," she said. "I'm loving the spring weather here."

He gave her time to sip and smoke and say inconsequential things about the shrubs and flowers. The diluted light wasn't kind to her. She'd pulled her hair back into a low ponytail and wore no makeup. She looked plain, ordinary. He wanted to paint her like that. He said as much and she glowered at him. "You can do better," she said.

"Did you ever paint after college?" he asked. "You were at the Institute, so you must've done it while you were there."

"They made art history majors do studio classes their first year," she said. "I could draw fairly well and had fun throwing a few pots and decorating them, but I painted as little as I could."

"You just loved art."

"And artists." She smiled and didn't look plain at all. "No, seriously, art history required more writing and critical skills than artistic ones."

"Things I would've hated." He took another one of her cigarettes. "Those classes would've been good for me," he said, knowing that he was talking about everything but what he should.

"No, they wouldn't," she said. "Classes would've clipped your wings." She stood. "At one point, when you'd been living at the studio for a while, Nick was ready to kick you out. He wanted the place to himself. For me mostly. It was while Joe was living with him at the apartment." She smiled. "I told Nick I'd break up with him if he made you leave. That unfettered painting was what you needed, not classes."

"How did you know?"

"Know what?"

"Know that I had potential."

"I'm good, Tommy. I can recognize talent. Is there more coffee?"

They both were ignoring the larger issues. He asked about her gallery. She asked about the pieces he'd recently sent to Devonie. When they went inside, Dana wandered through the house, admiring this and that although he doubted that Brenda's taste was in any way similar to hers. He could picture her liking elegant, European antiques or stark, modern furniture. "Don't you have any photos of your wife and children?" she asked.

He looked away.

"God, Tommy. You've paid."

"Not as much as Brenda and the kids," he said. "I thought I was protecting them, but I never knew how to stop hiding, how to make things normal." He'd lied so long, the truth felt foreign.

She touched his cheek. "Did you love her?"

"Not at first."

"And later?"

"With all my heart."

Dana slid her fingers down to his lips. "I'm glad. She deserved it."

"Yes." He caught her finger between his teeth. It was an obvious question, no longer important, perhaps, but he wanted it answered nearly as much as the ones they were avoiding. "Did you ever love me?"

She turned saucy then, fluttering her eyelashes and looking away. "Madly." She shook her head and met his eyes. "I loved standing close to your art."

Near noon Brendan called, and Dana went outside where Leon was mulching the flowerbeds. "Are you all right?" he asked Brendan.

"Yeah. I locked up tight last night. No problems. I just talked to Kinley and thought you might want to hear how she's doing."

"More than anything."

"She talked to the police, said she had no idea who'd want to burn her house down. She's been in touch with her insurance company, and they've arranged to have someone clear the debris."

"Good. Michael?"

"He's still in the hospital, but he's up and moving around a little. Kinley's met his parents. Said they were sweet to her, but they're anxious to take him home." Brendan's voice had about as much expression as a newscaster.

"When will they do that?"

"Kin didn't know, but they're making plans. His mother is going to fly with him while his dad drives his car to Michigan." His voice had turned dark by the end of the sentence. "She says she won't marry him now. She's afraid he'll get hurt because of her."

Keith shut his eyes. His reticence had to end. "Has she told him yet?"

"No. She says she can't do it while he's so weak."

"Try to persuade her to wait," he said. "I'd hate for her to be too hasty."

"Is something in the works, Dad? Because Kinley and I need to know what's going on. This isn't just you anymore."

"It's in the works. That's all I can tell you right now."

Chapter Twenty Three

KINLEY

Michael's parents were all but camping in his room. Both were jolly, anxious, and a little loud, but Michael seemed glad to have them there. Although they'd been nothing but kind and expressed how happy they were that she was joining the family, Kinley felt like an interloper. And a liar. She wouldn't be joining the Belli family. She couldn't chance it. Michael was too sick to notice her discomfort. He gave the same wan smiles to all of them. She'd taken care of business most of the morning and popped in to see him around noon, but she didn't stay long. To tell the truth, she could hardly look at his damaged body without remorse choking her.

And fear, for that matter. She felt as though everything she touched was at risk. After leaving the hospital, she drove to the gray house to check on her tenants. What if the arsonist returned to torch her other properties too? Dad's enemies were well-informed. They probably knew she owned other houses. She knocked on doors. Finals were this week; both downstairs apartments would be empty soon. She would offer to pay for hotel rooms for the two girls who lived on the right and the guy on the left whose windows must have glared with fire on Wednesday night. The girls took her up on it and started packing. She had to use her key to get into the other one and found it dirty but empty. When she called the tenant, he said he was crashing with a friend. All things considered, would he still get his deposit back if he didn't clean the place? She told him yes. It was the same story with one of the tenants upstairs. Kinley agreed to everything.

Outside, she surveyed the war zone that had been her beloved yellow house. She could sell the lot, she supposed. Even though she wouldn't be moving to Cincinnati, she didn't want to rebuild. She didn't know what she wanted to do. She felt like she'd fallen off a mountain. A shuddery sigh spread through her body.

From across the street she heard the neighbor lady calling her name. She turned. The woman was struggling with Kinley's canvas and sketchbook along with a large tote bag. Behind her came the husband, carrying something tall and wooden. "Are you ready to have these back?" the woman asked.

Kinley met them at the curb. Not really, but she nodded. "Thanks so much." She was always on the edge of tears these days.

"Your work is wonderful." The woman nudged her husband. "Show her, Bill."

Bill set the end of his leggy burden on the asphalt. "I thought you probably lost your easel in the fire," he said, shrugging. "I like to work with wood." He unfolded an easel, large, well-balanced. It was a beautiful tool.

The tears did come then. "I don't know what to say," she choked out.

Bill said, "We hope you'll stay in the neighborhood. Somehow or the other." His wife set the tote bag at Kinley's feet. "And we've been cooking. Some cookies. Mac and cheese. Soup. Maybe you've got a microwave and refrigerator where you're staying?" They both had anxious smiles.

Spilling tears onto their shoulders, Kinley thanked and hugged each of them. Her hotel room had neither a microwave nor a refrigerator, but she knew where to find both, along with space for the easel and light enough to use it, if she could still paint, if her hands were steady enough. Without thinking any more about it, she headed toward the downstairs apartment the guy had abandoned, her neighbors following to help carry what they'd given her. She'd need to buy a bed and at least a table and a couple of chairs. Bunches of cleaning supplies. Towels and sheets. It wouldn't be much more than subsistence living, but at least she'd have a home until things were sorted out. She could hit the art supply store after she checked on her tenants in the brick house. Then she'd walk down the long hospital corridor to see Michael again. He had no idea how much he was breaking her heart.

BRENDAN

At quitting time on Friday afternoon, Beverly marched into his office, dangled a sheet of paper from her fingertips, and barked, "Finals week work schedule." She let go of the paper and was out the door before it floated onto his desk.

During exams the library was open until midnight with various employees sharing the longer hours. Nobody wanted the late shift, but they all did their one night with good grace. It was just the way it was. Brendan looked down at the sheet and blinked twice before anger grabbed him by the throat. She'd scheduled him for three of the five late shifts. He reared out of his chair to find her, but she'd already left. When he passed the circulation desk, the librarian there gave him a cheerful wave. "Nice of you to take on so much of the finals schedule. You know I always feel out of my comfort zone over there in reference."

He nodded at the woman and strode towards his office. Beverly was punishing him again. Still. He almost walked into Hannah who was leaning against his office door. "I was afraid you'd already gone," she said. Her smile wavered. "How's your sister?"

"Okay. As okay as she can be right now, I guess." Her presence took his anger down to a simmer, but he knew his expression must be dreadful. He'd called her the night before, told her his troubles. All of them, except for his father. She'd been sweet. The sympathy had felt good. "Sorry. I just got the shaft again from my boss. Nothing to do with you."

"The world's really dumping on you these days, isn't it?" Such a soft voice.

"Yeah. I'm the universal dumpee." He smiled at her. "What can I do for you?"

She gave a little shrug that moved her hair across her shoulder. "Nothing. It's Friday. I'm done with classes forever, or at least until grad school. I thought maybe you might like to have somebody to eat dinner with."

For a second he felt like Kinley, wondering if dire circumstances would descend upon anyone he associated with, but that was insane. There had to be a difference between caution and paranoia. "Sure. Seems like you'd want someone more cheerful to celebrate with, though."

She'd picked up on his hesitation. "Just dinner," she said. "Things are still too complicated for you."

He grabbed his bag. "You have no idea how complicated everything is."

Just walking with Hannah helped his mood. He felt even better when they went outside into warm sunshine. "It's like it just turned spring," he said.

"It did, didn't it?" They crossed the campus plaza, nearly the only people stirring at that time of day. "Where do you want to go?" she asked.

They settled on a beer and burger pub down near the river. It was early for the restaurant's usual crowd, so they grabbed a booth near a window with a view of the Ohio's muddy water. They ordered beers and Brendan drained nearly half of his the minute it arrived. "So, are you doing commencement?" He didn't want to talk about Megan.

She wrinkled her nose. "My parents want me to, but I'd rather get out of here. My last exam is on Wednesday. I figure I'll leave that afternoon." She fumbled in the pocket of her jeans and pulled out a crumpled slip of paper. "No pressure," she said, "but here's my email and address in Columbus."

He took the paper. "Thanks. I have no idea what the next few weeks will bring." That was an understatement. "The divorce. Custody."

"My father got custody of us, my brothers and me. It worked out better than most people thought it would." She gazed out the window. "My mother's sort of a mess."

"I'm going to try for it. Megan's not exactly a mess, but I wonder how much her rich boyfriend will want a toddler hanging around."

Hannah nodded. "It'll be tough with your job, but my dad managed. My younger brother was only three."

My job, Brendan thought. Now there was something else to complain about, and he did. Poor Hannah. He relayed, in detail, all the frustrations of the job and his supervisor. "When my mother was dying and I was at hospice a lot, the head of reference must've been bad-mouthing me all the time."

"Is that the woman with the really short dark hair who always look like her feet hurt?"

He chuckled. "Yes." He ordered another beer for himself. Hannah shook her head. "One day when I called in, another librarian said that my supervisor had said, 'Isn't that woman dead yet?' Can you believe that?"

"No. God."

He was whining and knew it, but she was so easy to talk to, so sympathetic that he found himself telling her more about Kinley's fire, about Kinley's boyfriend, and it went on through his second beer and the cheeseburger that followed. "I'm sorry. I shouldn't be talking so much about myself," he said.

"I don't mind." She wiped her mouth, a pretty mouth that turned up at the corners even when she wasn't smiling. "You have every reason to be unhappy."

"Still."

She tilted her head until the sun lit up copper hints in her hair. "What would make you happy?" she asked.

There was no blatant seduction in it this time, but it was attractive. He thought for minute, gave the question the consideration he thought she intended. "I'd like to quit my job, go out to Colorado to help my sister, and then I'd like to come back here and fight to get my daughter." It was true. Every word of it.

If she'd been hoping that he'd say something about her, there was no indication of it. She gave him a bright smile. "Sounds good, except it might be difficult to get custody if you're unemployed."

He shrugged. "Oh, I'd get another job."

"Like what?"

"Maybe corporate research." It was easy to return her smile. "You know what I've always wanted to do? Be a fact checker for a news magazine or television network. Something like that." He felt his cheeks reddening. It sounded silly. "Or I could work in a book store. Anything."

"Then you should do it," she said, squeezing his hand. "Walk away from the university, go see your sister, and start putting out your resumé. Why not?"

"Money, for one thing."

Her nose crinkled. "Overrated. You can manage. Sell some stuff."

It was crazy, but she made him think it was possible. When they left and went back to their cars, he kissed her. It was brief and didn't promise a whole lot, but it made Hannah smile. "Good luck on your exams," he said. "I'll call you. Really."

Her smile stayed with him through the Friday evening traffic, all the way to his silent house where he felt tension creeping over him again. He wanted to call his father to ask exactly what he was doing about this mess. He also wanted to call Kinley, but he did neither. He locked his doors and brought a pry bar up from the basement. It sat next to him on the sofa while he watched ridiculous shows on TV. When he couldn't tolerate any more of the nonsense, he carried the heavy iron to his bedroom and tried not to feel absurd about it. He doubted that he'd sleep, but he would run again in the morning and that would make everything better for a little while. Like Hannah did.

Chapter Twenty Four

KEITH

Somehow the entire morning passed before he was able to pin Dana down to ask questions. She changed the subject, found something to do, or just avoided answering him. At noon, they made sandwiches, and Dana insisted that they take their lunches outside to sit in the sunshine. It was the kind of day when Brenda would've fluttered through the house like a trapped wren, opening shades and windows, and pleading that it was just for a little while, just to get a little fresh air into the house. Keith ate one bite of his sandwich and put it down. "Okay, I've waited long enough. How did you find me? And how long ago? And how can I protect my children from Nick?"

Dana lowered the chip she'd lifted and clenched her hands into a double fist against the table. "I found out that Tommy Vickers had turned into Keith Owen years ago, after I'd divorced Nick and opened my first gallery in New York. I got to know Devonie and saw your paintings. It didn't matter what the signature said, I knew they were yours."

"How?"

"Oh, come on, Tommy. I'd studied your work for quite some time back in Chicago. I recognized the brushwork, the techniques. You'd changed your subjects, become less abstract, but I knew the style. Remember that still life you did for Nick so he could convince his father that he was working? Joe wasn't the only one to figure out that it was yours. I'm good at this."

She unclasped her hands. "Devonie told me you lived in Cincinnati. She's never made a secret of that, nor that you were married and had two children. I did nothing about it for years, not until this past January when Donald Collins died."

"Why then?" He could hear Leon rolling a wheelbarrow on the driveway around front. It seemed such a common, everyday sound against Dana's revelations. Leon had left them alone, steered clear, but Keith knew he was being vigilant.

"Because then Nick had a real reason to search for you, and it wasn't for a happy reunion." She lifted her shoulders. "Mr. Collins looked for you after you stole the money. I told you that. But he eventually gave up and took it out on Nick. He thought Nick was a fool. He blamed Nick for botching the operation by hiring someone he shouldn't have trusted. Ultimately, he blamed Nick for Joe's murder."

Keith cringed at the word *murder*, but it was the right one and he, not Nick, bore the burden of it.

"Donald's disgust with Nick never let up. Instead of letting Nick take over the tasks Joe had done or training him for some other aspect of the business, Donald washed his hands of him. Nick was little more than a flunky, driving his father places, running errands that the little people had usually done. It drove Nick crazy. It drained all the sweetness out of him. And there was sweetness; you know there was. After his father turned on him, Nick hardly drew a sober breath. Either booze or coke. Sometimes both." She shrugged. "It wasn't pretty. After four years of marriage, I left. And Donald thought even that was no more than what Nick deserved. He settled a nice sum of money on me. And it was Donald who sent hefty child support checks every month."

"How many children did you have?"

"Just the one. Vincent. And no, he was named for Donald's father, not Van Gogh." Her mouth creased into a brief smile. "Eat something, Tommy. You need it."

She bit into her sandwich and motioned for him to do the same. He shook his head.

After a few more bites, Dana pushed her plate away and lit a cigarette, blowing the smoke away from Keith. "Donald loved Vincent. Only grandchild. He used to come see him at least once a month, first in New York and then when we moved to Boston. He would take him to parks, movies, buy him ice cream and toys. Donald did many horrible things in his life, but he was good to Vincent. And me, for that matter."

"Did Nick ever come see his son?"

She shook her head and sculpted her cigarette's ash against the ashtray. He smelled the pungent, earthy scent of the mulch Leon had spread. It reminded him of his father's pastures.

Dana started again, looking down now at the edge of the table. "So Donald died in January and when they read the will, Nick freaked out all over again. Or maybe still. I had very little contact with him during those years. All I heard was what Donald told me from time to time. Nick had remarried and lived out in the suburbs. Donald said he gave him enough for a down payment. But the will was a shocker. Donald left Nick nothing. Cut him out completely. It was punishment, pure and simple. Donald never forgot."

"Who inherited the bulk of it? Mrs. Collins?"

"No. She died years ago." Dana looked up to meet Keith's eyes. "Vincent did. He's a very wealthy young man."

Keith felt dull, like his brain was slogging through molasses. "That's good, though, isn't it? For Vincent?"

"Sure," she said. "He's a good kid, man now." She smiled like a mother. "He's invested the money wisely and works full time at administrating the properties, all legal now, entirely legal. Years ago, his grandfather urged him to get a business degree, and he did. Vince knows what he's doing." She frowned. "I'm happy for Vincent. But none of this was good for you, Tommy."

"Because Nick blames me for being cut out of the will."

"Yes. The money of course, but more because of losing his father's affection. For years." She ground out her cigarette and immediately lit another one. "And I'm to blame too." Her voice lowered, became tentative. "I told him I'd slept with you dozens of times. I taunted him with it, described how I was always going to the studio behind his back."

Keith stared at her. She stared back. A trickle of breeze loosened a strand of her hair. "He hit me, Tommy. I wanted to hurt him, so I lied."

Keith stood. He walked away from Dana, heading to the very back of the yard where a buckeye tree spread its massive branches. No wonder Nick hated him. Keith had been the cause of everything bad in the man's life. There was nothing he could do to make up for it, not money, certainly not a simple apology. He was Nick's worst nightmare. Out of somewhere the word *nemesis* flashed into his mind. He craned his neck to gaze at the top of the buckeye. Stooping to pick up a couple of them, he rolled them in his hand like dice, aware of the stiffness in his fingers. He still yearned to paint as long as he could. He wanted to live. But he couldn't see how anything less than his death would satisfy Nick. He threw one of the buckeyes against the tall fence at the back of the yard. It pinged and ricocheted into the grass. Then he threw the other.

When he turned back toward the patio, Dana was gone, along with their uneaten lunches. In a couple of minutes she returned, carrying two glasses and the other bottle of wine. He wondered where Leon had gone. He needed to square everything with him and his children. Soon.

"Thought this might help," she said, pouring the wine.

Keith pulled a cigarette from the pack lying on the table and lit it. "Okay," he said, weariness dragging down the syllables. "After Mr. Collins died, you started searching for me. You knew I was Keith Owen and you knew I was in Cincinnati. How did you figure out where I lived?"

"It took a little while," she said. "When I did the interview, Devonie said that your wife was very sick. Actually she was complaining about how long it'd been since you'd sent her anything. So I read the Cincinnati paper every day on the Internet. I scoured the obituaries. I would never have known Brenda Williams was your wife, but the survivors, your children, had the name Owen. Sick wife, two kids, Owen. I put it together."

The obituary. He'd had a bad feeling about that.

"It also said she was a teacher. It took some research to find the right school, but they all list their faculty on their webpages, so I knew I'd eventually come up with it as long as they hadn't deleted her the minute she passed away." He had to keep remembering that Dana had done all this prying to warn him. And because she felt guilty.

"I called the school and said I was friends with Brenda in college and that I wanted to send a condolence card to the family, but I'd lost her address. They gave it to me without a second's hesitation."

"So why did you think you needed to warn me?" He crushed his cigarette. She'd emptied and cleaned the ashtray.

"I went to Donald's funeral. After all he'd done for Vincent and me, I thought I owed him the respect. After the service Nick came up and asked if I knew where you were. I said no. It was mostly the truth at that point. He said he was going to find you and make you pay. At the time I wondered why he wanted to dredge up ancient history, but I didn't know about Donald's will. Nick did. I'm sure he had it in his hands before Donald was cold. When I found out about it, I knew I had to warn you." Her lipstick was gone, rubbed off on her napkin, wineglass, cigarettes. She looked pale and exhausted. Her hand rested on the table, and he touched it, feeling a tremor in her fingers. "I knew he'd find you somehow, but I didn't tell him where to look, Tommy. I swear it."

"It's odd that he found Kinley but not me."

"I don't know how he found her. I think he knows where you are, but he hasn't managed to get past your gates literally and figuratively. I waited out there for hours before Leon came through."

Maybe Nick had come while Keith was down at the lake or on Leon's days off or something. He supposed it made as much sense as anything. "Do you think he followed the same trail you did?"

She shook her head. "He doesn't know Devonie, but I guess Nick could've figured out that Tom Vickers became Keith Owen. Anyone who knew your early work. . . ." Her voice trailed off for a second. "Beyond that, I'm sure he hired a detective. His business is mostly legit now. According to Vincent, he can't afford all the creeps his father employed."

"Mostly legit? What does he do? Vincent inherited the properties, right?"

"Yes. But Nick owned a couple of restaurants before his father died. There's probably some gambling. Vince thinks so. And Nick has a few rental houses. Nothing big, but his wife isn't clipping coupons."

She'd meant to make him smile, but he was thinking too hard about what she'd said. "Yeah, probably a detective," he murmured. "But he hired somebody not so legit to set my daughter's house on fire."

She closed her eyes for a second. "True. God. I don't know everything."

He didn't suppose she did. Keith's fingers tightened around the wineglass. "You have his number?"

Dana nodded. "For emergencies. For Vincent. Do you want me to call? Maybe I could calm him down. I used to be pretty good at that."

"No." He held out his hand.

She reached into the pocket of her slacks, pulled out her phone, scrolled, and then clicked. "You're sure?" she asked. "You could hide somewhere else."

"No," he said again and took the phone from her. It was warm from her body. She stood and walked toward the house, leaving him alone and in the open.

Keith recognized Nick's voice say, "Dana?" Caller ID of course.

"Tom Vickers," Keith said. "It's time to talk, Nick. I'll give you whatever you want, but you're going to leave my kids alone."

Silence. "You son of a bitch." Nick's words were as quiet as a prayer.

Keith said, "We'll talk when you get here." He gave him his address even though he figured Nick already had it.

"Not so fast," Nick said. "You feeling the heat a little, Farm Boy?"

Anger choked off Keith's voice.

"I hear that she got out alive. Just a little singed around the edges. Lucky girl," Nick drawled.

He wanted to kill him. He wanted to torture the skinny asshole until his fingernails hurt. But he didn't say anything.

Nick knew what he was thinking. "I don't feel real comfortable talking on your turf. We'll meet someplace. I'll call you back. Is Dana there?"

"Yes."

"How sweet." He cut the connection.

Sweat trickled down Keith's back. A hammer pounded inside his skull. He had the stray thought that he might be having a stroke or maybe a heart attack. He took a deep breath and set the phone on the table.

●●●●

"Neither of us ate lunch," Dana said. She added mushrooms to chicken sizzling in a frying pan. "This will be good, really. You have to eat."

179

Nick had called back three hours after Keith phoned him. At first he whined about having to travel from Chicago to Cincinnati. Then he'd said they'd meet the next night at the bandshell in Devou Park, over in Kentucky. Midnight. Keith had argued, saying he never left the house. "Too bad," Nick had crooned. "I'll get your boy next time." Keith had said he'd be there. "Alone," Nick had said. Keith had asked if Nick would be alone. He'd laughed, if you could call the eerie, baying noise he'd uttered a laugh.

"I'll eat. What can I do to help?"

"Cut up a salad."

All afternoon they'd talked about it. Dana wanted to go with him; he said she absolutely would not. As much as he loved having her there, he'd prefer it if she went back to Boston tomorrow morning. She said she absolutely would not. He opened the refrigerator and found the lettuce, tomatoes, carrots.

"Do you know where this park is?" Dana asked.

"Yeah. Brenda and I went there a couple of times before we married."

Dana quit stirring. "Do you think Nick knows that?"

"I don't see how. He probably found it on a map. It's isolated. The roads getting up to it are narrow and twisty. That's what he wants." He had to get the cutting board out of the dishwasher. It was clean but still wet. He opened the drawer to get a dish towel and Dana saw his pistol. She raised an eyebrow.

"You're taking that with you, aren't you?"

Keith shook his head.

"Do you want to die?"

The chef's knife bit into the head of lettuce. It felt good. "No, but I don't expect to get a chance to shoot."

Dana gave the chicken a vicious stir and lifted the lid on the rice. "Oh, he'll want to talk first. Nick loves confrontation. He'll want to yell and scream and accuse you of everything from sabotaging his fine career in crime to killing the Kennedys. That's his way." She slammed the lid back on the pot. "And then he'll shoot you."

He put a fistful of lettuce in each bowl. "I have a plan."

"Okay."

"First I'll apologize for taking the money." Keith looked over at her. The stove had flushed her cheeks a subtle pink. He wondered what tints he'd need to reproduce the color. "Were you ever tempted?" he asked. "On the runs you made, did you ever think about taking the money?"

"Of course I thought about it." She poured some wine into the skillet and a little into her glass. She'd been drinking all afternoon, but it didn't show. "The first time or two, I thought I was sending a box of drugs and I was scared as hell." She laughed. "Pretty stupid, huh? But when Nick told me it was cash, yeah, I was tempted. I just figured I'd end up with more if I married the jerk."

"You didn't think he was a jerk back then." He peeled a carrot.

"No, you're right. I thought he was sweet. Silly and sweet and all kinds of rich." She shook her head. "So you're going to apologize for taking the money. Fat lot of good that's going to do you."

"I've put $250,000 in a duffel bag I'm going to give him. That's more than twice what I took." He used the peeler to shave off strips of carrot, taking care to make them thin and consistent.

"If you think money will satisfy Nick, you're crazy."

"I don't think it will either, but it'll give him something to consider." He rinsed the peeler and chose a knife for the tomato. "Then I'm going to remind him that his father killed Joe by dicking around with the Bolivians. He should've sent that money right off and figured out what the problem was later. Nick didn't do it, and I didn't do it. I'm sorry about Joe," he looked up at Dana. "But that wasn't my fault." She nodded. "And I slept with you twice. He may not believe me, but it's the truth."

He held her eyes until she looked away.

"And then, I'm going to bluff," he said.

"How?"

Keith paused and took a drink of his wine. He liked whiskey, even beer, better. Until this weekend, he hadn't drunk wine since Chicago. "I'm going to say the guy he hired to torch Kinley's house cut himself on the can of gasoline he used. He bled enough for them to get his DNA. I'm going to tell Nick that I've sent a letter to my lawyer saying as much and telling the cops where to look for the arsonist. To be opened in the event of my death. Or if anything happens to my kids."

"Is it true?"

"No."

●●●●

Everything took on a new clarity. Keith remembered the arty group at the bar in Chicago debating what they'd do if they had twenty-four hours to live. He hadn't contributed; he rarely did. Most had said they'd fly somewhere exotic which had struck him as stupid—why waste those hours in an airplane? Others had said they'd paint the whole time. That he'd understood. But when the hypothetical became real, he didn't paint at all.

After dinner, he asked Dana to give him an hour or so alone, and he wrote short, painful letters to Kinley, Brendan, and Leon. He'd already told

Leon to take tomorrow off. He emailed instructions to Devonie and his bankers. Afterwards, he went downstairs to fill a duffel bag with money. While he had the safe open, he cleared out his important papers and stuffed them in a large envelope. He started to hide these under the spare tire in his car and reconsidered. Nick might search it, and he would know all the hiding places. If the papers were going to be any use to him, he'd be alive and able to come back to his house. Maybe. He hid them underneath the lawnmower and put the duffel in the passenger seat. The bag he'd packed days ago for running tempted him, but he slammed the car door shut and went inside.

He ran his fingers over the cool, smooth granite. He sniffed the lingering garlic from Dana's cooking. He absorbed the color of the dark cabinets, his eyes flickering down to the top drawer near the sink, the dishtowel drawer. Over dinner Dana had asked, "Why don't you just shoot him, Tommy? That would end it for sure."

Her face had been earnest, not cruel. "I can't do that," he'd said.

"Then call the police, come clean. Tell them about the arson." He'd never seen Dana plead for anything.

"I can't prove anything," he'd answered. "They might prevent Nick from doing something tomorrow night, but it wouldn't keep him from trying something else."

She'd covered her face with her hands for at least a minute. Then she'd asked again, "Do you want to die?"

Maybe he did.

Chapter Twenty Five

BRENDAN

Saturday morning he decided to run farther than he usually did. God knows he had the time. After the first block or so, he felt his legs warm up, and he began to notice the neighborhood and the sky. Dawn broke a bit earlier every morning, and soon it would be daylight when he ran. Yesterday's bright weather had given way to leaden clouds, though, so there was little change from dark to dawn. If he could beat the rain, he needed to mow the lawn today, maybe go to the store. He was looking for things to do.

Once again he'd made it safely through the night. Nobody had come after him. He wondered what his father would, or could, do about the situation. He felt as though he was constantly breaking through cobwebs. Sticky, creepy. His feet pounded the pavement with a satisfying rhythm. He'd mow and then make phone calls—Kinley, Dad, and Rhonda. God, he missed his baby girl. Maybe Hannah, although he didn't want to push it. Keeping busy was the best way to cope with this madness. The sky on his left paled to a lighter gray. No sunrise today. It figured.

The old mower coughed and hacked like a veteran smoker, but he got the grass done by mid-morning. After showering, he called Rhonda. It was the same as every other time. Cassie was fine. They were doing all right. She hadn't heard from Megan and didn't know what would happen when she returned from the cruise. "Next Wednesday?" he asked.

"No, Thursday," Rhonda said. "They have to fly back from Florida."

Kinley had just left the hospital. They'd released Michael, and he was leaving for Michigan that afternoon. She sounded down, and Brendan didn't know of a damned thing he could say to cheer her up. She must've felt the same way about him. "Have you talked to Cassie?" she asked.

"Well, I tried to. She's not much on conversation yet."

"But she recognizes her daddy's voice, doesn't she? That's important."

"I guess."

"I'm so sorry, Brendan, but I never . . ." Her voice wound down.

"You never liked Megan. I know. I was stupid."

"No, not stupid."

He changed the subject. "You didn't say anything to Michael yet, did you?"

"No, I wouldn't do that in front of his parents, and they're always around. Anyway, I want him to feel better before I do it."

"So you'll have to go to Michigan sometime."

He heard her sigh. "I don't want to, but yes. I'm not enough of a jerk to break it off over the phone."

"Maybe a two line text. That would be sensitive." He meant for her to laugh and she did. A little.

"That's how you ought to tell Megan what you think of her," she said.

"Nah, I'm planning to hack one of those computerized interstate signs and type in 'Megan Owen is a world-class bitch.'" He heard a real giggle this time.

"We're a pair," she said.

Of miserable, sorry-assed losers, he thought, but he made his voice upbeat and asked, "So what are you doing? Are you painting?"

"I'm trying. I had to go out and buy everything all over again. My hands are a little shaky, and I cry almost as much as I paint, but I'm trying."

"We don't know how this is going to turn out, Kin. Maybe Dad can make things okay."

"Right." Acid dripped from her voice. "He'll just run again. I'm surprised he hasn't already. I don't understand anything, Brendan."

"I don't either, but hang tight. No trips to Michigan yet, okay?"

She was crying full out. "Okay," she whispered.

Brendan agreed with Kinley. He couldn't imagine what his father could do to fix their problems or if he would do anything at all. Vague assurances didn't cut it. Maybe it was the librarian in him, but he hated when things were unclear and uncertain. God, what if Dad's solution was suicide? He had an arsenal in the house. A good son wouldn't sit on his butt and let that happen. He doubted it but was afraid to ignore the possibility. He called his father.

"Hey, Dad," he said, using the same breezy tone as when he talked to Kinley. "How's it going?"

"Are you all right?" His father's voice was rigid.

"Yeah, sure. Just wondering what you were up to. Thought I might stop by while I'm out this afternoon."

"Stop by? No. That's not a good idea." There was something harsh and peculiar about the way he said the words.

Brendan tried again. "I was going to the store. Wondered if I could pick anything up for you." This was the man who'd begged him to stay a few nights ago.

"No." It was almost a grunt. "Do not come over here."

"Why?"

"I'm painting."

That was a lie. He wouldn't have answered the phone. "Okay, okay. Chill out. I'll talk to you later."

He stood in the living room holding the phone in his palm. Strange, even for Dad. Throwing on a jacket, Brendan picked up his keys and wallet.

KEITH

Saturday afternoon he and Dana pretended to watch television for a while, just like they'd pretended to eat breakfast. They didn't even attempt lunch, although they drank countless cups of coffee. As if they weren't jittery enough, he thought. They had both jumped when Brendan called.

After he got off the phone with Brendan, Keith made Dana pack up her things and put them in her rental car. She argued about it but finally agreed to go to a hotel that night after he left to meet Nick.

While she was gathering her stuff, he went to the basement to get packing materials. During the night, while Dana slept against him and he lay awake thinking of everything he'd done and not done in his life, he remembered his paintings from Chicago. While they picked at their breakfast, he'd asked her about them, and she'd said that Nick took them when Keith disappeared. He figured that Nick had probably destroyed them, but it was no great loss. Many were amateurish. He wanted Dana to have something he'd done, so he decided to give her the spider web painting. He hated that his kids had nothing of his now, but they'd get plenty of cash. Maybe they could buy one of the canvases he'd sent to Devonie. He was setting the packing materials on the table when Dana came back into the kitchen. Opening the door to his studio, Keith inhaled, for the last time, maybe, the scents that had controlled his soul for decades: pigments, turpentine, varnish, gesso. He took the painting to the kitchen. "I want you to have this," he said. "Maybe I should leave it for my kids, but there's just the one." He raised a helpless hand. "The painting I did for Kinley burned up in the fire, and Brendan's wife stole his. If I'm lucky, I'll be able to do others for them." He took a deep breath. "Sell it if you want to. Or need to," he said as an afterthought.

"Never," Dana murmured. "I'll keep it safe."

She took the wrapped painting out to her car and came back to stand behind him, rubbing his shoulders while he sat at the table, staring blindly at the refrigerator. He was glad she was there. She knew him like no one else, certainly not his kids, not even Brenda. She knew him through his art. The kitchen was silent, waiting. Midnight would be slow in coming. And then he heard something. A car was coming up the driveway.

They both rushed to the window over the sink. He stared between the shutter slats. It was a dark BMW. He didn't know the car. "Brendan?" Dana whispered.

Keith shook his head. It wasn't Leon either. "The gate?" she asked.

"It was locked. I know it was," he said. Only one person was in the car. He gripped the edge of the counter. "Did you close the garage door?"

"Yes."

The passenger got out, and it didn't take Keith but a second to recognize Nick. He seemed shorter, smaller, and much older, older than Keith and Dana looked, but it was Nick. He'd tricked them. Dana shifted to the left, moved away, but Keith couldn't take his eyes from the window.

"Are you going to let him in?" she whispered.

Yes, no. He wasn't sure. Keith waited for the doorbell or a fist thudding against the front door, but he heard the smooth snick of a key unlocking the front door. He left Dana standing at the sink and rushed to the hall.

Nick kicked the door shut behind him. He was smiling but it looked more like a skull's grin than friendliness. "My guy went to a lot of trouble, breaking into your son's house and making an impression of this baby." He held up the key in his left hand. There was a gun in his right. "But seeing you two freak out was worth it." He dropped the key on the floor. Waving the pistol at Keith, he said, "Disarm the system. Now."

Keith did. His fingers twitched.

"By the way, your security system isn't worth a damn. My guy could see the numbers on the pad light up as plain as day when your handyman came to work every morning." Nick looked like he was amused. "Over there." Again he gestured with the gun, pointing Keith toward the door into the kitchen.

Keith was breathing in short little puffs. He glanced at Dana. Pale. Still. He couldn't move. "Do it, Farm Boy," Nick ordered. "And no detours or I'll shoot the bitch. God, I've been wanting to do that for years."

Somehow Keith's feet moved across the room. His stomach churned at the thought of Nick's people breaking into Brendan's house. When had that been? He swallowed the extra spit flooding his mouth.

"When you told me Dana was here, I just had to come over before our rendezvous. Didn't want to miss seeing my lovely wife." Keith didn't remember Nick's voice being so gruff, and he'd never heard him speak with such venom. He was heavily tanned but didn't look healthy. There was a yellowish tint to his eyes. Keith glanced across the room at Dana. Her hands were curled into fists at her sides.

Nick's eyes darted back and forth between the two of them, but he kept the gun pointed at Keith. "You two been renewing your vows or something?" His voice pitched even lower. "Actually, bitch, it turns my stomach just to see your face." At the moment Nick was angled a little toward Dana, making Keith wonder if he had time enough to jump him, but Nick's head veered right back to Keith.

Nick nodded at the door behind Keith. "Is that your studio? A little nicer than the old one, hmm, Farm Boy?" Again, his face twisted into a horrific grin. "So this is where Keith Owen paints his masterpieces. People don't realize that he's just a stupid Indiana farm boy who made it big by stealing." Keith searched for a glimpse of the silly, generous kid he'd known but couldn't find it. "You stupid fuck," Nick said, his voice rising with every word. "Thinking you could outsmart everybody."

Keith kept his face blank, but his heart was pumping fire. He'd grovel. He'd beg. "What can I do to keep you from hurting my children?" he asked. He tried to remember what he'd planned to say that night at the park.

"Not a goddamned thing."

Keith felt sweat trickling down his ribs. "I have money." He tried to keep his eyes off the end of Nick's gun. The hole seemed to get larger by the minute. He'd been wrong. He didn't want to die.

He switched his focus back to Nick's face and could tell that Nick had expected a payoff. "You really think your cash can bring back my brother or the fortune I would've had if my father hadn't blamed all your shit on me?" Spit flew from Nick's mouth.

"I didn't mean for any of that to happen. I was stupid."

"Shut up, dickhead." He glanced at Dana and then back at Keith. "To top it off, you were fucking my girlfriend in the studio I let you use for free." Nick was shouting now. "I took you in. I gave you a place to paint and sleep. And this is how I got repaid?" He wiped his mouth with his empty hand. "Your dirty money won't change a thing. You gotta pay back more than that, Tommy."

"What, Nick? What can I pay?" He'd save the bluff for one more minute, not that it was anything more than useless. Nick had come to kill. He probably considered it a bonus that he could off them both at once. Dana's face was expressionless.

A sly look played around Nick's mouth. "You've started paying," he said. "Although the fire didn't toast your daughter quite as much as I'd hoped."

"Scum," spat Dana as Keith took a step forward. His hands ached to twist Nick's vile head off.

Nick sensed it. "Easy," he drawled, pointing the gun for a second at Dana and then moving it back to Keith. "Let's not get excited."

Dana's head jerked, and Keith caught a glimpse of movement outside the partially shuttered window. Nick followed his glance. "Car coming down the drive. One male." He moved his firearm in a slow arc between them like he was having a hard time choosing who'd be first. "Young guy," he said.

It had to be Brendan.

BRENDAN

The gate was open. That started his nerves jangling, and the strange BMW sitting near the front door made them go into overdrive. He slowed to a crawl. "Drive innocent," he thought, whatever that meant. He pulled way over, onto the grass, turned off the engine and slid out of the car. For some reason he felt leery about the front door. He punched in the code for the garage door and watched it climb. He paused at the door into the kitchen. A man was talking, yelling actually. It wasn't his father.

Brendan opened the door. There were three people in the kitchen: his father standing by the studio door, a woman he didn't know leaning against the sink, and a man standing between the two of them, holding a gun. His back was partially to Brendan, and for a minute he thought about rushing him. The guy was old. His skin looked like a prune. The minute passed.

"Come in, Brendan. Shut the door," the old guy said over his shoulder. Brendan didn't move. "Now," he ordered, "and don't make any quick moves or Daddy gets shot."

Brendan did as he was told. His dad's face was white, pained. It was like he was trying to tell him something, to run probably, but the pruney guy was sidling over toward the woman and swiveling the gun between the three of them.

"Move over to the table." He said this to the woman who glanced at Dad and then slowly shuffled toward that corner of the room, walking backwards so she could keep her eyes on the gun, pointed at her now. "Not that one," he said. "The corner chair. Move your ass, Dana." She was awkward with it, sort of hitching up her hip as she sat.

So, this was the mysterious Dana. She was okay, he thought. Brendan saw what the old guy was doing by moving her; this way he could keep everybody in view, at least peripherally.

"Let him go, Nick," Dad said. "He's done nothing to you."

And the old guy was Nick, whoever the hell Nick was. He had a wolf's grin and was definitely not okay. He spoke. "No, this is perfect. More than I could've hoped for." His dark eyes jumped over to Brendan. "Pass my thanks to your stupid wife, Brendan. She fell for my man's con and gave us your sister's address in Boulder. Much appreciated."

He felt his face go hot. "You son of a bitch." The guy ignored him.

"You like to run, don't you? Quite the athlete. Of course if you run just now I'll shoot you in the back." The bastard had a huge, ugly grin on his face. "You might consider locking your doors when you go out running, though. Anybody can get in. Make impressions of keys. Easy peasy." He rotated his gun from Brendan to Dana to Dad.

Nick exhaled a big, fake sigh. "You crashed our party, Brendan. So rude. But we'll include you. You see, I was going to meet your dad tonight and finish some old business. But when I heard that Dana was here, I couldn't resist changing my plans." He pointed the gun at Brendan who heard his father make a strangled noise.

"I had decided that we'd make this a murder/suicide. Dana kills your father and then shoots herself. Ex-lovers, so sad. Just like in the papers. But then you arrived. No matter. I said your boy had to suffer, Tommy. You get to watch."

Dad shouted, "No." But Nick did nothing more than flick his eyelids at him.

Brendan's mouth was dry. His heart was jumping out of his chest. The gun was absolutely steady. And pointed right at his chest.

"It's payback time, Farm Boy. You deserve every fucking bit of this."

Everything lapsed into slow motion. Nick turned a fraction toward Brendan. Dad moved toward Nick. The woman stood up. Brendan saw a flash, heard a loud crack and then maybe a second one, felt his body slam against the door to the garage, and slump down it onto the floor. His vision blurred, but he saw Nick collapse in front of him. The woman was standing at the table, a gun in her hand. Dad was where Nick had been standing, his hands out in front of him. Brendan felt a bizarre stickiness on his cheeks, mouth, nose. Then Dad was crouched beside him, shouting his name.

"I'm okay." His ears were ringing from the shots. Two.

Dad tore open Brendan's jacket and ripped at the shoulder of his tee shirt. He reached for the dishtowel that always lived on the oven handle. Brendan looked down and saw globs of blood and other grisly, unspeakable debris all over him. Was it his? Despite the fact that Dad was trying to shield his sight, he could see the old guy sprawled on the floor. He could've sworn he saw him twitch. God. Blood was everywhere. He was going to vomit.

Then the pain came like shards of lightning striking his shoulder. He must've made a noise because Dad murmured, "Hang on, buddy. Hang on." Brendan remembered him saying that to him when he was a kid. Dad had his phone out. The woman, Dana, had laid the gun on the table and walked out of the kitchen.

"We need an ambulance," Dad was saying. "There's been a shooting. A double shooting." The dispatcher must've been asking him questions. Dad said no, and then yes twice, and gave his address. The pain bore into Brendan's shoulder like a drill, and he couldn't help but think about the nastiness covering him. He shut his eyes. "You okay?" Dad kept saying between answers.

Brendan shook his head. "Get this shit off me, Dad. Please."

Chapter Twenty Six

KEITH

He left Brendan for only a minute and went to find Dana, sitting in the living room and gazing out the window. She'd opened the drapes. Even from the hall he could see her trembling. "Dana," he said. Her gaze didn't move. "Are you all right?" Ridiculous words.

She made a gesture that was more of a spasm. Tears snaked down her cheeks.

His shoes were tracking gore from the kitchen. He didn't want to walk on the pale carpet in the living room, and he was afraid to leave Brendan for long. "Thank you," he said from the hall. "With all my heart I thank you."

Her arms were crossed tight against her chest. He thought he saw her nod.

It was ironic that his house, the dwelling he'd kept safe and hidden from strangers, was suddenly invaded by hordes of people. They came with sirens and lights and drawn guns. When they arrived, Keith was back by Brendan's side, trying to stanch the blood from his wound while wiping his face. The boy had vomited twice and kept swallowing like he might do it again. "We've got help now, Brendan," Keith murmured. "It won't be long before they get you out of here." Brendan's eyes stayed closed, although Keith thought he was conscious.

Two uniformed officers appeared in the doorway, sweeping the room with their firearms and yelling at Keith to put his hands behind his head. He did and swayed as he stood. "Is there an ambulance for my son?" he asked.

The pair seemed more interested in what remained of Nick. They barked orders and questions, and Keith answered the best he could. He could hear others doing the same to Dana. One stepped over Nick's body and came to pat Keith down. "It would be easier if they took my son out through the garage," he told him.

"Right," the officer said.

"I'd like to go with him."

"We can't let you do that."

Eventually they allowed Keith to shift Brendan away from the door so the paramedics could open it and collect him. Keith grabbed his hand. "I'll get to you as soon as I can," he said. Brendan was white and sweating. Keith wasn't sure he heard him.

And then it was nothing but an ordeal. They allowed him to change his clothes, with a guard accompanying him upstairs. When he went up, he saw Dana sitting in the living room with two officers; she was gone when he came back down. They put him in there then and started with the questions. He couldn't recall ever sitting in his own living room. Reflections from photographic flashes strobed the room. He answered the same questions again and again. And then they took him away. Thank God there were no handcuffs. He hoped Dana hadn't been cuffed. Television cameras and journalists had entered the open gate and crowded the yellow tape around the house. He hadn't thought about that.

The motivation for all of it was a long-standing grudge, he told them. He didn't tell them that he'd changed his identity and hidden for thirty-two years. The first two officers didn't blink at Donald or Nick Collins' names, but once they'd taken Keith to the police station, the detective there didn't hide his recognition of them. Keith admitted to stealing from Collins. He mentioned a brief romance with Dana, although he wasn't sure this was the truth.

The interrogation room suffocated him. He wondered about Dana, asked if he could see her, but they ignored his request. He hoped they wouldn't mistake his jumpiness for guilt. He kept telling them about Dana's heroism. He kept bringing up Kinley and the fire in Colorado. When he felt rather than saw that night had fallen, he asked to call Leon. They let him but didn't leave the room.

"I'm in a hell of a mess," he said when Leon answered. He told him briefly what had happened. "Could you go to University Hospital and check on Brendan for me? I don't think he's badly hurt, but I don't know."

"Jesus, Keith. Yeah, sure. I'll go. Are they going to arrest you?" Leon sounded as shocked as when they'd heard Brenda's diagnosis.

"I don't know."

"But you didn't do the shooting?"

"No."

"Do you need me to come to the police station?"

"No. I want someone with Brendan." The detective was absorbing every word.

"Right. On my way."

Keith folded up his phone and set it on the table. "A family friend," he said.

The detective nodded. The man had the most asymmetrical face Keith had ever seen. No faces matched, half to half, but one of the detective's eyes drooped, the other didn't. One cheekbone was higher than the other. Even the tip of his nose listed to the right. Intriguing.

"Okay," said the detective. "Let's go over where everybody was before Collins arrived, and again while it was the three of you, and then where you were situated when your son came in." He frowned and pushed his legal pad and pen toward Keith. "Do you think you could draw me a picture?"

Keith almost smiled. "Sure. I can draw."

BRENDAN

He didn't remember much about the ambulance ride. He was hurting too much to care what they did to him, although he did recall asking if he could change his shirt and the paramedic saying, how about this, cutting and peeling it like he was a banana. Then they put a blanket over him. He still shivered, though, and he thought he might've been yelling. Embarrassing.

At the hospital he had a vague recollection of warm medicine traveling up his arm from the IV and then everything going blank. When he woke up he was in a room, and Leon was sitting by the bed.

"Hey fella," he said.

"Hey."

"How're you doing?"

Brendan took inventory. Just under his drowsiness, there was a stinging sensation in his left shoulder, up high. For a minute he wondered if he'd been stung by a hornet. It hurt like that, sort of. Then he remembered. He raised his right arm, studied it, and brought his hand up to touch his face. Clean, thank God. "Fair," he said. His voice sounded funny.

"You're still kinda drugged up," Leon said. "Which is probably a good thing. Careful with that arm. There's an IV in it."

Brendan turned his head toward the window. Dark. "What time is it?"

Leon glanced at his watch. "Nearly ten. Are you hungry?"

The scene in the kitchen flashed behind his eyes, and he didn't think he'd ever be hungry again. He shook his head. "How's Dad? Where is he?"

"They're still asking him questions at the police station. Don't worry. They're not going to arrest him."

"Or her either, I hope." Brendan licked his dry lips. "She saved our lives. She did." Leon stood and poured water for him. There was a straw, and he sucked cool liquid into his mouth. It tasted good.

"You'll be able to tell them that later," Leon said. "A cop came by while you were still out of it and said they'd want to talk to you when you're able."

"Not yet," murmured Brendan.

"No, not yet."

The next time he woke up he was more alert. It was still dark, but his father sat in the chair where Leon had been before. He was texting. Very slowly. "Hello," said Brendan.

"Good morning." Dad smiled. "How are you feeling?"

"Sore but okay." He moved his left arm a little and felt it burn. At least it was his left. "They let you go?" He turned his head and saw a uniformed cop standing by the door. He decided to ignore him.

"I don't think there was ever any question of that, but they took their good sweet time about it. I shouldn't complain, though. They drove me back to the house and let me have my car." He frowned over at the cop. "They said they'd come later this morning to talk to you. Are you going to feel like it?"

Brendan nodded and used the remote to angle up the head of the bed. "Who were you texting?"

"Your sister. I told her that we're all safe now."

Brendan wondered if it was true and then decided it probably was. "When am I getting out of here?" he asked.

"Soon. The only reason they kept you was because you went into shock and were pretty agitated. They told me you're going to be fine. No permanent damage. The bullet just tore out a chunk of muscle."

Brendan grimaced. He'd never considered himself squeamish, but he'd never witnessed and been a victim of a shooting before. "Dana?"

"They kept her overnight."

Brendan shook his head. "She was shooting in self- defense. And in our defense."

"I've told them that. I think they're waiting until they talk to you."

The cop didn't move. He didn't say anything either. But his presence freaked Brendan out. It was another hour or so before the detective arrived to ask him questions. He guessed the guy was fairly sympathetic because he didn't stay long. Dad said they made him repeat everything a dozen times. Not long after that, a doctor came in and said Brendan could go home. He had antibiotics and pain pills and instructions for wound care, but he could dress and go home. Brendan turned to his father. "Okay. Great. The doctor said somebody needs to stay with me, and what in the hell am I going to wear? I hope they burned my clothes."

Dad picked up a plastic bag. "I'm staying with you, and I bought you some clothes on my way over here." His face lit up. "Did you know that Wal-Mart stays open all night? I didn't." He concentrated on pulling the tag off a pair of jeans. "They may not fit well, but they'll do to get you home. We'll stay at your house until at least tomorrow. I can't go home yet anyway."

Brendan nodded and tried to move to a sitting position without causing himself too much pain. They'd given him a bag with his keys, phone, and wallet in it. He checked his phone. There was a text as long as a novel from Hannah that would've sounded like a good case of hysteria if she'd spoken it, all about how the shooting had been on the news, and what was going on, and he should call her immediately. He couldn't deal with that just now. As he eased himself into the cheap polo shirt Dad had bought, it suddenly struck him. His father was driving around and shopping. Out in public. And he was going to stay in Brendan's house which most definitely did not have a security system. "Dad?" There were about thirty questions in the word.

"I'm a free man," he said.

KEITH

Not long after he helped Brendan get settled into his house, Dana called. Brendan was sleeping, so Keith took his phone and coffee to the backyard so he wouldn't disturb him. Daylight had finally come, and dew made beads on Cassie's little swing set. "They're letting me go," she said.

"Thank God."

"They're not going to press charges." She sounded like she was convincing herself it was true.

"Brendan and I both told them you saved our lives." Talking to Dana made him want a cigarette.

"I saved mine too." Her voice was quiet.

"Yes, you did. God, Dana." He wished he were better with words.

"Anyway. Can you come pick me up, Tommy? There's the rental car, you know, and all my things are in it. And I have to book a flight."

"You could stay. Not at my house, I know that would be hard, and besides, they haven't let me back in yet." He expected them to say he could now that they'd released Dana, but there was serious cleaning to do. His stomach lurched at that. "But you could stay at a hotel or over here at Brendan's."

She said, "You're sweet, Tommy, but I want to go home." There was a yearning in her voice. Maybe she had a guy up in Boston, or maybe she wanted to forget she'd ever seen him. Nobody could blame her for that.

"Okay, I'm on my way."

Keith left a note for Brendan and headed out. Dana said little when she got in the car, nothing along the way. The gates were open. He drove cautiously up his long driveway, but no reporters jumped out of the bushes. There was still yellow tape across the front door but none on the garage. He was glad that Dana had packed her car Saturday afternoon. "Did you check on flights?" It wasn't what he wanted to know, but she looked so haunted that he feared saying anything more.

"There's one late this afternoon."

It was still morning. "Would you want to go over to Brendan's for a shower? Some food?"

She shook her head. "I'll check into the hotel next to the airport and stay there for a few hours. Change." Her voice ran out of gas, and her eyes were glassy. "I'm not sorry for what I did, but I'll never shed it."

"Never's a long time, Dana. I hope we . . ."

She interrupted him. "Not now. Maybe never, I don't know." She turned away, got into the rental car, and started the engine, raising her hand but looking straight ahead as she passed him.

His car ticked as it cooled. In the garage everything looked normal except for the bullet hole marking the door into the kitchen. He thought of what was behind that door. Leon had said there were companies that did that kind of cleaning. Keith rolled the mower forward a foot or so. His papers were still there. He picked them up.

Throughout the day, Brendan dozed and woke, always anxious. Keith kept telling him that eventually it would all go away, and that it helped to stay busy. Whenever he thought of Dana, he told himself the same thing. He was plenty busy taking care of Brendan and trying to get him calmed down.

The next day the police allowed him in his house, and he and Leon cleaned the kitchen. It was a nasty, gruesome job. That afternoon he took Brendan to the doctor who said he was doing well. And that evening Keith persuaded Brendan to pack some clothes and move over to his house. It looked normal, he said. Leon had even replaced the door into the kitchen. Brendan insisted that he was fine on his own, but Keith wouldn't hear of it. "We'll help each other," he said. "For once in my life I'm not sure I want to be alone."

That had convinced Brendan, but his face was gray and wary when they approached the gates. This time photographers and reporters blocked the drive. News had spread about who lived there and what he did for a living. Keith wasn't surprised, but it drove him into near panic anyway. Sharp pain hammered his hands clenching the steering wheel. The media people were shouting his name, asking questions that sounded like babble. He was steeling himself to get out of the car when Brendan murmured, "I'll do it." He cautiously eased himself out of the car to punch in the code. The reporters mobbed him. Keith felt guilty. He was supposed to be taking care of Brendan, not the other way around.

Inching the car forward until its bumper made contact with the metal, Keith made a path for Brendan who managed to get back in without allowing any of the mob inside the gates. He let out a gusty breath. "God. I didn't think we'd have to deal with this."

"They'll leave soon," Keith said with more optimism than faith. Grabbing Brendan's bag, he opened the door from the garage to the kitchen. "It's okay," he said. "Don't worry."

Brendan mumbled, "I don't know if I can do this."

He urged his son through the kitchen and into the den. "I'm going to make us some grilled cheese sandwiches and soup," he said. "And we'll eat them in here." He handed Brendan the remote. "Find us something good to watch."

Food calmed both of them down, along with goofy sitcom reruns that bored him silly but made Brendan smile at least occasionally. Keith waited for a little longer and said, "You need to tell your sister that you're safe."

"You texted her."

"Yes. But you need to tell her what happened. She'll believe you."

Brendan stared ahead at a loud Burger King commercial. "She should know, I guess." He didn't want to talk about it. Keith understood; he didn't want to live with publicity storming his gates.

"Yes."

"Okay." Brendan got out his phone.

"One more thing." Keith pressed the mute button on the remote. "I don't know what your situation is at work. You've missed a lot of days, through no fault of your own, and I don't know if you can take more off."

Brendan's eyes were opaque, like he was having difficulty understanding the words.

"I'd like you and me to take a trip," Keith said. "Out to Colorado to see your sister. Make a nice drive of it. See the country. Help her out." The idea had come to him while he was heating the soup.

Brendan frowned.

"I want to make things right," Keith said. "With both of you." Brendan still didn't say anything. "Please assure her that she's safe, that she can marry Michael without putting him at risk. Make her believe it. And ask if we can come visit."

"I don't know."

"I understand. We can't tell Kinley anything definite yet, but see what she says. I want to do this, Brendan. I need to."

A little light came into his son's eyes. Keith touched Brendan's good shoulder and left the room.

Chapter Twenty Seven

KINLEY

She'd never told Michael that the fire had been set to kill her. And she absolutely hadn't let on that she was breaking off their engagement. When she'd called Michigan the last couple of days, she'd put on a performance worthy of a friggin' Oscar. Cheerful, encouraging, oh, she was amazing. And it was easy because Michael acted the same way, except that his good humor was genuine. Kinley took a deep breath and picked up her phone. He answered like he'd been hatching his. "Hey, Sweetheart."

"Hey yourself. How are you feeling?"

"Super. Can't quite play yet, but that's okay. I deserve a break."

He'd hate pity. "You do. You really do."

"How about you?"

"I bought some dishes yesterday. Got tired of eating off paper plates."

"Cool. We'll need those when we move to Cincy." She never knew what to say when he made these references. She'd heard nothing from Brendan, although she'd been leaving messages and texts like crazy. It was worrying her. She'd received a cryptic text from Dad early on Sunday morning, but she didn't put much faith in it.

"Yeah. Sure. Sarah's coming down tomorrow and wants to go shopping. She says that all they have in Wyoming are cowgirl shirts and boots."

He chuckled. "That's good. I guess you two did lose all your clothes in the fire. She's doing okay?"

"It seems that way." Sarah still had bad dreams. She'd even thought about turning down the job in Broomfield. The shopping trip was meant to be therapy for both of them.

"How's the painting going?"

Here she could tell him the absolute truth. "Pretty well, surprisingly. The café picture is all but done. And I've made a good start on the one of your gorgeous face."

"As I recall, it focuses on my hands." There was laughter in his voice.

"They're gorgeous too. What did the doctor say about music camp?"

"He says I'm good to go if I feel strong enough, and I do. Plus I still have a few more days to rest."

"As long as you're healthy enough to fight off the teen-aged girls," Kinley said.

A long laugh. "You don't have to worry about that. I wish you could come up before I leave for camp."

He'd been saying this even when he was in the hospital, but it wasn't the original plan, and when she did travel to Michigan, it would be to break off the engagement. "No, I can't. I still have so much to handle here."

His voice turned soft. "I know. I'm sorry. It's just that I miss you so much." She didn't speak for a second, so he started again in an apologetic strain. "You've had such a rough time. Did you talk to a realtor?"

"Yep. All the properties are up for sale. I've called the tenants and told them. We'll see." She watched sunlight capture dust motes falling to the wooden floor.

●●●●

Although she'd bought a broom and swept every day, ash still crept into the building. The whole place stank of fire. Michael talked a bit more, telling her about seeing his nephews, describing the food his mother had cooked to pamper him. Inconsequential, but that was what most days were made of, she thought. Consequential things happened rarely but kicked peoples' butts when they did. She told him that she loved him, that she'd call tomorrow, and clicked off.

She sketched much of the afternoon, working on a still life consisting of detritus the former tenant left behind—a partially melted plastic bowl, bent coat hangers, a sliver of soap, and a dirty green wine bottle. The objects seemed sad. But she wasn't into painting happy just then. When hunger demanded it, she went out to get Chinese. She swept the floor. Again. She stared at her canvases. She thought they might be good, but she didn't know. And then her phone rang.

Brendan's voice sounded slow and odd, like maybe he was on drugs or had been crying. Damn that Megan. "What's wrong?" she asked.

"God, Kinley, what isn't? To start with, I've been shot."

"What?" Her voice was a screech.

He told a horrific story. Kinley ranted about their father and his lies for a good, long time before she demanded a full explanation, and then she let him tell it without interrupting. Much, anyway. "Who's Dana?" she asked. She didn't know why she latched upon this part of the story. Maybe because it was easier for her to comprehend than guns and gangsters.

"A woman Dad knew back in Chicago when he was Tom Vickers and just starting to paint. He doesn't say much, but I think they were lovers."

"Are they lovers now?" She'd been gripping her phone so hard her fingers hurt.

"I don't know. But he just saw her for the first time since Chicago a few days ago. This doesn't have anything to do with Mom, Kin, and Dana saved our lives. That creep had his gun pointed right at my heart, and she stood up and shot him while he was shooting me. Threw off his aim. Saved my life. It was amazing." His voice was shaking.

"Oh, Brendan. Oh, baby." Now she was crying again. She'd been crying over everything since the fire. "But you're safe. Dad's safe."

"We're all safe, Kin. You too. The danger's gone. It's a goddamned happy ending."

She heard a stifled sob that broke her heart. He couldn't talk for a minute so she cooed comforting words into his ear. She hoped she sounded like Mom.

He pulled himself together. "Sorry. Probably the painkillers. Anyway, you can marry Michael. Nobody is coming after us ever again. Hell, Dad's going out and doing things in the middle of the day. He took me to the doctor and went to Wal-Mart. Can you believe it?"

She had to chuckle. "No, I can't." At the very edge of her vision there seemed to be a clearing, a blue patch after all the storms. "Next thing he'll be buying a convertible and going clubbing."

Brendan's laugh exploded like a surprise. "I can see it now. Disco Dad." He paused and his voice became serious. "But he wanted me to ask you something, and it's really important to him."

She narrowed her eyes. Okay, he'd offered himself up to this Nick for their sake, but he'd still put their family through a special kind of hell their entire lives. She wasn't feeling generous. "What?"

"He wants him and me to drive out to see you. He says he wants to make amends."

"Why didn't he call and ask me himself?"

"He didn't figure you'd talk to him. Would you have?"

Damn Brendan with his insight. "No, I probably wouldn't." She could just barely imagine her father and brother locked into a car together, driving cross-country for a happy reunion, or at least a reunion. But it sounded as though Brendan wanted it, and she couldn't deny him. "It's okay by me. When?"

"I don't know when. Megan gets back from the Love Boat tomorrow, and I have to see what she's planning for Cassie."

"Bring her. Cassie, not Megan."

He chuckled. "That would be fun, wouldn't it? Diaper changing the whole width of the country. Anyway, I'll call you tomorrow. We'll probably know more then."

"What about your job? I don't suppose you're working yet. Do you still have vacation time?"

"No, I'm not working, but I've decided to quit my job."

BRENDAN

He hadn't fully known that he meant to quit until he said it to Kinley. But once the words were out of his mouth, he felt his entire body loosen up. By the next morning he felt even more sure of his decision. Hannah had said he should. She was right. After lunch, he called her.

She answered fast and started babbling. "Slow down," he said. "I'm fine now. It's all over. Are you still in town?"

She was. She didn't want to leave for Columbus until she knew he was all right. He smiled at the phone. "I was wondering if we could get coffee or something. But I'm afraid you'll have to pick me up here at my father's. I'm on pain meds, and I'm still a little sore for driving."

She could and she would. By the time Brendan cleaned up a little and told his father where he was going, Hannah called him to open the gate. "Is there anyone out there? Journalists?" he asked.

"Just me," she replied. Brendan gave his dad a thumbs up and opened the door.

"This is a mansion," she said when he scooted gingerly into her car.

"Yeah, the old man's loaded. That's the only reason Megan married me." It felt strange to be outside.

"I doubt it. Where do you want to go?"

Her hair lay soft against her shoulder. He wanted to touch it. "This sounds crazy," he started, "but what I'd really like is ice cream."

She smiled. "My dad used to say there wasn't much ice cream couldn't cure."

"Smart man." Like his daughter, he thought. She hadn't bombarded him with questions. He'd tell her some of it. He figured he could pare down the entire grim story to maybe five or six sentences.

She drove to Graeter's, which made him think of his mother. And Kinley. After they got their scoops they sat at one of the uncomfortable little tables, and he told the scaled-down version. He figured she knew most of it from the news anyway. "Now what?" she asked when he finished. "Nobody goes to jail or anything?"

"No. At least we hope not. Dad and I are definitely in the clear. The police didn't press charges against Dana, and they don't think she'll be indicted when the Grand Jury rules on her in a couple of months. Self defense." He let the creamy sweetness melt against his tongue. "But all this made me come to terms with some issues. I did decide to quit my job. And Dad and I are going out to Colorado to see my sister."

Hannah grinned. "I wish everybody followed my advice like that." She deposited a spoonful of chocolate chip in her mouth. "I assume the shooter had something to do with your sister's fire."

He nodded. "He paid people to set it. I don't think arson was in his skill set."

"God. And this Dana, is she still here?"

"She's gone back to Boston. Dad says he doesn't know if he'll ever see her again."

"That's sad. I get the feeling they're connected from way back, right?" He'd never known anybody better at reading between lines.

"Yes. And maybe they re-connected while she was here. He never said." He didn't want to go into any more detail, and she sensed it. "I don't know what I'm going to do about a job."

Hannah scrunched up her nose. "Don't worry about it. Take your trip and work on that when you get back. Do you want to stay in Cincinnati?"

"I think I'll have to if I want to see Cassie. The lawyer said that I have a chance at getting custody, but it's not a sure thing. It all depends on Megan."

Hannah's eyes flashed, and he thought it was the mention of Megan but it wasn't. "You were bored at the university library, weren't you?" He nodded. "What about a public library? They're busier. Of course you have to deal with little kids doing reports on presidents and homeless people looking for a warm spot to hang out, but still. You could start some programs, do computer literacy classes or book discussions, that sort of thing." She was watching him closely, judging how he was taking what she said. "I know you said you'd like a corporate job, but in the meantime. . . ." Her voice trailed off.

He'd never thought of it. Academic libraries were the pinnacle, or so he'd thought in grad school. But he could make the change. Easily. "You're brilliant," he said. She grinned and used her spoon to carve a ridge in her ice cream. He said, "Of course there'd have to be an opening. And my experience might not be what they'd want."

"Details, details. You'll get a job."

Despite her confidence, Brendan felt a tightness start creeping back into his spine. Unemployed. Even though he was glad he'd quit the university, he didn't like the sound of unemployed. He asked, "What about you? Do you have resumés out there?"

"Not yet. I'm going to give myself a week or two off first."

"Good thinking. How did your last exams go?"

She scraped up the last of her ice cream. "Fine, I guess." She looked straight into his eyes. "You know, I don't really care. I'm out. That's all that matters." She grinned. "What did we say back in high school? Stick a fork in me; I'm done."

He smiled.

"Anyway," she went on, looking down now. "I've changed my strategy. I was going to send out applications all over the country, but now I think I'll limit them to Cincinnati. Do you think that's a good idea?"

He remembered how she'd come on so strong when they'd first met. She'd thought that was what he'd want, and she'd been wrong. Once. He could forgive the charade. "I like you better like this," he said.

Her cheeks colored. She knew what he meant. "It was the only way I could think of to get your attention." She looked down at the empty bowl in front of her.

"Oh, I was tempted."

She grinned.

"I hate to see you limit yourself, but it would be fantastic if you got a job in Cincinnati." His shoulder gave him a warning twinge, but he leaned over to kiss her. She tasted like vanilla. "Until I get back from Colorado?" he asked.

"Sure. Call me."

Chapter Twenty Eight

KEITH

He and Brendan left four days later. He would've liked to take off sooner; the occasional reporter hovering outside his gates suffocated his new-found sense of freedom. Leon bought newspapers and magazines. It wasn't just the shooting. The world had discovered where reclusive artist Keith Owen lived. But the delay gave him time to conduct some business, make some calls and plans, and pack up a good bit more than he had stashed in his emergency bag. He'd had time to shred the farewell letters he'd written and square away some details. He'd taken Brendan to another appointment with the divorce attorney and then visited the bank to withdraw a sizeable chunk of cash for their travel expenses. Four days had also given Brendan a little more time to heal. He could drive now and had moved back into his house. Best of all, Megan had allowed him to have Cassie for most of the weekend. The witch still hadn't admitted to stealing the cow picture.

Early that morning, he picked up Brendan who commented on the quantity of boxes and bags in the back of the Nissan. He told him that he was taking art supplies to Kinley. Brendan seemed happier than he'd seen him in months. That was good. Keith was driving when they hit morning rush hour around Indianapolis, bad planning on his part, but it wasn't too slow. Once or twice he caught himself looking in the mirrors to see if someone was following. Nice that he didn't have to do that anymore.

They were still in Indiana when Brendan asked, "Have you ever wanted to go back to Muncie? See how things have changed?"

"Not really. I left that behind years ago."

"When you changed from Tom Vickers to Keith Owen?" Brendan's eyes were on the road even though Keith was driving.

"So you know that part."

Brendan glanced at him. "I know that Tom Vickers was kicked out of school for plagiarism."

Keith grimaced. "It was wrong to do it, but all I wanted to do was paint. Writing papers took too much time, and I wasn't very good at them." He shrugged. "I was fool enough to ask a buddy if I could re-type his paper from the previous semester. That was the first time, and the professor flunked me for the course. Didn't figure lightning could strike twice, so I tried it again when I re-took the class with a different instructor."

He was surprised when Brendan smiled. "Stupid," he said.

"Yep."

"But you didn't want to go to college anyway, did you?"

"Not regular college. I wanted to go to the Art Institute, but my parents wouldn't let me."

It was spitting a little rain. Warm rain. May was a good month. Brendan turned to look at him. "Was that why you let Kinley and me major in pretty much whatever we wanted?"

"Guess so. I didn't want Kinley to go so far away, but it was her choice." He turned on the wipers. "I wanted you two to feel free," he said.

They ate lunch in Illinois and crossed the Mississippi soon after. The wide, muddy river reminded Keith of the run to Memphis with Dana. The heat. Her body. He'd tried to call her a couple of times before he left, but she never answered.

After hours of ordinary, occasional conversation, Brendan brought up the past again. "How did you manage to change your identity? Seems like that would've been difficult."

"Easier than now, I imagine." He loosened his fingers from the wheel and flexed them. "My last run was to Cleveland. I ditched the car and took a bus to Cincinnati. Stayed in a motel the first week until I figured out that I wanted to stay there. I got an apartment in Clifton. Went to a bar there. Mostly students," he said, glancing at Brendan. "I asked one of them where I could get a fake ID."

"For drinking, he thought," Brendan said.

Keith nodded. "The guy sent me to a Photo Bug. Ever heard of them?"

Brendan shook his head.

"Before your time," Keith said. "They were little booths situated in parking lots. Kinda looked like bugs. They developed film, that sort of thing, back when photos required processing." He paused to pass a semi. "Anyway, I was supposed to talk to Walter. Funny that I can remember his name." He saw him in his head. Big guy with long hair. Pudgy hands with bitten fingernails. Heavily into the Grateful Dead. Probably stoned most of the time. "I told him I wanted a very good driver's license with a different name. Not just for bars. I was twenty-two anyway. Walter looked at me funny. Asked me if I needed a birth certificate too. I hadn't thought of that, but it made sense. I said yes. Social security number too. I told him I might need a passport eventually. He said it would cost me and take a while. I said I didn't care about the cost, but I was in a hurry." Keith glanced at Brendan. His eyes were wide, deep. "I got it in a week. Keith Owen. I didn't choose the name."

Brendan was quiet for a long time. He was probably trying to figure out how it had been accomplished. They'd driven out of the rain. Missouri was very green with slopes and hills and lots of trees. It looked like Kentucky. The Nissan ate another thirty miles before Brendan asked another question. It was okay. He'd figured that being trapped in a car together would give his son a chance to get information. That was his trade. "So how did it work? The jobs you did for Nick?"

Brendan had trouble saying the man's name. Couldn't blame him. "There were probably four or five of us working as runners, couriers for Collins. I never knew exactly how many. Collins would use a different person, car, identity, city, and carrier each time to send packages of money. We'd take the box to the airport freight carriers for shipping. The addresses were different too, but all the boxes contained payments to Bolivians sending drugs to Collins for distribution in Chicago. The drug people mostly worked out of Florida. Some in Texas."

"Which drugs?"

"I never saw the drugs, but I imagine it was mostly cocaine. Maybe grass. I got paid $200 plus expenses per run, and I had one every six weeks or so. It was a lot of money back then, especially since Nick let me use his studio and sleep there for very little, sometimes nothing at all." He shrugged. "I didn't know how much money was in the boxes, although Nick hinted that it was a lot. But I figured I could steal one package and set myself up for life. It was wrong to steal; hell, it was wrong to be part of the drug trade in the first place, but it didn't seem too horrible to rob drug dealers. Besides, all I cared about was painting." He realized that he'd already said that. "I never dreamed stealing that money would have such repercussions. I just took it and ran." Brendan didn't say anything. "So, that's when I became Keith Owen, not when I left Indiana."

"Yeah, Nick called you Tommy." Brendan's voice was tight. He didn't like remembering the scene in the kitchen any more than Keith did.

After a few more miles he offered to drive, and Keith let him. They'd be stopping for the night soon anyway. The sky had turned the color of orange sherbet with flares of bolder color at the horizon. Keith shut his eyes and saw how he might paint it. Devonie said critics raved about his skies. He never read the articles.

Keith relaxed his fingers and sipped from a Coke they'd bought when they switched drivers. "How much did Mom know?" Brendan's voice was quiet.

"Very little. She didn't ask. I think she was afraid it would hurt too much if I didn't answer her." Keith turned his head to look out the side window. "I tried not to lie."

He thought about Brenda for a minute but forced the memories away. She would've been appalled at everything, especially the injuries done to her children. As the light faded, the trees picked up shades of black and gray. He and Dana had once argued about whether there were shades of black. He was sure there were. She said black was black. "We could stop anytime now," he said to Brendan.

"Might as well drive another hour," he said. "I'm feeling okay."

The next day they moved into Kansas, and the drive became monotonous. Brendan called the girl he'd gone out with for ice cream. Keith hoped she was kind. Later, while Brendan was driving, Keith called Kinley. He was apprehensive about it, but she was civil and asked where they were, how the driving was going. She said she'd be ready for them, although the apartment she was using was sparsely furnished. Keith told her that was fine.

BRENDAN

He didn't think they'd ever get through Kansas. Although it was probably a very nice place to live, the drive was boring as hell. Dad still didn't talk much. He'd changed, relaxed, but he hadn't turned into a witty conversationalist. It was a long trip.

When they were about an hour out from Boulder, Dad called Kinley. She said she'd be watching for them. Brendan absorbed the foreign terrain, grand as the mountains were, with impatience. He wanted to see his sister. Obeying the GPS, he made the turns, stopped at lights, and led the car deeper into Boulder, wondering how close they were. But, even though he knew the reason for their trip, nothing could've prepared him for the shock of Kinley's gutted house. The street was pretty, lots of comfortable old houses and mature trees. Charming, some people would say. The burned out lot was a deep gash.

"We'll take in our stuff later," Dad said, opening his door. He stared at the ruins.

It still hurt to get in and out of a car, so Brendan was slower. By the time they walked up the steps to the porch, Kinley had opened the door. She looked worn, bruised, but she was smiling. Dad hugged her, and Brendan wondered how she felt about that. He must've whispered something in her ear because she pulled back, looked him in the eye, and said, "Really? Really and truly?"

Dad nodded and she hugged him again. Her eyes were closed.

She squeezed Brendan, hugging hard and then saying, "Oh God, did I hurt you?"

He said no, although it wasn't quite true, and they all went in. The main room of the apartment was spacious with a kitchen area against the inside wall and a futon against the front. Other than a small table with four chairs in the middle of the room, there was no other furniture. The outside corner, full of light that seemed brighter than anything back home, held an oversized easel and a rolling metal cart full of supplies. Dad went straight for the easel. There was a painting on it.

Brendan held back beside the table that had been set for lunch. Kinley stood beside him, her index finger in her mouth. She stared at Dad's back, nerves radiating off her. But she must've wanted him to see it or she wouldn't have had it on display.

The painting showed a young man lying on his side in bed, his head propped up on his hand. The focal point of the work was his other hand, draped against the sheets. A pianist's hand. Brendan remembered the fire. A heroic hand. Brendan was no artist or critic, didn't pretend to be, but he'd grown up with Keith Owen's work. He knew good, and Kinley's painting was outstanding.

Dad finally turned around. Tears wet his cheeks. "Oh, Kinley," was all he said.

She blinked, fidgeted. "You like it?" She had a marvelous grasp for the obvious. "When I got into it, I changed what I'd done in the sketches."

Dad nodded. "I often do that. Sometimes sketches don't translate to paint." He turned back to the canvas. "What you've done with the sheets," he said. "Your brushwork. Light. Shadows. Composition." It was like he couldn't put an entire sentence together. Finally he turned back to her. "It's brilliant. Do you have more?"

Kinley beamed. "Two. And a few sketches."

KINLEY

Dad needed a haircut. Brendan had lost weight, probably from running more than the shooting, but he looked like hell. Lunch didn't help his color, and finally Dad noticed it too. "I'm hurting a little," Brendan admitted. They made him take a pain pill, and she led him to the bedroom.

She felt bad that it was only an air mattress on the floor. She'd decided that Dad could have the futon she'd been using. "Will this do?" she asked. Her tenant from across the hall said it was fine if Kinley wanted to

209

sleep in her apartment, but she felt funny about putting her brother over there. "If you'd be more comfortable in a hotel, we can do that." She'd bring in the extra kitchen chair. That might help when he was putting on his shoes.

"Chill, Kin. It's fine. I've just been in a car way too long." He slipped out of his shoes and knelt to get on the mattress. She unfolded a blanket. She'd bought two yesterday. A weird way to build a hope chest, she thought. "You're amazing," he murmured. "The painting is Michael, isn't it?"

She nodded. Of course he couldn't know; he'd never met Michael. "You don't think Dad's just blowing sunshine?"

"He may be the new, improved Dad, but he still wouldn't compliment art if he didn't like it." He struggled to lie down. "God, Kin; he cried. What do you want?"

Dad asked to see Boulder, so while Brendan napped, they took off in her car. He kept marveling at the mountains. "I told you," she said. "Have you noticed the light?"

He nodded. "I could see it long before we reached Denver. Crystalline. Now that you're painting, it's a shame you're leaving it."

She concentrated on the traffic.

"You are still going to marry Michael and move back to Cincinnati, aren't you?"

She glanced at her father and then back at the road. "It nearly killed me to see him lying in that hospital bed. I won't have him hurt again because of me."

"Because of me," Dad said.

She shrugged.

"There is absolutely no danger any more. Nick Collins is dead. There's no one left to remember what I did or blame me for things I didn't do." She glanced again. He looked sincere.

"What about Dana?"

"What about her? She's no threat. Surely Brendan told you what she did." She could feel his eyes on her. "Or do you mean Dana and me? There's nothing about our relationship that could possibly hurt you and Brendan." He looked out the windshield. "I don't think there's any relationship at all."

Kinley pulled into a parking space near Pearl Street. Might as well show him the heart and soul of Boulder. "Do you wish there were?" she asked.

He met her eyes. "What? A relationship? Yes."

"You love her?"

He shrugged.

"Did you love Mom?"

He smiled. "I came to love her very much. That's God's truth. "

She believed him, on this at least. They strolled up and down the street, pausing to go in the consortium where some of her painted glassware was still for sale. He didn't comment on it. At an art store he bought her more brushes along with tools and a better palette. "You sweetening me up?" She tried to make it sound like she was joking.

"Trying to. I brought a few things from my studio too. They're still in the car."

He agreed quickly when she suggested getting a drink. She took him to the bar she'd painted. As soon as they sat, he grinned. "I recognize this place. Remarkable." He paid for her wine and his beer. "So, when's the wedding?"

"We've only just started talking about it. Early September, I think."

He nodded. "Cincinnati or Michigan?"

"At first we thought Michigan, but we changed our minds. Cincinnati. Neither of us wants the production that a Michigan wedding would entail. He has a huge family."

"Makes sense." He took a healthy slug of beer and leaned his elbows on the table. He looked tired too. "Why don't you have it in the backyard of our house? Leon's got everything looking beautiful. It'll still be that way in September."

It was a thought. With her being Protestant, after a fashion, and Michael a Catholic, a church wedding was way too complicated. Besides, Dad might even attend it there. Before she could answer, he went on. "As a matter of fact, why don't you and Michael plan to live at the house while he's in school? Rent-free, of course. You say your stay in Cincinnati might be temporary. If it is, maybe Brendan will want the house after you and Michael leave. Or maybe you'll stay. It doesn't matter to me. You and Brendan can work that out." He looked sane, but she was wondering if he'd lost his mind. "Oh, I won't be there," he said quickly.

"Where are you going?"

"I'm not sure."

She narrowed her eyes. "Seriously, are you trying to buy me?"

He looked a little pale. "I'm trying to love you," he said.

"Then I want to hear the whole story. All of it. Totally honest. From the time you left the farm until last week. I deserve it." She heard how stern her voice had turned.

It didn't seem to bother him. His eyes were mild, even if dark circles lay beneath them. "Okay. Stop me if it seems like I'm leaving anything out."

He talked for a long time, pausing just to order them each another drink. It didn't exactly sound rehearsed, but he'd told it before, probably to

Brendan. The sun sank until the light in the bar was the same rich gold as the evening of Michael's recital. He'd proposed here, she thought as she listened to Dad's tale. She'd started painting again, in her mind anyway, in this very place. Witchy, she thought. And although her father's story seemed ugly and hardly credible in spots, she thought it must be true. It was the place, she thought. Strong magic.

When he'd finished with the shooting and its aftermath, she just said, "We need to get back to Brendan. He'll wonder where we are."

Dad stood, his body hitching a little as he moved.

She hadn't asked a single question during his story, but she had one now. "You really plan to leave the house?"

"Yes."

"I'll talk to Michael, but it sounds great."

On the way home, Dad couldn't take his eyes off the mountains and asked if there were books describing trails up into them. She explained that the ones he saw were technically the Flatirons, not the Rockies. He shrugged and said that didn't matter; he just wanted to hike. She understood. Some Colorado people were content to have the mountains as a postcard backdrop for their lives. Others wanted to get up in them. The next day she took them to a bookstore where Brendan bought novels and Dad grabbed everything he could find about hiking the Colorado Rockies. They read all afternoon on the porch while she painted. The next day Dad headed out to buy a backpack and hiking boots, and that very afternoon he left to try an easy trail near Boulder. For the first time since they'd arrived, Kinley and Brendan were on their own.

She told Brendan that she was worried that Dad might fall or have a heart attack. He wasn't exactly young, but Brendan laughed at her. "For years Dad's done daily workouts more strenuous than my runs. He's in great shape."

"Not that we'd know about his health," she retorted. "He never would leave the house to go to a doctor. Worried Mom to death sometimes."

"Quit, Kinley."

"These are the Rockies, Brendan. Not some dinky state park."

She was making bread. The week before the fire, Michael had shown her how, but this was the first time she'd tried it on her own. Okay, she was showing off, but otherwise her cooking wasn't much. Might as well play to her strength. "So, I've been wanting to ask you, what's this about Dad moving? He's offered Michael and me his house."

Brendan's head jerked up. "He didn't mention it to me. Where's he going?"

"I don't know. Thought maybe you did." She poured dissolved yeast into the bowl and added flour and bits of salt and sugar. She thought that was how Michael did it.

"Do you suppose he's going to move down to the lake permanently?"

She shook her head. "I can't imagine him doing that."

Brendan watched her work the dough. "I don't think he'd go to Boston."

"What's in Boston?" She dumped the gooey dough onto the floured counter.

"More like who. Dana." He shook his head. "I don't think so."

"Then where?" She folded the lump and used the heel of her hand to knead it.

Brendan scrunched up his face. As a kid he'd done that when he was thinking. "I heard him muttering something about the reporters. That they were going to make his life a misery. I know Leon chased them away from the gates a few times. It'll be easy now for people to find the reclusive Keith Owen. Even if the threat from Nick is gone, Dad would hate that."

She turned over the dough and shook her head. "I guess we'll find out eventually." She looked up at Brendan. "Do you mind about the house? We'll probably only live there a couple of years. Dad said you could have it after that."

He grinned. "I don't care. Honest. Besides, I don't need a studio."

When Dad returned he swore it was one of the best days of his life. He loved the mountains, loved the hiking. He loved everything including the grocery store lasagna she served and the loaf of crusty bread she sliced. It was good. Brendan had made a nice salad, and the wine was just right, although Dad drank only a sip or two. She should buy beer for him, she thought. He insisted on doing the dishes so she could call Michael and brag about her bread. Brendan sneaked away to phone some girl named Hannah. Kinley needed to quiz him about her. When she finished talking to Michael, Dad was outside, rooting around in his car. He brought in a box and set in on the kitchen table. "I could've left this for you at home," he said, "but I thought you might use them this summer." He looked apologetic. "I hate to give you more to move." His face was pink from mountain sunshine.

She glanced around the bare room. "There's not much, and I don't need much if Michael and I are going to live at the house."

She'd rarely seen her father more pleased. He stood straighter and beamed. "Michael likes the idea?"

"Michael loves the idea." She hesitated. She'd never liked talking money with her father. He always wanted to give it to her, and she always felt weird about taking it. "If all these places sell, we'll be more than okay. Wealthy, actually. Boulder property values must be the only ones in the country that haven't declined for a minute. But I don't know how soon they'll sell." She glanced out the window rather than meeting Dad's eyes. "With no rent coming in right now, I'm living on insurance money." He started to say something, but she wouldn't let him. "I'm fine. Really. But knowing we have a rent-free place to live, a rent-free place to live with a studio, takes the pressure off." She leaned toward him and touched his cheek. It was warm. Sun-burned.

"Good." If anything, his cheeks turned even pinker. "I'll let Leon know. He'll be tickled."

She smiled. Dad opened the box. "Brendan told me your neighbor made you the easel. He did a fine job. But I figured you lost everything else."

She nodded. "I haven't replaced much of it yet."

"Maybe this will help."

It was a treasure chest of even more brushes, specialized ones that would be perfect for certain situations, exotic pigments—the ones that cost the moon, glazes, varnishes, and other wonderful tools. There was a box of expensive watercolors and even pastels. "You might want to try other media," he said. "I've never done much but oils, but you never know."

She hugged him, touched all the fine things, and hugged him again. Brendan came in and peered into the box. "Look," she said. "It's amazing."

Dad shrugged and said, "Something else. I wrote Devonie Goddard, and she's willing to display a few of your pieces when you're ready."

Okay, this was too much. She knew her face showed it because the light went out of Dad's. "I don't want special favors."

"It's not. If they don't sell, she won't accept more. She made that plain."

Brendan was watching her. He knew how she felt. Sort of. "I don't want anyone to know I'm your daughter," she said slowly. "I don't mean to be rude, but I have to make it on my own."

Brendan said, "I noticed that you haven't signed yours yet." It was a question.

She'd delayed that on purpose. "This is all too much, Dad, even though I appreciate it more than you'll ever know." She took a deep breath. "But I'm signing my work with Mom's name. It'll be Williams."

If it bothered him, he didn't show it. "I'll be proud no matter what," he said. "I'll know my daughter painted them." He turned toward the kitchen. "Are there any of those cookies left? I need a bite of sweet."

She carried the box over to her cart but didn't unload it. She wanted to do that by herself and savor every item, like a kid at Christmas. When she glanced up, Brendan was looking at her. For a second she felt guilty. There'd been no gifts for him, no big house to live in. His face was bright, though. "You're on your way, Sis, whatever name you use," he said. "And I'm glad."

Chapter Twenty Nine

KEITH

He'd already been up for over an hour, poring over the hiking maps when Kinley came into her apartment the next morning. She spoke and headed to the coffeepot. Brendan was still asleep. "You're not hiking today, are you?" she asked.

"No."

"Good. It's best if you give your muscles a rest between hikes." She yawned. "Two days in a row isn't smart when you're getting used to the altitude."

"That's what I thought." He looked down at one of the maps. "Some of these look wicked. What if a hiker got lost?"

She sat at the table. "I hope you aren't thinking about hiking those."

He shook his head.

"That's why you sign in at the trailhead. If a family reports a hiker missing or the register indicates he's been gone too long the rangers start searching."

"What if they never find the hiker?"

"Usually they do," she said. "Or they find remains." Her face darkened. "A bad fall. Once in a great while snakebite or bears."

"Grim."

She peered at him over her mug. "The Rockies are nothing to play around with."

"I could see that even on the baby trail."

"Was there ice? Probably not on that one, but if you go high enough some of the trails still have patches of snow or ice this early in the season. Double treacherous." She put down her coffee. "Honest, Dad, I'm glad you love the mountains, but I do want you to be careful. Are you planning to hike tomorrow?"

He nodded.

"I figured."

Brendan came in then, looking bright-eyed. He was definitely feeling better. "What's everybody doing today?" he asked. He ran his hand over his wound. Must be starting to itch.

"I have no plans," said Kinley. "Whatever you two want to do."

Keith looked at Brendan.

"I'd like to get something for Cassie," he said. "Just a little something."

"Okay, that's easy," she said. "Dad?"

"You two go on and do that, get lunch, spend the day. I'm going to mess around a little in Boulder. Just sightseeing on my own."

Just as Kinley had said, the next morning Keith printed in all the required information at the trailhead. Date, time, name, car make, model, license plate. And the fact that he was by himself. He loved his kids. He was glad they, for some reason or the other, still seemed to tolerate him. But he liked being alone. Always had. He shifted the backpack onto his shoulders and took off up the path. It wasn't steep yet, but it would be.

It was a Monday, surely not much of a hiking day. He wanted the mountain to himself. He hadn't told Kinley which trail he was taking or how difficult it was. She would just worry. His muscles bit into the incline. It felt good. The sky was a brilliant blue, one so vibrant that it wouldn't look realistic on canvas. More like one of those sofa paintings people bought for fifty bucks. He noticed that he was breathing hard and slowed his pace. High altitude was a tricky thing. He might get light-headed if he wasn't careful. Kinley had warned him about that. She'd also told him to drink lots of fluids. His backpack was much too heavy, and part of the weight was the water bottles she'd made him pack. She was turning into a motherly woman. He hoped she'd become a real mother soon.

He walked for nearly an hour before he took his first break, sucking down water and catching his breath. Trees blocked any vista he might've seen. He touched the bark of an aspen, trembling in the fresh breeze. No wonder Kinley loved them so much. He gazed at the spindly trees for a good while and decided the painting of them he'd done from a photograph was decent, but the colors weren't right. You couldn't get that from a photo. Maybe he'd try again and replace the painting Kinley had lost in the fire. Although maybe she'd prefer to do one herself. Kinley puzzled him. She'd had every opportunity to paint, at college, later. How had she choked it off for ten years? Incomprehensible.

He began trudging up the mountain again and wondered what he could do for Brendan. Not the ass end of a cow this time. That had been done at least partially in anger at his son's contrariness. Keith smiled. His father had used the same word to describe him.

217

Pebbles slipped and trickled away under his boots. It was steep now. And colder. He knew it looked as if his generosity was aimed only at Kinley, like he was leaving Brendan out. He wasn't, but, other than the trust he'd set up for little Cassie's education, he could do little until Brendan got rid of that witch he'd married. Keith didn't want her getting one penny more than she had to. The attorney had said that Brendan might have to sell his house and split the proceeds with her. Keith shook his head. He'd paid for that house. It should be Brendan's. Oh well. It would all work out. He just hoped his son didn't feel neglected in the meantime.

He looked at his watch. He'd been walking two hours and was feeling it. The mountains were magnificent from a distance, but rough and, frankly, fairly uninteresting up close. He studied the rocks and tried to transfer them to a painting. It didn't work. He supposed the postcard pictures, the sofa paintings, were really all anyone could do with such scope, although he wished he could capture the mountains' strong personalities. He had the ridiculous thought that they were defying him, defying any human who tried to conquer them. He shook his head. He wasn't sure anybody could capture that.

The book had said that another trail intersected with this one, but the path he was following no longer had the attributes of a trail. Just rocks and more rocks. He would need to stay alert to find the junction. He'd read that trail junctions were marked with piles of rocks, but there were rocks everywhere. Out here in the middle of the mountain it was hard to tell whether man or nature had organized the stones.

Up ahead, it looked like his trail curved to the right. He guessed. After he made the bend he got the vista he was looking for. Down a sheer, rocky drop that fell for what looked like miles, the earth spread out before him. It was a God view, he thought. The wind found him there and whipped the few scraggly pines clinging to the edge of the precipice. On beyond the valley were more mountains. Layers of them. It made him wish he knew something about geology, about how these craggy beasts had formed.

And still he climbed up. Not too many yards ahead was the marker for the intersecting trail. It was more obvious than he'd thought it would be. He went beyond it. The incredible view was still on his right, and a wall of rock bordered the left side of the trail. The path narrowed. Thin air chilled his face and burned his lungs. He needed to rest. He could hear his heartbeat in his ears. He'd walk just up to the boulder jutting out on the left. It was nearly a bench. He'd sit and eat the sandwich Kinley had made him. Maybe it was time to backtrack. He looked at his watch.

As he neared the big rock, he ran into ice on the trail. He hadn't noticed it; he'd been looking at the view. His boots slid, caught and slipped again until there was only air under his feet. His arms splayed out, and the shifting weight of his backpack pulled his body to the right, to the very edge of the mountain. As he fell, he must've hit his chin, because when he raised his head a couple of inches, he could see blood on the dirty ice. It had happened in seconds. If he slipped again, he'd end up rolling down this bastard of a mountain.

Fighting off panic, he tried to move but his knees and hands could get no purchase on the slick path. Now most of his right leg was hanging off the edge. Pebbles he'd disturbed scattered down the steep mountainside, down into the abyss. Now what? This wasn't how he'd intended the day to go, but a person could plan only so much. His interlude with Nick should've taught him that. He'd been ready to die then, but he hadn't. Maybe the mountains had plans of their own. Okay, he was scared. His hand clawed at his pocket for his phone and found it, but his frozen fingers were too crabbed to grip it, and the motion shifted him even closer to the edge. The phone skittered across the ice and fell down the cliff. He could hear it bouncing against the rocks. It would take only the slightest motion for him to follow. He was very, very cold.

BRENDAN

By late afternoon Kinley was bouncing around the apartment like a pinball. "Where is he?" she asked. "Do you know which trail he was hiking? Should we call the rangers?"

"Maybe the trail took longer than he planned or he stopped somewhere on the way home. He could be drinking a beer somewhere."

She tried calling Dad's phone again, but it went to voicemail like it had the previous dozen times. He was worried too. Dad had left a little after nine that morning. Brendan couldn't conceive of him trying a hike that would last this long.

Kinley stopped and got very quiet. "What address do you suppose he used on the trail register?"

God, he could see where she was going. "He wouldn't be stupid enough to put Ohio, would he?"

"Not stupid, just habit. I bet he wrote the Ohio address. They'd never know to get in touch with us."

He thought she was going to start tearing her clothes and hair any minute. "Do you have the number for the park rangers?" he asked.

Her eyes were huge. "No. I've never needed it." She picked up her phone. "911?"

"Hang on," he said and started typing on his laptop. In a minute or two he had the number.

She called and gave them Dad's name. "Ohio license plate," she said. "I don't know the number, do you, Brendan?"

There'd been too many cars. He shook his head and took the phone from her, giving the rangers all the info he could about Dad's vehicle. Then there was nothing to do but wait. Night came, and Brendan wondered how the rescue people could search without daylight. The phone stayed silent. To keep hers free, Kinley used his cell to call Michael and cried while she was talking to him. Brendan sat very still imagining what it might be like to be stranded overnight on a hard, cold mountain. Dad had no tent, no sleeping bag. There were animals up there too. He made himself quit thinking. He asked Kinley if she was hungry. She said no. He wasn't either.

He jumped when Kinley's phone rang. She grabbed it. The rangers reported that they'd found the car and Dad's registration. They'd hiked the trail and looked for signs of him but couldn't promise to do a thorough search until morning. Kinley squeaked out a breathless thank you and looked at Brendan.

"What?" he said. "There's nothing we can do."

Finally he made sandwiches that neither of them did more than taste. They drank coffee and then switched to tea. Well after midnight they unfolded the futon and curled up on it, the phone between them. When dawn crept in they started on coffee again. They took turns taking showers so someone was always by the phone. Kinley gave up hope first. "All the disappearing Dad did, and this time it's forever."

"We don't know that."

Her wet hair hung in strands. "Sometimes they can't find a body. Nothing."

"How long do they search?" he asked.

"Days. Until they're sure nothing can be found."

Hours later they jumped again, but it was the doorbell rather than the phone. A uniformed ranger stood on the porch, holding a blue backpack. Brendan shut his eyes and took a deep breath. The ranger came in but wouldn't sit. "Is this your father's bag?" he asked.

Kinley nodded.

"We found blood on a patch of ice. Signs of a fall." The man was young, looked anxious as hell at having to deliver such news. "It's a deep ravine there. No outcroppings to speak of. We caught a glimpse of this bag, and one of the guys used a rope and hook to get it." His adam's apple jerked up and down. "Look inside. Make sure it's your father's."

Kinley's hand shook as she worked the zipper. She pulled out two water bottles, one full and one empty. There was a granola bar and a sandwich. A spare pair of socks. Dad's. They both knew it. Brendan nodded at the ranger.

220

"We can't get very far down in there," the ranger said. "It's some of the roughest country around here. But we're going to take the chopper out and see if we can find him. "The pilot's probably taking off right about now."

"And then what?" Brendan had to clear his throat.

"He'll have a spotter with him. They'll make passes for quite a while." Brendan could tell the guy didn't hold out much hope. "Did your father have a phone with him?"

Kinley nodded like a puppet. "He did," said Brendan.

"Maybe he'll call," the ranger said. "Let us know immediately if he does."

They all knew that Keith would've called already if he'd been able.

They waited all that day and night. Nothing happened. By the next day, they'd both turned numb. Kinley even didn't cry when an older ranger came to the door and said they'd discontinued the search. If their father had fallen where they'd found the backpack, there was no trace of him. But it was a sheer drop that fell forever, he said. No hope. Sorry. They'd be sending paperwork so a death certificate could eventually be issued. What address?

But late that night, she cried, talked to Michael, and cried some more. For what might've been, she told Brendan. They'd just found Dad, she said, and now they'd lost him. He sat up with her for a while and then poured most of a cup of tea down the drain. He said that he might as well go home. Kinley said she'd go with him. There was no sense in staying.

The next couple of days were mercifully busy. She saw her realtor and hired painters. He worked at cleaning the empty apartments the best he could with one arm and unplugged a couple of drains. While she called her remaining tenants and told them where to mail their rent, he boxed up her belongings and shipped what wouldn't fit in the two cars. He called Devonie and listened to her try to hold back tears. Still at her parents' house in Wyoming, Sarah agreed to visit Boulder once a week to check on the apartments until she moved back, and Hannah said she'd drive to Cincinnati from Columbus the minute he got home. This brought the first smile he'd managed in days.

Nobody bothered them while they were preparing to leave. Fortunately the press didn't know where to find them. Word had gotten out, of course. Big time. It was all over the Internet. Kinley bought newspapers from New York and Chicago and Los Angeles to read Dad's incomplete obituaries, supplied mostly by Devonie, Brendan figured. All of them reported the death of an artistic icon, a painter of "sublime talent," one said. "The entire artistic world mourns the death of Keith Owen." That was from Devonie herself. Photos of some of his paintings accompanied the articles. But there wasn't a single picture of Keith.

The night before they left, they sat on the floor and ate Thai takeout. Kinley kept glancing out the window at the mountains. He wondered if she still loved them. Brendan was very glad that Michael waited for her at the other end of the trip. Cassie and Hannah for him. He'd called Megan and told her about Dad. "She actually sounded sorry," he said.

"Probably sorry she didn't stay married to you." Kinley's comment was sharp.

"Why?"

"She'll figure there's a big inheritance."

Honest to God, he hadn't thought of that. "We'll have to work our way through all of that when we get home, won't we?" His spirits fell even lower.

She nodded. "I guess there's a will."

"There is." He still had the combination to Dad's safe in his wallet. "It'll be complicated as hell." Will, divorce, the interminable drive. Brendan was exhausted just thinking about it.

She was silent for several bites. "What time are we leaving?"

He'd told her twice already. "Seven-thirty."

"And we'll try to keep our cars close?"

He halfway wished they had walkie-talkies. He'd almost suggested they buy some. "Sure, but we'll get separated sometimes. Just call me if you need to stop or if you get lost or something."

She nodded and looked at her spring roll like it was a snake. "Does Leon know we're on our way?" she asked.

"Yeah, I called him. And Aunt Lily and Uncle David. They all wanted to know if there was going to be a funeral."

"There can't be a funeral," Kinley said. "We don't have a body." She was pale, Brendan noticed. Hell, he probably was too.

"Well, a memorial service."

"What's the point?" she asked. "Dad would've hated the publicity." She set down her carton of food. "He tried to be a real father there at the end, didn't he?"

He wasn't hungry either. "He was willing to die for us, Kin. That was the plan with Nick. I'd call that trying. And the way he took care of me when I was shot." He shrugged. "Your painting."

"Are we making Dad out to be better than he was just because he's dead?" Her eyes were huge.

"I don't know." Brendan wanted to leave right then. He wanted home and Cassie and Hannah. "At least Dad doesn't have to run anymore," he said.

She let out a huge sigh. "I miss him." She smiled then. "He was impossible, but I miss him. And I think he liked running."

It didn't matter. They'd never know. He dredged up a smile and put it in his voice. "We start fresh now. Your art. Michael. My divorce. A new job, I hope."

She raised her eyebrows. "You forgot Hannah."

"No, I didn't." This made her grin. "And us. We'll have each other close."

She reached over and hugged him. "That helps, doesn't it?

Epilogue
DANA
<u>July 2008</u>

Telling Vincent that she'd shot his father was the hardest thing she'd ever done, more difficult than actually shooting Nick, which had seemed both instinctive and logical. He'd threatened three lives; it had made sense to take one instead. She'd used these words to the detective when he interrogated her, but she couldn't say them to Vincent. She remembered sitting on a bed at the Cincinnati Airport hotel and calling him. She remembered how her voice had shaken.

He'd been a sweetheart. "Let's face it, Mom, he was never much of a father to me," he'd said. "I'd much rather have you alive than him," he'd said. "You live by violence, chances are you're going to die by it. I've got a pretty clear view of what the Collins side of my family has been up to over the years."

They talked often anyway, but Vince had requested that she call him the minute she heard the Grand Jury's verdict. "Not guilty. Self-defense," she reported.

"As it should be," Vince said. "Good."

Later in the conversation he asked if she could come to Chicago. "I have something to show you," he said.

"From your father?"

"From Grandpa's office. Dad never got around to cleaning it out. Mandy asked me to sort through the files and 'boring stuff.' Her words. She's sold everything but Dad's underwear and already left town. So much for the grieving widow." Vince laughed. "But I found more than files. You'll see when you get here."

She couldn't resist either the opportunity to see her son or the mystery. He picked her up at O'Hare, took her to dinner, and drove her to his loft, a beautiful place with high, open ceilings and a few good paintings she'd given him over the years. He talked about a girl he was seeing. They discussed his job. He refused to show her what he'd found until morning.

The next day he gave her coffee and bagels and brought a package loosely wrapped in brown paper into the bright kitchen. It didn't take much imagination to see it was a painting. Vincent started unwrapping it. "This was locked in the safe at Dad's office. That struck me as odd." He lifted a shoulder. "I think the painting's weird, but I Googled the artist; his stuff brings outrageous prices." He handed her a framed painting of a field full of cows. The most prominent one had its rear end facing front. The picture was signed KOWEN. Of course.

She smiled. Impudent. Playful. She hadn't known Tommy was capable of that. None of his work had ever showed this mood. She chuckled.

"The artist died a couple of months ago," said Vincent. "So I guess that makes it even more valuable, doesn't it?"

Dana nodded. "Incredibly valuable." Within two weeks of his death, Devonie had sold every one of Tommy's paintings at double, triple their usual high prices. Dana asked, "Do you have any idea how Nick got this?"

Vince shook his head. "I asked Mandy, nothing specific because I didn't want her getting her greedy hands on it. All she said was that one of the guys who worked for Dad brought it to the house back in the spring. He'd been doing some kind of job for Dad. She thought the painting was ugly." Vince grinned. "I guess Mandy's never heard of Keith Owen or she would've thought it was fabulous."

"Do you think it's ugly?"

Vince shrugged. "I guess not. You've taught me enough for me to realize it's fine work. But cows?"

Dana looked at the canvas, was tempted to touch it. Nick must've told his man to steal any paintings he saw when he broke into Brendan's house. She said, "Yes, cows." She smiled. "I know for a fact that it's stolen. You could never sell it."

"Really." His eyes narrowed. "So Dad stole it."

She looked away.

"Do you know who it belongs to?"

"Yes."

"Then make sure it gets back where it belongs, okay?" Vincent lifted the painting, began to rewrap it.

Back in Boston, she packed it more securely and sent it to Tommy's son in Cincinnati. She'd been tempted to keep it. When she gazed at the spider web painting in her bedroom, she couldn't help but think how fine it would be to have two of Tommy's paintings. Tommy's remarkable paintings. She'd tried to keep him and his art alive, but, as far as she knew, he hadn't painted anything in the few months she'd given him. The silky web glowed from the canvas. Devonie would've salivated over it, but she'd never get the chance. Tommy's last picture was just between the two of them.

LEON
<u>September, 2008</u>

It was about time something happy happened in this family. He scrutinized the tables the caterers had scattered across his perfect lawn and decided they would pass muster. He'd added pots of pink roses and yellow chrysanthemums where things were a little bare and figured the place looked about as good as he could make it. You couldn't make September look like May.

But then he didn't want to think about May. He missed Keith. What a sorry way for a man to go out, dying at the bottom of a cliff a thousand miles from home. Leon hoped that when he passed, he'd have his wife and boys around him. His boys. Keith had educated them—one a chemical engineer and the other an architect—paid tuition for five years on each of them. And Keith had provided a nice berth for his old pal too. Leon reckoned he could retire, but he didn't want to. He'd stick around the place as long as Kinley wanted him, and she said she did.

Leon strolled back to the gazebo where the preacher would stand. From a Presbyterian church out in Colorado where Michael had played, Kinley said. Early that morning he, Kinley, and Sarah, the maid of honor who'd also flown in from Colorado, had attached vines and ribbons to the latticework on the structure, and it looked fine. He tweaked an ivy leaf and thought about Brenda. To tell the truth he missed Brenda more than Keith on this special day. Brenda would've eaten this up, choosing flowers and buying dresses and getting excited. She had missed a lot and not only because she died so young. He shook his head. At least she'd been part of Brendan's wedding, although Leon was just as glad she hadn't been around to see how it turned out.

He went in the kitchen, and all the catering people were real nice to him even though he could tell he was in their way. He'd need to dress soon; he was walking Miss Kinley down the aisle, a real honor, but he wanted to check everything one more time. The living room looked fine, especially with that brand new baby grand sitting all black and shiny in the corner. Michael had just about cried when he got a load of it. Keith had ordered the piano right before he left for Colorado. Leon had taken delivery on it not three days before Keith died. It was a nice wedding gift for the kids.

The doorbell rang. Leon couldn't get used to that, but Kinley said she never wanted that front gate closed, let alone locked, again. After the

226

wedding, she said she was going to have it taken out completely, and that was fine by him. The daggoned thing hadn't done what it was supposed to do anyway. When he opened the door he expected to let in another one of the army of caterers, but it was a UPS guy with a big package. "Another gift for the bride?" Leon said.

The guy grinned. "More like the groom. Leon Perry?"

He sure as heck wasn't the groom, but he took the package back to the den. Getting out his knife, he tore into the packing, thinking how much it looked like the canvases he and Keith used to box up. He glanced at the sticker in the corner. Goddard Gallery, New York. That was Devonie. What in the sam hill was she doing sending something to him? It was probably a wedding gift for Kinley, but maybe Devonie thought it would be safer to address it this way.

He figured it was a painting but was surprised that it was Keith's. One of the last ones he'd done. He remembered packing it. Keith had called it "The Lady of the Lake," and it showed Brenda on an island looking like a ghost. Sweet Brenda. He couldn't figure out why Devonie had returned it to him. On the back, an envelope was stuck in the frame. He opened it and found a note from her saying that shortly after she'd received the painting, Keith had asked her to send it back in the fall. He'd wanted Leon to have it. Devonie mentioned that she could get a fine price if he ever wanted to sell. She considered it one of Keith's best.

Leon gazed at Keith's depiction of the shadowy female figure nearly hidden by spring trees. Other people might not know it was Brenda, but he did. Brenda, who'd baked Thanksgiving pies for his family and sent them home with him. Brenda, who'd looked at her feet when she'd asked him to teach Brendan how to dribble and shoot a basketball. Leon dabbed at his eyes and called himself an old fool. He cleared up the packing and took the painting into Kinley's studio where it would be safe. He'd like Kinley to see it. Brendan too. But sell it? He'd put a price on one of his sons first.

BRENDAN
December, 2008

Christmas Eve afternoon, he was trying to put together a miniature plastic shopping cart while Hannah packed a small tote bag with pretend food, clever stuff like tiny boxes of cereal and fake cans of applesauce. "I would've loved having something like this when I was a kid," she said. They sat by a Christmas tree encircled with gifts for Cassie.

"What time is it?" Brendan asked.

"Nearly two. Why?"

"I'm supposed to pick her up at three, after she's had her nap. How are we doing on the other stuff?" He set the bright cart upright and Hannah put the tote in the basket.

"Everything's done but her stocking."

Brendan surveyed the pile of loot. "Kids with divorced parents make out like bandits, don't they? Double gifts." Megan had given him a list he'd mostly ignored, choosing instead the toys and books and stuffed animals he wanted his daughter to have.

"Sometimes." She picked up Cassie's scarlet Santa stocking. "And sometimes one thinks the other is going to buy things, and neither one does."

He kissed her nose. "Sorry. I forgot."

"It's okay." She touched his face. "A few packages under there are for you."

"Really. A couple are for you too. I figure after we take Cassie back to her mother tonight we can have a little Christmas drink and open our gifts. Yes?" After the divorce was final in October, Hannah had moved in with him. He'd been gravely disappointed that he hadn't been granted full custody of his daughter, but it probably had been for the best. He and Hannah were doing fine, especially since she'd snagged a job last month writing copy for a union publication. Not what she wanted, but a start. Still, having a two-year old all the time might've tried the patience of the relationship. He wondered how much Scott Klein liked having a toddler around. He and Megan hadn't married yet.

"Did your family open on Christmas Eve or Christmas morning?" Hannah asked.

"Christmas morning. We can do that if you want."

"We did both, Eve with my dad and morning with mom if she wasn't too hungover." She grinned. "Tonight's fine, especially since we're going to your sister's tomorrow."

"That's not until afternoon." He stood and picked up rolls of wrapping paper and scissors. Hannah grabbed the ribbon and tape.

"Yeah, but I plan on keeping you awake until really late tonight." Her hair had dipped across one eye. She looked silly and seductive. He loved it.

"You planning on staying up to catch Santa?" he asked.

"Yep."

There was a clatter at the front door that had nothing to do with Saint Nick, he thought, although later he changed his mind about that. "Mailman," he said.

"Poor guys, working on Christmas Eve."

He grabbed the stack of mail. It looked like a couple of Christmas cards and the water bill, crummy to get a bill on Christmas Eve. Scroogey. And there was a large yellow envelope from his attorney. All the divorce paperwork was done. The guy had been paid. Brendon had no idea what it could be. It was as mysterious as the package from Boston a deliveryman had brought him several months ago containing Dad's cow painting with one of Dana's business cards tucked in the frame. No explanation whatsoever. He glanced at the wall above the mantel where the painting lived now. He didn't care how Dana had managed to get it. He was just glad to have it back.

"Anything good?" Hannah asked, nodding at the mail.

He opened one of the cards. It was from his supervisor at the public library. Typical of her to send cards at the last minute, but she had a sense of humor and appreciated Brendan's skills. He liked this job even though it paid no more than the one at the university.

"What's the big one?" she asked, picking up the water bill and filing it in their 'in' basket. God, she was as obsessively organized as he was. This made him smile.

"Don't know." He ripped it open. There were several sheets of paper topped by a letter from a bank, a Swiss bank. He read the first paragraph and sank into the nearest chair. "Jesus," he breathed.

"What's wrong?"

He kept scanning, stopped, went back to the first sentence. "Jesus," he repeated. Hannah came over and sat on the arm of the chair.

"Brendan, what is it?" There was worry in her voice.

"No, no. It's good." He swallowed and grabbed her hand. "Last spring, in April this guy says, my father set up an account, a Swiss bank account for God's sake, in my name. He says Dad instructed him not to inform me of it until the divorce was final and gave him my attorney's name. He's just heard from the guy in Switzerland."

"A little slow wasn't he?" She was smiling now.

"It's a million dollars, Hannah." He couldn't have stood up if the house had come tumbling down. He could just see Dad smiling at his surprise. He wouldn't have said a word, just smiled.

"Good God," Hannah breathed.

"I thought we'd divided everything up already. Cash, property, accounts. Done everything just how Dad's will said we should." That had netted both him and Kinley more money than he'd ever had.

Hannah said, "But this was separate, wasn't it? Set up before he died." She grinned. "Merry Christmas, Mr. Millionaire. Megan will really wish she'd stayed now."

"But I don't." He kissed her.

KINLEY
December, 2008

Christmas Eve. She'd dug out her mother's battered recipe box and found the card for sugar cookies. Decades of buttery fingers had browned the edges. She and Brendan used to sprinkle colored sugar and jimmies on the Santas and stars and reindeer their mother cut out of the dough. Michael was doing the turkey, potatoes, and everything else for tomorrow's feast. The least she could do was bake cookies. She figured she might just manage those without messing up.

He was in the living room practicing for his Lutherans' Christmas Eve service. She'd asked him if he ever mixed up all the denominations he'd played for, but he'd said they were all pretty much the same. She loved having the piano. It was bliss listening to him play and even better that he stayed home to do it rather than going to a practice room. "Thank you, Dad," she whispered as she worked sugar into fat sticks of butter.

Everything was going well for her family and friends. Sarah had moved to Broomfield and loved her job. They talked every week, and Sarah had promised to come to Cincinnati next summer. Kinley's realtor had found buyers for both the vacant lot and gray house, although the brick house hadn't attracted much attention. And just last week Devonie had called to say she'd sold the first of Kinley's paintings, the one at the bar in Boulder. Kinley had titled it "Recital," not that it really made sense, but Dad's titles hadn't always made sense either. She thought about him more than she ever dreamed she would, wishing she could ask him things, wanting to show him her work. The night after Devonie's call, Michael and she had drunk champagne with Brendan and Hannah. Dad would've been pleased, she thought. Turning, she looked through the glass door into her studio. His studio. She was an orphan now, but there'd been a legacy, a huge legacy.

From the living room came a muffled curse, and she smiled. Michael loved grad school, even though he had to work very hard. Life was good. Kinley stirred in an egg, vanilla, and flour and gathered the dough up into a messy ball to chill before rolling it out. Michael would probably tease her about being picky and artistic when she decorated the cookies. He'd said the same about the wedding flowers and the comforter it took her a month to choose for their bedroom. She always retorted that he'd been positively obsessive about the wedding music. And then they'd laugh. They laughed a lot.

She was washing cookie dough off her hands when she spied a DHL truck coming down the drive. She dried her hands and rushed to the front door before the deliveryman could ring and disturb Michael. The DHL guy wore a Santa hat, probably way against the rules, but hey, it was Christmas. She dug in the pocket of her jeans and pulled out a five to tip the fellow. Crappy to have to work on Christmas Eve. He handed her a large package and grinned when she gave him the money.

Michael was playing "O Holy Night," and it sounded like heaven, like what angels would play if they had pianos in paradise. Not wanting to interrupt him, she scurried into the kitchen and used a paring knife to open the box. Inside there were layers of bubble wrap and then pieces of linen. The kitchen was warm, so warm that condensation made decorative fog on the window. She felt a chill, though, when she saw the linen. Dad had always packed his canvases like that. She checked the label to see where the parcel had come from. There was a Customs declaration on the front. It had originated in Colombia. She didn't know a soul in South America. Stripping away the cloth, she found a framed painting of aspens, spring aspens standing erect under Colorado's translucent sky. She could feel her heartbeat in her throat. The signature on the painting said TVICKERS. "Son of a bitch," she murmured. Then she screamed it: "Son of a bitch!"

Michael's ethereal music turned into a discordant jumble, and he galloped into the kitchen. "What?" he asked.

She already had her phone in her hand. When Brendan answered, she screeched, "Dad's alive, Brendan. The son of a bitch tricked us." Her voice snagged. "He's still running."

TOM
January, 2009

Colombian light was different from any he'd experienced. It had a glare, a harshness that made vibrant colors even more vivid. During the rainy season, the sky was often nearly white. Now that the breezes had come, it was milky blue. He stepped back from his canvas and squinted, making the paint blur. He liked the effect. Sometimes he tried to imitate it. He was

231

playing with different styles. Some might criticize him for this, but he chose to think of it as versatility. And necessity. He must not paint as Keith Owen had.

He left the room he used as a studio and went onto his patio. From there he could smell the sea. Wild parrots jabbered from the bougainvillea clinging to his house. He liked Cartagena. He liked the feeling of barely tamed jungle. The house was all right, not quite as fine as the pictures he'd seen on the Internet before he'd gone to Colorado, but it would do. He liked the way the tile floors cooled his bare feet. A woman named Lidia came three times a week to clean them and do other chores. Her brother Enrique kept the patio and flowers neat. They didn't understand English, and he couldn't comprehend much Spanish, but it worked.

Sometimes Lidia cooked for him—chicken and rice, baked fish, flan—and she bought him pastries at a bakery in El Centro. But he often ate his dinners at one of three restaurants on Boca Grande. He met an English artist at the El Dorado for drinks a few evenings a week. He sensed that Julian drank more than he painted, but that was all right. They never showed each other their work. That was all right too.

One night in late September he'd called Dana. She didn't let on that she was surprised he was alive. She'd just said, well, hello there, Tommy. And she'd told him that her son had found the cow painting. He was glad that Dana had sent it to Brendan.

He'd finally gotten up enough nerve to ship Kinley the aspen picture, ripping open the veil again. Dana had said she'd keep his secret from the world. She'd even agreed to exhibit his new work. But she'd said he should tell his children that he was alive. He didn't see the sense in it. He was never going back. He couldn't work with everyone knowing where he was. But he'd done what Dana had said, in his own way.

He shaded his eyes against the relentless sun and looked toward the Caribbean. He'd been wrong. Water could be blue, even aquamarine. Skies looked different over the sea too. He'd play with that soon. He also wanted to capture some of Cartagena's colonial buildings and their shadows. Mysterious. Intriguing.

Dana had laughed when he asked how she was doing after the shooting and all. It hadn't been a pretty laugh, but she'd said she was fine. Maybe. Truth was fluid, he thought. She laughed more gently when he asked if they could meet in Miami sometime. No, Tommy, she'd said. That ship has sailed.

He wondered what Kinley had thought when she received the painting. He hoped she liked it. He was sorry for the trouble he'd caused. For about a minute he'd considered including his kids in his plans for killing Keith Owen. They could've helped. Brendan could've met him with a car and taken him to the airport. Kinley could've shipped things to his new address. But he wouldn't make his children lie for him. That's why he'd never told Brenda anything. Besides, it wouldn't make much difference if they knew; he'd never see them again anyway.

The escape from Colorado had scared him pretty good. He'd nearly died for real, although he supposed the evidence of his fall had given credibility to his disappearance. After struggling for what seemed like hours, he'd finally rolled his backpack and body to the left without dropping off the cliff. He remembered scooting his body by inches, staggering to his feet, trying to keep them on the other edge of the path where his boots could get a grip. Then he went through with the plans he'd made. His phone had already gone where he'd intended to throw it, and, as planned, he'd tossed the larger backpack into the ravine, keeping the smaller one with his money and papers inside. He'd kept his Tom Vickers driver's license and passport current the whole time he'd been Keith Owen. That had been smart, although getting current photos for his documents had made him physically ill every time he'd done it.

In Boulder, the day before his hike, he'd shipped the painting supplies he'd brought from Cincinnati to the house he'd purchased in Cartagena and bought a bicycle. He'd hid it in his SUV. When he'd limped back down the mountain, he'd pulled the bike and another small bag from his car, locked it, and left. Riding back to Boulder had been painful. He remembered how bruised he was and how his chin had dripped blood onto his jeans. In Boulder he'd caught the shuttle for the Denver airport and flown to Mexico City, where he bought a car and a few clothes. It had taken days of driving to get to Colombia. A grand adventure. Beautiful sights. Brendan would've liked it.

He flexed his hands. Colombian weather had improved his joints. He loved the flowers and colors. Early on he'd painted the plants and banana tree bordering his patio. They weren't quite right. He needed to work on them. And then maybe he'd send a couple to Dana. Maybe. And he'd like Enrique to sit for him. He had a strong face, proud cheekbones. There was something essential, something primitive about him. He probably wouldn't want to do it, but Tom would pay him. Lots if he had to. There was so much to paint. Kinley and Brendan wouldn't understand, but nobody ever had. Except maybe Dana.

Acknowledgements

My thanks go to the Wise Women—Annabel Ihrig, Cheryl Eschenbach, and Joyce Hurst who have been with me from the beginning. For their sharp ideas and fine suggestions I'm grateful to Susan Johnson and Maura Isaacs. I appreciate Steve Atkisson's generosity in showing me the ropes with grace and knowledge.

Several people have shared expertise that just can't come from Google: Chad Sloan for music, Suzie Pellegrini for art, Bob Roncker for running, Lt. Kevin Vogelpohl for firefighting, Detective Craig Burris for police work, and Evan Sharfe for creative design. Many thanks to all of you. Any errors here are entirely mine.

I've had the opportunity to learn about writing and experience the nurturing atmosphere of the Appalachian Writers Workshop. Many talented people offered me wisdom and encouragement including Lee Smith, Mark Powell, Marianne Worthington, Sharyn McCrumb, Silas House, and Maurice Manning. How I loved sitting on those porches for late-night discussions!

Special thanks go to Tiffany M. Williams, a fine writer and wonderful friend whose insight gives true depth to, 'let's swap stories.'

And to my dear friend and mentor, Gwyn Hyman Rubio, I offer my deepest gratitude for your unwavering support, insight, and phone calls that lifted me over the rough spots.

Lastly, I thank my husband Jim and my son Matthew for your love, patience, guidance, and assistance. No writer has ever had a better team.

New

NOW AVAILABLE: J.T. Cooper's new suspense novel

VIRAL

A PASSENGER DIES on the Barcelona-Cincinnati flight. EMTs and Customs officials suspect biological terrorism and lock down the Cincinnati Airport. Although some of the exposed passengers have already cleared and exited, the remaining ones, as well as TSA and other airport employees, Customs officers, and one airport policeman are flown to a moth-balled Army post for quarantine. Just before they take his phone, the policeman, Luke Davies, calls his wife Maggie and tells her to take their son to his parents' home in rural Appalachia. Luke, isolated with strangers waiting to die, and Maggie, isolated in a world she hardly understands, hunker down to wait out the terrifying crisis.

PRAISE FOR VIRAL

J.T. Cooper has crafted a riveting tale of a near apocalyptic pandemic and the actions and attitudes of the people caught in it....As the focus turns to simply survival, they work at maintaining integrity, humanity, and faith in the face of disaster. –Annabel Ihrig, author of *A House in the Country* and *Full Circle*

Available in paperback and ebook formats at most booksellers world-wide.

Visit
https://jtcooperauthor.com

CPSIA information can be obtained
at www.ICGtesting.com
Printed in the USA
BVHW040210260523
664933BV00012B/117